PRAISE FOR THE *MEN ON MEN* COLLECTIONS OF GAY FICTION

MEN ON MEN

"Some of the best gay fiction,
—Martin D

MEN ON MEN 2

"Some of the hottest (in other words, coolest)
stories I've read anywhere."
—Brad Gooch, author of *Scary Kisses*

MEN ON MEN 3

"A rich mosaic of cultural diversity.
A groundbreaking collection."
—*Lambda Book Report*

MEN ON MEN 4

"Rich and complex . . . heartfully and boldly tells
us stories that need to be told."
—*The Advocate*

MEN ON MEN 5

"This exciting book is the pot of gold at the end
of the rainbow coalition."
—Edmund White

MEN ON MEN 6

"The range of these stories marks the vitality of
contemporary queer life."
—Frank Browning, author of *A Queer Geography*

David Bergman, a leading gay scholar, critic, editor, and prize-winning poet, is the author of *Gaiety Transfigured: Gay Self-Representation in American Literature* and the editor of *Camp Grounds: Style and Homosexuality* and *The Violet Quill Reader*. The editor of the *Men on Men* series since 1992, he lives in Baltimore and is a professor of English at Towson University.

MEN ON MEN

7

• BEST NEW GAY FICTION •

EDITED AND WITH AN INTRODUCTION BY
DAVID BERGMAN

Ⓟ

A PLUME BOOK

PLUME
Published by the Penguin Group
Penguin Putnam Inc., 375 Hudson Street, New York, New York 10014, U.S.A.
Penguin Books Ltd, 27 Wrights Lane, London W8 5TZ, England
Penguin Books Australia Ltd, Ringwood, Victoria, Australia
Penguin Books Canada Ltd, 10 Alcorn Avenue, Toronto, Ontario, Canada M4V 3B2
Penguin Books (N.Z.) Ltd, 182–190 Wairau Road, Auckland 10, New Zealand

Penguin Books Ltd, Registered Offices:
Harmondsworth, Middlesex, England

First published by Plume, an imprint of Dutton NAL,
a member of Penguin Putnam Inc.

First Printing, November, 1998
10 9 8 7 6 5 4 3 2 1

LIBRARY OF CONGRESS CATALOGING-IN-PUBLICATION DATA:

Men on men 7 : best new gay fiction / edited and with an introduction
    by David Bergman.
        p.   cm.
    ISBN 0-452-27734-5
    1. Gay men's writings, American.   2. American fiction—20th
century.   I. Bergman, David, 1950–
PS648.H57M48   1998
813'.01089206642—dc21   98-19321
                                                                          CIP

Printed in the United States of America
Set in Janson
Designed by Julian Hamer

PUBLISHER'S NOTE
This is a work of fiction. Names, characters, places, and incidents either are the products
of the author's imagination or are used fictitiously, and any resemblance to actual per-
sons, living or dead, events, or locales is entirely coincidental.

for John, once more

CONTENTS

INTRODUCTION

DAVID BERGMAN

This is the third time I have had the honor to edit and introduce a volume in this series. It continues to be a pleasure. Yet the longer I have served as editor, the more difficult it has become to make the final selection of stories to include in *Men on Men*. One reason is that I get so many wonderful stories to read. Yet another reason is that rather than operating from a false position of certainty, I am always waiting—indeed, hoping—to be thrown off balance and cast into a state of critical confusion. For the very best stories, the ones I find most stimulating to read, are those that open up new areas of pleasure and experience—literary, linguistic, formal, or representational—and when confronted by the unprecedented (or at least what is unprecedented for me), I feel daunted and uncertain as well as exhilarated and excited. The power to disturb our sense of assurance is what literature—rather than mere entertainment—does; instead of giving us what we have come to expect and know as readers, it challenges us with unaccustomed thoughts, feelings, and experiences. This power to provoke us with different perspectives and unexpected insights is why literature—rather than propaganda—can't be written to serve a particular cause or provide a particular social service, except the service of stretching our responses and imaginations. So when I find a story that pushes me off balance, offends me in some way I can't immediately recognize, I am forced to consider whether my reaction is a sign of my own or the story's limitations. Although I have selected what I found to be the best of the stories I've read in the last two years, I am fully aware that the selection is a highly individual one because my basis for selection is constantly evolving, altered by the very stories I read.

While you may not like all the stories in this collection, I hope that at least some of them will throw you off balance, delight and surprise you, move you in ways you hadn't anticipated, and even offend you by challenging your treasured assumptions. W. H. Auden in a prayer asks God to "prohibit sharply the rehearsed response," to keep him from habitual and deadening reactions. It is a prayer that should be repeated not just by every editor and every writer, but by every reader (and every critic) as well.

So what's new? One of the new things I've been noticing is a growing number of writers working from the perspective of the laboring classes. Gay fiction in the past was divided between the world of Proust and that of Genet, the upper classes, as in Brian Sloan's "Sex with Teenagers," and the demi-monde of petty thieves, prostitutes, and pushers, whom we find in Emanuel Xavier's "Christ-like." Writers of the seventies and eighties depicted middle-class gay life—and such accounts were at the time a breakthrough—but they often left out working-class experience or, when they did depict it, viewed it from the outside. But in the last few years I have found more and more stories dealing with blue-collar lives: Keith Banner's frightening and hilarious "Holding Hands for Safety," Shawn Behlin's hauntingly inconclusive "Mullinville," Michael Bendzela's painful "Marriage," or C. Bard Cole's surprisingly upbeat "Anniversary." Although the narrator of Christopher Lord's "Graffiti" is clearly middle-class, even upper-middle-class, his awareness of the insecurity of his class position is something new; indeed, it is the first time in my memory that an essentially gay story has addressed the economic and psychological uncertainties of the new professionals whose careers have been shaped by the downsizing and corporate reorganization of the last twenty years, changes that have made even those in management nervous about the future.

Some old themes are dealt with here with a new psychological subtlety and originality. Michael Carroll's "My Senior Senior Year," which is a retelling of the coming-out story, maps with enormous precision a new pathway to the love of men. Brian

Sloan deftly handles a teenager's coming out from the point of view of the "older" lover. David A. Newman's expertly constructed story, "Calendar Boy," shows in unexpected ways how humiliation can lead to a sort of freedom; Andrew Holleran's "The Married Man" is yet another, but quite different, approach to the same phenomenon. Greg Johnson and Ernest McLeod give us very different reactions families have to their sons' announcement of their homosexuality. Allen Ellenzweig's "The Athena Galleria" returns to the Greek tradition of an older man's love for a younger man, but he updates it in marvelous ways. Perhaps Ellenzweig and Banner also represent something else that's new—the impact of television on the life of gay men. In both stories, the narrators are involved with occurrences that are not merely public but broadcast over the airwaves. Keith McDermott's "Sweet Thing" returns with tenderness to the various and surprising ways one can be queer in suburban America.

In the past, I have been disappointed that gay writers seem to leave out of their fiction their valuable and important relationship with lesbians. In the last two years I have gotten a few stories that have begun to tackle that relation. Ernest McLeod's "Frankie's Wedding," another coming-out story, shows a gay man's debt to a lesbian in a particularly fresh and heartwarming manner.

And there are other stories that fall under no clear rubric at all. Alex Jeffers's "The Strait" deals with the conflicts of an American-educated Turk returning to his country, and Kevin Killian, the biographer of the gay poet Jack Spicer, tells the tale of the son of a gay poet confronting his father's biographer.

More stories in this volume are sexually explicit than in any of the preceding volumes I edited. Not that all the stories focus on sexual experience—the ones by David Newman, Keith McDermott, Christopher Lord, Greg Johnson, and Aaron Jason are not concerned with sex. But in all the others, authors write about sex to some extent. Since there has been a lot of controversy lately about the propriety of sexually explicit gay fiction, the increase in sexual explicitness needs, I suppose, some explanation. (For me, nothing human could ever be an improper subject of fiction.) The simplest explanation is that I received more good stories that contained sex scenes than ever before. In fact, six years ago, when I started editing Men on Men, I was surprised by getting very few stories that contained any explicit sex. I explain the dearth of sex in those stories as a result of the trauma that AIDS has inflicted on our communities. AIDS is not forgotten in the stories in this volume: Emanuel Xavier's "Christ-like," Felice Picano's "The Geology of Southern California at Black's Beach," Greg Johnson's "The Death of Jackie Kennedy," and C. Bard Cole's "Anniversary" all deal directly with AIDS and its impact. Indeed, there are more such stories in this volume than in the last. But the concern about AIDS no longer seems to keep writers from writing about sex, and more important, they do not write about the two as separate issues, but as experiences intimately entwined. Although some may be harshly critical, I see this as a positive development, because it has not been dictated by some commissar of community health or morality, but derives from the internal driving force of the artists' imaginations.

Because of the controversy about sexual explicitness, it is important once again to distinguish between the literature about sexual experience and masturbatory writing or pornography. Pornography is writing whose central purpose—sometimes sole purpose—is to arouse the reader sexually. Literature about sex is not meant to excite the reader sexually (although admittedly it sometimes does), but rather to depict sexual experience from the inside, what I call the "phenomenology of sex." How is sex experienced? What does it come to mean to the various participants? How is it used by them? How does it alter them? How are they altered by it? These are important questions that should interest any writer. In story after story, characters try to figure out the meanings of sex, meanings that keeps changing whether you're Brian Sloan's teenaged or Andrew Holleran's fiftysomething or Reginald Harris's African-American protagonist.

But in gay writing representing sex is especially important. In straight literature we can assume what the heterosexual characters are doing in bed. Literary tradition gives them a "default position," to use that computer term, and when authors write more explicitly, it is usually to show how far their characters have moved from that position. In gay writing, there is no default position. Oral sex registers differently than anal sex, which is different from mutual masturbation. S & M presents an entirely different range of experiences. As readers we cannot automatically assume who is on top and who is on the bottom, or if the characters are reversing positions, or as in the case of Shawn Behlin's "Mullinville" whether they are touching at all. The specifics of the sex act are vital to our understanding of character; indeed, in Caleb Crain's story, "Cocksucker," the different sex acts are the important key to the protagonist's changing state of mind. Moreover, in Crain's "Cocksucker," in Reginald Harris's "A Tour of the Collection," and in Emanuel Xavier's "Christ-like" race and sexual power merge in complicated ways that get embodied by the act of sex. It is not because gay men are more obsessed with sex than straight men that it is such an important part of our writing; it is because we have not developed the social or literary conventions—and happily we won't— which would erase our need for such explicitness.

One of the things I have consciously tried to pursue in my time as editor of *Men on Men* is to open its pages to new writers, men who have published little or nothing. I have tried very hard to make writers aware that *Men on Men* is not a closed shop and to assure them that I will read every manuscript that comes to me. Only by opening up the selection process can I hope to offer readers the range and quality of work they rightfully demand. *Men on Men* 7 contains stories once again by unknown authors and up-and-coming writers. Two authors are publishing their fiction for the first time. But nothing could be served by *excluding* established authors, and I am happy that some of the most distinguished gay authors have new stories in this volume.

Moreover, these established authors are beginning to tell a story we have heard little about until now. What has been nearly absent in gay writing is how openly gay men of the Stonewall generation are coping with growing older and reaching middle age, how they survive and prevail over the devastation of AIDS. But it is not a subject only for older writers. Aaron Jason, a young writer, has in "Grace Under Lashes" written a particularly funny and moving account of the relationship between an older drag queen and "a young thing in curlers." I find it exciting to see how we have begun imagining growing older and not fading into either premature desexualized dotage or *faux* heterosexual marriage. As a man quickly aging, I am perhaps more interested in this issue than younger readers; nevertheless, I think it is one of the community's great imaginative challenges.

But the proof of writing is in the reading, and these stories argue for themselves much, much better than I ever could. My hope is that they will give you pleasure, not as a mere diversion, but as something engaging, challenging, moving, and, yes, enjoyable—in short, as something not very different from love.

HOLDING HANDS FOR SAFETY

KEITH BANNER

That night Trent, my cousin, came over, he did not act like anything. Just kind of lounged around the living room of our apartment like the god of beauty he must've thought he was, or would always be, all five foot, seven inches of him, with his bleached-out crew cut and public-pool tan and the easy, confident grin of a shark in a cartoon.

His glass of Pepsi, though, the one I got him without him asking, shook when he brought it up to his mouth. His eyes were swollen and red. He could not really "lounge," either, as much as shake his legs and drink nervously from his glass, every so often commenting on what I was watching on the VCR, which happened to be *Mad Max Beyond Thunderdome*.

"This is pure grade-A shit, Clyde," he might say. Or: "Bor-rrrring."

Me, I just thought it was drugs.

I just thought, Great, Mom and Freddy are gone, so it's just me and Trent. And Trent was on drugs, which might mean he might let me you-know with him. Might allow me the privilege—who knows? There is always hope in little hearts. Sometimes Trent would get pissed right in the middle and kick me away. I'd kick him right back, and we'd start fighting, and the fighting would lead back to what we were doing in the first place. I was only sixteen, and he was all of eighteen. People were always asking him, "Why don't you join the army, Trent-O," or "Why don't you go to trade school," or "Why don't you at least get a job and help your mom, who you happen to be bloodsucking off of." He answered back almost always with the same poem—him holding his crotch, sticking his middle finger into his mouth, pulling it out of his mouth slow and showing it wet.

So, like I was saying, he did not really act like anything had happened that night. Quiet as hell mostly, sitting there, any other night. That grin coming out when he said something smart-assed, then closing down. I crawled over to him about a half-hour into his stay, sat up beside his legs, as he was sitting in Freddy's La-Z-Boy chair, the one no one was supposed to sit in but Freddy ("I have got one rule and one rule only . . ."). Big fat Freddy was Mom's latest boyfriend, a little older than her, and he worked at the hospital in maintenance. Trent and him could get along enough to hunt deer.

I am sitting on the floor next to Trent's hairy legs, watching *Mad Max*, Tina Turner wearing a screen door, and I look up at him. I just expect him to pretend to spit at me or maybe even fucking *do* that. But suddenly Trent slides down the chair onto the floor right beside me. He waits a second. Then just starts kissing me.

The front door was open, the screen letting in night noises, brakes going out, car axles bumping up over speed bumps, kids screaming, sometimes a bash of head or fist against concrete. I imagine what the ignorant and the small-minded neighbors we got in this complex would think: bleach-blond crew-cut high-school graduate with no future french-kissing his cousin, the black-headed, slightly overweight sixteen-year-old boy who works part-time at Burger King on Pleasant Avenue and tells people he gets good grades when he is only but average (if even that).

Kissing, this time, Trent used tongue and teeth. Now usually it was a quick peck and then down to business. That was okay, but this kissing was like it was being videotaped for the Kissing Channel. He had his whole mouth wide open, and I tasted the sourness of a sore throat starting, a storm brewing way off, the bruised goodness of his warm breath like something overripe kept in a hot kitchen out on the counter. I kissed back deep. We did this for about five minutes approximately before I got up to breathe and to shut the door.

I did not say one thing. Did not want to ruin my good luck.

Trent stayed on the floor. He did not really look that incredibly horny. He looked tired, stupid, beautiful, and something I had not seen before in his arrogant ass: he looked scared. Scared-shaken like a dog gets and you don't know what to do. Dogs are not supposed to be scared, right? I leave all the lights off. I close the curtain, turn the sound down on the TV.

I sat down beside him again. This time he got up. Turned around and looked at me.

"I killed Courtney," he says. Then he laughs like it is just so unbelievable.

Courtney was his little half-sister. They did not have the same daddy. Trent, Courtney, and their mom, my mom's sister, lived in the same apartment complex as us, as this was one of the few that took Section 8. Borderline retarded, Courtney was tiny and had stringy brown hair and always wore dirty sundresses in the summer. Ten and still shitting herself almost every other day. She'd always be running around the complex, poop stains leaking out the back of her sundress. Always too excited playing, it seemed, to go inside to the toilet. Talking and babbling a lot, and although she was borderline retarded, she had the same exact obnoxious ways of all ten-year-old girls in dumpy apartment complexes, a sort of stupid-ass but frilly pride that made her talk back to people in a high pitch and paint her toenails out on the sidewalk like a show and wear lip gloss from her mom's purse and throw rocks at parked cars and steal all the mail flyers from the shelf under the locked boxes up front, throwing them around and into the air like birds getting caught in a jet propeller.

"I just killed Courtney," Trent repeats, still laughing in disbelief. He can't say nothing else, coming over to me, swooping down like Batman. I ain't believing it, of course. It's another dumb-ass game of his, a way to trick me.

But he looks at me close then, saying, "She's in the dumpster, Clyde."

(He calls me Clyde because he says I look like a Clyde he once knew. My actual name is Brian.)

Then Trent laughs again. This time though with sadness leaking out of his closed teeth as he does it, the sadness like a crazy voice in a shut garage. Then he stands up and goes down the hall to where my bedroom is.

I laugh too. It *is* kinda funny: Courtney, Little Miss Retard

Bigmouth, her panties full of shit, dead in the dumpster. I mean, some things vulgar and sick like that can often be funny, like Marilyn Manson or Howard Stern or *Pink Flamingos*. But still there wasn't any reality to it right then, that was the main reason I could laugh.

Or maybe it is just some things, no matter how serious, how dumb and how serious, you have to laugh at or you lose your mind.

Plus all I was thinking right now was how Trent had gone down to my bedroom. I mean, "butterflies" was not the word for what was in my stomach. Fucking Steven Spielberg pterodactyls. Trent was in there getting into my bed. Like he loved me.

But for a second I just stand there, shocked, contemplating my good fortune, looking at the godforsaken brown vinyl couch, the spools for electric cable Mom had painted and antiqued to turn into end tables, the shelves filled with Mom's romance novels and my horror and sci-fi ones, the TV screen with *Mad Max* still going on it a little fuzzy, Freddy's big tiger picture framed in chrome he bought as his gift for Mom letting him stay here. . . .

I take a deep breath of all the air we usually breathe, stale and corn-chippy and like all our feet have left a smell combining into Family capital F: thinking of family and what me and him were about to do, and then too about Courtney. Was she dead? Of course not. It was Trent's sick sense of humor. I thought of Courtney in a flash, how one time she begged and begged me to walk with her to the store because she had a food-stamp dollar she found in the kitchen drawer. How she stood in front of me while I was watching I think it was *Hellraiser 3*, me getting pissed, but then finally I got up.

"Jesus Christ, okay," I told her.

And she wanted me to hold her hand. This time the sundress was orange with pink straps. She looked at me as I got my shoes on, and she said, "We got to hold hands. Mom said. For safety."

I kind of laughed at her, tying my shoes. Her mom did not give a shit about holding hands for safety. Still, though, I let it go. She was fresh from her bath and clean and kind of sweet, her stringy hair still dark with water.

"Come on," I told her.

I took her hand. It was very warm, like inside she was always hot, always "on."

We walked together. It was one of those half-rainy days, still hot, though. She pulled on me, and I tried not to be mad at her because she was borderline retarded and hyper. I tried, but soon I let go of her hand and told her to go on by herself. Told her to get lost. I wanted to finish *Hellraiser.*

"*You* get lost!" she screamed. But she ran on ahead.

I turned back, went home. Later I saw that she had got Reese's Cups with her food-stamp dollar. She ate them both off by herself, over by where the chain-link fence started, by the back woods. She was still pissed at me. Sitting there outside.

Now I hear Trent from back there, the back bedroom where I sleep.

"Come on," Trent says. "What the fuck are you waiting for, fag?"

I can tell by his voice he is lying down.

I go.

He is in my bed, naked, not muscular, just skinny, but him not having muscles makes him prettier. He has never got all-the-way naked before. My face turns red and hot, and I stand there. He looks up at me, just the sheet over the bottom part of his legs. He needs me, it looks like—needs me like he has not needed me, or maybe anybody, before. Like I am his version of safety. This scares me back and gets me suspicious, but I cannot pass him up, of course.

"Come on," he whispers. His eyes are shiny. He has a little-kid face, a little kid who wants something but he can't tell you because it's embarrassing.

"Get in bed here," he says. He strains his voice. "Honey," he goes.

The next morning, of course, Trent is gone, because we don't want my mom or Freddy knowing what we do. Alone, I rise feeling all elegant. There is that specialness to waking up after getting exactly what you want and not having to explain it to nobody. This one hundred-percent-pure happiness. That's kind of what I liked about living here and being sixteen and being gay. Oh sure, eventually I would get sick of hiding it and have to run away maybe to San Francisco or somewhere I don't know, but right now the secrecy of it is what makes it so special. So original. That and this afterglow feeling and not having to explain it to nobody. My own secret world inside my head after getting what I want. Still naked, I held my gut in as I stepped from bed into my clothes angelically.

I know I had a smile on, cruising down the short hall toward the living room, where Mom and Freddy were already up.

There on the morning news was a picture of Courtney.

Mom says, in her frayed-out pink housecoat, "She didn't come home last night, Brian." It was one of those serious whispers she gets when she wants to show how terrible things are. But in reality I saw her the way she would kick Courtney's little ass out of the apartment and the way too she talked about how Courtney needed somebody there to discipline her because Peggy—who was on disability for her back—was too damn lazy for raising kids. Plus Dean, Courtney's dad, was in jail for writing bad checks.

But now, with Courtney's picture on the TV, Mom was all feeling about it.

Freddy goes, "Wipe that stupid grin off your face."

I guess I was still smiling. From satisfaction at first, then from shock. I wiped it off.

"All the news programs have showed up, because Peggy called the police at five this morning. I was trying to wake you up but you had your door locked. I swear you sleep like a damn corpse. I guess the TV people watch the police scanner for situations like this," Mom goes.

Then on the TV is Peggy, who lived four buildings down. There she is in predawn light on her patio which overlooks the high school and the front of the complex. Peggy in a big T-shirt, no bra, her hair graying out from her black dye job, her mouth unlipsticked, eyes baggy.

"I don't know where she could have gone. I called everybody that could," Peggy says on TV. There is this picture of police taking down information from neighbors in the complex.

What the hell am I thinking? Of course what Trent told me. I stand there, and Freddy says, "Peggy has let her go unsupervised way too much. You don't know what kind of trouble a girl like her can get into. The freaks out there who pick little girls up and—"

Mom busts into tears.

"I am going over there right now!" she screams. She goes into the bedroom and comes back out with a pair of old sneakers and socks and sits down on the couch to put them on angrily, like she is going against what Freddy has told her. That's their relationship: him laying down the law, her going against the law but also not a lot of the time so mostly it's just him and her getting along smashingly. Which is all Mom has ever wanted from her men: a smashingly successful relationship. Do not ask me about my dad, who lives in Kentucky or Tennessee and is a truck driver and sends me twenty-dollar Sears gift certificates for Christmas.

"Dorothy, you go over there now and you ain't gonna be able to help her no how," Freddy says, in his chair, in his work uniform, white pants and white shirt and black shoes. Maybe it's that he is jealous of Peggy, that Peggy and Courtney are getting all the attention. He has the biggest head, like a mongoloid, and yet he doesn't look retarded. He looks like a big white genius, even though I know mostly he is a stupid racist asshole who when he gets drunk sometimes brags about the KKK and hunting niggers like deer. But then on TV he watches *Cosby* and Urkel and laughs and even has a black friend at work named Roy. Roy and him even go drinking sometimes.

Mom slides her feet into her shoes hard.

"I am going, Freddy."

"Fine," Freddy says. "I gotta go to work anyways. Go over there and bother her. Go on. That's what you're good for. Get your goddamn picture on TV."

"You can shut your mouth right now," Mom says, standing up, and then she looks at me.

"They are gonna have a search party," she says. "You go get dressed and you go with me, you hear? Thank God you finally woke up, Sleeping Beauty."

Her face, that serious desperate mascara-eyed face with its blond curly hair and black eyebrows and those double chins, I want to slap it for some reason. Then I see Trent in my head, his face so alive as he came while I was jerking him off.

I felt perverted, I felt stupid, but the secrecy came back. No one would know anything anyways, right? So the beautiful secrecy of what we had done before and did last night comes back to me, like someone opened a door and right outside that door was Saturn spinning closer and closer till it gets in through my eyes into my brain.

"Get in there and get dressed. Get you a Pop-Tart," Mom tells me, fat in her pink housecoat and black sneakers and big tube socks. Caring about my breakfast.

"You got to work today?"

"Yeah. I have to be in at two," I tell her.

"Well, that's three hours anyways. Get dressed."

Freddy is grunting, sitting up out of his chair. He comes over to me.

"You sit in my chair?" he asks me.

It pisses me off how accurate Freddy can predict stuff. Like his ass has telepathy.

"No."

"Who did?"

"Trent," I blurt out. I walk back to my room and get dressed slowly, and then I hear him say, "You tell Trent to keep his lazy ass out of my chair, you got it?"

"Yeah," I yell back, through the shut door.

Then Freddy leaves, and I come out in my Nikes, T-shirt, and cut-off sweat pants. Feeling dirty from the sex last night but also liking the glazed fishy quality of it all over my body. Like I am trying to prolong what me and Trent did. Then I picture Courtney like I had done last night: in a dumpster. Dead.

I need to tell Mom what Trent told me. I need to. But don't have to.

Mom gives me a packet of these watermelon Pop-Tarts I had her get. I bite into one as we walk out into the hot hot sun. It tastes so sweet my teeth almost start to ache right off. There are still TV trucks and vans here. It makes you wonder why would anybody care about old Courtney anyways? Some retarded white-trash girl with an unnerving face and shit-stained sundress throwing rocks? I mean, she isn't Princess Diana, obviously. But they are all lined up to report on finding her, like she has fallen down a well. Like her life meant anything.

Serious business, all them white vans and trucks with big primary-colored logos on them (CHANNEL 13 ACTION NEWS— WE *CARE*; CHANNEL 6, YOUR AWARD-WINNING 24-HOUR LOCAL NEWS STATION, etc.). Satellites, police cars, all surrounding Peggy and Trent and Courtney's apartment. Trent's Chevette, yellow with a WIBN frog-mouth sticker on it, ain't out there. I am walking beside Mom, like we are in war-torn Bosnia.

Mom says to me, "Trent is gone. Ain't that just like him? Leaving right when he is needed. Courtney is his sister."

"Half-sister," I say, not thinking, eating the goddamn Pop-Tart, gagging on it.

Mom just looks at me in bewilderment.

"Some people are saying he did something to her," Mom whispers as we walk.

I realize at this point that I am involved in a conspiracy. Trent told me because he knew he could trust me, did he not? He told me then let me have my way with him because he had to tell somebody. Plus he needed someone to love him after he told them. Like religion, like being saved. He knew that I would not tell no one because I wanted him so bad, and that makes me feel trashy but also full of hope again because it will be only me and him who know.

It's so damn hot and sticky, the sky above the complex smoggy from the interstate. I finish my second Pop-Tart just as we go past the police cars.

A policeman is standing outside the apartment.

Mom goes, "Peggy Stewart is my sister. I need to see her."

The policeman has a big mustache and a gut and he stands back not saying nothing.

"This is my son, Brian. He is going to help with the search party."

Mom smiles, all take-charge and shit. I remember when I was six, and Dad had left. It was just me and Mom in the kitchen on a bright winter's day. She held me out of school, and she got blitzed, sat me down at the dinette set. In her bra and her panties, she said to me these speeches of bizarre gut-wrenching sadness that did not make any sense. Just like she was talking to some adult who could pity her for being so fried she couldn't put two sentences together.

Now she was with AA. Now she had Freddy to keep her ass in line.

Peggy was in her living room, looking doped up. There was a couple of other fat women, neighbors, and also a blond and thin reporter in a professional skirt-outfit with a microphone, a tall cameraman in a T-shirt and jeans behind her. One of the obese ladies was holding Peggy's hand, one of those instant friends you get when you go through a real glamorous tragedy like losing your kid. You could tell by Mom's face she was hurt, that she thought she should be the one on camera with Peggy holding hands. If Freddy hadn't held her back before, she could have been the one holding her sister's hand on TV.

The blond woman had that husky, reporter way of speaking. It was not live, it was being taped for the noon edition, the other obese lady whispered to Mom and me.

"So, Peggy, when does the search party begin?" said the professional reporter.

Peggy says, "Soon as everyone gets here." In a spooked victim voice. "It's so nice. All these people."

Positioned by the front door, I saw some kids coming from beyond the front buildings, men and women too. Neighbors you don't talk to really, just pass by on your way to work or school, but here they were showing up to find a little girl no one liked.

Mom says then, interrupting, "I am Peggy's sister. I just live down the way there. I think what's happened is that Courtney just forgot to tell her mom, and as soon as she wakes up or one of her friends sees it on TV, they'll call."

Mom smiles, like she knows deep in her heart.

The cameraman doesn't turn the minicam on her, and people in the room just act like what she said was nothing.

Peggy and Mom, though, get together after the interview. Peggy busts into tears and Mom does too. The other people let the sisters have their time together. I notice people I know, people I don't, all of them pulling together in this desperate time of need.

I wondered where Trent was hiding.

When we passed that mustached policeman I thought of just telling him. Thought of saying that Trent told me he killed Courtney and put her in the dumpster. I mean, when we went to bed together last night he did not mention anything else, not even after, and I just let it slide, but I was an accomplice now. And that almost had a beautiful sound to it, to me then.

All this searching was a lost cause, people. I was a know-it-all.

We got organized outside little Courtney's apartment, and we searched.

I thought about going to that dumpster by the back of their building first thing. It has a brick encasement around it, brown, big as a grand piano, the lid shut tight. But I didn't. I got caught up in the search. It was like an Easter-egg hunt, people walking around, yelling her name. Some going across the way toward the big ditch, some in the parking lot of the high school, some down a hill toward the water tower.

I walked around and called her name too, feeling foolish but also part of something important. Mom and Peggy sat outside the front door of Peggy's apartment, like the queen of tragedy and her tragic sister, two of them ruling over this little colony of searchers. I walked in the grass and looked in the weeds and in the trees, knowing that inside the brown dumpster was where she was. Finally after an hour, I got so sweaty and stupid with the hunt, and with the feeling that I was all the way completely evil, that I walked over toward the dumpster where they lived.

I heard my mom say, "What are you doing?" Still sitting there on the lawn chair next to Peggy, supervising.

"I just thought I'd look," I said, not turning my head around. I felt my stomach go out of my body like it had raised up and levitated out of my eyes. I was caught. Why had he killed her? This hit me, as I stood there. What was the fucking point? She was just some dumb little girl. Right there staring at the brown dumpster with the rusty door handles, I felt so stupid with sorrow that I did not want to see nothing, not her body, not her face, the guilt of thinking it was a great big joke last night transforming automatic into that deep shock you get right when you see the car you're in about to hit the semi in front of you.

Mom says, "Look where?" She comes over to me, fast. "In the dumpster?" she whispers. Her breath smells of old damp cigarettes.

"Yeah."

I am shaky, like a diabetic. I have had too much sugar. I need some insulin. Freddy is diabetic, and he does his own shots like a junkie in the bathroom. Talking real loud the whole time, stupid bullshit, because he says talking real loud gets him over the fear of needles he has.

"No, don't look in there," Mom says. Like it would be in bad taste somehow. Her face loses its seriousness and gets a silly absurd expression, like no way no one could do that to a little girl, kill her and put her in a dumpster. No one would do that. But then I thought of that one time Freddy brought home a big deer on his car hood and then out in the goddamn parking lot he cuts the damn thing's head off with a saw and brings the head into our apartment and boils the head in a big pot of water in the kitchen. The smell was not of this earth, hot and coppery and tangy like a chemical, singeing into your face and eyes and nose. He wanted to make the skull into a sculpture to be hung on a wall. "A European mount" is what he called it. He threw the parts he did not want into the dumpster, did he not? But then again Courtney wasn't a deer, was she?

"Mom, she could be in there," I say, hot gray sun in my face, her smell of cigarette breath and old sleepy housecoat, stale and yeasty like grocery-store bread.

"She ain't," says my mom.

"She could be," I say.

I start walking over to the dumpster again. She grabs my arm. I pull away. I open the door. Four or five big oily black birds scatter. Inside, cushioned on white bags of trash, not even hid by them really, is her.

She was in her nightgown, and her neck was bruised. Her eyes were open to look out at where she was. Her mouth was bloody from coughing up blood. Her skin had the color of that sky above us, hot and cold both at once, gray-hot, gray-cold, her body puffed out from the heat, and she was not funny, she was not funny to me, and I did not cry and I did not laugh.

Mom was behind me.

She sobbed out. Her cries were great big, and I remembered her yelling at Courtney one day when Courtney came in without knocking into our apartment. "Who do you think you are, you little bitch? You knock. You hear me? Did somebody tell you this is your apartment? This ain't your apartment to run in and out of. You hear me?"

Mom doing that in front of Freddy to show Freddy that she could mean business too. But Freddy told Mom to calm the fuck down. Freddy took Courtney onto his lap, because Courtney was crying at Mom's display. Freddy smelled her, though. She had done it on herself, of course. Freddy had this look of betrayal upon his face.

"Go on and change yourself, sweetie," he said, putting her down.

Courtney just ran off.

*   *   *

I call off work at Burger King. I have the excuse of being in shock, being the one who found my half-cousin in a dumpster dead like the deer Freddy cut the head off of. The reporters wanted to talk to me, but Mom talked to them for me, as they all came over once we found her. Mom said she was the one who really saw her first, which might be true. She was the one who talked to the police, telling them it was her who found her because I told her I could not handle it and she already knew I was a kind of an emotionally messed-up kid.

I stayed with Mom for a while after the ambulance came, after all the people parted away. Stayed with Peggy who had gone into shock too of course.

Peggy said, her eyes glazed over, "Where's Trent?"

"Nobody knows," Mom says.

"Where is he?" Peggy says, like she did not hear Mom.

Nobody knew. Not even me. And I did not say nothing to nobody. Everybody was talking, though. Called him names. I wondered if he had left his fingerprints on her neck.

"You don't think . . ." Peggy starts, her eyes zombielike. Big and empty.

"I'm beginning to," Mom said back.

They talked about how Trent had always treated Courtney like his own personal little-girl slave and how sometimes he would hit her in the head hard, as a joke.

"Jokes can get out of hand," Mom, in all her infinite, housecoat wisdom, said.

Peggy was too sick and tired to listen to her. She closed her eyes and opened them, but looked like she was staring into a volcano.

Soon I just went home, leaving Mom at Peggy's, and as soon as I got back I collapsed on my bed in my room and flipped through some old Clive Barker novel I'd read last summer. Then I remembered last summer, the first time Trent had come over to our apartment after Dean, his stepdad, had been sent to jail, and him and his mom and Courtney had moved in here close to us.

That first time Trent was over, my mom and Freddy were gone off to the horse races in Kentucky, so it was just me and him. He was bored, and he had pot.

I had loved him since I knew how to love people. Trent, who

I loved since I was seven maybe, in the little-boy way of looking up to him, wanting to kiss him even then. Trent, who never paid attention to me never, but then he let me take a toke that night.

"I didn't know you smoked, Clyde," he said. Last year he was not a crew-cut dyed blond, but had longer, dirty-blond hair shaved on top, with strands hanging down off his neck. He had a major tan, though. No shirt on. I was breathless when he arrived. Funny how easy it is to lose yourself, but really I wanted to be lost. I guess everybody does.

"I smoke," I say, letting my lungs let go of it.

"Hey," he says then, taking another toke. He breathes it in like it is the nectar of the gods. He looks at me and laughs at his own pleasure. I take in his laugh as something we are sharing, he is letting us share, and the laugh becomes ours. I taste the hickory leftovers of the pot in my mouth and feel the pot eat into my thoughts like tickling little mice-mouths.

"Hey," he says again, relaxing onto the floor. At this time, Freddy's chair wasn't here. Relaxing, shirtless on the floor, Trent grins.

"Are you a fag?" he says. "I mean, I heard you were."

The question did not even hurt my feelings, because I have been called that a lot at school and here. Even if I wasn't, I would still be called that from the way I look. I don't act like a fairy, I don't think, but I have the look in my eyes of someone who likes things too much. It is that look they are labeling "fag," I'm sure. The fact that I can't hide how much I want things. But right then, still drunk off the sound of his pot laugh, I go:

"Who wants to know?"

Trent laughs more. He pulls down his cutoffs slightly, just to show the start of his pubic hair. I am shaking from the desire of him. Remembering family cookouts at dusk with him being thirteen and me being eleven and him the center of all attention, arm-wrestling all the deadbeat dads and eating all the potato salad and all the moms getting pissed at him and him charming them right back into giving him brownies.

"I do, fag," says Trent then. "Me. I want to know."

I see the way the muscles go under his underwear and cutoffs. My mouth is open. I don't even care that Mom might be able to smell the fucking pot tomorrow when she gets back. I go for it because that is who I am.

*   *   *

It was close to sundown when I sat up, and there in my room, just sitting on the floor, the door closed, was Trent. The Trent who had killed Courtney just yesterday, that Trent.

I thought he was a vision, something I had cooked up, but he was sitting on the floor Indian-style, his eyes wide open. "You awake?" Trent said. He smiled with kindliness. He was a changed man. He was a little boy all over again, this little sweet boy hiding from his mommy and his daddy. "I snuck in," he said.

"How?" I said, getting up.

"Through the front door," he said. "I just like ran in. I left my car at the Shell station on the corner. I didn't know where else to go. I heard they found her."

He was just half-talking-half-whispering, sitting there. His face was peaceful, not scared like last night. Peaceful from drugs or peaceful from insanity, I was not sure.

"I found her," I said, standing up then and walking to him. "Me and Mom did."

"I thought so," he said. He looked up at me. He looked up and he grinned. "Fucking traitor," he says, laughing nervously.

I sat back down on my bed, and he sat beside me on the bed. He was tender, like once you kill a little girl you can allow yourself the luxury of not being macho no more. Not being the guy who gives the finger to passers-by, you can be this weird fucked-up boy in the same clothes as yesterday, five-o'clock-shadowed, sitting on the bed next to your gay sixteen-year-old cousin. Maybe you are gay too, but gay and a child killer, so you are no longer that much of a human being. You are this dumb-ass demon, this shadowy thing, this ghost of a person. I loved the ghost, I think, almost more than I loved the real thing.

But there was pity mixed in with it. Pure pity. And also this new thing I had not ever known around Trent: a hatred and a disgust, which only made the love feel deeper.

"She was on the phone yesterday morning and Mom was at work and I had to call somebody 'cause we were going out that night," Trent says to me now. Right beside me. He has to tell.

"She wouldn't get off the fucking phone. She wasn't even talking to nobody real, the little retard," he says, but even calling her names did not seem bad, because he did that anyways, all the time, when she was alive. She would hit him back and yell at him, which tickled anybody who saw her do it: some scrawny little pigtailed girl trying to beat up on him.

"She was just pretending to talk to someone and just carrying on, you know."

Trent then imitates her. Holds up an invisible phone to his ear, goes borderline-retarded-little-girl in the face, babbling in this high voice, "Yes ma'am we do have that in stock. Yes ma'am I can have that out to you tomorrow."

Trent laughs, "She was fucking playing Service Merchandise or something. I needed to call my friend about what was up that night. I tell Courtney to get off the phone at least ten times, but she won't."

His face gets mad and he is staring off into outer space then. It's like something that happens a million times, his killing her. He is seeing her on that phone being stubborn, and his anger unveils itself like a big trombone that he is going to blow into, shiny and shaped strange. He sits there and gets that pissed-off face back and he stands up and he says, "You fucking bitch get off the goddamn phone you ain't even using! You're playing!"

He starts crying but he stops. He goes on.

"And so I grab her and fling her onto the couch. She starts screaming bad. I grab her around the neck, Clyde, and I lift her up to the ceiling. Up there man. She squirms. She squirms and like just doesn't fucking shut up and then I like hear her neck goddamn crack."

He stops. No crying, no anger left. He stops himself from putting on a further show. He climbs back onto my bed and he looks to me again. His eyes flash out of themselves, and I can tell he doesn't understand totally that what he did is wrong. All he knows is he will be caught, and that is what is making him scared and peaceful both at the same time. Nobody liked her anyway, right?

But now everybody loves her. Even me.

I stood up then.

I go, "Her eyes were open, Trent. When I opened the door. To the dumpster. You should have shut her eyes, man."

He lies back, like he's sick, resting his head on my pillow. He can't say nothing for a second, like he is thinking of them eyes, hers, open. Eyes that look at him and he knows exactly who he is. Eyes that make him want to kill her all over again.

"I know," he says. "I know that."

We don't do anything, except kiss.

I can't do anything else, but this kissing is scary and beautiful, his mouth ripe from being bitten into over and over, his breath really bad but even that is beautiful. I don't think he snuck into my room to do it as much as to tell me it all so that he could go on. He was going to make his run for it soon.

He got up from my bed and he stretched after we kissed. I got up and stood by the closet, standing there, dumb and scared and hating him, but also loving him that way I always had because no matter what he did that love protected him in my eyes, even while I saw Courtney's open eyes, her eyes open and seeing the world for the first time for what it was.

He yawned. A murderer can yawn, I thought. A murderer's got feelings.

"So you telling?" he asks, like it's some prank he pulled.

"I don't know," I say.

"You found her, so if you tell they could get you on something, I bet," he says, his voice going back into its middle-finger meanness.

"Yeah," I say. "But I think they already think you did it anyways."

Trent comes up to me. "It was an accident," he says. "I fucking have thrown her against like cement walls, man, and she bounces right off."

When he kisses me that last time, I think of Courtney. I think of three ambulance guys pulling her out of a dumpster, and then I remember how she used to like have this old Operation game she'd play with by herself on the front stoop—you know, the game where you pull out the bones from some guy with a red light bulb for a nose, with electronic tweezers. If you hit the sides, it buzzes. Courtney made the thing buzz on purpose, buzzing out there all the day long. I see them pulling her dead white body out, and I feel myself suddenly shaped from that pulling.

Trent pulls back and I miss his mouth automatic.

Mom is out in the living room, because suddenly I hear the TV. Shock brings me back to life.

"Go out through the window," I say.

"You ain't telling?"

"Go out the window," I say.

He does. The screen takes a little time to get off because they painted over the hinges, but finally it falls to the ground outside. He slips out, then turns back and reinstalls the screen, which is stupid but he does it. I see his face while he screws it back. He is stupid and he is beautiful and he is lost. Maybe somehow he is looking forward, in a way, in a sick way, to being hunted down.

My stomach has that empty feeling. I won't ever see him this way again. This close.

He doesn't say anything else. He goes. Disappears into the woods behind the complex.

I go past Mom in the living room.

"Peggy may be put up on charges," Mom says. It is that same serious voice. She is in her smock from the grocery store. She is tired and curled up on the couch. Maybe she has abandoned her sister.

"They may get her for neglect," Mom adds, and she starts to cry slowly. I stand in front of her, wanting to run away.

"They think that Trent done it," she goes, still crying. On TV right then: a picture of the ambulance guys pulling her out.

I go outside, ignoring her.

There are candles lit by the dumpster where we found her. There are stuffed toys and flowers hanging off the dumpster's sides in plastic sacks, stuck there with duct tape, and big pieces of paper with her name on them, and cardboard with curlicues and her name and WE LUV YOU!!! REST IN PEACE DEAR SWEET COURTNEY.

People are standing by the dumpster, people who probably don't even know her, or who when they did would run away from her. It seems like another sick joke, that dumpster fucking decorated for her, like it was her coffin or something. But people don't get jokes this serious.

I stand back, a little ways off. A fat retarded man is standing in the candlelight, maybe he is not retarded, who knows? He has on dirty clothes and he speaks in a strange lispy stutter, holding a big Bible. People are both scared of him and listening to him. They wonder where he has come from. He looks like he is out of his mind suddenly, standing there, buzzed-headed with big eyes and a thick-lipped mouth.

"Oh dear Courtney," he says in his way. "Dear sweet little angel! Dear dead Courtney, what has the world come to? Why?"

He reads from the Bible, reads a verse: " 'Blessed are the children . . . blessed are the meek. . . .' "

He stands there and people laugh, but nervously. He drops the Bible to the ground then, this freak, and he starts speaking in tongues. Babbling like an idiot, his face jerking, his mouth wide open, letting out the bullshit of God. Her name comes out of his mouth sometimes, inside all the gibberish.

I see Courtney with her eyes wide open, looking out at what people did, what people do, see her looking at me and then at them. Her eyes are almost crossed but shining like stars that have the ability to read minds. She is reaching out to grab my hand. She wants my hand.

The fat guy opens his eyes then, stopping his tongue-speaking. He is deadly serious, looking at me, then looking at the others, but it seems like he has me targeted, or maybe it's just my paranoia.

"We are all gonna pray now," he says. It is an order.

MULLINVILLE

SHAWN BEHLEN

So, like a lot of men, I'm sitting at a bar with a decision to make. The dark-skinned bartender is allowing me to call him "my brother," and with his approval I've formed a pyramid of martini glasses on the bar. The light seen through them is better than itself, refracted and beautiful. I'm rather impressed with myself for this.

This place is called Frank's, and I've never been here before. It's an odd conglomeration of drinking establishment/eatery. Up in front is a dark space filled with comfortable-looking chairs and glossy tables. They're perhaps too close, each topped with a metal vase and a red blossom. In the corner, there's a blind man with black shades and a guitar, crooning the blues. I like that: melodic loss from someone who's lived it.

He launches into a slow, deep-voiced version of "At Last," and I think of Etta James. By the age of twenty-one, she was a full-blown heroin addict, the regret of her love for Harvey Fuqua simply too great to face without a little help. And on her version of this song, on the final "And here we are in heaven, for you are mine at last," the cry of her voice is enough to make me wonder if their location, some vision of perfection, is instead meant literally. Can love transform any particular place into heaven? Or was this man hers only after death?

Of course I trouble myself with similar questions about myself and Eric. Tonight, I'm supposed to tell him if I'll tag along to Mullinville, Kansas. If he'll still have me, that is. But for me, the dilemma is this: Do I do that to him? Or do I stay where and who I am? At the moment I have little faith in there being a right choice because of something my third-grade teacher told me.

She was a tall woman named Miss Evelyn Brozowski, whose eyes weren't quite horizontally even. One afternoon she caught me mashing Robert Geiger's face into a chain-link fence because he'd thumped my ear. She clapped, demanded I stop, and threatened a paddling. I didn't really care. I was a mouthy boy, wound up and oblivious to such things. But in the end, all she did was tell me this: "Mitchell Ray Malone, you don't understand. Life's about choices, and you better be certain of every one you make. Each move leaves other ones behind, ones you might have liked better. Young man," she said.

Tonight, I'm unable to get those words out of my mind. I'm thinking what Miss Brozowski gave me that day was an evil little present.

Eric is Eric Reade, a man who meets the world with whatever's required always at the ready. I admire him for that more than he can know.

Sometimes when I'm around him a sliver of how I was as a boy works itself to the surface, and I question why I am this person I am now. But that's not something I ever do on purpose. At times, Eric calls me Pretty Boy, Muscle Boy. He jokes about the money I spend on my hair and the hours I've accrued at the gym. He's wiry himself, and shorter, with a mashed-in, pugilist's face. His manner suggests that he finds my occupation, my wardrobe, my haphazard ways all a source not only of humor but, at some level, also of astonishment, and certainly of annoyance. He's thirty-four, and I'm twenty-five.

We met early on a Sunday morning, on a side alley a block or so from Cedar Springs. I was drunk to the point of stumbling, hunting for my car, convinced for some inebriated reason that I could sing. I remember the sky was flat and moonless, a just-washed towel with the nap all fluffed. Ragged blasts of distant music drifted from the nearby clubs where I'd spent the night with my shirt off and my butt wiggling, having a grand, good time. From a line of dumpsters, the stench of rot settled with the alcohol in my gut and suggested a mighty rough morning ahead. The alley was uneven with potholes, gravel shifting under my feet. I wasn't even sure it was the right alley. Mostly I was laughing at a stupid joke I'd just heard—How does a gay man fake orgasm? He pulls out and spits on the other guy's back!—and trying not to fall because of the Miyake pants I wore on this, the night of their grand debut.

So, the bottle across the back of my head was a complete surprise. I remember kicks at my ribs and my stomach, right in my balls, and the realization that what I felt on my face was blood. They yelled, too. Three teenaged boys in Cowboys caps kicked and yelled at me what I was. In response, I rolled into a ball, a sort of lowest-common-denominator style of self-preservation, and waited for their legs and mouths to grow weary. But they were determined, heated little 'phobes, and the end arrived only when Eric did. He didn't know me, but he knew my situation and fought in my stead.

Afterward, I said something about noble knights, and swords, and even a word or two about fiery dragons. But Eric wasn't entirely impressed. "Jesus, you're a grown man," he said, "twice the size of those kids. Why'd you let them do that to you?"

It was a good question, but a stumper as far as I was concerned. Eventually, he frowned at my silence and walked away. Who could blame him?

Weeks passed before I saw him again, although I certainly thought about him enough. When he came into Neiman Marcus, I was seated at my desk in the designer room, the afternoon a slow, ponderous, unprofitable one. I looked up to see him fingering Armani slacks, pretending not to notice me, although it's not a big room and I was the only person in there. He wore jeans and a white shirt, both paint-splattered, as were his tennis shoes and the backs of his hands.

I thought about thanking him again, but asked instead, "Looking for anything special?" He ignored the bait and replied with a muttered, "Hope so." He said he had a party to go to that night, where everyone would be dressed nicely. "I never dress up," he said.

In the fitting room, he failed to close the door, undressing before me. His briefs were too large, the elastic weak, and the skin on his thighs pale enough for the veins to show. Weeks later, when I finally asked, he told me he'd left the door open to teach me of our differences, the extremes of them, and that even our bodies made testament to the fact. And though it's true his is not a beautiful body, I saw that day that his posture and the proud jut of his sternum were things I immediately wanted to know, to touch. He tried on only one set of the clothes I'd picked. He stepped in front of the mirror and said, "It's fine, this is fine," before returning to his own clothes, visibly relieved. At the register, he paid with cash, a rarity in my department, then said I could join him at the party if I wanted. "I can bring someone," he said. "It's a guy I painted for. He's like you, the clothes and all."

It wasn't the most romantic of invitations, but it was enough. Looking back, I know I've rarely felt so unable to understand myself. Men approach me regularly, but Eric made my skin tingle and my chest clench. It was a strange, humbling response for me to have.

That first date, we had a decent enough time, even though the ratio of our words was markedly uneven and I stubbed my toe on a table, forcing me to spend the rest of the night without a shoe. But we never discussed how we met, and haven't since. It's as if, both afraid we saw too much too fast, we've waited while current emotions attempt to catch up and overtake that first heat of shame, admiration, shock, connection, whatever it was we felt.

At the time of that first date with Eric I lived where I do now, rent-free in a penthouse on Turtle Creek. Eric still believes I pay money, still thinks my landlord is an old family friend. The rooms are large and exquisitely appointed. On the walls are moody abstract canvases with famous names painted in a bottom corner, a few of which I've chosen. The Diebenkorn in the dining room is my favorite.

Through the windows, almost all floor-to-ceiling, I can see the Dallas skyline, which isn't particularly grand or expansive, but is at least lit up nicely at night. The place is owned by a man named Howard Clenellan, and there are those who would say he owns me, too. He's quite old, a world-class talent in the giving of promises, and the spender of enough inherited wealth to make grown men weep.

I met Howard my second day on the sales floor when I sold him a Zegna shearling with horn buttons, a very nice coat. He returned the next day with a blue box from Tiffany's, a gold bracelet inside. That night, he took me to dinner at The Mansion and home. Since then, our arrangement has never been verbalized. We've let it evolve into its own quirky little demon by itself. He swears one day he'll fund a store for me to run and, in the meantime, I live here and travel, accepted in a world quite different from anything I've known before.

Prior to Howard, I lived paycheck-to-paycheck and, as a kid, a teenager, I watched while my parents tossed a checkbook around like a hot stone, explaining to my sister it was too expensive to be a cheerleader, regardless of the perfection of her jump kicks. To me, they swore that a boy needed only three pairs of jeans, and that white T-shirts were as acceptable and interesting as blue, green, and black, all colors I coveted.

So, obviously, being Howard's young companion has its advantages. And in return, what Howard wants most is the company, a reinforcing of the notion that I would be with him regardless of the promise, the life, and will continue to be so until he's gone. He can't understand that when I date other men, they're not anyone he knows, and he can't fathom why I work. For both of these, I have reasons, although he won't hear them because he's not someone I'd ever wish to hurt. I work at Neimans because it's something of my own. I choose men beyond his circle so he'll never know how their touch exposes a need in me I ignore whenever I can.

Because what Howard also wants, and what I've also become a master of ignoring, generally, I think, is for me to perform as I did our first time together. When he set up the scenario, his voice careful and his manner deferent, I was glad I'd imbibed at dinner. Now, though, it's rote.

What I do is this: with gold silk cords, I tie him at the wrists and ankles. He's fully dressed, as he remains. A third cord goes around his waist, so that he's strapped to an old wooden chair that otherwise sits half-covered in the closet. The chair's in poor condition, the joints rickety and the finish marred. It's the only thing left of Howard's father, because the money, all from Howard's grandfather, came with the stipulation that the generation between them be forgotten. Then, once Howard is secured, I strip and masturbate for what sometimes feels like forever. I'm careful not to touch him or speak. There's not a sound in the room but our breathing. Howard prefers that I rotate, giving him a view of all sides while I alternate hands, keeping the other always busy, rubbing my chest, my ass, my face. He stays perfectly still as I do this, a satisfied Buddha who desires constant motion on my part, the hitting of poses that never seem posed.

I'm not the only man who provides this show for Howard, but I am the only regular. I assume that's because I'm good at it, this unnecessary skill.

Today was the first day of Last Call, the final clearance sale at Neiman Marcus. Already, I've been there three years longer than I planned, my original estimate a reasonable and what I thought to be a wholly generous six months. In the meantime, I was supposed to find a better, more suitable job, whatever that might have been. But then I met Howard. And it's not as if the business world of the Metroplex was impressed with my English degree from Aggieland, my lack of experience, and my many proclamations that I'm an organized self-starter and a fine communicator. That's why I ended up at Neimans in the first place.

The truth is that I appreciate the insulated nuttiness of where I work. On the surface, my job requires the ability to stand for eight hours in a small room, to animate a piece of cloth and offer well-timed assurance. But what I'm really doing is convincing whoever stands before me that this ridiculously expensive item of clothing is necessary to a life.

Let's face it. What we put on our bodies has little to do with function, everything to do with how we desire ourselves to be perceived, the world all a show. This is nothing new. It's the same with cars, houses, boats, whatever. And an insane price can actually help.

So, if a man holds up a Versace shirt and says, "Price?" I don't say, "Two thousand," I say, "Two." I simplify.

Some men become fidgety and say, "Dollars? Hundred? Thousand? Jesus." But other men, the ones who cause me to have a paycheck, become smug. They say, "No problem," and hand me a card. I've decided that it all comes down to worthiness, what a man thinks he deserves.

Only one shopper from the day stands out to me now, which isn't so uncommon. After a zillion people, laziness sets in and it becomes easy to see them as faceless, all the same. But this man,

Mr. Anton Kepler, has bugged me all season about one ridiculous shirt.

Actually, it's happened before. I've watched it. A man will see some piece of clothing that is completely unlike anything he owns or has ever owned before, and will covet it. It's an irrational desire, but true and heartfelt all the same. The shirt or pants or jacket might represent a new position in life, or symbolize a fit, more virile past, or any number of things.

For Mr. Kepler, the Versace shirt of his dreams seemed to encapsulate—with just fabric, buttons, and thread—all the things he's never allowed himself to have. It was the antidote to a lifetime of being reasonable. He's come in the store for two months now and tried it on. The shirt is silk, a brilliant gold on a black ground, the pattern a complicated series of medallion rosettes with a Greek key border.

It's not a subtle or necessary shirt in any way. And it requires a wearer just as obvious or it tends to look cheap and overwhelming, which is exactly how it looked on Mr. Kepler, a short, fiftyish man with wire-rimmed glasses and little hair. But he loved that shirt.

This morning, I told him the truth, that a client called before we opened and asked me to stash the shirt away for him. Still, Mr. Kepler wanted to try it on, lamenting that he'd never broken down and bought it. I said I understood, but explained again that the shirt was someone else's, that he couldn't see it. But two hours later, Mr. Conklin phoned to say he didn't want the shirt after all, and this afternoon, when Mr. Kepler came in to question me one last time, he found it wadded on the sale table, thrown in with everything else. He was furious, and in a room that remains fairly quiet, he yelled at me, his face red and clenched as tightly as his fists. He did not buy the shirt.

Instead, he caused the words of Miss Brozowski to come to mind after all these years. I have the nagging suspicion that had Mr. Kepler been in her class, she would have considered him redeemed today. Because even though he failed to act until it was too late, until the object of his desire had been relegated to nothing special, he made his decision to walk away with pride.

But all I can think is that if every decision presupposes regret, and even no decision is a decision of sorts, then how does any human discover the bravery required to move even a finger?

* * *

For four and a half months now, Eric's been the only man I've dated, the only man other than Howard who's seen me naked, the only man to see me unprepared, or nervous, or anything but glib. Four nights ago, he drove me in his pickup with "Reade Painting" on the side to White Rock, a small lake within the city. We watched joggers, ducks, and the setting sun.

When it was finally dark, he told me that three weeks earlier, back in Kansas, his father had died. I'd seen no signs of loss or mourning. He said also that he'd been born and raised there, in Mullinville, that his father's liver failure was not a great surprise considering the alcoholic life he'd led, and that his mother wanted him home.

With my own odd life in mind, I find it best not to pry. Therefore, the death was new information, as was the explanation that Mullinville rests off Highway 54, ten miles from Greensburg, home of the world's largest hand-dug well, and half an hour from Meade, home of the Dalton Gang. But Mullinville itself, Eric said, is home to nothing except assorted generations of wheat farmers and their interwoven families. He deemed the place "tiny," "backward," and the inhabitants "beyond fucked up."

"I almost went out of my mind growing up there," he added. "Everybody knows everybody, everybody's got their nose up your ass, sniffing for shit so they can use it against you." He said he wouldn't even think of what he was considering except for the chance at good money. "And for Mom," he added, his voice suggesting this might be the real reason.

His plan concerned his father's junkyard, Eric's now, and the ideas he had to make it as profitable as he'd always been convinced it could be. "We grew up poor," he said, " 'cause Dad was embarrassed about being the junk man. But it didn't have to be that way. It could have been a business. I always used to tell him if he would just sell off parts instead of the whole damn car, and pull in business from Larned and Greensburg, which wouldn't be hard, and haul certain kinds of shit to Dodge City, then we'd have money to get into recycling. And then, yeah, it's every man for himself." He slapped his hand on the steering wheel and looked at me. "That makes sense," he said. "Right?"

It didn't, but before I could think of anything to say, he faced the front window again, squinting as if he could see what he described there, rising from the lake. His excitement filled entirely the cabin of that pickup. It seemed to gobble every bit of available air.

So, I should have found it simple to join in, to exclaim and wave my hands, to ask questions and prove I understood. But it was such dispiriting news to hear, this talk of him elsewhere. I kept my face toward the water, reflections of the new moon winking from there without any junkyard heaven I could see. All I could picture was trash and pinched-looking elderly people staring aghast. If I wanted to be cruel, I'd swear Eric babbled, ideas coming almost too fast for his mouth to handle.

When we got back to his place, Eric surprised me again. He lives in a duplex on Abbott. It's not a fancy place, but it's nice enough. He has a full-sized bed in the tiny bedroom, a three-foot stack of magazines beside the commode. In the living room is a recliner and a television off to the side, the rest of the space saved for a huge rectangle of plywood he's glued together for his jigsaw puzzles. Currently, he's working on a five-thousand-piece picture of St. Peter's Cathedral. It's sixty-two by forty-one inches, and the colors are mostly drab, with just a touch of red. It would drive me insane.

As we walked inside, I was telling myself how stupid it was to be angry and climbed atop the recliner, stretching my legs over the sides. After all, what could I expect? I'd asked Eric once why we worked well together and he'd said our differences gave him a reason to wonder about things he normally wouldn't, that I challenged him. But surely a mother and a new business could easily supplant that.

Eric turned on the light and squatted over an unfinished corner of the puzzle. "We'd be good there," he said.

"St. Peter's?"

He laughed. "No, of course not. In Mullinville. We'd be good in Kansas."

I didn't have a clue what to say. Honestly, not through his whole speech at the lake or during the drive back did I ever consider going with him, did I ever think he would ask. "Yeah, I'd fit right in," I blurted. "Just transfer me to the Neimans there and I'd give that designer customer a few lessons in real style. They'd love me."

Eric completed the bodies of some people at the base of a col-

umn. "You'd work with me," he said. "For us." He twiddled
another piece between his fingers. "Of course, you couldn't wear
some of those clothes. But you could be you," he said as if he
believed it. "I'm not going to lie, not going to hide, that's for
damn sure." He gave that sharp intake of breath that means he's
seen the piece he wants. "I wouldn't let anything happen to you,"
he said, looking up, his face sincere enough to kill me. "You
know that."

Wes the bartender thinks I mope too much. He's told me this,
and also that I should give him a chance to cheer me up. I tell him
thanks, but no. "My brother, it's all too complicated already," I
say. But I do take another beer, listening while the blind man
hawks his cassettes, proving he's not so different after all, and
three young women with way too much hair fight over their bill
behind me. Everyone in this place doesn't seem quite so perky or
at ease anymore. I don't know if the difference is mine or theirs.
I assume alcohol's had something to do with it.

After I left Eric's that night, with his offer still a thing I couldn't
or wouldn't believe, I drove back to White Rock. I knew that
before he offered again, before I could answer, he needed to
know certain things, namely that Howard wasn't merely a family friend who gave me a room, a man so elderly that Eric and I
needed to spend our time at his duplex or out somewhere. Eric
needed to know everything.

But as I searched again the surface of that lake, waiting for some
fine vision of a combined future to break the waves, I realized I
didn't have the nerve. I'd ignored the truth for so long I couldn't
imagine explaining it, especially not to him. I wondered where any
nerve I'd ever owned had disappeared and remembered how I'd
been forceful and rambunctious the first half of my life. I might
have understood Eric's father better than Eric had, my own dead
father an excellent teacher of shame. I cried that night, but only
enough to know how much more I could if I wanted.

The next morning, I was running late and gulped a piece of
toast almost as it leapt from the toaster. It was Luisa's day, so I
left the saucer and a glass in the sink, knowing she would take
care of it. I hurried down the hallway, past Howard's room, and
then stopped. He was twisted on his bed, still asleep, but beside
the closet door I saw something I'd forgotten.

Weeks earlier, Howard had decided to have his bedroom repainted again, had even had the paint mixed to match some remembered cat's nose. He'd put the actual job off only because his usual painter was in the midst of another job, a long one. I stood there, staring at that paint, and the idea came so fully formed into my head it seemed I'd always had it.

At work, I immediately phoned Eric, talking before he could say hello. I told him I understood he already had something lined up, but this would be a favor to me. I told him it was the only way I might be able to leave behind my old family friend with a clear conscience.

"Tomorrow," I said. "You have to do this. You have to."

And so, two days ago, Eric met Howard. I worked pre-sale that morning with a markedly low number of brain cells focused on my job. I disappointed the determined Mr. Kepler, and by lunch I knew I couldn't stay away from Howard's anymore.

Still, I drove slowly, surprised it had begun to sprinkle, and parked carefully beneath the building, saying hello to the parking attendant and the security guard inside. I was pleasant on the elevator, and when I stepped into Howard's foyer, I gave Luisa a quick hug and explained that I was just darting in, that I needed nothing, thanks. I walked as quietly as possible to the door of Howard's room and sat in the hallway just beyond it. The afternoon before, Howard had hired two men to move the furniture several feet from the walls and drape it all. Now, the third of the room I could see looked ghostly like that, the drizzle beyond the windows spattering the glass and wavering the sights beyond it. I couldn't see either Eric or Howard, but their voices were clear.

"Yeah?" Eric asked, and Howard answered, "Yes, exactly."

I heard a metallic thump and Howard say, "Careful." My eyes traveled the blotched skyline too quickly.

"Mitch was beautiful in Paris," Howard continued. "I took him there one summer, so pleased with the reaction. He speaks the language, and led me around for two weeks. It's wonderful to see the world through a young man's eyes. At night, we walked in any direction, wherever our feet and wits took us. Mitch is a fine boy."

Howard's a fine boy, too, I thought, one who never grew up because he never had to. There are times I envy him. He coughed, and I imagined the folds of flesh at his neck and jaw stretching with the thrust of his face. It was a sound I would have recognized anywhere, one I will remember the rest of my life.

I'd always considered the trip to Paris a disaster, my poor French able to get us only into trouble. That he'd been proud of me felt good, felt like a hand on my shoulder, just the firm, warm pressure of it. I leaned my head against the door frame, thinking that he kept me afloat, somehow even with the water's surface.

After a moment, Howard continued. "Mitch always knows what he likes, too. He's quite decisive," he said. I shook my head. It was clear how little he and I actually talked, how limited we kept each other. I couldn't remember the last time I'd voiced an opinion about anything other than clothing or meals or rooms or furniture or paintings, about anything that wasn't made by other people, bought by other people. I looked the length of the hallway into the dining room, at the Diebenkorn. It's price had been in the high six figures, but Howard bought it because I liked it. I still do. The colors are mostly green and blue, and seem to hover, to glow, the light somehow trapped inside. But it belongs to Howard. It's part of my life only as long as I'm in his house, in his life.

"But I don't think he knows what he wants," Howard said. "Which makes it difficult. I only want to see him happy." He paused. "And you think this Mullinville, a junkyard, will do that? I must say I can't really see it. Mitch in a junkyard, in some little town. It sounds horrible, not like him at all."

"I think I can make him happy." Eric's voice was soft, but not unsure.

"Ah," Howard said. "But you are a different kind of man, Mr. Reade. From Mitchell and myself. You work with your hands, whereas Mitch is a creature of his senses. Every day, he tells people what is beautiful and what is not. And people listen to him, they believe him. I think you've misjudged yourself."

At that, I leaned through the doorway to see Eric in the center of the room, faced away and bent over. In the corner, Howard sat in his father's old chair. He was slouched comfortably, his legs crossed at the knee, one foot barely swinging. I watched his face as he watched mine, and it became obvious what he learned there. I thought of turning to Eric and proclaiming that I knew precisely what I wanted, even though I didn't deserve it. But I knew Howard would finish explaining all about me now. He would say whatever it took to make his point.

When I left, Eric's body curled in almost the exact same position mine had been on the first night we met.

At a commission of eight percent, I made almost $1,800 today. It took fourteen hours with only one short break, but that's a Last Call record for me, and I think for my department. Which proves little except that I can work as hard as the next guy and that I'm not wholly dependent on Howard for things.

I got the note this evening. Judy, a co-worker from the Polo department, brought it back to the fitting rooms. "He wouldn't let me transfer the call," she said. She is older and cherished department-wide. She mothers us all, and we let her. "He made me take this down exactly," she said. She handed me a folded piece of ripped paper and asked, "Are you okay?"

I lied that I was, stuffing the note in my pocket and returning attention to my customer, a man named Johnny, who had huge, cartoon muscles and a blue tattoo of a bird on his neck. I was frantically trying to sell him Mr. Kepler's Versace shirt. All day, I'd shown it repeatedly, without any luck, beginning to crazily believe the shirt was haunting me. But now that it was on this guy, the best body for it I'd seen all day, I knew I had a real shot to see it go. He was modeling it for his girlfriend, Amy, flexing his biceps against the fabric. She was short and giggly, with no hips to speak of, but perfectly conical breasts.

And when she handed me a credit card, I pulled her close, hugging those man-made breasts right to my stomach. I was amazed by how sweet she smelled. "The service," she squealed. "It's so friendly."

As they left, I stepped into the office and pulled the note from my pocket. "Still deciding," it said. "Midnight at Frank's on Fitzhugh. If I'm brave enough to ask again, you have to answer." Since he'd failed to call before now, to leave any sort of message with Howard, my assumption had been that I'd never see Eric again. To learn now that decisions were yet to be made, that I still had a part in this, gave me a hope that felt too large, like how a whole pie in five minutes might taste to someone starving.

Yesterday, after I left for work, Eric had stoically returned to

Howard's and finished the job. Howard said he watched Eric paint the whole afternoon, and though Eric didn't seem to mind being watched, he refused to talk about me or anything else. "He does have a plain, methodical something about him," Howard told me last night. "I see that. But enough for a life?"

I knew Howard wanted me to argue, to give him a reason to speak and tell me everything to think. But I concentrated on work instead, readying thank you notes and making lists of who might buy what.

In the past, I've suggested that the jobs Eric and I hold are similar. He makes buildings look better, and I do the same for people. But his silence in reply to this has always made clear what he's too nice to say. He doesn't show paint to the houses and say, "Here. You like it?" And even on a successful day like this one, I don't zip the trousers, or button the shirt, or weave the clothes around someone who stands there patiently nude.

Tonight, as I finish a third beer, these strike me as unfortunate, vital differences. It's after midnight, which is fast becoming all I can think about, and Frank's has begun to thin. Worker bees need to rest before tomorrow, or maybe they know of a better place to go this late.

The blues singer has been silent for a while, the last request called out twenty minutes ago. Now, he sits atop a stool two down from mine and shakes hands with anyone who stops by, all saying something nice. He looks conspicuously healthy up close, his skin coffee-colored and smooth, his hair lustrous. He grins when Wes gives him a drink and says, "Good man."

"Sounding real strong tonight," Wes tells him.

"That's true," I add, staring at the clock above the lined-up bottles, feeling weak and surly. "Incredibly strong," I say.

The singer removes his shades and looks at me, nodding. I watch him for a moment, then wave my hand before his face like an idiot, flinching when he blinks. His eyes are light blue and look entirely normal. It's only after a moment that I realize there's no focus to them, no change, as if they've been painted on by someone more concerned with color than function.

"You know, I can still feel," he says and waves his hand between us. "The air?"

Honestly, it makes me want to reach over and thump him. "So?" I ask. "What's with the lack of sight?"

He doesn't even pause. "Jerking off as a kid," he says. "Isn't that how it happens? Too much and you'll go blind?"

It's perfect, and I love it. I laugh until I cough, slapping the bar like some drunken old geezer. Wes joins in, and the guy on the other side of me, too, all of us so damn proud of a blind man with a sense of humor.

But when he adds, "We do what we gotta," I think of Howard, of standing before him with my dick in my hand, my legs spread, and my mind off God knows where. Suddenly, it's not so funny anymore. It's unbearable, and I can't feel anything. I know beyond any doubt that Eric's not walking through that door, not giving me another chance.

And who can blame him? It took courage bordering on stupidity just to leave the message at work, just to give the two of us another thought. His mother's counting on her implacable son to return, not me. She doesn't want some fancy boy, and I don't want a junkyard. Seriously, if Eric and I were to work together, live together, take on a town together, I couldn't rely on my usual shtick. It's not like I'd be showing off rusted tools, or a beat-up tub, or a mountain of tires and saying, "This season, worn rubber is a major statement from Goodyear."

Eric said I could be myself in Mullinville, but could I? Over the past decade, I've learned a way of life that sits like a watched pot, never boiling. I ignore the highs and lows. I concentrate on the middle. But in Kansas, I imagine life would force water, even blood, to bubble up.

So, thirty minutes after the appointed moment, I give up and leave. I tell Wes and the blues singer to have a grand, good night, then head for the door, assuring myself I would have told Eric no. I would have been brave and saved him, smart enough not to attempt the impossible act of peeling layers of learned indifference, like skin and muscle to the marrow of my bone.

Still, he lifted me above what I'd known, and I won't ever forget that. He bore me up.

It's muggy and noisy when I step outside, cars taking off when the stoplight changes as if it hurts to be still. Above me, the moon is a sleek crescent, stark and yellowed, the stars so distant. I cock my head back and stare, wondering still about Miss Brozowski and hard decisions. Maybe the simple act of making one was the important part of this, but I can't believe that. No matter how hard I try, it feels impossible to spin this night into something I can live with. It's all about regrets again, how life is full of them no matter what's decided, and what's done.

The 7-Eleven store across the street is lit up and promising convenience. I think about hurrying over there to find caffeine to counteract the beers I've had, but I should probably just go home and go to bed. Sleep might be the only thing to help.

I turn to my left and walk toward the parking lot, stopping when I hear the blind man start up again. I'm sorry I was rude to him, sorry he's the better, wiser man. I glance again at the 7-Eleven, but go ahead around the corner, and there's Eric. He's backed his pickup into the space beside my car, and sits on the tailgate, scratching dried paint from the handle of a brush. His posture suggests it's just a night, one of many. He's in a ratty pair of jeans and an old T-shirt. He looks the best I've ever seen him.

Staring and silent, I think again of Miss Brozowski. When I knew her, she was probably near the age I am now. Yet she was certain enough to tell an eight-year-old boy that a life could be mapped, each decision building on the last.

But how could that account for this man before me? A sudden shock of instant, delirious hope overcomes me, and I believe, completely, at least for this moment, that if we're lucky, inexact and unknowing as we are, our decisions are rarely made autonomously. That's what Miss Brozowski either didn't know or had forgotten. Suddenly, I feel sorry for her.

"Why didn't you come in?" I ask.

Eric shrugs. "This way I could still leave when I saw you coming." He laughs at the look on my face and says, "Oh, come on. It'll be harder with you, but impossible without." He fiddles with the paint brush and looks at me, scrunching his face into something still amused, but wary.

He's thinking about his own set of decisions, I bet.

MARRIAGE

MICHAEL BENDZELA

Lydia

I could hear an engine humming out in the snow, so I parted the drapes and looked out. There they sat in that little truck, like they were waiting for someone to come out and see what they wanted, like a couple of Siamese twins. Their little tailpipe gave off white puffs that looked solid in the frigid air. I was surprised the little SOB even had the nerve to show up in the dooryard with him. At least he knew better than to set foot in the house, no matter if it used to be his. If he tried such a thing with Carolyn around, there's no telling what might happen. I was thinking: That other one better not even get out of the truck if he knows what's good for him.

I didn't know what to do: I just let go of the drapes. I had this funny, panicky feeling. It was like some bad prediction come true.

"Carolyn?"

Should I tell her he was out there and that he'd brought that other one with him, knowing she might have an attack? She heard the catch in my voice when I said her name, and pushed herself up off the couch and stomped over to the window. She stood there a minute looking at them, sizing them up, like figuring out the range and angle for the best shot. Maybe she was taking in that other one—the one who turned her husband's head around till he was looking out over his backside. The one she hadn't seen yet. Kimberly didn't even look up from the TV.

Just then the driver's door opened: There he stood, just as gangly and beaky-nosed and pimple-scarred (with the little beard to try and cover it up) as the day she looked at his sorry mug and said "I do." I always thought he was a dub. Maybe I should of told her that before she decided to marry him: Why would you want to marry something like that? Maybe I should of done a lot of things. I can just imagine how she would of taken it. Things seem simple when you look back on them, but at the time I figured better just to sit back and let things take their course, hoping by not interfering she'd see the error of her ways herself. Huh!

"Look at him," Carolyn said, wrinkling up her nose. "He's going up to the garage."

"Probably looking for that snowblower."

"Well, he's in for a little surprise." I've never seen a woman make such an evil face before. She said at the window, "I got rid of the goddamn thing, you old faggot."

"Carolyn."

"Well *I'm* certainly not going to use it."

"I meant, watch your mouth in front of Kimberly."

She let go of that curtain like it bit her. "What the hell did he bring *him* here for?"

"Maybe he thought he'd need a hand loading the snow-blower."

I could appreciate her disgust, but I was afraid his presence was upsetting her too much, so I decided to take matters into my own hands. I wrapped a sweater around my housecoat. And me just out of the tub.

"Where do you think you're going?" she said.

"Someone needs to go out there and tell him whatever he's looking for ain't here. Then I'll tell him to get back in his little truck and beat it. I don't want him coming up here to this house causing a commotion with you in the condition you're in."

"It's not like I'm going to die, Mother."

"No, but you act like you might." I slipped on my snow boots. "And there are some things medicine can't take care of."

"You're not going out in that cold with a wet head."

"Just lay back down. It'll only take a second. I have no intention of socializing with him."

Fact is, I hadn't seen him since he dropped his little bomb and sent Carolyn into her latest tailspin, and I'd be darned if I'd let him get away before I gave him a little piece of my mind.

Vic

We'd been dumped on, first storm of the season. The air afterward was so cold it snapped. Or, as we used to say, if you let a fart you'd have to chip it out of your shorts. But the cold and the snow didn't stop that old woman from coming down the snowy walkway in just a housecoat and sweater, with wet hair yet, yelling at Barry as he was trying to get into the garage to get his snowblower. *His* garage, *his* snowblower.

"Oh shit," I said out loud. I wondered if I should hop in the driver's seat and shift into reverse for a quick getaway. Barry was still trying to fit his key into the door lock. Apparently the bitch had changed the locks already. She didn't waste any time, that one. I'd even swear she was counting on his leaving all along, but Barry says that's ridiculous. He says she never had a clue that anything like this would happen. "Uh-huh," I say, skeptically. "What do you mean, 'Uh-huh'?" he says. "I just mean I find it a little hard to believe she didn't have any idea that something was, shall we say, amiss."

That woman, the bitch's mother, walked up to him at the garage with her mouth moving a mile a minute, biting off chunks of cold air and spitting them back at him as steam. He just stood there while she got it all out. Then he said something back, and she began chewing the air again before he could finish what he was saying. He just made a quick about-face and came back to the truck and got in.

"She *sold* the goddamn thing." He slammed the door on "goddamn." "I don't know how much more of this shit I can take."

That woman came toward the truck, mouth still ratcheting. She was tugging that sweater tighter around her housecoat, as if she had some wild animal hidden under it that she didn't want to let get away.

"Why is she coming to my side?" I looked over at Barry, but he was gazing out his window. She thumped her finger against the glass and said, "Open this window." I grinned, cracked it a little, and leaned back, thinking she wanted to take a parting shot at Barry.

She looked me up and down the way she might look at a snake before she grinds her heel into it. She said, "Finally, I get to *see* what you're like." There was now ice in her wet hair. "I've certainly *heard* enough about you. For some reason I thought you'd be . . . *different*."

I could feel a smile forming on my mouth like the ice forming in her hair.

"Disappointed?" I said.

She just ripped her eyes away from me and threw them across the truck at Barry. It was like I'd slid off the face of the earth as far as she was concerned. "I'm glad that little girl's not out here to see this." The cold flooded in through the window as she launched into Barry.

"You've really lowered yourself this time, you know that? There she lays, deathly ill up in that big house, while you snoop around here with *this*"—flicking her eyes at me—"trying to steal stuff out of the garage."

"That snowblower was a gift from my father," Barry said.

"So why don't you go and tell your father why you don't have it anymore? Or maybe I could tell him for you. Would you like me to call your father, Barry, and tell him the whole story about why the snowblower's not in the garage anymore? I bet he'd get a kick out of that story. Unless he's heard it already. Did you tell him that story yet? How you left behind a sick wife and daughter for a sick lifestyle—"

Barry put the truck in gear. "Goodbye, Lydia."

I cranked up the window, and we spun out of there. I reached over and turned up the heat, waiting for the right time to say what I wanted to say. We drove a long time before I realized there is no right time to say such things.

"You know, Barry, you have this way of sitting there and taking abuse like you like it."

"So we use shovels," he said.

Lydia

I sat in a kitchen chair while she went at my hair with the blow dryer. She tsk-tsked me as she rubbed my head, thawing out my hair. I could see that Christmas tree of theirs—by "theirs" I mean hers and Kimberly's—going right up into that pretty cathedral ceiling like some kind of statue in a museum. It had been set up in the living room since Thanksgiving. Me and Carl made sure that tree had just as many Christmas presents under it this year as last. Weren't no way we'd see Kimberly disappointed just because her father decided to have a midlife crisis during the holidays. Carolyn made most of the ornaments herself: she'd taken half the old ornaments off the tree and thrown them into the garbage the day he left, so she and Kimberly had to spend a lot of time at the kitchen table making new ones, using ideas from one of the several decorating magazines she gets.

It's too bad all this had to happen right before the holidays. At least with the ornaments she's got something to busy herself with so she don't have to think about it all the time and sicken herself. She says she's going to hold on to all they got, even if it kills her. She's already started selling stuff off or throwing it out, like it's all hers. She says if he was so concerned about who owns what he wouldn't of dumped them so quick.

She lifted my hair and whipped that stream of hot air back and forth across the back of my neck, yelling over the screaming motor, "Did it look like either of them had AIDS?"

"My goodness, Carolyn! . . . Watch that thing, you'll burn my neck. I got enough to worry about without wondering if you might of picked up something in addition to all this."

She just laughed. "There ain't a *thing* to worry about, Mother. I hope he does have it. That way me and Kim will just inherit everything instead of having to take him to court." Her fingernails scratched my scalp as she rubbed the wetness away.

"You're doing a good job of making sure there is no more 'everything.' "

"Whatever he left behind is mine as far as I'm concerned. I'll sell it all off if I want to, or cart it to the dump."

"You'd better wait and see what that Portland lawyer says first."

"Possession is nine-tenths of the law. If that lawyer can't see that, then I'll just hire me a better one."

She clicked off the hair dryer: suddenly the sounds I don't normally notice in that big house were magnified—the Frigidaire, the furnace, the television babbling at Kimberly in the other room. Our voices seemed too loud, and I was afraid Kimberly would hear some of the awful things her mother was saying.

"You can barely afford this one, so how do you think you're going to be able to hire a better one?"

"I expect to make it all back in the settlement. That's why they call it taking him to the cleaners. You clean out his bank account."

"That's putting an awful lot of trust in lawyers."

She wound up the cord and put the dryer back in its box. "What judge is going to side with someone like him? They'll be as disgusted as I am." She dropped the box in a drawer and slammed it shut. Then she picked up a brush and started brushing out the snarls. "The no-good son of a bitch, doing this to his daughter at Christmas time."

"Christmas is still three weeks away," I said. After she'd been brushing awhile, I said, "Carolyn, I've been wondering."

She stopped brushing. "About what?"

"About if there were any signs. All those years—couldn't you tell that something was wrong with him?"

She just began brushing again. "Mother, he had us all fooled. Do you want me to braid this for you?"

"Yes. I'd think a serious thing like that would show somehow. You said yourself you had nothing to worry about as far as catching anything from him, so doesn't that mean—"

"Mother, I haven't been well, remember?"

"Yes, but didn't he even *want* to—"

"Look." The hairbrush hit the countertop. "Whose side are you on anyhow?"

Vic

Bouts of insanity arrive as regularly as weekly installments of the soaps. Somehow Barry glides through it all as if asleep and dreaming. Paralyzed is more like it. Sometimes he just goes to bed when he hears the latest artifact hitting the rubble heap of his falling-apart life. And he won't stand up to the big bitch or her mother but just lets them walk all over him. I expect it's guilt.

We'd been living in my one-bedroom apartment in Portland with the kerosene space heater going. Things were okay for the first few weeks, then when the shit hit the fan he'd just lie there for hours looking up at the ceiling. Still trying to figure out where that cathedral went, I suppose. Imagine spending over ten years of your life building something for yourself and then having to sit back and watch while the whole thing falls down around your ears. That'll teach him for building his life around a lie.

I was lying there, my knees hooked over his shoulders—the thing he abdicated wife, daughter, cathedral ceiling for—when it occurred to me how similar it must be to having sex with a wife. Fucking is fucking. How absurd the whole business really is. All this pain just because you want something a little different. And yet it's worth risking everything for.

"Barry?"

He gave a grunt of acknowledgment.

"How much better is it with me than with her?"

He sighed, gave up, got off. Feeling guilty now, I swore I was in earnest and just curious. He said he and his wife stopped having sex a long time ago, and they were both satisfied with the arrangement, though I think "satisfied with" is a poor choice of words. She supposedly has all these back and female complaints that she has to take pills for, and that make things difficult for her. How convenient for him. I wanted to know how he could stand spending all those years without any sex.

He didn't say anything while he got back into his underwear. Then: "I didn't."

This was news to me. I pictured anonymous encounters on Portland's Western Promenade, a certain movie theater in town. I cringed, seeing as we'd made do without rubbers for a while now. And I thought I'd be safe with a married guy.

"So that's your method, just drop the bomb and see what happens. Like the way you went, 'Hi, honey, I'm gay, la-di-da,' and walked out. Now you go, 'By the way, I've been having anonymous sex all these years, tra-la-la.' "

"As usual you exaggerate."

"So it's not true, then?"

"I haven't been as much of a slut as you think."

"Just enough of one."

"Look at me—I'm healthy."

"Is that like, 'Look at me, honey, I'm straight'?"

"All right! If you really think I should be tested—"

"Yes, I really do."

And that's how we live, crisis to crisis. It's to the point that I wake up and look at myself in the mirror and say, "Honey, something's in store for you today. Don't know what, but . . ."

Makes a person just want to stay in bed and watch the soaps, or videos. Safe.

Lydia

Whenever she has one of her spells, I want to go out and find that SOB and shoot him myself. And I can still remember when they used to come up the sidewalk together, Kimberly between them, swinging from their hands. She'd see me and break out of their grip and come running at me, calling out "Nana!" through gap teeth. Meanwhile the two of them would just stand there looking at her while I bussed her cheeks and made her laugh. I remember how they devoted all their attention to her, gave her all their energy, like she was the one thing in their life that mattered. Funny how I would remember that now. It seemed perfectly natural at the time. Now it looks to me like things were shot to hell even back then.

"You should be glad he's gone," I say. "Do you want someone like that in your bed?"

She swings her head around at me, her hair flying out at the ends like a twirling skirt. "I *am* glad he's gone."

"Well then, I'd think you'd be relieved."

"*Relieved?*"

Yes, she's my daughter and I'm firmly on her side, but something's not right about all this. I just can't figure it.

When she storms out of the room, you can hear her feet reverberating in the metal heating ducts, but only in the kitchen, as the rest of the place has this gray plush carpet that absorbs the sound. I thought that carpet was a big mistake when they first got it—it's too expensive just to have people tracking snow all over it—but she loves it. I really have no right to complain about it while I'm staying here. Soon as things settle down, I'm going back home to Carl.

She's been in and out of the hospital so much lately that I don't want to leave her here alone. Seems like those pills the doctors give her don't do a damn bit of good. One minute she's a maniac stamping the floor and planning that SOB's demise, the next she's got all the drapes drawn and won't get out of bed.

This must all be really hard on Kimberly. I try to talk to her about it but she's too young to really understand what's going on. I keep having to refer to the SOB as "your father," which I do through grit teeth without making it seem so obvious. She's got the basic facts down: He's gone bad, and once he's out of the picture, they'll get everything, including the house. "Then will you *and* Bumpa come live with us, Nana?" "We'll see," I tell her. She needs to hold her ground, not let him sweet-talk her over to his side. I know she's doing all right because she's taken to calling him "Barry the Fairy," which I don't think she even knows the meaning of, but at least it shows she's in the right frame of mind. I'd say she's going to grow up to be just like her mother, thank God.

Whenever I see the two of them at the kitchen table carving ornaments out of bars of soap or scissoring the ends of each other's beautiful long hair, it's like nothing has gone wrong in their lives and I almost think everything's going to turn out all right after all, though I don't know how long Carolyn's going to be able to hang on to this house with just her job at the beauty parlor. I always did think they were a bit extravagant, even when they first got married, what with that reception they had afterward. I thought Carl would die. He even refused to cosign on some loans. Now those expensive chickens are coming home to roost. What a blow, to lose the man in the family.

On TV the other day they had this talk show with a man in a wig and a dress. He had shaved his legs and put them into pantyhose. (I hate wearing them myself, I feel like a water balloon.) He crossed his legs like a lady and acted like he was serious about it. Carolyn can't cross her legs like that, she's too fat. She was looking at the screen like her eyes wanted to pop out of their sockets. She turned to Kim and said, "*That's* what your father is. Isn't that disgusting?"

"You mean Barry the Fairy dresses like a *girl*?"

"Yes. Do you see why he's never setting foot in this house again?"

That's as close as she ever got to explaining to the girl what's been going on.

"You can't even expect prayer to help someone that far gone," I said.

Things were never like this in my day. Nor in Carolyn's, for that matter. Bad enough losing your man to another woman. This way it's double bad. Triple bad. How do you explain it to a child? I tell them to go to church, keep the sacraments, ask for God's blessing. I remind them the devil's in all our lives, and when you see it that way it don't seem so bad. Just another one of Satan's many disguises.

Vic

I knew these bisexuals.

Like clockwork: You meet a guy, he says he's bi, you and he hit it off well. He begins to confide things in you, like that you're the only one who knows about his . . . even his wife doesn't know he's . . . You have incredible sex, after which he sits on the bed rail and says, "I hope this doesn't mean we can't still be friends." To which you respond, "Why would you think otherwise?" And a week later, he still hasn't called. So you take the initiative, call, and he's so *icy*. You remind him that he's the one who said he wanted to keep communications open, to which he responds, "It's not like we're *married* or anything." And so you slam down the phone and cross out his number so hard you tear the page of your address book.

Yes, I knew these bisexuals. And I was attracted to them, nevertheless. But after growing weary of the lies, enduring a midlife crisis, and undergoing several months of therapy, I knew something had to change. With Barry, things were different. When I got a load of that bad goatee, that cornered look in the eyes, I knew I'd be taking a different tack. So when he said, "I think I'm bi," I said, "I think you're full of it."

After Barry and I finally had sex, which was anything but "bisexual," he gave me the lowdown on the two of them: They were twenty and twenty-two. She was pregnant, he was in the closet. He'd done what many people believe cures fags: he found himself a woman, impregnated her, and married her (in that order). When I ask him why the hell he had to get her pregnant first, he says he had to find out that it could be done. Apparently, doing it with a rubber wasn't enough of a public statement of his alleged normality.

"There's something powerful about being loved so intensely by a woman for so long. . . . Why are you crying?"

"I just am, okay? We don't have to analyze everything."

"I'm sorry. I'm just trying to explain what it was like. It was largely a lie, but there was something undeniably powerful about it."

The unrepentant fag wipes his eyes. "Love's love, I guess."

"And yet I don't understand how love—her love, especially—could turn to hate so fast. Regardless of the, uh, circumstances."

"Barry, love turns to hate the way milk turns to cheese."

"But milk needs a culture to turn to cheese. What does love need to turn to hate?"

"Lies, Barry. Lies are the culture that turns the sweetest of milk into the stinkiest of cheese."

"Some people like stinky cheese."

"Yeah, well, *I* don't. I hope you're through with the lies, Barry."

"I hope so, too."

Here's a lie: "Family values."

The bitch apparently doesn't know you don't side against flesh and blood just because you think he might be wrong; that's exactly when you've got to stand by him. And what they're doing to that little girl is about as far from family values as you can get.

He's partly to blame, of course. Not because he decided to end that false life of his but because he doesn't put his foot down while they cart away his life. If you let them get away with their shenanigans, it only looks like you must think you deserve it. It takes a man to follow through on what he's started, and I think what pisses me off the most is this half-assed way of going about things. He needs to stand up for himself, and the fact that he just lies there like a dog taking a kicking like he deserves it makes me want to lean down and give him a good kick myself.

The way I figure it, she's been a party to the lie all along. What kind of woman puts up with a husband who hasn't fucked her in years, even if he keeps the mortgage paid?

Everyone sides with her, of course. He walked out on her (rather, he had to leave because she began throwing coffee mugs at him), she did nothing to deserve it, and he committed adultery. What's worse is people believe his leaving her for a man instead of a woman is somehow the worst thing he could have done. What was he supposed to do, stay married to her? There are those who believe so: to spare his wife and child the embarrassment—that is, to keep that expensive cathedral ceiling over their heads—he should never have told her about me. Never mind that their marriage, that so-called sacred institution, was a facade covering up the truth—he's a fag, she's a leech.

Supposedly his leaving her for a man is an insult to her womanhood. So if he had left her for another woman that would have been, what, a compliment to her womanhood?

Then they say: "You're the one he left her for, you'd say anything to justify it."

In other words, I'm the fag that broke up their marriage, so none of what I say has any validity.

My ass.

Lydia

Maine may be a large state, but it's small people-wise. These small towns sometimes feel like a shoebox with about a dozen people in it. It don't take long for the parties involved in some personal affair to cross paths, and it always happens when you least expect it. Or want it.

I can just imagine how it happened. I'd been dreading all along something like it happening.

I sometimes wonder if she hasn't always wanted to behave like this, only there was a lid on it as long as they were married. I can't really believe that about my own daughter, though.

Carolyn took Kimberly out to the Maine Mall to try on some new shoes. This after having maxed out the credit cards for Christmas. Usually the man has control of the finances, but since he up and left, she's been taking charge, you could say. This was before he realized what she was up to and canceled the credit cards. Maybe he really did let her keep those cards out of concern for the child, just like he said he did. Little did he know she'd take it as an invitation to go on a revenge shopping spree. She'd wait in line with the cards (I've seen her do this) and if they rejected one she'd just hand them another.

They tried this new store at the mall where Kim found a pair of the ugliest shoes you could imagine a girl wanting. They looked like what we would have called clodhoppers in my day, but they were what she wanted. Big and black and ugly as sin, with steel toes. Now what a girl in junior high wants with steel toes is beyond me. It wasn't until Carolyn saw the price tag that she was convinced Kim should have them.

Then who walks in but the SOB himself. Come to find out that other one works there at the shoe store (luckily he didn't try to put those shoes on Kim for her) and I guess Barry had come in to wait for him to get off work so he could drive him home.

Now I know Carolyn must of said something first. That's just the way she is. She shoots from the lip, says whatever's on her mind, no matter if it isn't the right place or the right time, let alone the right thing to say. I can just see that girl standing there with those new clodhoppers on her feet, looking around for someone to come save her. I would of if I'd been there. That other one just walks away like he's got more important things to do than listen to the two of them snap at each other. I can hear her voice rising while the SOB just looks at her like he can't believe what he's hearing. And Kim crying in those ugly black shoes she wants so bad. Then, from what Carolyn says, he told her to shut her fat mouth, that it was a public place, and she shouldn't behave in such a way. He didn't come there to listen to her, and so on. Now maybe that girl just decided she'd had enough—what did she know, really?—so she walks up to him and kicks him in the leg with one of those clodhoppers. Hard. Metal toes, too, so he's nearly crippled. She leans over him and shrieks, "I hope you *die!*" hair winging out like her mother's as she turns on them ugly heels and runs off.

Now the store security guard thinks she's trying to shoplift those new shoes and heads out after her: he has basically to drag her back into the store. That other one was standing there with a customer's high heel in his hand, open-mouthed. After a long argument, the guard sees that Carolyn was indeed intending on paying for the shoes after all.

See? Here's the credit card, and here's her old shoes right here on the floor. Barry backs her up, too. So they run the card through—and the machine won't take it. So Carolyn turns and smacks the little SOB right on that little beard of his. Barry offers to pay cash for them, but Carolyn says she'd rather die than have that girl walk out of that store with those shoes after he embarrassed her by canceling the credit cards without telling her first. But he didn't listen, he just asked that other one for some cash and gave the checkout lady the money. I can just see him sitting on one of the shoe-trying-on benches, raising his pants leg to see where Kim kicked him, Carolyn's red hand print glowing on his cheek. He looks up at his daughter like he doesn't know who she is anymore. The other one stands there with that high heel in his hand like he planned on putting it on himself. Good Lord, talk about a scene.

Vic

The worst thing is, she has succeeded in turning that girl against him. The justification being that because he's a fag, he deserves it. The family split right down the middle (or rather into two-thirds and one-third), their side blaming the split on him, on me—us.

I'd told him he was asking for trouble by letting her have those credit cards. If the girl needed new shoes that bad, he could have bought them for her. Then I saw for myself just how far gone that bitch is. Barry was waiting for me to get off work when she and the girl came into the store. The girl tried on the most expensive pair of Doc Martens on the shelves while Barry hid in the men's aisle. Maybe it was because I said, "You're really being pathetic, you know that?" but he finally came out of hiding. Words were exchanged. Then—I couldn't believe it—he gave her a piece of his mind. And when I saw his wife standing there with that useless credit card in her hand, fat and helpless and caught in her own little trap, I actually felt a little sorry for her. I saw her at last for who she is, and it wasn't pretty.

I wanted to say, "Doll, we all know your life's a mess right now, but why don't you just try and make it a little easier on yourself? Let alone the rest of us." But no, she's a black hole of hatred, dragging everything and everyone into it. Nothing worse for some people than having their meal ticket taken away.

I didn't actually see the girl kick him. I was on one knee, trying to remove some woman's flats to replace them with heels. I can only imagine what would have happened if he hadn't offered to pay for those expensive shoes, if he had just let the security guard deal with her. That would have only proved in the bitch's mind how depraved he is. As it was, he had to borrow fifty dollars from me and combine it with what he had in his wallet to get the girl off the hook. But that, too, only proved to her how depraved he is. Even after she'd smacked him. The girl never even took the shoes.

Barry was rubbing his sore leg when I tried to get that girl to apologize for saying what she said. I wouldn't let a child of mine talk to me like that. "Little girl, you didn't really mean what you said about your daddy, did you?" She just put her nose in the air and walked out, leaving me standing there with a high heel in my hand. My customer slid into her flats and got up. "I believe I'll check the other stores," she said.

That's when he started to cry. Just hung his head between his knees and bawled. I dragged him off to the stock room (we'll never get over that knee-jerk response of retreating from the public eye), where I told him that this family is no longer two-thirds, one-third, it's half and half, and now I guess they'll have a fight on their hands.

MY SENIOR SENIOR YEAR

MICHAEL CARROLL
(FOR PATRICK E. RYAN)

Sun, moon, rain, and corn gods.

Pyramids.

In that hired Chevy Suburban, Larry and I cruised along, "doing" the pyramids and villages. Larry made frail attempts at Spanish, bargaining over the carved wooden toys, a mask and a necklace which he bought me, little fired-clay charms of ancient deities strung with beads of malachite on strips of leather.

When we walked through the villages together, the people thought, Father and son—not because I looked so young or because he looked that much older (he didn't), but because there was no other way for them to explain us.

"*Hijo,*" he began calling me after a lady in the marketplace referred to me as "your boy, señor. . . ."

"That could've meant anything," I said. "It could've even been her way of saying she knew what we were up to."

But, of course, there weren't very many gays, or very many obvious ones, touring through the desert-dry countryside, and in the city of Oaxaca, where we stayed in a little guest house, there wasn't a single bar for "us" that we could find—though we cautiously asked around.

We had come from Atlanta, seven hours by plane, with a change in Mexico City before final touchdown in Oaxaca State, in the southwestern part of the country where the Sierra Madre mountains roll abruptly to the sea. He'd given me the trip as a gift for my upcoming graduation—one of those dread, double-edged gifts, I feared, meant to please and make the recipient feel guilty. We both knew, even if the two of us hardly ever talked about it, that whatever I did after college it probably wouldn't keep me in Georgia.

Though Larry was only thirteen years older than I, his hair early on—long before I'd met him—had turned from salt-and-pepper in high school to dove gray in college, until finally he'd arrived with the thick, clean snow-white head of hair I first saw him with that time he wouldn't stop staring at me during a party at my fraternity. I learned the same night, moments before he introduced himself, that Larry was our most successful alumnus—a banker, a thirty-six-year-old personal investment whiz kid working on private accounts, at minimum, of five million dollars each.

Now I was in my second senior year at UGA and drove two hours from Athens to Atlanta to be with him on the weekends. I got there on Thursday afternoons. Noon educational psychology was my last class and I would take off out of town immediately afterward, full of excitement because of the suddenly new draw of Atlanta, where I'd grown up but without ever once having seen its gay side. Now I traveled "home" each weekend to be with my first male lover—happy to be leaving behind the dreary, abstract world of academic educational theory for another week.

The only tricky part was concealing my car, a distinctly huge, manila-colored LTD station wagon (left over from my mom's years of transporting food for a family of five). I didn't want Atlanta friends, my sister or parents to see it, since I was supposed to be cloistered away back in Athens studying and making up the coursework I'd failed or left incomplete during my first senior year, spent on acid.

Because Larry lived in Midtown, in a mostly gay highrise where I could park, there wasn't much chance of running into my dad, who taught at a suburban college just north of the city. But Mom volunteered in a hospital attached to Emory, not far from the gay district, and she liked to shop in the afternoons at Midtown boutiques because she thought they were nicer and cleaner. She would've put two and two together and figured out I was "playing the funny field" (her phrase for what had happened to Patricia Hochworth, a girlfriend from high school who turned out, when Mom caught up with her again in middle age, to be a lesbian).

Besides, I was supposed to be in Athens in the apartment I shared with my girlfriend, Kate, with whom I still slept—though that in itself had started off in high-drama fashion for my family, who didn't want their younger son shacking up so early in life. We were still conservative Catholics on my mom's side—Dad pretended, but really could not have cared less—so everything was about either working your way up to marriage or, as in the case of my sister, out of it again with a genuine, expensive papal annulment. Moving in with Kate had started innocently enough, since I swore to my folks I didn't have any sexual interest in her. Two years later, I was spending four nights a week with Larry and three more with my sometimes girlfriend, Katherine Anne Reinglow, whose money and means—it's my suspicion—had begun to win her some acceptance, and even a little affection, from my mother.

I didn't know what I was. All I knew was that I didn't want to end up like Pat Hochworth, the head nurse my mother had rediscovered after their thirty years of being out of touch. Mom had gradually come to piece together her old schoolfriend's life from all of the women who called and left messages with Mom at the oncology desk, these Jeris and Betts and Susans and Margarets wanting Pat—who lifted weights, went to AA, didn't smoke, and drove a giant four-by-four—to call them back if she got a chance. But she never did. Not even her kids could get through, which my mother registered as her worst crime by far. "She never talks about them . . . ," she sighed, quite pensively.

I suggested she go out with her sometime.

I romanticized Pat, much as I shuddered to imagine how painful—for her and her family—it must have been for her to come out so late in life. Though I wasn't sure about myself, at least I knew I wasn't going to marry and have kids with Kate. Our relationship was already sliding on the downward slope of its bell curve. We were ending as we'd begun: knocking on each other's bedroom door in the middle of the night or on a bored Sunday, "roommates" ostensibly, though it's probably true that we'd both felt closer before agreeing to go in together on the lease. Our relationship had never felt so intense for me as when we first moved in together, whereas for her, I could tell, it was the end that hurt. Hurt, for me, because I'd already learned that a lover always turns out to be a loser—a truth Kate had already figured out for herself, but which she punished herself for over and over again.

Kate and I had started out during her junior year and my chemistry-set days of my fraternal disorder, misconduct and misconstrued ideas of anarchy; kid's stuff, university Indian-summer term (for want of anything else to do but go home and cut the lawn for the folks), the season giving over to autumnal equinox, when animal nights begin to outweigh buzzing, heat-stifled days. Heavy nights ralphed into the toilet bowl behind pool halls and indie bars, brought up in the weak and freezing light of raw winter mornings. Kissing with vomit lips to smooth away the chills, the headachey eyes and the stabs of fear and doubt, everything young and sad but sweetly so, the smell of our dirt and funk— the odor of sex and grub we'd put into our mouths the night before, exuded in the hangover gray of wasted church hours. One of us reaching to put on another tape, smoke from a joint, diddle limply with our jaded or at least chafed genitals.

On into the following summer, missing classes, fucking from behind in the men's bathroom of the pedagogical basement. By June, in a haze of pot-clouded judgment, speed-read thoughts firing lightning-quick through burnt-orange and gray nimbostrati, we both knew it had begun playing out, moving toward its logical, last horizon, as we moved on to the other side of a storm-drenched summer.

At the start of my final year at UGA, the one my fraternity brothers and friends liked to refer to jokingly as my "senior senior year," I knew I needed to do things differently if I was to get my degree, but by then I'd come seriously to doubt that I would ever graduate. Also by then the bloom of telling myself I loved Kate had long since faded. Not that I'd ever made my feelings common knowledge around the frat house or to many of my friends. With the brothers I'd always said, "I love Kate . . . to go down on me." But I was a coward, since even after coming to know my true feelings—of affection, but also of a detachment from her deeper needs and emotion—I was still cooing in her ear all the words she wanted to hear.

Which is how I met Larry.

I went to one of the rush-week parties to say good-bye to the house and the life I'd lived in it. I'd always been told that once you were in, you could never get out—it was like the Klan or the

Mafia in that way. What I had planned was a slow fadeout: to make myself less and less desirable by making my presence gradually scarcer and more boring.

I confided my plan to only one or two of the brothers. Anyway, I didn't have the guts to withdraw far enough from house activities so that we'd end up having a showdown, or I risked looking cheap. I couldn't get completely out, anyway. My father had raised me never to quit things.

Tonight I sounded out my gripes, heard their advice, and proceeded to get drunk directly from the house keg and the taps of my newfound sense of freedom. Though I felt camaraderie for some of the brothers, I did not feel sentimental or smarmy. I expounded on my just-announced theory: that the phrase *rush party* perfectly characterized the irony of it all. These freshman boys, barely torn from their mothers' laps, thought they were speedily heading for adulthood, whereas they were just shifting into another form of adolescence—going from one shelter to another, from home to a house. By "rushing" they thought they were getting a taste of the speeded-up routines they would one day actually—no doubt rudely—be forced to submit to in the real world, but all they were truly getting was a mere exercise in comparison: a game.

"I think you're right," came a voice from somewhere among a crowd wedged between a grill on one side, on top of which roasted two dozen wienies, and a stack of aluminum beer barrels on the other, but at first I couldn't tell whose it was. A flare roared up out of the grill when grease from the hot dogs dropped to the coals and sizzled. We emerged from the smelter cooling and gold-fused and surrounded by the starless-skied darkness of the frathouse patio.

"But I think," he said, not taking his eyes off me, his teeth bright and perfectly formed as new-minted coins, "I think your days of being a pledge are *way* in the past, am I right or am I right?" His accent was certainly country-cured, like a Virginia ham left in the window for display. "Could be you're even close to graduation. . . ."

"I'm not as young as I look," I joked, hoping he'd get just my brand of irony—and share it.

"Now, you're not all that young!" The accent. The smile. I could see even then how Larry might be able to use both of these to perfect effect and get away with almost anything. He had my brother's same teasing air, an almost flirty sweetness and freedom around me, which confused me at first. At times it was almost spooky. Things progressed strangely, so—*easily*. I'd never felt that kind of willingness to know and be known by somebody. Never with any girl had I had the confidence to let her drive, to let her conduct what was happening—nor the same curiosity, like a rubbernecker approaching what he knows is a car wreck, to see what will happen as it's happening. What I'd longed for, or needed, was someone to take over—someone I could trust. I don't even remember how, with this guy, it all unfolded, or how I got over the initial worries of what it all looked like to the others, or just when I instinctively let go.

Nor do I remember how we made our way closer together, how one of us got from one side of the grill to the other. Did we maneuver like a pair of self-conscious straight guys, slowly making our approach with baby steps or subtle laughs and jokey gestures learned from the tube—the heterosexual guys' form of flirtation with one another?

(Though I remember some of our first words, because Larry, who told me later he'd started to feel like he had no more time to waste, liked to be direct and to the point, and in those first few minutes simply turned to me and said, "So what are you doing here?" then pounded it down with a swig of beer from its plastic cup.

"What am *I* doing here?" I said grinning, looking him straight in the eyes. "What are *you* doing here?"

"Good point.")

Larry was a chapter alumnus and how we'd never crossed paths once in all my time at UGA was simple: though he'd been living in Atlanta, interning in graduate school at Deloitte, Touche in a branch office before moving on to the bank where he was now vice-president of financial services, he'd been sequestered at work or at home—answering calls and screening client portfolios behind his desk, or decompressing at home from the events of the day blurring past him, leaving him exhausted but strangely restive. His sex life he'd left, if not quite neglected, then at least to chance, as much as that was possible while still observing the rules of safe sex.

His great period of sexual experiment, he was amazed to

reflect, had actually been his years in college: in fact behind the doors of his room in this very house (a room whose window overlooked the patio, its door three down from the one to my old room). By the end of sophomore year, everyone in the house knew he liked men, since he'd decided he could no longer hide it. That was in the late seventies, a time when people were already fed up with Anita Bryant, a time before AIDS when people in the South had decided, "Why shouldn't people do what they want behind closed doors?" (In that song the thick-waisted, piano-tinkling singer had never said exactly what it was he'd done there with his baby, and most had been grateful enough to him for this to make it a hit.)

Besides, Larry's good grades and model involvement in all the club's charities and community services had helped his brothers overlook his unashamed activities in bed. Not to mention the good trade he'd gotten off some of the other hard-up Greeks. No, in the end he was the one who'd thought he'd been had when all those straight boys and not so straight boys marched off after graduation to live their staid lives with jobs in other states, intent on marrying, while Larry stayed behind, alone with his feelings.

Now he joked to himself that he was back after five years of staying away from the blast site of his imploded heart. Or maybe that wasn't it. All he knew now was that his frat loves hadn't boded well for those first years just out of school, when he was cast into the work world and became once again (just as he'd been as an arriving freshman) the studious misfit, a nerd in need of friendship and warmth and sexual consideration.

We estimated the last time he'd been here was two years before my arrival. Since then he'd started making the weekend rounds in Atlanta bars, and he'd had two or three steady boyfriends—exactly how many or for how long each had lasted I couldn't tell. Lately, working harder than ever, he'd become sentimental and lonely. Tonight he had wanted only to get out of town, as far away from whatever it was that was clouding his head. Oh, and he was pretty horny, too.

Maybe the first thing to attract me was that when he took me, he took me in a truck: his Ford F-100 pickup, 1973, two-tone beige and flat army green, rusted and battered, badly kept inside and stinking of camping and hunting trips of summers and winters past with his father. It ran fast with a tiptop-sounding engine moan, and he swore, as we tore along the backroads toward the place he'd inherited, that the paint job was kept, according to the wishes of its previous owner, waxed smooth enough to see your reflection in and even to skate across the hood in your sock feet.

In the high, clear light of the moon I had doubts about the shine. Still, giving him the benefit of the doubt, I waited till we reached the house in the country, which from the outside hardly seemed to have fared much better. We got out looking at the miserable, low-roofed structure, a shack really. I asked him, "So who's the previous owner?"

"It was my granny, left me everything on the property. Ended up she had scads and scads of money stuffed away in banks all the way from here to Charlotte, North Carolina! Typical country, Depression-era mentality."

He laughed. He would waver between nostalgia-deflating jokes and sentimental one-liners washed down with pulls of canned beer. After the death of his grandmother, when Larry became lord of this ragged estate, he and his father had used it as a hunting lodge, fishing shack, and drinking pit-stop. Only when Larry went away to school, far from his "country boy" father (by then his father had retired from his job as a papermill foreman), did he start to feel like his own man for the first time. And it was then that he started questioning why he was still carrying on with girls, and the worst kinds of girls: cheerleaders and debutantes.

He'd gone to a private high school run by the doyen of associated Southern "nondenominational" churches, a hard-packed, fat-bodied, bull-necked shrimp who'd once been the star defense for the Falcons. While playing for the school team, Larry had prayed on the sidelines and talked pussy with the guys at gametime, then serviced a couple of the harder-ups afterward. The University of Georgia had marked a slow evolution from all that: a limbo between the former hell of life among smalltown, church-attending rednecks and a future paradise of living with his lover in the Emerald City, making money, never going to church again. (Of these two twin-tied Southern spectator passions, only football had stayed with him, but the cleaned-up TV version you need never leave the house for.)

Now he planned to renovate and move into the attic some

things of Granny's he couldn't part with completely. "I'm going to do most of the work on my own and make it a weekend place for myself and whoever ends up being with me. . . ."

Larry talked a lot, speculating on the future and inviting me to do the same. I told him I planned to "evacuate" as soon as I graduated, then trade my "book larnin' " in for real experience. I told him I'd gotten jumpy and claustrophobic, that I'd started to take things for granted without ever questioning whether or not it was the way they really should be. I see now, and was even beginning to see then, how it was possible for him to misinterpret or misunderstand everything I was saying. But I didn't begin to see fast enough. He was subtle and merely nodded at what I said.

"Well, are you actively seeking candidates?" I asked.

He laughed and said, "Oh God, of course I am. I think it's time."

Not that I was looking to fill a "position." If he'd asked me, straight off, "How 'bout it?," I could've told him right away, "Not interested."

But it never came up, although starting that night, in Granny's great iron bed, we began our fascination with each other, spending our time together, lying in bed—clumsy me and perfect, expert, blue-eyed Larry. We seemed to know, or find interesting or funny, how oddly paired we were. So this was it: the hardness of his body, the uprightness of his back, the thickness of his chest, which became my favorite part. He was not tall. He stood three inches below me, and yet everything about him, his dick too, was full-sized, and nothing, not an inch of length or thickness anywhere, was short of just right.

When we fell into bed together, laughing, trying to relax, and he urged my clothes off me, running his warm hand along my back, telling me my back was warm, he kept things in motion for me, so I wouldn't have to guess or fumble a move. But he asked if each one he initiated was okay.

He smiled. "Now don't tell me it's *not* your first time, 'cause you'll just go and disappoint me."

"I won't," I laughed.

He looked at me. I pressed back my lips to prevent a smile.

"Not even when you were a kid?" he said hopefully.

"Well, a couple times of touch-peepee, I guess."

He looked at me strangely. "You guess?"

"You know that twilight line between what's real and fantasy, you don't know which? But then you decide it doesn't really matter which?"

"I think." Another strange look. Then he gave me a testing look, running his hand under the covers. "Touch . . . peepee."

At the same time the big mud god of Kate-and-me had already begun falling to its knees, crumbling and dissolving into a pool of straw, earth, and hurt. I was coming home less often. And already we'd retreated into our separate bedrooms, spending the night together only on inspired occasions, until finally not at all. I can't even recall what she asked me.

My mother would call and if I was gone, or even if for some reason I wasn't, she'd always talk to Kate awhile. After volunteering downtown (she had never traveled much and had stayed pretty naive), she wouldn't admit it but she had probably come to the conclusion that downtown Atlanta was the center of sin, at least in her native Southeast. She seemed to enjoy marking the decline of American civilization. Because of her friendship with Pat Hochworth, she had become more sophisticated and at the same time a bit more leery about things. If she'd known I was spending all my time with an older man with money in the center of corruptest Rome it wouldn't be long before she started to catch on.

"That Pat," she'd say, before telling me the gossip gleaned from the sometimes cooing, sometimes desperate messages she'd had to take for the head nurse, messages left by Pat's myriad lovers. "She's got such a busy life. Maybe I should turn gay."

I wondered if suddenly she was sounding me out. My mother wasn't normally funny; not that this was any occasion for me to laugh. When I reported it to Kate, sounding *her* out, Kate told me, "Maybe she's bored with *her* life. I mean, she did decide to go out and volunteer as a hospital receptionist." But it had never occurred to me a woman who'd spent all of her life, and ours, seeing to her children's needs could be bored or lonely.

"You don't know my mom—she never makes jokes like that."

"Maybe you don't know her either, anymore."

I knew all about Kate's father, who'd had to be taken away, and her horror of him and of ever being alone with him again. Eventually she'd figured out that what her brothers had done to her had been no better, but not before she realized that in some ways she'd enjoyed their furtive coaching. Yet it was wrong because she could never get it out of her mind, wrong because it still made her feel guilty, and wrong because it made her irrevocably distant from her mother.

I'd been surprised by these confessions and then—on the far edge of our candid, wrecked wanderings into the darkest corners of our souls—by the places we'd reached together in bed, those places only accessible with heavy gear and the bright helmet-lamp of trust. For her, sex was as much invested with her fears of the penis as it was with her attractions to me. For me, it was merely a plowing-back of the dark strata to get at my desires.

Kate, the little woman with her tremendous heart on fire, stoked on the hardest, blackest coal; Katie the hurt child; the faithful daughter; the cool, ambiguous sister with hot liquid silver coursing through her veins; Kathleen the student racing to finish her master's before running out of undergraduate-loan bucks, running long on reserves of guilt, running cool; Kate the burrowing machine; my sister-mate Kate; my one-in-the-morning warmth and quiet understanding; Kate the insane, even terrifying lover at six a.m.; Kate hurling scorn and wielding marital aids; valiant Kate willing to jettison breakfast from the apartment window to help make her point and save our relationship: the Kate I could no longer take.

And then there was the Kate who knew, instinctively, though she need not have relied on instinct, what was going on between Larry and me when she finally met him. She needn't have relied on instinct with a clue of considerable length and weight at hand. She kept it in a drawer next to her birth-control pills. ("Charms," she'd said, "of another life," not knowing at the time she could apply that description to either one of us.)

Not for years had she needed for their intended use the pills in their little plastic calendar case. It had taken us months to work up the trust needed for penetration. "I've been taking them," she said, "to keep things running inside. They help clear the plumbing." She'd gone on to explain how endometriosis had slowed things down, given her cramps and robbed her of her period; before she'd gone to the doctor to discover it, she hadn't menstruated in twenty weeks. It had been four or five years, she explained, since she'd let someone inside her.

When I saw the vibrator buried beneath an assortment of graphic-art supplies—the detritus of yet another abandoned major—something stirred in me. I was going in, at her bidding, to find the calendar case so the two of us could begin our amorous new adventures, not knowing what depths we would soon enough descend to. The pencils and pads laid aside, the thing seemed to find itself suddenly, all Easter-egg pastel and shiny plastic, in my grip. We would get into the habit of calling it things: Blue Dawn, for its pale sky-blue and its way of making the user sing a faint aubade if it was inserted during the just-violet minutes before sunup; Bonnie, Bunny, Bonnie the Bunny, Wee Willy, the Whopper, the Thing, and geyser-making Old Faithful. We would get into the habit of a lot of things once it was all out in the open, but for that first moment, as I stood there in the bedroom next to the drawer, holding the vibrator, a thrill of uncertainty and shame, as if I'd actually turned it on, paralyzed me.

Kate walked in, saw the vibrator in my hand, and made a joke about my finding her "drawer of Venus," and I apologized.

"Why apologize?"

"I didn't mean to unearth it. It just popped right out at me when I was looking for your pills."

Kate laughed and said she hardly ever used the thing. "I mean, except lately," she remarked after a pause, in her dry monotone. Then she asked me: "You ever use one?"

We began with our fingers, hers in my anus, mine in her vagina, and afterward, cooking rice, making eggs, and slicing onions, we smelled our hands and laughed about the sauces of our bodies.

In another week we shared the vibrator and took turns sliding it in and out of each other—first into her, then into me. She was working up to the point when I could enter her, and then the feat came to mind: Let her "enter" you, I told myself, with her hand and the thing. Then, with it still inside you, get on top and enter her.

A tiny charge of static blossomed in my entrails, leaving a spray of bright waving flowers in its wake to float me toward gradual orgasm as I fucked and was in turn jabbed and fucked by her, the two of us ramming and being rammed until finally we came together, a springtime flourish of baby's breath and primrose buds sent out from the root system down in our dirt to the surface of our skins—leaving us surprised and smiling all over, our faces and flesh burning with sexual blush.

"Didn't you ever turn it on?" Larry asked me when, months after he and I began fooling around, he finally learned I'd been more intimate with Kate than I had originally let on. I was consciously keeping it from him for as long as I could, but when he started asking me questions without the slightest hint of jealousy in his voice I saw no reason not to tell him the truth. Besides, he had a matter-of-fact way of pulling the dirty facts from me, detail by detail, and learning everything before I stopped to wonder if I should be keeping the things that had happened between Kate and me a secret.

"Kate had already killed it," I replied. "Plum wore it out. . . ."

Things between Larry and me were well under way, had even reached their high point, when Kate caught on. Sex with her and the dead vibrator had all but dried up, and I had already begun to doubt whether sex with both Kate and Larry, even on different days, was possible. So early into my bisexual days, as Larry drily called them, I hoped to compartmentalize the two sides of my sex life and keep them separate. But it was Larry, claiming to be envious of me, who encouraged me to think of it all as a function of my being AC/DC, with fully convertible energies.

Yeah, I countered, tell that to a woman scorned and abandoned, which was how Kate had begun to act: afraid that I might slip away.

Having begun to view my inner self, deeper than my heart, as deep down as, yes (as Larry often liked to remind me) my "electric rectum," I realized I was then seeing everything through a telescope: with objects at the greatest distance appearing most clearly in the overall picture.

He coached me in bed, bringing a set of dildos with him: thinking, I supposed, it would help warm me out of the frigidity he must have taken my fears and intimidation to be.

"Take this," he said brightly, "with plenty of this."

He started by slathering K-Y onto the smallest, most flexible one. When it was halfway in—already as far as it would go—it brought my dick to immediate attention. Then, just when it seemed it could go no further, without feeling like a hot spike driven into the core of me, Larry turned it, twirling it in and out a little more and starting a fit of twitches in my penis, which lolled and pointed about the room, jerking and hardening with each thrust. He took the dildo out and worked it back in—back and forth until it was finally in me up to the little rubber testicles. He turned them like a dial until they rested against my balls, then scooted closer to me in bed with his face in my crotch and began sucking me off as he worked the dildo in and out. I came in another two or three minutes.

He picked up where Kate and I had left off. But he reached something deeper than she'd helped me find on previous excavations.

Sometimes, too, he would use the same method to tease me toward near-orgasm, watching my face while he went down on me for signs not of pleasure—that was constant—but agony, as he got deeper and deeper with the thing, jabbing and fucking while the wet, warm inside of his mouth went up and down on my merely human penis. Just as I showed my usual signs of climax, the sounds I made with my mouth, the rolling-back of my eyes like a shark's when it maws the flesh of its prey, he watched and waited, then pulled his face up from my cock, the rubber member still stabbing me through with uncomfortable but mounting sensations, and he slid up flush beside me (still pumping) and kissed me—pressing and forcing his face and lips and tongue into mine as I reached down and pumped myself in front while he handled me from behind before my penis began to shrink, as it always threatened to do with so much pain, or not enough sensation, the roughness of his face against mine, the smell of his breath, the stabbing rhythm of the dildo as it pulsed through the center of me.

At those times, putting my orgasm off for a moment, he maneuvered his free hand onto himself while he kept the other one stirring my insides. He kept grabbing and teasing his cock until it was erect and ready to move him toward his own orgasm. At that moment I was ready and came, and as I was doing so, giving the usual signals, he turned excitedly to me, bright with a smile and shining eyes. Keeping both hands busy still with our ecstasy, he craned his neck around—painfully, it seemed, but maybe this was why he'd stayed in shape—to slide his face down my chest toward my belly to begin lapping my already-shot load. He caught the rest on his tongue and lips. He finished by licking me clean and using the taste of it to hurry himself on to orgasm, jacking and pumping his cock. Usually by then he would've pulled the dildo from me already, replacing it with two fingers, and together with the taste of my spunk and the touch of his fingertips inside my anus, the sensation of his other hand lightly and slowly chugging up and down on his erection—it was enough to send him racing home for the finale. Afterward he lay on his side lifeless and spent, immobilized from exertion, nesting his flushed face against the damp, smelly hair of my crotch.

Neither was better than the other, I told myself; the trip I took with each partner was just different. The things I thought and felt varied, but as I explained to one of the brothers, my only true confidant from the frat house, who caught up with me early that spring, it was the same striving toward sensation—the same sensation, of modulated intensity.

Yet I began to prefer Larry's hash of salty, unshaved skin, his tongue on fire from alcohol and spice and hot pepper, the burning force he applied to the thing as he slammed it up into me. I'd become bored with Kate's softness and curd. Still, I went back to her from time to time for the coolness inside the slick mouth of her pussy. And one Sunday night when I tomcatted back home, conveyed by Larry, my master on the sly, my mistress saw me climbing out of the expensive Japanese contraption he'd bought himself.

Larry and I were both conservative about the things we did together in public: no displays of affection. I got out to say goodbye and saw the light on inside the apartment, but no clear figure in the window. I wasn't sure if she was looking or not. I played it cool. We always shook hands when we parted, and I thought everything looked innocent. But then later in bed—another knock on the door—she snuggled up close to me, and once there chilled into position, growing quiet.

"Your mother broke down and asked me to tell her the truth about what was going on with us," Kate said finally. "I told her I had no idea. But you know she already found out that you're never here on the weekend. . . ."

"No problem," I said. "I can handle her."

"What are you doing to Kate?" my mother asked me the next time I went home.

"I'm not doing anything at all."

"She sounds upset, and anyway, where are you going every weekend? I call and you're never there. And she tells me *she* doesn't even know."

"I don't have to tell Kate everything. She's my roommate."

"Are you telling *me* everything?" she said.

"We're roommates."

"She sounds upset. I can hear it in her voice."

"Well, to be honest, Mom, Kate is a little bit messed up."

"So what's going on between you?"

When Larry asked, I explained to him that I'd told my mother nothing, except that I had tried to make her think Kate was messed up.

"But she *is* messed up—from what you've told me," he said.

"No," I said, "you don't know her like I do. She's got her problems like everyone else, but she isn't any more fucked up than I am."

He laughed and put his arms around me. "I can deal with that."

Just before spring break of my last semester, the letter arrived from Washington. I stood opening, then reading, it next to my post-office box at school, memorizing phrases ("We would like to *invite* you . . . must hear from you *by* . . .") from its two succinct paragraphs, and realizing this was what I'd been moving toward all along.

At the end of the week Larry planned to get off from work late, as usual during that period, and called home to ask if we could meet for dinner at a bar not far from his office. "No problem," I said, though, too, I distinctly remember standing there in his living room—wet from the shower and naked but for a towel—at the same time thinking, Oh, except for this one other thing . . .

I chose a Friday night, when I knew we would have the entire rest of the weekend to talk it through and get him used to the idea of my leaving. That Friday night he met me at a Mexican restaurant, where we drank a lot of tart margaritas. Afterward we went barhopping and drank some more, then returned home good and drunk together, tumbling into bed for a lot of sex. All the while I was thinking of my news and how to tell him, I could never get my lips around the words—words were the only problem—and then before I knew it, I had been stunned into a thoroughly fucked silence and fallen asleep.

But in the morning I knew I had to tell him. We lay in bed, slightly hung over in the sunlight splashing through the half-shut curtains, both of us remembering what we'd tried and each time abandoned the night before. I didn't think I could make things worse by finally telling him my news, but still I decided to soften it by telling him I'd gotten a phone call from Washington saying I could expect a letter with their offer any day now.

He rolled over behind me, sliding his naked arms around me, and told me he thought it was coming anyway. "After all," he said, "you did warn me . . ."

And it's true, I'd told him about my fantasies of teaching in South America or Guatemala, traveling around in my spare time, hitching rides in Volkswagen vans while eating some nice mushrooms, and seeing what the poets and visionaries copying down their trances had seen. I still wanted to float among the reed canals on the Day of the Dead, sleep in a hammock beneath a palm shelter on the beach near Puerto Angel, drink mescal; keeping one foot in the sand as I swung and swayed, and watch violet dawn coming on after an all-nighter spent inside a mosquito net and a gold-leaf haze.

He held me and squeezed me, whispered he didn't want to lose me but it seemed like he had to, then sighed and said for spring break he'd planned to take me to Mexico—did I still want to go?

"You can work on your Spanish and maybe it'll help you decide if you really want to volunteer," he said.

Larry didn't want me to go—he admitted to having a daydream in which I stayed behind in Atlanta to teach, and either moved in with him or into my own place in Midtown near his. A part of him believed I wouldn't go. At times he seemed to play along with my fantasies while he was waiting for his own to come true. Given my lazy ways of sitting around his apartment among all the copied Eames chairs, splatter paintings, and the spectacular twelfth-story view, and particularly the way I dipped into his grass supply on a Thursday afternoon when I should've been studying, I understood why it was hard for him to believe I'd ever actually leave him.

When I told Kate about the vacation, I decided to level with her completely. I let her ask me questions that had been going through her mind now for months.

"Well, who *is* he?" she said.

"Just a boyfriend," I said, trying out the sound of it. "You met him once, but you probably wouldn't remember because the house was crowded and he was the last one you'd suspect. . . ."

"That older guy, the one hanging around looking all out of place and pathetic and maladjusted?" she said, after I'd described him by his hair ("really white") and his eyes ("really cool blue") and told her how much I loved these.

"So you're in love with this guy?"

"Larry? No, not in love. He's just—well, like I've always considered you—a lover," I said.

There was a direct flight from Atlanta to Mexico City, where we'd planned to stay for a night at the Hotel Emperador—our last, as he called it, "fancy fling" before flying the next afternoon to Oaxaca State. It was Larry's idea to do the main part of the trip as cheaply as possible, to see what it would be like for a volunteer living on a budget. In the Emperador we had a mile-high luxury view of the city suspended in grayish pea soup, and we woke the next morning to the first light coming in through smoked glass to see what had been a mere dim silhouette to us the night before: a church cupola of piecrust-colored stone rising, pushing toward us from invisible street level. It was lit up and beginning to glow, as if thin gold foil had been beaten and smoothed into every pore and acid-etched scar the instant the sun came out from behind the maroon-and-silver mountains. Later that afternoon, pulling away in a commuter plane that kicked up hot dust into the unclear air, neither of us suspected the real adventures we'd thought we were starting were left behind before takeoff in Atlanta.

The Jacarandas (Larry immediately dubbed it the *¡Ay carambas!*) was a modest house from the time of the hidalgos with a garden, courtyard, and carriage entrance. The courtyard had been halfway filled in with a two-story fifties box structure that provided a common dining room and extra guest rooms—and left just a postage stamp of lawn and narrow strips of garden blooming with spiky-leaved daisies, magenta-tinged geraniums, and gaudy petticoat ruffles of bougainvillea shimmering on the far wall toward the high ripening papayas growing on the next property. Along the top of the wall, the bougainvillea entwined themselves around the dagger edges of broken bottles cemented into place to keep out intruders. Their blossoms were cinnamon-tinctured red.

On the second floor of the old house, ours was the only room to look out both onto the street and also down onto the tiny limeskin lawn, at the center of which stood the single jacaranda tree—its trunk broom-pole-skinny, its tiny purple flowers like watercolored kernels of popcorn, sweetening the breeze that intruded between buildings at the end of another hot afternoon.

All day, and deep into the evening, in a room opening directly onto the street beneath us, the family ran a sidewalk cafe, serving burritos in chocolate mole sauce. The two brothers, one sister, and their mother were always coming and going from parts of the guest house we could not see, where, incredibly, all of them managed to live and sleep.

Behind it, a tiny clinic for mestizo children breathed in the scent of the restaurant fuming with the smoke of the tortilla ovens, the steam of the pots filled with boiling tomatoes and chicken stock, and the burning oils given off by the caustic jalapeños. The odors saturated the cramped waiting room directly adjacent.

We came and went. At siesta, when we returned from the museums and ruins, the clinic was empty, or an old man and a young woman with her baby and small children were lined up on a wooden bench next to the shut door to the doctor's office. Their feet dangled above the oxblood tile as Larry and I passed upstairs for our rest, stunned after another dutiful march through the heat. They must have wondered, as they sat there waiting to ask the doctor for antibiotics, what these sunburned gringos were doing here to begin with, always looking so busy though we obviously accomplished so little.

We immediately slowed down. It was as if the sun and the climate—which served locals and mestizos as the ideal pacer for a life to be lived slow and easy and had fired the heterogeneous people over five centuries of conquest, cohabitation, and ambivalence into a hard-cured, reddish race knowing when to

work and when to rest—served only to drain the energy from us
and make us restless and lazy. We must have looked crazed, on
the run from our own country. Each morning we combed the
village markets and countryside in search of bargains, returning
with the odd carved doll and handmade rug. As soon as the sun
crossed the midday mark, we hid from the other Americans staying at the Jacarandas, who met for tea under the porch of the
addition, looking into the garden. Their voices, the honking
Midwestern ones and the loud and educated-sounding North-
eastern ones, reverberated off the walls of the courtyard and the
privacy fences. Our windows stayed open for the cross-breezes;
from the street side came relative silence, save the occasional
crepitating VW Bug or a truck barreling along on its delivery
route from town. On the sunny garden side, we closed the curtains, telling ourselves it helped cool the place and muffle the
noise. We fooled around a little, when we fooled around, fell
asleep damp, warm, and tired, woke up, went downstairs all
groggy but vaguely content and satisfied, and sitting in the
restaurant began over coffee to hash through the thick and
lugubrious dreams we'd just emerged from.

Now, too, began a new agitation between us.

In the cafe two Zapotec sisters wearing hairnets served
lunch each day, whipping up fruit drinks for the old men,
dressed in their dark suits and hats, who stepped in from the
street for shade. The girls were pretty but plump, and so
sweet, even servile, that they gave off the air of enjoying nothing more than serving camomile tea with its Spanish name,
manzanilla, printed on the paper tag trailing out from the tops
of the local ceramic teapots, black as cast iron. And at noon
each day we came in, after our morning tromps around the
city and surroundings, for enchiladas drenched in pepper and
chocolate *mole*.

"Do you think they're pretty?" Larry said on the third or
fourth day.

I snickered, "No."

I was enough of a body fascist to know he already knew the
answer. But I also knew he was fishing for attention. I don't
always understand myself and I don't know what had caused my
silences. But I knew that in my head any silence coming from
him—at an awkward juncture, or when we'd flopped in bed

again and I just couldn't come, though I wanted to—I could use to justify my own silence.

Mornings we went off to the villages and pyramids, seeing the tombs and ball courts and the recently unearthed stone buildings of Monte Albán, Mitla, and the other Indian sites still standing in defiance and giving up none of their secrets. (Were the carved people in bas relief lunatics, figures in primitive medical charts, or just dancers?) Afternoons, returning in the midday heat and glare for lunch, we argued about the siesta. Or did not argue: observed another standoff in our differences.

By the fifth or sixth day—or some time about halfway through the trip—he was too hyped up, saying he was not used to a nap except occasionally on the weekends. While I still felt like sleeping, he went off to wander over the hot stones of the city. The city, dead and carved out of the earth and hiding its figures, seemed to speak to him, allow him rest; but finally it was the separation for hours at a time—we'd never spent so much time together before, and it was telling on us—that saved us. He came back late in the afternoon, lay down on the bed beside me, our individual differences softened, or bent slightly, and untold what he seemed to be saying had just been revealed to him, as if everyday life for him back home was merely mute and here he was surprised into understanding.

"There was a concert suddenly. I mean, I was walking along one of those main streets leading to the *zócalo* and went past this courtyard and suddenly there was all this music."

"Mariachi, like with violins and horns?"

"No, it was chamber music—with violins and horns."

And churches, endless churches, with rows of statues of the martyrs glistening on the wrists and foreheads with painted-on stigmata. But he'd been raised Protestant and now protested against the idea—one I'd been made to accept and swallow before I'd forgotten it. He'd brought out two or three dildos from his kit and said in the hot, anxious minutes before dinner, when we decided we were finally talking again, though words had become unnecessary, he planned to turn my anus on one more time.

And later that night, after eating, after wandering the town, where he showed me the things he'd passed and looked at in those two or three days we couldn't be around each other, couldn't speak, we drank a bottle of mescal we'd bought at the side of the road returning from our first day of ruins, amber tequila-like mescal with the agave worm preserved in it like a lab specimen curled plump and white at the bottom. We lay for the second time in bed that evening, after our stroll among the night muchachos. Larry had been looking at them more and more closely, amazed at their pretty limbs and faces, or just amazed at how much he suddenly wanted them. I also knew how much he liked my skinny boy's body and toneless abs (not as washboard-defined as his), but when he came over to me on the enormous bed he was thinking of other boys.

The curtains were drawn, the Americans chattered in the courtyard of honeysuckle and jasmine below, and he pulled from the black leather bag the odorless lubricants.

"And put the bottle away," he said, laughing, pointing to the mescal. "We've already drunk half."

In this state, his words slurred back into their native mush. Those molasses-slow words took on the pale yellow and soapy lime green pollen dust of spring until the whole room was heavy and pressing down on me: preventing me from getting up, slick and sticky in my bath of clear sex gel he'd spread across the insides of my thighs and crack. "Go," he said, pushing me bare-assed across the bed with his strong running-back legs, pushing the mescal bottle into my grip as my hand dragged behind me. "Get it on outta my way."

He was a redneck love, a hunter cocksman, a farmhand from when he was a kid.

A country fuck, I suddenly laughed to think, then I said the words.

"Oh yeah?" he said, making to come at and attack me. Then fell back and breathed hard, his breath racing to overtake his laugh, which died away.

Next I remember waking up early the next morning freezing to the sight of him wrapped in a cocoon of blanket, bedspread, towel, and sheet, his face blanched and soaking in sweat.

"Allergic," he said, shivering, burning, a sweat rivulet running from his forehead tracing the curves of his facial bones, collecting along the squared outline of his jaw.

"What're you talking about?"

"Allergic to alcohol," he said.

"Larry, you drink all the time."

I smelled shit and he shook to get the words out, a frightened look taking him over. "Jesus, I'm sick."

"I think it was the food," I told him, sure of myself. I hovered over him wondering how I could take over and get him cleaned up.

"It's the turista," he said.

"That's right. Are you okay?" I asked, with plenty of visual evidence to the contrary.

"I haven't slept all night," he said, and turned in bed just enough to stir up the smell of his diarrhea. Then he made one of his dear and humble faces that cracked me up. "Did I do that?" We laughed. "I've been chained to the toilet all night"—in my drunkenness I hadn't been able to notice—"but about an hour ago, or whenever the sun was just starting to come up, I finally thought I could just slip out a—oh God, *sorry*. . . ."

He lay in a puddle of it under the covers and the smell when he lifted them immediately began pounding into my hangover.

"Larry, get up so we can get you into the shower," I said.

I fought both revulsion and self-disgust. When I touched him to help him into the bathroom, he felt smaller than the night before, but more real than ever. He was burning through clammy skin, radiating heat through cool, almost lifeless flesh. Was that a life trying to abandon a fading, disposable shell? He felt more real to me than ever. I could understand things like worth and love again, I could feel what was valuable and great about him, feeling him leaning against me. But at the same moment, I felt frantic, chastened, confused, lost in this place, and no longer me.

And still he was hot, until he reacted suddenly as if his temperature had turned on a dime. He began to whoop and howl and beg me, even as I told him not to make too much noise. "Larry, they'll think I'm killing you."

"Turn it off! Come on, turn it off!" He panted and tried to catch his breath, drawing himself up and ducking from the stabs of cold water. I turned it off, and he sat balled up and shivering, his face pushed down into the folded-up strength of his chest. I grabbed both towels in the room and began to cover and dry him as he sat there curled and dripping on the tile, moaning with relief with each half-moment his skin slowly returned to room temperature. I stripped the bed, helped him back onto it (naked but getting warm and comfortable again, he said), then rolled him into the still-clean blanket, threw the sheets together with his dirty drawers, and dumped them in a pile at the bottom of the shower. I turned on the hot water and let it run to get the stains out. I worked to get the last traces of shit out with a bar of soap and a bottle of shampoo, scrubbing and rinsing, alternating the two until they disappeared. I rinsed and wrung out the laundry, then hung it across the shower rod and went out into the bedroom to find him sleeping quietly.

I went out to find bottled water, aspirin, and something for Larry's diarrhea. When I stepped out into the sun, that feeling which had struck me before I could get him into the bathroom, just an hour before, came back. It was part hangover, part depression, pure doubt. I found a pharmacy and for an instant forgot it wasn't my own symptoms I was here to treat. My high-school and college Spanish returned to me.

"There's an English-speaking doctor just across the street," the man told me. "Do you need a doctor, *muchacho?*" He pointed to a clinic located across the street—one I hadn't seen. "Go and see the doctor at the clinic, then you will want to come back."

I crossed the street, wondering if I wasn't the delirious one. But at the clinic I was finally able to exercise my textbook Spanish.

"*Por favor, ¿aquí hay un medico quien habla inglés?*" I asked at the front desk. The more I was directed to the next desk, then the next, in the heat, the more I began to panic and get dizzy. Before I found the doctor, I'd already decided I was catching the bug, too, and was about to collapse in a puddle of my own filth.

If anything happened to me I would be alone, with only a plane ticket to get back on. Then I'd have to explain things to all kinds of people. I'd told my parents I was skiing in Colorado with some of the brothers. I knew that if I fell sick, I would get better, but unexplainably a part of me worried for Larry. I realized that for me Larry stood for strength; he was the man I'd never quite felt inhabiting me. Of course I'd played football in high school, too, and gone through all the same masculine motions as he had. But I'd kept a secret of something else playing inside me. Then there had been a point when he'd put down his false macho side forever. But I could not; I was split. Now, in a hair's breadth of time, I felt stabbed by—his love. For an instant I loved back, cared only about him, fearing the worst, yet wanting to show him everything.

ANNIVERSARY

C. BARD COLE

Marty Lefaivor had no clue what homosexuals were supposed to do to be romantic. On his drive home from work, he stopped at the liquor store and bought a bottle of New York State champagne, then stopped at the grocery store with the idea of buying chocolate and strawberries. Except the store didn't sell fondue pots, which it belatedly occurred to him was the essential missing ingredient of that scenario. So he looked at the tankful of live lobsters instead. He imagined the ordeal of bringing these disturbingly buglike creatures to their boiling deaths while Edgar hovered behind him, wondering aloud if he knew what he was doing. He pictured sitting down at the dinner table and watching Edgar screw the back off his cooked lobster with his hands, picking at the many-legged, beet-red corpse with entrails and fat and roe tumbling from his plate. He pictured Edgar snapping the large red claw with a nutcracker and dangling the pink-edged piece of meat in front of his open mouth, finally slurping it in like a live goldfish. He imagined the butter all over Edgar's fingers, most likely dripped down the front of his shirt as well, the garlic smell permeating his hair and breath and skin.

Trying to force these thoughts to the back of his mind, he put some strawberries and grapes and onions in his shopping cart and then selected a couple nice beef filets. Marty knew how to cook steak with little fuss; Edgar knew how to eat steak without making himself disgusting. Marty got back in the car with his groceries and drove until he reached another liquor store, where he bought a case of Bass Ale in bottles and a Lotto ticket. He played 4/18 (Edgar's birthday), 10/23 (his birthday), and 9/11: the day's date, the anniversary of their first meeting, three years earlier.

Marty found a decent parking place at the end of the block and walked home with his groceries. Edgar had beaten him home from work and was watching TV on the sofa, wearing a long-underwear shirt and boxer shorts. His jeans, inside-out socks, and tennis shoes were tossed in a pile by the door. He was sprawled back, resting a bottle of beer between his legs. "Hey," he said as Marty fumbled to open the inside door. "How was your day."

"Okay," Marty said. "I got some steaks. There's a case of beer in the car."

"Oh shit," Edgar said. "Should I put on some pants?"

Marty carried the groceries into the kitchen. "If you want to get it for me."

"Steak. What's all this for?" Edgar stood in the doorway, sliding into his jeans.

Marty unpacked the bags on the counter. "Where were you three years ago tonight?"

Edgar looked blank for a minute and then smiled. "Three years ago tonight right now?" he asked. "I think I was wondering why I was going to let myself be dragged to half-price night at Allanté."

"You remember, you asshole," Marty said.

"Of course I remember," Edgar said. "I picked up a couple videos on my way home. With that Romanian guy you like."

"You got porno? Edgar, you are foul. You're a dirty boy."

"I picked ones you'd like," Edgar said. "You're the one who likes porno anyhow."

Edgar went out to get the beer from the car. This was true, that Marty was the one who liked porno. He was a little older than Edgar, but he had not had many boyfriends. He was in his twenties before he had been with a man, and even then hadn't liked it so much. He never acquired a taste for meeting gay guys. Instead of learning how to meet people, he studied how to work up the nerve to rent dirty videos and buy magazines without feeling obvious or guilty.

He had become somewhat attached to looking at pictures of

different sorts of men having sex. Sometimes it was boring to have sex with the same person over and over again, especially because there were two or three things Edgar liked and he always liked them the same way. And Marty had become annoyingly familiar with every square inch of Edgar's skin, from the mole on his shoulder blade to the ingrown hairs on his throat to the exact lines and folds of his circumcision scar. The only thing to watch, really, was Edgar gaining weight and losing the adolescent smoothness of his skin, and he took no pleasure in that. Noticing those things made Marty feel like he was a bad person.

Sometimes Marty blamed himself for having been shy and ashamed in his search for love. He had wanted to be done with it all, and settled on the first guy he met who also wanted out of the looking-for-sex racket. Other days, he'd be sitting with Edgar having coffee in the kitchen, watching the gray smoke curl from Edgar's nostrils, and he'd say, "You're not using the patch still? 'Cause that could give you a heart attack." And Edgar would say, "I'm not a moron, for fuck's sake. I'm not using the patch anymore. It wasn't working. I don't feel like quitting right now. You don't have to nag me." Marty would realize that he was saying these things to Edgar because Edgar was the most perfect person who had ever walked across his life, and the thought that this person might die and leave him alone was the most terrifying thing he could imagine. He loved Edgar. He liked their life together.

"How much did you pay for this? Bass Ale?" said Edgar as he carried in the case of beer. "I hope it was on sale."

"It wasn't *on* sale," Marty said, turning the steaks in their Worcestershire sauce marinade. "But it was *for* sale. You like Bass."

"I like *Beck's*," Edgar said with little apparent concern. "I hope you like Bass."

Marty looked at his boyfriend. Edgar's hair was growing back over his ears. He had buzz-cut it for the summer, mostly to get rid of the bad bleach job he'd given himself earlier, angrily resisting the darkening of his white-blond hair. The stripping agent brought it close to its former color, but his hair looked thin and fried and fake and made Edgar feel, he said, "like an old faggot." He was twenty-six. Sometimes Marty liked them getting older and sometimes he didn't. Marty was turning twenty-eight the next month. He had a decent job he intended to keep, and a house of his own, and a boyfriend he intended to be with forever. Sometimes thinking about these things made him happy, and sometimes these things made him think he might as well be dead already.

They had sex that night. They had anal intercourse for the fifty-eighth time since they had been together as a couple, Marty on top and Edgar lying on his back with his left leg hooked around Marty's waist. Marty was using a condom. He was not aware of it being the fifty-eighth time. He had not been counting. He would probably have guessed a higher number. It seemed like they repeated this act fairly often, but really their sexual activities had come to be confined to the weekend nights, and most of the time less intrusive interactions satisfied them both.

After they had orgasmed and Edgar was almost asleep, his face buried in Marty's armpit, Marty said, "Do you think . . . I mean . . . I was just thinking. . . ."

"Huh?" Edgar said.

"I was thinking, what's the point of us using rubbers at this point? You know? It's not like we're being, you know . . . with anyone else or anything."

"Mmmm," Edgar said, eyes closed.

"It's been three years," Marty said.

Edgar didn't say anything.

Marty looked at the ceiling, an ugly plaster ceiling covered in stucco icing whirled in a circular, raked pattern. One corner was chipped where Edgar had experimented to see how easily the stuff would come off. "That shit reminds me of my parents' bedroom," he'd said. "We keep that and next thing you know we're putting painted screens in the window, china cats climbing the lightpost, and going full *Bawlamer*, hon." The outside light threw shadows across the ridges, and if you stared at them while going to sleep, you could hallucinate small creatures moving around up there.

The next morning, Marty got up and found Edgar in the bathroom standing nude on the toilet, trying to look at a big pimple he had near the center of his back. He had obviously been picking at it.

"That's a prizewinner," Marty said.

"No," Edgar said, hopping off the toilet. "It's weird. Doesn't it look weird? It had black in it."

"That's from your T-shirt," Marty said, running his finger around his lover's sore. "You scratched it and it got goopy and some schnibblies from your T-shirt stuck to it." He displayed some of the loose fibers on the tip of his finger.

"No," Edgar said. "That's just threads there. That's from my T-shirt. But there was different stuff before."

"You're crazy," Marty said.

"No, I'm not," Edgar said seriously. "You didn't see."

Marty yawned. He wanted some coffee.

"Listen," Edgar said. "What you were saying last night. If you wanna start, you know, doing that, then I think we need to go to the doctor and all."

Marty was surprised. He thought Edgar had been sleeping through those comments. "You want to get tested," he said, "in other words."

"Don't you think we should?"

"Yeah. I mean, it wouldn't hurt." Marty had gotten a blood test a couple years ago when he'd gone to the doctor after stepping on a nail at work. During the examination he suggested to the doctor that maybe he ought to take an HIV test, "seeing as he was there already and all." The doctor paused and asked him why he thought he ought to take a test like that. Marty shrugged, said he didn't know, really, and the doctor shrugged and said if Marty wanted one . . . And so they did. When the tests came back, there was nothing unusual, and the doctor told him he shouldn't get all worked up. It was hard to get AIDS and there really was no call for someone who wasn't doing any of those things you *had* to do to get themselves in a state. Marty gathered that the doctor thought he was being overanxious about a one-night stand with some girl he didn't know too well.

"I mean, if you want to," Marty said. "I've got no problem with it."

Edgar nodded.

"That's just a zit, though. You know that, right?"

*   *   *

Marty had his second cup of coffee at work, listening to the crew foreman describe the extent of the drywall that needed to be hung by the end of the day. This project was a couple floors of an office building on St. Paul Street. They were making smaller rental units out of some floors formerly occupied by offices of the corporation which owned the building. Everyone was downsizing these days. Most of the crew's work lately had been renovation jobs like this rather than new construction, and their contract for this job contained rigid deadlines.

Marty often ended up paired off with the one female on the crew, Trini Coulburn, a short-haired, well-muscled black woman about thirty-one or -two. He suspected Trini was a lesbian, and to that end had earlier broached the subject of his upcoming anniversary with Edgar. Trini had been unsurprised and sympathetic but she had not returned the courtesy of admitting to being a homosexual. Not that Marty had said point blank that he was, either. He'd actually said, "Yeah, um . . . well . . . it's sort of my anniversary coming up. You know my friend Edgar? We been together three years this Wednesday." Trini had nodded without any expression in particular and said, "That's a long time—I mean, for a guy your age." Thursday morning, when they began cutting the drywall for the bare aluminum-stud framing that outlined a bank of office cubicles, Trini asked Marty how his big night had gone.

"Okay, I guess," Marty said. He was hoping that she would pry beneath the surface to inquire why, for example, Marty only "guessed" that it had gone okay. Which of his hopes had gone unrealized. But instead she nodded and smiled a little and went back to slicing the hole for an outlet box near the bottom of the panel.

"He just got me a little edgy," Marty let out a little while later, as if there'd been a far shorter pause in their conversation. "He got it into his head somehow that we need to get blood tests all of a sudden."

Trini wiped her forehead and her nose with a blue bandanna, then returned it to the back pocket of her jeans. "I had a cousin that died of that," she said matter-of-factly.

"I'm sorry," Marty said. If he were stupid he might have concluded Trini meant her cousin died of a blood test, but he knew they agreed on what they were actually talking about.

Trini shrugged. "It's something you don't wanna mess around with," she said.

"I know," Marty replied, somewhat abashed. He had wanted to talk about anxiety, not about some person dying. "I just don't know why, all of a sudden," he said. "He wasn't worried about it six months ago. He wasn't worried about it two days ago. But now he's got a notion."

"You know people," Trini said. "I got a sister-in-law like that with brain cancer. Sometimes it's cell phones and sometimes it's power lines but it's all gonna give her brain cancer. At least for a couple days after she's seen it on the news."

"Your sister-in-law?" Marty wanted her to tell him whether she meant a brother's wife or whether she meant a woman who was sister to a person Trini considered her spouse.

Instead Trini just squinted at him like he was deaf or a moron. "Yeah, my sister-in-law."

After work, Marty stopped for a beer with a couple guys from the crew. There was a game on the TV at the end of the bar, and they watched it and talked mostly about baseball. Jimmy Elsrod was having problems with his wife and announced he should have stayed single like Lefaivor. Then he could see any woman he wanted. Marty figured he based this assertion on the masculine beauty he might have possessed ten or twelve years ago when he was still a teenager. Considering Elsrod's present appearance, he was lucky if his wife wanted him. And after all, it seemed she didn't particularly.

Sometimes Marty actually said these things. Sometimes a guy from work would mention an attractive sister who could use a steady, responsible guy—usually in place of the reckless, irresponsible guy she was currently quite happy seeing even if her brother wasn't. Marty would decline the date and sometimes a guy like Elsrod would say, "What the fuck's the matter, Lefaivor—you gay or something?" And Marty would say, "Yeah. I am gay. I have a homosexual lover and everything." And Elsrod would say, "Yeah. Right. You're gay and I bet you butt-fuck all the time." And Marty would say, "Yeah. That's right. We do. We have anal sex."

By then an involuntary smile would be pasted across Marty's lips and the truth would be working as a better lie than a lie would. None of them believed he was gay. They were incapable of believing he was gay. Elsrod was okay, though, mostly. He was a fat, balding jerk who thought he possessed some natural charisma, but he was an all-right guy besides that. And the other guys on the crew, Roy Schaeffer and Pat Donaldson and Mark Joyce, were nice. They had their little bits. Roy was a racist, and Pat talked about the strange magazines he liked to read about ghosts and UFOs, and Mark told too-explicit stories about his swinging sex life. Mark's wife liked to stick a finger up his ass when she gave him head, and once he had persuaded her to get a girlfriend to join them in bed. Everyone found these stories both believable and disturbing, unlike Marty's deceptive admissions, and they liked Mark, but in a condescending way, as if he were mildly retarded and could not be expected to exercise a socially acceptable restraint on the things that occurred to him to say.

Marty thought Mark's sexual life, as revealed through his banter, sounded pathetic and sad. How could you love your wife and do things like that? And if you didn't love her, what did you get out of it, chained to one person but not even pretending to be faithful? The other straight guys did not seem to envy it, either. On more than one occasion, Elsrod had said, "Did you ever hear of anyone bragging about that kind of thing? I think that damn Joyce is a closet-case queer. Wanting us to hear all about where he's sticking his dick."

Sometimes, Pat Donaldson suggested, people who have these compulsive abnormal sexual drives are just experiencing the side effects of the brain experiments the aliens do. It was probably Mark's way of crying out for help.

Roy and Marty and Elsrod agreed that this was as likely an explanation as they could come up with. Why they didn't think Pat was nuts is another issue altogether. For one thing, he didn't seem particularly intent on believing the things he enjoyed reporting. That his knowledge demonstrated some admirable devotion to reading and the intellect was another reason. Plus, it was interesting to hear about. It was interesting to imagine that behind closed doors, people would admit to being kidnapped by creatures from other planets; to knowing that our genetic codes had been manipulated back in prehistory to help us walk upright, develop our brains and our society so we could one day join our ancestors in space. More interesting than hearing about Mark Joyce and his wife's finger, anyhow.

Edgar was mad when Marty finally came home around nine-thirty. He had the television on and would not look at Marty. "There's a whole stack of bills that need to get paid," he said.

Once a month they sat down to go over their finances. Except for the mortgage payments, which Marty alone covered, they split everything down the middle. They added up all the expenses and divided them in half and then sorted the individual bills into the two piles which most closely approximated the halved sum. There was always a tie-breaking bill for which they would need to write two checks. Edgar had his name on Marty's MasterCard account, but other than that they had no joint finances. To get the credit card, Marty had only needed to send in a form to the company's address in Delaware. The form did not ask why you wanted this other person to be able to use your card. But to get a joint checking account, they would both have had to go to the bank branch and probably explain what they were.

Edgar finally looked at Marty and said, "I guess you're too drunk to do it tonight."

Marty made an irritated sighing noise and went into the kitchen.

"Did you think about what we talked about this morning?" Edgar said loudly. Marty was looking over the bills. He wasn't too drunk. They weren't that hard to figure out.

"Yes," Marty said. "I thought about it."

"And . . . ?"

"Well, I'm ready to do it," he answered. "It's perfectly fine with me. I don't think it's all that necessary, but I guess we should."

"What do you mean it's not all that necessary?" Edgar was being pissy. "Do you think you know everything about me? Do I know everything about you?"

"No. I don't know. I'm just saying, you know. We're healthy and I trust you."

"Trust? Jesus shit, Marty, do you think people *want* to give each other AIDS? It's people who don't bother worrying about it who end up getting it."

"I said we should do it, so I don't know why I need a fucking lecture about AIDS tonight. You're not sick, Edgar, just because you got a goddamn zit."

"I know I'm not sick, asshole. But wouldn't it be nice not to worry about it every time one of us gets the flu or a rash or a zit? Not to have to worry about dying all of a sudden every time something stupid happens? That's all I'm saying."

"Did you hear me say it was fine? I said fine. It's stupid. I don't worry about zits. You're out of your mind. *You* don't worry about zits."

"I don't know what's up with you, man," Edgar said. "I don't know why you're freaking out about this."

"I'm not freaking out about it," Marty said. "I'm freaking out at you. You're pissing me off. I'm sorry I stayed out and didn't call, I can understand you being mad. Why do you have to turn it into me not caring if I give you fuckin' AIDS for chrisssake?"

"Fuck you, Marty. Not everything's *about* you." Edgar's voice had a sharp, quavering tone to it. Marty slowly turned around. Edgar had his legs folded up on the couch, his hand over his mouth. He wasn't sobbing, but there was a visible tear or two on his reddening cheeks. He looked sidelong at Marty, then darted his eyes away again.

"You aren't the only guy that's ever fucked me, you know," he said.

"I can take care of these bills tonight," Marty said. "I only had a couple beers. Let me relax for a while, and I'll do it during the news."

"Marty . . ." Edgar said plaintively. "I'm sorry. You know? I've just been putting it out of my mind is all. I love you. I don't want to make you sick."

Marty had a hard-on when he woke up. Edgar was asleep with his back pressed against Marty's left side, snoring softly, dusted with sweat. He remembered one of those dreams where you're stuck back in school, feeling as small and overpowered as you used to but with a nagging, uncertain refusal to accept those conditions—you almost recall that you graduated years ago. One scene of the dream had occurred in a locker room that wasn't quite like it should have been. Nothing sexual had occurred, but he watched the boys undress, noticed a porno magazine in one of their lockers. A magazine from a dirty bookstore—the kind that comes in a pack of three for five dollars, not a slick monthly one that a kid could shoplift from a convenience store or something. The vague boys of his dream made him think of several people to whom he'd been mildly attracted. When he had been that age he had never let himself think any of the boys he liked were within his reach, sexually. He had fantasized, sometimes in quite specific detail, of going over to a friend's house, hanging out on a strange bed listening to music when something accidental and electric happened. He never picked his own friends for such a daydream. They were always boys he admired but knew slightly. Sometimes they weren't even on friendly terms. He enjoyed making up what their bedrooms might look like.

Edgar, on the other hand, had begun to sleep with men when he was rather young. He had slept with men who had no business even talking to a teenage boy. "I thought someone would show me what I was supposed to do," he'd said of those experiences. "It was nice to have someone think you were important because you were young and inexperienced. No one else thought that way when they looked at me. You were just some worthless kid."

When Marty made love to Edgar, he felt like he was protecting him.

"How many lites do we need, Mar?"

Marty and Pat Donaldson had volunteered to run down to Wawa's to pick up coffees for the crew. Pat was ordering at the counter while Marty wandered down the magazine rack, reading cover lines.

"Marty?" Pat asked again. "How many with milk?"

Marty looked over. Both Pat and the clerk were looking at him. "Oh. Four. Five, I guess."

"Everybody like regular donuts? Or should I get a handful of these Danishes and shit?"

"Just get the donuts. We had that argument last time, remember."

"Yeah," Pat conceded. "If I get a Danish to eat in the truck, you want one too?"

Marty laughed. They'd been given ten bucks to go to the

store, were supposed to bring back change. "Okay, sure," he said. He prodded a tabloid magazine with the headline "Astronomers Discover Ancient Air Force Base on Mars." "Hey, Pat," he said. "You want this?"

Pat cocked his head back. "Man." He scrunched his nose up. "What, do you think I'm an idiot?" The clerk finished packing a cardboard tray full of steaming coffee cups and pushed it across the counter. Pat handed over the ten-dollar bill. "You ever look at that magazine? It's got a sentence right on the inside cover says, 'For entertainment purposes only.' "

Marty pulled the tabloid out of its slot. Beneath the Ancient Air Force Base blurb was one that read, "AIDS Scare for Baywatch Beauty." He let go of it disdainfully. "You mean you don't believe in the chicken boy?" Marty teased.

"People in this world," Pat exhaled, picking up the tray of coffees, "still believe in an ancient sky god gonna send them to hell, and I'm a freak for thinking somewhere in this infinite universe there's another planet with living creatures on it."

"I'm just pulling your chain, Pat." Marty held the door open for him. They'd driven down in Pat's white Ford pickup. Pat handed off the coffees for Marty to hold. "You know I don't mean nothing by it."

Rings of burning hot coffee swirled around the plastic lids on the cups, splattering a few drops on Marty's jeans as Pat backed the truck out. "Shit!"

"Sorry. Watch yourself," Pat said. He squealed into the intersection, but by then the coffee spillover had cooled down a little.

"Man," Marty said, rolling down the window and resting his arm there. "You don't believe in God, Pat?"

"Well," Pat said. "I mean, I don't believe in God with a white beard. I don't believe in God parting the Red Sea. I don't know what the fuck's out there. Maybe there's some kind of God, but I don't know him." Pat pushed in the lighter, smacked his new pack of Marlboros against his thigh to tamp down the tobacco in them. "Does that surprise you?" he asked.

Marty shrugged. "Kinda. I don't know."

"You surprise me," Pat said. "I woulda thought you'd be a little skeptical of the whole thing."

"What? God?"

"Yeah, religion and all. Organized religion."

"What would make you assume that?" Marty asked.

"I dunno. I guess I just think certain kinds of people get skeptical about things. About being told how things are supposed to be."

"What kind of people? What are you talking about, Pat?"

He exhaled, a slight snort, then shrugged. "I don't know, Marty. Nothing." He rolled the pack of cigarettes between his fingers, undoing the cellophane wrapper with one hand. "I'm not Elsrod, you know. It's cool with me, man."

"I don't know what you're getting at, Pat."

"Okay. Sorry," Pat said. "But it's cool with me, Mart. I just wanted you to know that."

"Yeah, okay," Marty said. "It's cool with me too." He chuckled as if he were bemused by the conversation.

"You're such an asshole," Pat said, beaming. "You know exactly what I'm talking about."

Shortly into the morning, Mark Joyce was horsing around with a nail gun and drove a one-and-three-quarter-inch galvanized steel nail into the meat of his forearm. Trini Coulburn sat him down in a chair and straddled him to pull it out. Marty felt his head go light as a thick trail of blood oozed out the dark hole in Mark's arm. He had to sit down and look away.

Trini wrapped a sheet of clean chamois tightly around Mark's arm, and Roy took him to the emergency room, but the image—and the red dots on the floor where Mark had done it—made Marty uneasy for the rest of the day. At lunch Pat apologized if he had made Marty uncomfortable about anything and Marty assured him he hadn't. Pat said that on Saturday he was going to the ball game with his brother and they had a couple extra tickets if Marty had twenty bucks. Marty said thanks but he had some chores he needed to take care of at home this weekend. After work everyone stopped off for a beer as usual but Marty only finished half of his before he said he needed to get along.

There were some groceries out in the kitchen but Edgar did not seem to be around when Marty came home. The back door was sitting open, though, and after fixing himself an ice tea Marty heard Edgar talking with one of the neighbors outside. He stuck his head out the screen door.

"Hey," Edgar said. He was in the Gristlers' yard next door, leaning against the cinder-block wall that divided the area behind the houses into their individual pens. Matt Gristler was starting up his grill. "I was just over here helping Matt put up the crib for the nursery. He was dragging it in from his car when I got home from work."

"Hey, Marty," Matt said. Matt was a married guy about their same age. His wife, Jen, was pregnant. "I told Edgar I could put on some burgers for you guys. I appreciate the help and all. Had to go up to Jen's mom's this afternoon and bring down this old nursery furniture Jen wanted. She's been bugging me for weeks."

"Oh yeah," Marty said. "When's she due?"

"First of November. Not too long now, right?" Matt said. He shook the grill a little, settling the charcoals. "Goddamn. I'm looking forward to it and all, but man. Kids."

"It's a big step," Marty agreed.

"Shit yeah, it's a big step. I'm going to be somebody's dad." Matt put the lid back on the grill. "I gotta get the burgers from inside. You want a beer while I'm in there?"

"No thanks, man," Marty said.

"I'll take one," Edgar said. "Shit. Hey, Matt. You like Bass Ale? We got a whole case we're never gonna drink by ourselves."

Marty was a little put out by Edgar giving away their beer, but he came out with a six-pack and walked around the gate with it. Matt was still hung up on how much money the baby would cost but shut up about it once Jen came home. She waddled out to the back door, a huge pinkish gray sweatshirt tight across her belly but baggy and huge in the neck and arms, waved hi at Marty and Edgar, and smiled with genuine pleasure when she saw Matt had fixed dinner. "Someone's been a good boy today." She pulled the elastic off her dark blond ponytail. "I saw what you done upstairs."

"Edgar gave me a hand," Matt said.

"I wonder if they'll love us so much when we've got a baby screaming through their bedroom walls all night," Jen said.

"I can sleep through worse than a baby," Edgar said.

"Him too, I'll bet," Jen said, kicking at Matt's leg with her sneaker. "I can guess who's gonna be getting up at night." Matt smirked as he flipped the hamburgers. Jen laughed like she was offended and lowered herself gently to the picnic bench. She shook her head as she caught Marty's eye and said, "Men," with a pouty groan. She winked at him then and he did not know how to react. "Go on, drink your beers in front of me, you sons of bitches. Damn, I'd like a beer."

Edgar took a dramatic swig off his beer bottle, wiping its mouth on the tail of his T-shirt.

"You know, Dr. French says I shouldn't start drinking alcohol until the baby's done breast-feeding, can you believe it? Oh, I sound like a drunk, don't I? But not even one beer for the last six months. I suppose if I hung out with a different crowd I might not even be noticing, right, hon?"

"I told you I'd stop if it'd help you."

"I know," Jen said. "He quit smoking already," she said over to Edgar and Marty, "so I let him have his beer for the time being."

"I have a cigar now and again," Matt said. "I figure it does less harm."

When they finished eating and Marty had helped Jen take the dishes inside, Matt brought his cigar paraphernalia up from the bar in the basement, arraying the coat-pocket-sized leather humidor case, the wide brass lighter, and the cigar cutter on the picnic table in front of Edgar, who examined each item with interest. The cutter was of surgical steel in a matte finish, square with a round hole in the center, from which two blades emerged when you squeezed the two levers between your thumb and forefinger. It looked partly like a nail-cutting tool and partly like a guillotine. "Jen's brother got me these for Christmas," Matt said as Edgar rolled one of the cigars between his fingers.

"You're not going to have one of those," Marty said with a little irritation. Edgar looked at him and raised his eyebrows in an expression of uncertainty.

"Go ahead," Matt said. "Don't worry about it. I got a whole box." Which wasn't really Marty's concern but made it hard for him to object further. He just wanted to be getting home soon. He liked Matt fine, of course, but he and Edgar had things to talk about.

"Seriously?" Edgar said. Matt nodded enthusiastically and got himself one as well. Edgar smiled as he and Matt began unraveling the cellophane wrappings at the same time. It was a flirty, pleased smile that lit up his face, Marty observed—they were about to do something naughty together—though he was only a little bit jealous because it didn't mean anything. Edgar liked to be accepted into the rituals of guys. He'd fallen in love with Marty because Marty was a guy, but this was a difficult impression to keep fresh now that they'd been having homosexual sex for three years, keeping a household together. Anyone seems to be a queen once they start bitching about the smell of your pee drying on the tile where you missed the bowl a little.

Matt showed Edgar how to draw in on your cigar to get it lit, and Marty wondered who Edgar thought of when his mind wandered having sex. It didn't bother him, because he did it too, but he wondered who. They talked about certain famous actors being cute—Keanu Reeves, Brad Pitt, the guy who played Becky's boyfriend on *Roseanne*—but actors were something you masturbated about, maybe, when you were alone. Marty thought of real guys when he had sex. The boys he had liked in high school, guys he had known since, and past sexual experiences that had been hot. He assumed Edgar did likewise. He wondered if Edgar had ever thought about Matt. It was no big deal: Marty had.

"Marty," Matt said, shoving the open cigar case down to his end of the table. "You want one?"

Marty frowned. "Not a whole one. I'll take a drag, though, I guess."

Both Edgar and Matt began to offer their cigars in his direction. Matt put his back in his mouth and puffed vigorously when Marty accepted Edgar's.

"I guess he's more used to my spit," Edgar said, as if he'd won a contest and needed to be magnanimous, deferential in victory. Matt grinned bashfully—as he did any time his neighbors referred, however obliquely, to the nature of their relationship—and turned his eyes away when Marty brought the cigar to his lips.

"Gee," he said awkwardly. "Look at all the stars out tonight. Sometimes with the lights from the harbor you can't see anything."

The night felt kind of cool so Marty put on an old T-shirt before getting into bed. Edgar smelled him and made a face. "You dig that out of the bottom of the closet? Makes you smell like socks." Marty snorted. Edgar pressed his lips against Marty's armpit and bit his flesh through the cotton fabric.

"It's real nice how Matt's got the nursery set up," Edgar said, his hands on Marty's stomach. "I mean, they got this big wardrobe with a fold-out changing table pushed up against our wall. Matt said he figured it'd buffer against the noise. I thought that was real considerate."

"We'll see how well it works, I guess."

"It's just a baby," Edgar said. "I don't imagine we'll hear much out of it."

"I'm not sure," Marty said. "We heard them make it, didn't we?"

Edgar giggled, hooking his leg around Marty's. "Do you think they can hear us?"

"I guess. We can hear them, right? I can't imagine they're so much louder."

"I think they're a little louder," Edgar said. "Jen's a little more dramatic than I am. Or maybe Matt gives her more to yell about." He had his hand down Marty's shorts now, squeezing him gently. Marty switched off the lights and closed his eyes. Edgar moved his head to Marty's chest and planted damp kisses on his shirt.

"Marty?" he whispered. "Honey?"

Marty moved his hand to Edgar's head, stroking the short, fine locks of hair. He traced the curve of Edgar's ear with a finger he wetted on Edgar's lips. "What?"

"I'm sorry I was so stupid before. I guess it just freaked me out. Even the idea. Thinking about drawing blood makes me go light in the head. To think that we're filled with . . . veins and shit."

"Don't worry about it," Marty said. "That's natural. It's scary to think about."

"It's just, you know . . . us thinking about making a decision like that. It kind of scared me. Because that's it, right? That's the last step. That's us saying we really mean it, isn't it? I mean, Jen and Matt, they're married, they're going to have a baby together."

Marty softly hummed in agreement.

"Marty, I want to have a baby."

Edgar listened to Marty's heart beat.

"Marty?"

"You can't have a baby, you silly old girl," Marty said.

"How do you know?" Edgar said, pulling Marty's underwear down past his knees and climbing on top of him. Sliding his hands up his lover's chest until he had him by the shoulders. "We've never tried."

COCKSUCKER

CALEB CRAIN

The wind was rising. Two blocks from the train station, Stitch took out his wallet to reread Jesús's address. Flakes of sawdust drifted to the door of a bodega; at the sill they leaped up and scattered. Draped over handscreens in the windows of an SRO, shirts and stockings were swaying heavily, or twitching like nervous sleepers. A beggar with a greasy wound in his face sat Indian-style on the sidewalk, an empty coffee cup tucked into the nest of his legs as he counted lottery tickets.

Jesús's address was a large, square building of pale yellow bricks. The corridors were empty, and the elevator clanged when it shut. Stitch checked himself out in the elevator's buffed steel ceiling; he ran his fingers over his crewcut. He didn't feel safe. The elevator trembled; it was rising, but too slowly for Stitch to feel any vertical tug. His reflection in the metal stared down at him, scumbled, staring up.

Stitch thought about how he'd met Jesús, three months ago. Stitch had been Jacob then, his old name, before the crewcut. It was his first time in a sex club. He had paid fifteen dollars and then stepped through a short U-tunnel, like the light trap at the entrance to a darkroom, to enter a tall, dim warehouse. Black paint greased the walls. Blurry, silent porn shifted and bled one orange man into another on a large screen over the bar. A bald, muscled dancer in a dog collar spread his legs over a chair, on a stage raised foot-high in the middle of the room, and played with himself.

Jacob's voices had hissed at him: *This is what you deserve.* Men stood staggered through the warehouse, drinking silently. They glared at the go-go dancer and the porn. *They can see how bad you want it.* From time to time, when one finished his drink, he walked with studied casualness toward one of the dark corners of the room, where he disappeared. Jacob sipped a lemonade, then emptied his hands and walked toward a corner, too.

Jacob could see a short, unlit corridor full of men. They lined the walls, one or two deep; many had tied their shirts around their waists. A man slouched at the entrance watched him uncuriously. Jacob smelled fresh sweat and something oily and chemical, like a rotten jar of olives. To walk through, you had to touch them. You had to wedge your shoulders between theirs and inch your thighs around their buttocks and feel their hands pinch your ass and squeeze your cock. You could push the hands away, but they would come back. Jacob's face was in the face of a fat bleached blond with one nipple ring, then a pretty, tan thirty-year-old with bulging shoulders. He stepped on someone's foot. "Sorry." The corridor stayed silent, jostling, breathing, rubbing, unbuttoning. He was thrust behind a shirtless man who was jacking off another shirtless bodybuilder; he laid his hand on the man's shoulder, to anchor himself as he passed, but the man's shoulder was smooth and wet with sweat, and Jacob's hand clamped down as if he'd touched a live wire. He pulled away, scared. He didn't know what the man had felt, because he couldn't see his face. Maybe the man didn't want Jacob's touch, because he was busy with his friend. Jacob stumbled; he was out.

The next corridor was longer, narrower, and less crowded. He found a spot along one wall. His eyes slowly adjusted to the ultraviolet light; flecks of lint starred men's shirts, their eyeballs gleamed, and their hair looked dusty and metallic. The men became negatives of themselves, or solarizations, filtered in blue. He remembered UV light is supposed to be bad for your eyes, and here he was squinting in it. He didn't leave. The corridor slowly crowded with men. They pressed Jacob against the brick wall. He took off his shirt, and the bricks' edges cross-hatched the ribs of his back. Some of the men who passed touched his crotch, or touched theirs while watching his. Sometimes Jacob reached out, but he touched people too gently, too inquiringly— he would stroke a shoulder or a forearm, but too tenderly—he alarmed them, and he immediately felt ashamed. You fucking sissy. If you want it, make like you want it. The men shuffled past. He wasn't going to be Jacob if they asked.

Finally he noticed that a Latino leaning against the opposite wall was cruising him. Wiry, grizzled hair curled out from under his flowered baseball cap. He tried out a smile on Jacob—or was it a trick of the light? Jacob couldn't see well. Other men shuttered their line of sight, in long, irregular stops. The man had turned his head; now he turned it back. He fixed Jacob with serious, angry eyes that broke when Jacob met his stare. He waved Jacob over to him.

"You having fun?"

"I guess."

Hesitantly Jacob placed his palm against the man's chest. He held it there delicately and felt goose bumps rise on the man's skin. The man put his hand over Jacob's and ground it against his pecs. Suddenly Jacob was all over the man; he stuck his tongue down his throat, in his ear, pushed his fingers against his nipples, his hands down the back of his pants. The man unzipped Jacob's jeans and took out his cock to massage it. The men around them were watching.

"What's your name?" Jacob whispered. His cock was hanging there in the other man's hands, where anyone could see it.

"Jesús," the man said out loud.

"Do you want to come over?"

"No. I want to get off here. Touch my cock, baby."

You could hear the man's accent in that one word, "baby;" his lips stuttered thickly over the repeated *b*, and he shortened the vowels. He wasn't hiding it; he said it again. "Go ahead, baby." Jacob tugged open the man's fly. He peeled down the man's white briefs, and his fat cock bounced free. Jacob wanted to suck it, because it was magnificent and hard, but that was against the rules, so he spat on his hands and worked them up and down Jesús's cock. While they kissed they still stared at each other, with glassy, wide, unfocusably close eyes, like a whale's eye on his harpooneer. "Yeah, baby," said Jesús. He didn't even know Jacob's name. Jacob didn't know if his name was really Jesús, and it didn't matter. The hair on Jacob's balls prickled; he was going to come. "I'm going to shoot." "Yeah, baby, shoot. I want to see you shoot."

They turned slightly, with their temples pressed against each other and their dicks pointing at the same brick in the wall. Jacob watched the muscles in the man's chest tense and rise, and then the man let go; he sank a little; and then Jacob saw him racked with coming, and felt the man's come leap through the cock in his fist, and Jacob came, too, loosing it, throwing it out of him, poison and love; it fell against the wall and on the floor.

"Jesús is a beautiful name," Jacob had said. And the man had told Jacob his phone number.

The elevator clanged open. At the end of the hall, a door was ajar but dark.

"Hello?" Stitch said.

"Come in," he heard.

Stitch edged into a small, unlit room. He couldn't see anything. This must be the foyer. The narthex. A man, not Jesús, flapped open a curtain, rushed past him—"Excuse me"—and shut the door as he left. Stitch shuffled toward the part in the curtain. To keep from tripping, he scanned the dark with his hands.

When he passed through, he saw he had arrived in a kitchen. Jesús's cap was off, and he was grinning. "Baby," he said.

"Who was that?" Stitch asked. "Your last trick?"

"Ay, no. She was taking a piss outside the bucket. Did you see her? I told her she had to leave or you would beat her up."

Hoping for a clue, Stitch looked over his shoulder, but of course the man was gone. "I don't understand."

"I said you were my boyfriend. And that you are very jealous, baby, a violent man."

"It was your last trick, wasn't it."

"Ay, you *are* jealous. No, baby, no. He said on the phone that he was six foot, blond, muscle"—he air-kissed the tips of his fingers—"all that, yes? He is a friend of my friend, that is how I know him. Not the phone sex line. Don't get the wrong idea. You want a drink, baby? All I have is water."

"I might need something stronger."

"I never drink, baby. It is bad for the exotic beauty. I have cook wine. Or the bodega on the corner."

"All right, water."

"I can go to the store. Are you despairing for it? For you, baby, anything you want. You know that."

"Please, water is fine."

"I don't want it to be just fine. I want you to have what you want."

"Give me water."

"Okay, baby, if that's what you want. You know I can go to the store." He poured a glass out of the tap. "There. Do you want ice?"

"Sure."

Jesús shook his head. "Ay, and she wants ice, too." He had to dig to pry free an ice cube. "I am just kidding, baby. What is your name again?"

"Stitch."

Jesús's apartment was a large, L-shaped studio; the kitchen was in the small leg of the L. Stitch wandered into the crook of it, the living room. One wall was stacked with rustic-style wool blankets and cardboard boxes. Along the other wall, plate-glass windows looked uptown. A television murmured and giggled to itself in the far end of the apartment.

"Do you like my garden?" Jesús asked. He took Stitch by the elbow and brought him to a jagged row of potted plants. "I did not buy any of these. Each one I made grow, with my especial care. I take branches. This one from Central Park. This one from the Rambles, baby. This one from the middle of the street, in a Madison Avenue. You see, this one, with flowers, from the box outside my restaurant."

"You have a restaurant."

"I am a waiter," he said, with matter-of-fact pride. "I will tell you about it, but not yet, baby. I am showing you my garden. I put the branch in water first, until I see roots."

Some people took in stray cats; this man took in shrubs. The leaves were tightly curled, grayish and wary, as if the plants hadn't forgotten the street yet. No fresh sprout had grown too far away from the stiff-barked twig it had hid inside when Jesús first brought it home. But, however cannily, they were flourishing, all of them.

Stitch remembered the question he was being distracted from. "Who was that man, anyway?"

"I told you, a friend of a friend."

"And why was he pissing in your pot, or whatever."

"That is Venezuelan expression. Taking a piss outside the bucket. It means, not even close."

"And?"

Jesús paused, frowned. "Are you jealous, baby?" he asked as if he were afraid Stitch were allergic to something he had cooked. "I just want to know. No, forget it. If you want to, forget it."

"No, I tell you, but you cannot be jealous. Salvador, my friend, told this man I like Brazilian boys. So the man calls me and say he is Brazilian. Not only that. He say he is Troy Aikman, but really he is Julia Child. He lie because he think that I will fuck him anyway. No, baby. He was not pissing in the bucket. Not anywhere in the neighborhood of the bucket."

"Got it. So he *was* going to be your trick."

"But thank God, you came. I am so happier to see you." He paused to get the English right: " 'Happier' or 'happiest'?"

Stitch eyed Jesús's salt-and-pepper curls and loose smile. What am I supposed to learn from this sweet-talker? The Venezuelan crouched over one of his clippings, weeding stray clovers out of the soil. He hadn't built up any showy muscles in a gym; instead, his body was lithe and casual, like a wild cat's. He glanced up at Stitch, who took his grin to mean, It doesn't matter what I say, in the end, because there's no reason we shouldn't take as much pleasure in each other's bodies as we can. And I plan to take my pleasure. Was that the attraction? Since his old self, Jacob, had panicked, Stitch's first loyalty was to the body, not to who he thought he was. He was curious to know what this body wanted.

They kissed. When Jesús's soft, bitter tongue snaked into his mouth, Stitch remembered everything they had done in the sex club. Kissing a man you hadn't fucked in a while was like speaking a foreign language you thought you had forgotten. It turns out you never forget. He knew to bite the corner of the man's upper lip and to stroke his thumb along the unshaven line of his jaw. Back then—Stitch had quit smoking Jacob's cigarettes—he hadn't been able to taste the stale smoke in Jesús's spit. He reached down to hold the man's cock and felt blood coursing evenly into it. Through the denim of Jesús's jeans, Stitch felt Jesús's cock widening across his palm.

"You like?" Jesús asked.

"You've got an amazing cock."

"Once I fuck you with it, you won't want anybody else."

"That's what I'm afraid of."

"No, don't be afraid. I go slow. I take you so easy, baby. It will be so good."

Jesús unbuttoned Stitch's fly, to loosen the waist of his pants. He pushed a hand down along the small of Stitch's back. "I'm not a bottom, really," Stitch said. "I've never really done that."

"I'll show you."

"You'll show me. Does that mean I fuck you first?"

Jesús glowered. "I don't get fucked." He pronounced each consonant. "Put it *out* of your mind. It is not possible."

"If you want me as bad as you say, you'll let me take you first."

"Ay, baby, you don't give up."

"Neither do you."

"We could have so much fun, baby. Let me have this ass," he said, squeezing it. "Give it to me."

"No."

Jesús yanked his hand out of Stitch's pants and walked behind a folding partition of shellacked brown particle board into the bedroom. Stitch followed. The television threw red and yellow flickers across plain walls. The Venezuelan sat on his bed and lit a Merit. He kicked off his shoes, swung his bare feet up, and patted the pillow beside him. "Not even my boyfriend fucks me. I can't let you fuck me. Now watch TV, baby, until I get tired, and then you can go home."

Stitch unlaced his sneakers and crawled up onto the bed. "You have a boyfriend. What's his name?"

"No, nothing. I can't fuck you, I tell you nothing."

"Come on. How old is he?"

Jesús kept his eyes on the TV. "Nothing," he repeated.

"Is he older than I am?"

The studio audience laughed. Stitch glanced at the screen. A vintage rerun; it looked like *The Mary Tyler Moore Show.* "How old are you?" Jesús asked.

"Twenty-five."

"He's younger."

"Aha."

"No more," Jesús said. The bluish light of the TV phosphor blinked and fluttered over his face. "You are jealous, and there is no right for you to be jealous."

"And how old are you?" Stitch asked.

"Forty-five."

"You are *not* forty-five."

"Whatever you say, baby."

"You aren't."

"Like you like it."

"You look much younger than forty-five."

"Because of my exotic beauty."

In a commercial for douche, a waif model skipped across a dewy field. Her linen skirt trailed damply behind her through the grass. She'll get ticks, Stitch thought. The bickering reassured him. So did the rhythm of the television—crass, then chuckly, then sentimental—and the solid warmth of the man's body at his side. He turned his head to admire Jesús's olive skin, aquiline nose, the malevolence pooled in his eyes.

"No way you're fucking me if you've got a boyfriend. You're trying to addict me to a cock I can't have."

"If I fuck you, I will take care of you. You will have all the cock you need, baby."

"What if I want it the same time your boyfriend wants it?"

"I'll take care of you. I promise."

It was a transparent lie, so appealing it didn't have to be true. A promise to be reliable and present: it was more intoxicating than any fuck could ever be. He knew Jesús would bed whomever he wanted, whenever he wanted. And so would he. Here they were, watching sitcoms in bed, lying to each other like an old married couple.

"No, I'd be jealous," Stitch said.

"There is enough. You don't have to worry, baby. Besides, my boyfriend is away. He writes to me, only."

"What do you mean, 'away'?"

"He's on tour. Baby, I'm not going to talk about him with you. It makes me sad. I want you to relax, okay? Let's watch some nice television and have a good time together."

Jesús stared straight ahead. He gripped Stitch's hand and firmly pinned it to the mattress. Stitch laid his other hand on the fly of Jesús's jeans.

Jesús peeled the hand off. He explained: "You have to be nice to Mary"—he pointed to his face—"if you want to meet Jesus"—he pointed to his cock.

"I am nice to Mary."

"No. You have not done nothing for Mary. Where is my ring?"

"Your ring. You're the one who's forty-five."

"Baby, I'll tell you what to do. All you say is yes. You give me that white ass and you say yes yes yes."

"I've tried before. It's too complicated."

"It is no hard, baby. It is no harder than taking a shit, and you do that every day."

"You're an incurable romantic, aren't you." He climbed on top of Jesús. He clasped his hands over Jesús's and crushed them into the pillows. He forced open the man's knees.

"What you doing up there, sweetheart? You'll get dizzy."

You'd love to let go, wouldn't you, Jacob? Lean out over the precipice until you feel yourself in the arms of your own weight, and then tumble into those arms, the only sound a small gritty scratch, your sneakers scuffing gravel as they lift off the ledge. He wasn't dizzy, exactly, but he felt something a little like panic. When he read a story where a man got fucked, it set the character at another remove. He couldn't think of the man as a man anymore, but he didn't think of him as a woman, either. Stitch might be a bottom. He read about it as something human, something he knew people enjoyed, but although it sounds like a bad joke, once a character let himself be fucked, he was no longer a character Jacob could enter.

"I don't know what I'm doing," he admitted. He focused on one of Jesús's eyes, then the other. The man tilted his head back, to meet Stitch's gaze, and his curls screwed themselves vainly against the bed's white sheets, like tendrils wound into springs and grasping for a hold. "I don't know who I am, either."

"I tell you," Jesús said.

"You don't know anything about me. You haven't asked me one question, except how old I am."

"I tell you who you are," he repeated.

He rolled Stitch over, got up, and switched off the TV. Behind his bedside table was a Victorian cheval glass, which he wheeled out to the foot of the bed. A vine was carved as if clinging to the dark oak frame. The old glass nodded heavily in its hinges; Jesús tipped it back to a slight angle. Silently it repeated the rumpled bedclothes, the pillows, the pack of Merits, and Jacob or Stitch. Jesús climbed onto the bed and walked across it on his knees, entering the frame.

"Kiss me," he ordered. "Look at yourself while you kiss me."
They kissed, kneeling together, parallel to the mirror. With one eye Stitch could see a glassy picture of Jacob, furtively watching himself kiss a middle-aged Latino man. Even kissing, Jacob had a worried smile. Please don't look.

"Who are you?" Jesús asked.

Stitch watched. What would he say? A tendon in Jesús's neck stood out, taut, like a mallet raised by a struck piano key. He bit at Jesús as he kissed him; he could see his own teeth rake along his chin. "I'm kissing you," he said.

"Who are you?" the man repeated.

He knew Jesús had done this with hundreds of men, and he would do it with hundreds more. The cheval glass had seen all these self-discoveries, impassively. Jacob or Stitch or someone else. It didn't matter who was making the discovery.

"Who do you see?" Jesús asked. The curls behind Jesús's ears were salty with sweat; he licked them instead of answering, let the tang cut his tongue. He didn't want to have to put it in words. There was someone here who didn't speak. "You don't know yet," Jesús said. He tugged Jacob's shirt out of his pants and stripped it off him, over his head. The inside-out T-shirt veiled his face the same moment white cloth blocked his sight. When he could see again, he watched the man's dark hands rubbing his pale, naked skin. The hands' callused, dry touch trailed after the sight of them, the way the echo of a gun's report reaches you a few seconds after you've seen the shudder of it firing. The man bent down to suck Jacob's nipples. He bit them, too; they got hard.

"Look at yourself. Who are you now?"

He saw his own fingers untangling Jesús's belt. He guided his shaky hands by what he saw in the mirror, moving everything backwards. He unhooked the tongue of the buckle. He was taking what he wanted; here was Jesús's thick cock, hanging out of his fly, in my hands. If I ask him to, he'll fuck me with it.

Jesús stopped him. "Who are you now? Answer me."

"A cocksucker," he said. The voice startled him. It wasn't the polite, fine voice he usually spoke with.

"Do you like being a cocksucker?"

"Yeah, I like it."

"Say it."

"I'm a faggot and I like sucking cock."

"That's right, baby," Jesús said. He stroked Stitch's buzz-cut head, his eyes on his. "Now you know."

Several weeks later, Jesús fucked him. Afterward, Stitch lay stunned for a few minutes. He didn't think he could keep from shitting himself, so he didn't move; he felt like a child. He thought about the photos Jesús had shown him, just before they stripped and got in bed, of Jesús's wedding in Venezuela. White linen on a muddy beach. Jesús had married a lesbian from the United States, because he was in love with a man and wanted a green card so he could live with him in Manhattan forever and ever.

The pleasure had gathered along Stitch's spine like a corposant on a mast, pulling into a white collection the sparks Jesús's cock was striking into him, a weightless sphere that drifted upward, trapped in the hollow between his back and Jesús arched over him. When the pleasure reached the nape of his neck, it entered him and covered his brain, and he felt it in him and around him, a white ribbon circling his sight, tightening it. For a moment all of him was this bright static energy. Then he felt Jesús's cock again, and the pleasure broke; the electricity ran down it like a lightning rod. He screamed; his eyes poured tears; he drooled spit; come shot out of him.

"How are you, baby?" Jesús asked, settling onto the mattress beside him. "Was it like I said?" He tugged a Merit out of his pack.

"Oh yeah," Stitch answered. He felt pleasantly empty now. He gazed at the Venezuelan with silly, doting eyes. "You were fucking great." The blunt language they had fucked in—the take it and give it to me and you know you want it and it's all yours—wasn't adequate, but he couldn't break the mood by resorting to another. The overflow spilled into sentiment; he could have whimpered like a puppy.

A heavy swirl of smoke reeled backward down into Jesús's face. He blinked tears out of his eyes and pawed the air in front of him to clear it. He squinted at Stitch's look of adoration. "Don't fall in love with me, baby," he said. "I don't want to hurt you."

Stitch sniggered. He would have shook his head, but it was snug flat against the mattress. He knew he wasn't going to make that mistake. He'd had his fill, and he was through with something. He wasn't through with sex. He knew by the sweet, dull ache in his muscles that of course he would have sex again, and of course he would have some sex that meant very little to him, emotionally, but he was done with what you might call literary pornography. He was not going to try to invest sex with a meaning it didn't have; he was no longer interested in confusing his anxiety with punishment, or guilt with tenderness. He didn't know for sure that this attitude wasn't just the hormonal sense of completion and resignation that a man feels after coming, but he did know it wasn't an adolescent's remorse. In his head he was already planning to see Jesús again. He knew he would lose track of this insight and have to repeat this disappointment—because it was a disappointment—but now at least once he'd come this way. Next time he would have to admit it was familiar.

"Say you're my bottom," Jesús ordered.

"When I feel like it," Stitch said.

"No, say it now, baby," he insisted, jabbing the air with his cigarette like a teacher's fescue.

"I'm your bottom when I feel like it."

"Ay, you are so difficult. You are not grateful." He found the remote control and turned on the news. "Watch TV, baby, and I make you dinner."

Stitch continued to lie flat on his stomach. Today's important facts burbled out of the television behind him. He licked a salt streak of sweat off his own forearm. Pans clattered in the kitchen; water ran. On Jesús's nightstand, a bronze winged nymph thrust a torch skyward with both hands, a tree trunk strategically beside her to support the light bulb and lampshade her arms weren't burly enough to carry alone. At her feet were a *TV Guide* and a crystal ashtray whose rim was crenellated at one-inch intervals to hold cigarettes. Nothing to read, Stitch's insomniac sin. Jesús had left his pack of Merits, which Stitch reached over and grabbed. The cellophane crinkled; the flimsy package was more of a sack than a box. He sniffed the hole in the top, and the air the tobacco had embittered slashed a straight line up the membranes of his nose. He felt something in his sinuses shift; his mouth watered; and his heart beat slightly faster. His body remembered. He tapped out a single cigarette and drew it slowly across his nostrils like a violin bow, teasing himself. Forget about it, he told his limbic system. Down, boy. He slipped the cigarette back into the pack. I know this trick.

As he replaced the Merits, he noticed a postcard. A white concrete public building, as earnest and ugly as an overweight child, somewhere in the Midwest. As an afterthought, a landscaper had backed a few rangy maples up against the entrance, which they guarded awkwardly, like inexperienced bouncers. Stitch flipped it over. Michigan. A hockey rink. Jesús's name and address were printed in block letters, the message itself in a loopy, wide cursive. "Dear JC, We are here for another week and a half. The weather's nice. I miss you. I hope your fine, sexy. Love, Joey."

From the kitchen, Jesús asked, "Baby, you eat meat, yes? You like chicken?"

He heard the joke, but he fumbled it. "Yes," was all he answered.

"I thought so, baby, but I want to make sure."

So this was the boyfriend. What unfakable banality. He knew Jesús made other men lick his balls in front of a mirror, fucked anyone he pleased, and cooked them dinner when he felt like it, but he had been flattering himself, he realized, by believing that these other men were at least attractive and amusing. This boy wasn't. He was bland. He was one of those people who had chosen early in life to be uninteresting, who preferred not to offer the world anything salient to hold on to, who lived with a deliberate flatness, the opposite of everything Stitch valued.

He sat up. He propped the postcard against the nymph's tree trunk and hugged his knees to his chest while he examined it. He couldn't stand it. "Jesús, what does Joey do for a living?" he yelled.

Jesús silently walked in from the kitchen. He had tied a stained white apron on, and Stitch felt naked. "You were not supposed to read that."

"You should know to hide your boyfriend's mail when your tricks come over. What does he do? Why is he in Michigan?"

Jesús was solemn. "He is an ice skater. He is in a traveling show."

"What show?"

"*Barbie on Ice*. He is one of the friends of Ken," he said evenly. He stalked back to the kitchen, the loose ends of his knotted apron strings dangling over his ass.

All Stitch could think was, He's not even Ken. He made a dash for the shower.

THE ATHENA GALLERIA

ALLEN ELLENZWEIG

I doubt you can imagine my surprise on seeing Nikos Strapoudopolos holding a dozen people at gunpoint on the television news. Nikos, a young waiter, was committing his felony for the benefit of CNN at the Greek coffee shop I frequent on upper Madison Avenue.

I have been eating at the Athena Galleria for twenty-five years, ever since I began working in the somewhat rarified precincts of the New York art world. At age twenty I uncrated precious twentieth-century sculpture, Brancusis and Arps, then worked my way up the invisible ladder of sycophancy, seduction, and charm to head up contemporary sales for a gallery whose owner had an indulgent taste for conceptual art. Ten years ago I found a financial backer in order to open my own gallery, which happily specializes in more affordable art. I sell what are called "works on paper"—drawings, prints, artists' books, and photographs: small in the hand, intimate to the eye, easy to steal.

When I first started eating at the Athena it was run by Nikos's uncle Theo, who remains its owner to this day. Mild-mannered Theo made the most of his tiny space and location. The Athena began as a sliver of well-situated real estate whose owners came to America in the wake of the military takeover in Greece. The coffee shop and its staff were an immediate success. They made fresh roast turkey daily, their Greek salads used the best feta cheese, and Theo's cooks mastered a number of other international dishes in keeping with the desires of his cosmopolitan clientele. After all, the Athena's neighborhood was a heady mix of foreign embassies, art galleries, antique stores, designer boutiques, and the imposing apartment buildings along Fifth Avenue that house society gentry and business titans.

As a young man, I felt privileged to enter the narrow confines of the Athena, for during the midday rush a kid from the provinces could hear conversations in French, Arabic, Italian, German, Turkish, Ladino, Spanish, Portuguese, Yiddish, and, of course, Greek. Nor was it lost on me that famous people actually strolled into the place. There was the morning Robert Redford was taking out coffee and a roll; Jacqueline Kennedy sauntered in behind her bug-eyed sunglasses late one afternoon and sat in the deepest recesses over an ice cream soda; and Paul Newman with Joanne Woodward closed the Athena one misty Friday evening around nine.

In the early days, Theo treated me with an ironic mix of the courtly and the paternal—"And how are you today, my fine young friend?"—though he and his staff looked after all their regulars as one would a far-flung family. You greet them on arrival as if they are vastly welcome, never daring to let on that whether or not they prove amiable, you really haven't enough space and will be forced eventually to push them out with deepest regret. It would be unfair to say that I was ever rushed out of my seat during lunch, but the Athena's noise and hubbub— orders shouted in coffee shop slang, frantic patrons yelling for checks, waiters shimmying between customers standing in wait for takeout—never encouraged me to linger. Nor did the cigarette smoke and cooking smells, which clung to one's clothing long after a meal had been devoured with gusto.

In its way, the Athena's cacophony and beehive drone provided me a window onto a world I could never have known elsewhere. I began to learn the ways in which people operate when put to the test. Theo was like an orchestra conductor, commanding his staff to each play his part, and milking his audience so they should come back for more.

"You look most beautiful today, young lady!" he would address a female customer whether known to him or not, and it was with no cruel humor that he would say such things to women of sixty or seventy. Indeed, it was the custom at the Athena for Theo and his waitstaff to assume the Mediterranean prerogative—now lost in the days of our sex wars turned political—of flirting with his female customers while at the same time addressing them with a courtesy and respect which is nothing if not Old World. Theo's cousin Kris, for example, had the daily habit of preparing a take-out tuna on rye toast for a wizened matron known to be a rich widow of at least three decades' tenure.

"My dear lady," Kris would say, "enjoy your lunch. Perhaps you try our apple pie today?"

"No. My doctor says I have to watch my weight."

"Ah, but the doctor he only thinks of the heart like a mechanic. You must live too to take some pleasure."

"No," she would insist, "I simply can't. It's not good for me."

So Kris would say goodbye, and Theo would follow with "Goodbye, darling! See you tomorrow!"

Such courtliness made tolerable the otherwise abrasive conditions that held within the small luncheonette whose one aisle, ten tables for two, and fifteen counter seats were forced to serve hundreds within three hours. They all came: art collectors checking out the Impressionist sale at the old Sotheby Parke Bernet; functionaries of the French consulate who might that very evening dine on *saumon fumé* and Pouilly-Fuissé; golden teenage boys and girls in the blue blazers of their nearby prep schools; colored nurses from Lenox Hill Hospital in their starched uniforms and high-pitched laughter; tawny and slender male and female models between shoots in nearby Central Park; and the rest of the multitude, the local residents and workers and tourists just passing through.

Another agreeable feature of the Athena, and certainly the one that kept me loyal through the years, was the tender, ironic mocking that Theo and his waiters proffered their substantial homosexual clientele. Given the neighborhood's significant commerce in aesthetics—art and antiques of the ages—it was to be expected that men of classical tastes would range the fertile territory in search of beautiful objects both natural and man-made. In my early years at the Athena, I did not entirely know how such exchange operated, though I have had twenty-five years to become expert in the trade. Theo, Kris, and the rest of their extended family, however, seemed instinctively to know how to ingratiate themselves with their handsomer customer-dandies yet keep in check any untoward advances. I well remem-

ber the first time one extremely distinguished neighborhood
merchant of nineteenth-century salon paintings brought his
young male assistant in for a hurried repast.

"Ah, so this must be your nephew . . ." said Theo, maintaining a poker-faced sobriety which he held throughout the flushed
moment when neither of his customers knew quite what to say.
"Today, we have excellent beef stew. You like. Very nice."

"My . . . *nephew* will have the beef stew. A Greek salad for me,"
replied the dealer.

"Listen to your uncle. Smart man. Excellent."

As for me, the period came when Theo and Kris were wise to
my experiments in debauchery, for I was hung over one morning
as I stopped in for takeout coffee and a muffin.

"No look so good." Kris smiled. "But you are young. Is the
time to be crazy. Later, when you have wife and children, not so
easy stay out all night."

"I see you've planned my future," I replied.

"What? You *got* marry and have kids. Same for everybody."

Then Theo jabbered something in Greek to his cousin and
Kris looked back at me.

"Is no reason not to find wife." Kris smiled as he handed me
my breakfast order.

I paused and looked back at Kris with a shocking frankness
that made me breathless. He had large, deepset, and extremely
dark, soulful eyes of the kind you might see on an early Christ-
ian portrait panel from Egypt under the Romans.

"No, not me, my good friend." He gave out a little laugh.
"Too old for that. We look for you, though. Lots of nice boys
come in here, you know."

I had an impulse to act offended, but as I left the Athena I felt
rather kindly toward Theo and Kris for this exchange of confidence. They were the first outside my own circle to acknowledge
what still in those days was an outlaw reality. After some
thought, I found Kris's suggestion an elegant rejoinder, but I
didn't take it to heart. The charm of these Greeks was boundless,
I thought, but I figured sincerity was not necessarily part of
the mix.

Some weeks later I entered the Athena at the height of lunch
hour hoping at least to find a counter seat. Instead, it appeared
there would be an interminable wait, what with every table and

stool filled and a line of "to go" customers lodged in the aisle. Suddenly, a drop-dead beautiful couple in sunglasses and autumnal cashmere—agency models, to judge from the expertness of their grooming and the stunning streaks of blond in their his-and-hers hairstyles—arose from their table, snaked past the crush, and breasted their way out the door, leaving in their wake whiffs of cologne and perfume, and gazes of social envy. Alas, a lone luncher like myself would not get their table for two. Yet Kris made his way from behind the counter and pointed me toward the twofer, at the same time indicating the young gentleman ahead of me, the nape of whose neck had already caught my eye. I sensed the fellow's hesitation; he turned around to look at me with some embarrassment. He turned back around to Kris, who was already wiping the table clean in expectation of our approach.

"You sit," Kris said without looking up. Then, as if sensing our hesitation, he added, "I get menus right away. Sit, sit. You together, no?"

"Well . . ." My new companion hesitated.

"Thank you. Yes," I blurted out to Kris, then turned to the man with the exquisite neck. "Please. We'll wind up waiting otherwise. If you prefer, we needn't talk."

"No, of course not. My name is Brandon."

"Stefan," I said, careful to give it the Central European pronunciation my family insisted on and which, I hoped, lent me the faintest trace of the exotic.

We sat.

"That is a very beautiful name," said Brandon, but no sooner had he paid me this compliment than Kris handed us the Athena's oversized menus and, to me alone, a surreptitious wink.

That was the last time we sat in the Athena by mere chance. From then on Brandon and I arranged lunch together several times a week; it became Theo's running joke that we were "brothers," even after he well knew that we had taken an apartment together in a nearby brownstone, for we would occasionally wander in just before closing time if we were short on groceries and preferred the last of the Athena's lamb stew to our own paltry stocks. And should I chance to be alone at lunch, Theo or Kris would ask, "So where your brother today?" then slyly smile as if the question were the height of wit from the Periclean Golden Age.

Ten years ago, the small designer women's-wear shop that neighbored the Athena Galleria went out of business, though one might have thought a single sale of any of its evening gowns would have secured the owners their rent. But, for whatever reason, Madison Avenue has always had spaces that cannot hold any particular commerce for very long. Besides, so much has been in flux in the niches of the rich these past two decades, with greed and gall reaching new heights—or should I say lows?—that the avenue itself has seen remarkable shifts in taste that are at once de rigueur and arriviste. This has included an increasing interest by a broader clientele in the investment possibilities of art objects, and with this understanding has grown an increasing trade in stolen art. Almost monthly, the Art Dealers Association sends me notices with Xerox illustrations of the latest artwork to lose its way.

In any case, Theo himself seized the opportunity for change by expanding into the vacated dress shop, at the same time upscaling the Athena's interior so that the Parthenon wallpaper was replaced by smart postmodern colors and contrasting trims, while the electric candle sconces were exchanged for light fittings decidedly Art Deco in feel. Meanwhile, there was an unusual change in personnel. Old Jimmy, a man of massive forearms and sausage-shaped fingers who had sullenly worked behind the counter washing dishes, was from one week to the next gone from sight. At the same time, a stylish Greek-American woman said to be Theo's sister-in-law suddenly held sway at the cash register near the entrance, doing double time as a kind of hostess. She did not seem to like either Brandon or me until she got wise and saw that we were longstanding customers and favorites of Theo and Kris. She warmed to us slowly, though it was not the same when she said, in perfectly average speech direct from the borough of Queens, "Have a nice day." It did not have any of Theo's particularly theatrical majesty: "My dear friends," he once told Brandon and me on the first real day of spring, "go to Central Park and breathe the grass grow."

A few years ago there was more dramatic turnover in the Athena's personnel. By then, Theo had opened two additional restaurants on the Upper East Side, and it is no accident that I call them such. Theo was now commuting in from the Westchester suburbs in a forest green Jaguar, instead of dragging himself in by subway from Astoria with the rise of the sun. His grown children, Alex and Katrina, were being educated at Yale. His cousin Kris was managing a new Galleria II a few doors down from the Plaza Hotel, while Old Jimmy's son, Christopher, was taking in dollars hand over fist with a stylish French bistro which owed its success to contractual promises made to a graduate of the Cordon Bleu not three years out of school.

Soon a new young crop of immigrant relatives were working at the Athena, none of whom ever knew it in its more raffish days. Among them was young Nikos, who in his first week seemed as lost as any greenhorn ever come to the New World. He was no boy, however, and was most unusual for being a fair-haired Greek in the company of raven-haired but pale men whose smiles were, nevertheless, all tentative. As before, Theo commanded them in style, though because the customers were no longer at such close quarters, it was only by careful observation that I was assured the essential character of the place had not, in fact, much changed. Certainly, the food had not, though the prices were ever more inflated and the size of the menu remained of such gigantic proportions that it was as though I were back in Radio City Music Hall, where as a child on exceptional visits to New York City it seemed to me that the candy bars and sodas were scaled to the gargantuan size of the theater. No, some external features of the Athena had changed, but not its heart and soul. Theo was still there, after all, and he was bringing along a fresh generation of young Greek immigrants as he had nurtured his contemporaries.

Perhaps the biggest change was one in my own life. Brandon and I had parted; like a middle-aged married man with an itch, he had decided to seek out greener pastures. He found himself a perfectly inane art student with a gym body who lived in Chelsea and thought Brandon the height of sophistication for being able to say "déjà vu" without ceremony—and for paying every restaurant check with an American Express credit card. But we neither of us are dead of AIDS, so I find it in my heart to forgive Brandon his folly, meanwhile waiting for the day when he will know to come home. Till then, I wait, and eighteen months ago I found myself fixating on Mr. Nikos Strapoudopolos of the sandy hair and the thick chest and biceps, who, however, looks like he grew them the old-fashioned way: he *earned* them.

On my busiest days in these last few years—and there are many of them—I now call in my lunch from the Athena. So I became acquainted with Nikos who, at the start of his employ at the Athena, was not charged with taking orders but with busing tables or making outside deliveries. When he first came through my gallery door, he could barely speak English; instead, he gesticulated in an uncertain pantomime as he handed me my paper-bag lunch and the green bill that served as my receipt. I was immediately struck by his good-natured smile and by his unusually large stature, for unlike Theo and Kris, who are of modest proportions, Nikos is broad and fleshy in a way that might suggest relations to Old Jimmy. Nikos stood there that first encounter trying to decipher just exactly what I said as I disappeared into the backroom to fish for smaller bills with which to pay and tip him. He seemed genuinely relieved when I re-emerged, though I could tell he had been glimpsing the odd drawings on the walls. A look of far deeper perplexity now shaded his brown eyes, and he was happy to settle the bill, quickly compute the commission he had received, and find his way out the gallery's front door.

I passed him several times in the street after that as he ran around the immediate neighborhood making his lunchtime deliveries. Increasingly I was struck by his indifference to the weather, which is to say that as summer moved into autumn and then to winter, Nikos still managed to rush about with his collar open and his thick arms exposed to show off their muscles. I judged him to be in his mid-twenties, but he affected a boyish look by letting his fair hair fall over his forehead. On the other hand, he also carried substantial weight which threatened a future paunch. Over time he came to recognize me and offered a shy smile. Soon I found myself calling the Athena on an almost regular basis in the hope that Nikos would deliver my meal. Two out of three times I was rewarded. More and more I had the gallery receptionist send him back to my office where I could linger in my search for the proper amount of money while surreptitiously remarking his look of marvel at the odd images or objects that graced the walls and accented countertops in my severely decorated white-walled office. Here where I was accustomed to cultivating new clients, impressing upon them a sense of privilege as I opened a just-published portfolio of new prints or removed from one of the drawers an unlikely early work by an artist now grown famous, here where I conducted business in a cocoon of intimacy that was a seduction as well as a negotiation, here where two Barcelona chairs and an Eileen Gray screen lent the spare space a stark authority, I watched Nikos Strapoudopolos fidget in wait, shifting his thick trunk and substantial haunches in the white uniform of his trade that boasted across his upper-left chest a circular badge reading THE ATHENA GALLERIA.

Then one day he surprised me by pointing to a photo sequence by Duane Michals and saying, "Is crazy, this."

He had never before ventured an opinion, but I could tell by the cockeyed smile on his face that however crazy it was, he was also delighted with the sequence. It was one of Duane Michals's earliest photo narratives, *Paradise Regained*, in which a young urban couple face the viewer surrounded by the trimmings of apartment life: a dresser and desk, a lamp and ashtray, a clock radio and teacup. Little by little their contemporary trimmings disappear throughout the series of six pictures; ferns and potted palms overtake the surrounding space; the man and woman each lose articles of clothing. At last, in the final of the six pictures, they appear as Adam and Eve in an enclosed Eden, facing the camera in their splendid nudity, the jungle surround managing by an appropriate spray of leaves to hide their genitals.

Soon after, during his deliveries, I began to open for Nikos on their hushed casters the long print file drawers in order to elicit his reaction to some of the gallery's holdings—testing, for example, what his unspoiled eye would make of one of the "Braid" etchings by Jim Dine or the strict early geometries of Frank Stella. Of a large Jim Dine "Bathrobe" he said, "Is what you wear! People, they buy this in picture?" with a tone of astonishment and dismissal, as if anyone stupid enough to buy an image of a bathrobe would do better to have his head examined. Nevertheless, he added, "How much this?" as if he had grown sensitive to the possibility that in my world of art, so proximate to the one in which he labored, there were conventions of value that were still to be respected. And when I told him the price, he stared at me in wonder, shock, and awe; I was then sure he had never imagined that something drawn or printed on mere paper, however fine the weight or weave, could fetch such princely sums. Had I been dealing in Arps or Brancusis and quoted him *their* prices, I am sure he would have fainted dead on the spot.

Now when we met on the street I would engage him in conversation, and though he was passing in obvious haste, for he was carrying bags and boxes full of meals for rich shut-ins, or consular employees, for prep school administrators and dealers in rare antiquities, he nevertheless paused long enough to smile and say cheerily, "Hey, boss! How's business?" He had picked up this locution over a matter of months. I knew well enough it was borrowed from Theo and Kris, who often used the honorific "boss" less as a sign of the social hierarchy, though that may have been a part of their address, than as a sign of fraternal amity. It was also true that they seldom knew their customers' names, though there were exceptions. I, for example, was eventually addressed as Mr. Stefan.

The day came, however, when it was no longer Nikos who delivered my lunches. The first few times I was hardly aware of the difference, though a mild disappointment lingered like a melody in the background you hardly know is on the radio. But after several weeks of some other Greek stranger passing into my office compound, I began to worry that Nikos had found another calling. I made my way over to the Athena for the next several days, mildly surprised to find that I had forgotten how in its new space the coffee shop was twice as crowded and dense with noise.

I quickly spotted Nikos working behind the counter, ably and swiftly taking orders and bantering with customers in an English that had grown vastly since he had first assumed his duties under his uncle Theo's thumb. He fairly glowed with self-confidence as he shouted the lingo: "Grilled Jack whole wheat! Bed of lettuce!" I took the first seat that emptied at the counter and was delighted when he greeted me with smiling recognition.

"Hey, boss! How you doing! Is nice to see you. Business okay? What I can get for you?" He already had his pencil to pad and took my order without a blink.

Now that I knew where to find him, I made it my business to keep more lunch hours free than had recently been my custom. Soon I returned to the Athena with my old regularity, positioning myself at the counter so that Nikos would take my order. From my vantage, I would watch him as he commanded his side of the counter with a sort of exuberance, scooping ice into large glasses, setting a tuna sandwich before a client at the same time as he plopped a small coleslaw onto the plate and greeted a new army of regulars and transients with sly good grace. He had all the moves down. The women were called "darling" and "my dear." The men were all "boss" or "my friend." There wasn't an ounce of snobbery in his approach—the beautifully appointed doorman from the nearby Westbury Hotel, a large black man in a uniform of crisp pleats and epaulets, was given quite the same cheerful attention as a wealthy neighborhood burgher steeped in his *Wall Street Journal.*

After a number of weeks, however, I began to notice that there was a particular flirtation going on between Nikos and a stunning Greek woman of high breeding and demeanor whom I had often seen in the neighborhood without knowing anything of her. She would come in for a takeout order, dressed in clothes whose exquisite tailoring suggested less the best boutiques of Madison Avenue than the haute couture quarters of the rue du Faubourg Saint-Honoré or the Avenue Montaigne. She was by no measure typically beautiful, but there was about her a self-sufficiency of style and surety of effect, like a great stage actress of a certain age, or an opera diva just past her prime, who covers her deficiencies and claims the audience as her own. Her nose was rather too large, but since her mouth and eyes were likewise proportioned, she offered her viewer a face that was striking to behold. She was clearly over thirty, but not, I thought, by very much. She spoke an English that bore the traces of British schooling, and seemed always to order either a Caesar salad with extra Melba toast or a large fruit salad with a decaf. Theo called her "Mademoiselle Melina" and Nikos followed suit.

"Is especial beautiful today," Nikos complimented her one noon when she entered in a tightly tailored black ensemble that showed off her figure without at any point permitting actual flesh to be revealed.

"Yes, yes," she sharply replied. "Go back to work, Nikos. Keep your eyes in your head."

This swift reproach delighted him and he continued, "In the village no girl dress like that."

"I'm sure there are other compensations for the simple life. Not too much ice, Nikos. It's diet, that?"

"What? You say 'Diet Coke.' Is what I give."

"I'm just checking that you're paying attention."

"Mademoiselle Melina, I pay attention," and he smiled as if she should know better than to doubt him, that he indeed hung on her every word and, as well, her every glance and gesture.

"Yes, I know you pay attention. But to what?"

With that, she grabbed her lunch, paid her check, and swept out with a smile on her lips.

I witnessed this sort of banter for weeks, wishing always it were I who imposed on Nikos such dashing high spirits and erotic wordplay. Eventually, though, I noticed that his uncle Theo would cut Nikos short in his conversations with Mademoiselle Melina, spitting out between his teeth a garble of Greek that would send Nikos spinning around to some customer who had been waiting too long to place his or her order. Once, however, Melina herself spat back to Theo under her breath a barrage of Greek, then ended with, "Leave the boy alone! He lives on hope! Hope! Don't you answer for me. I speak for myself!"

When the commotion had died down, Theo's eyes happened to glance my way and he sighed heavily. He pointed me to a just-emptying table and joined me for a cup of coffee.

"My nephew, Nikos. This boy gonna kill me, is so stupid. My sister's boy. She lose her husband just after Nikos is born. I raise him with my money, my American money I send home to Greece. I want to send him to university in Athens, but no. Don't want to go to school, he got big ideas to get rich. But my sister, Sofia, she die, so I send for him to come here. Now look! He crazy for that Mademoiselle Melina. You know who she is, Mr. Stefan?"

"No. I have seen her around the neighborhood, though. She's something special, I would guess."

"Special all right. Her father build the ships. Big man, very rich. She live all over the world. Go to Paris La Sorbonne. Married once to French movie star. They divorce. She has little girl with her. Owns art gallery Eighty-first Street. You must know!"

"What's the name?"

"Is that . . . is funny name. Not hers." He shouted out something in Greek to his sister-in-law the cashier/hostess, who answered him in Greek, though less volubly. He turned to me. "Minotaur Gallery! Is good name, I think."

I had certainly heard of the Minotaur Gallery, but it had never been on my list of local visits. I knew from the monthly *Gallery Guide* and from the evidence of my own eyes that it specialized in small antiquities, a field in which I had no commercial interests and barely any expertise. It was upstairs in a townhouse on a row that ran between Madison and Fifth Avenues, the sort of place that one could look up at from the street and see in its windows, especially at night, a small but beautiful male torso in marble, the trunk broken at the thighs and shoulders, lit dramatically by a spot. Such relics as it exhibited and sold may not have been of the first rank; it was doubtful their lineage stretched back directly to Praxiteles. Yet such a fragment and others like it were choicely displayed and credibly "antique." It had never occurred to me that I should pay the Minotaur a visit, though my curiosity was now piqued.

"He want to marry her!" Theo continued. "He say he is in love with Mademoiselle Melina. In love! What a woman like her want with a boy from the village, no education, nothing? But he make love with words to her. I tell you, nothing good gonna come from this. I'm trying to stop this. He is crazy. She ten years older than him, a woman with a child. She can pick any man she want."

I looked back at Theo sympathetically, as if to say that the antics of the children we raise are never to be understood, but it occurred to me that it would be better not to offer an opinion of his nephew's behavior. I surmised only too well how a lusty young man of no means like Nikos might well be impressed by so self-possessed a woman as Mademoiselle Melina, a woman who carried both a pride in her gender and a confidence in her sexual appeal like badges of honor that might serve either to seduce or to defend.

Then, curiously, Theo leaned in closer to me and under his breath spoke in tones of highest confidentiality.

"Nikos, he think very much of you. You give him consideration, speak to him in friendship. Maybe you counsel him? Me, I am like the father he does not listen to. Whatever I suggest, he do exactly opposite. But you, Mr. Stefan—oh, this would mean very much from you. I send him to you, is okay?"

This struck me as an extraordinary request which implied a degree of trust that nearly shamed me to my scalp.

"Oh, I don't know . . . these are family matters. Perhaps it is best if they are settled in the family. Why don't you get Kris or—"

But Theo cut me short. "Is exactly right. Is a family matter. But Nikos, he don't want to listen to the family. Shouting, shouting at home. I tell him to leave. He live alone now in Queens near my cousin Spiros. Nikos, he have no friends. No girl. He just dream of Mademoiselle Melina and how he gonna get rich to marry her."

"But surely she herself has made him understand . . ."

"No. She tease him. She flirt with him. She speak to him like maybe there is chance. Please, Mr. Stefan, you talk to the boy. He respect you."

I reluctantly agreed, despite the eager attraction that the opportunity to share intimate conversation with Nikos obviously held. But my diplomatic "portfolio" in the matter seemed dangerously compromised by that very fact, and I was ashamed to think that I did not deserve Theo's trust. Nevertheless, we agreed that he would have Nikos come around, though I insisted there be no pretext for the visit other than friendly concern and the chance for him to discuss his life prospects with someone who might better guide him. We agreed, Theo and I, to put it more on the basis of young Nikos's professional future, allowing that any such discussion would surely touch on personal matters as well.

Nikos came to visit the following week just after closing time at the gallery. My staff were gone by then, so there was no chance for interruption, or, as important, for arousing their suspicions in any particular direction. He no longer had on his white uniform with the insignia of the Athena Galleria over his left breast. For only the second or third time, I saw him in civilian clothing. He wore a cheap black leather jacket over jeans and a T-shirt that stretched tightly across his thick chest. He entered somewhat sheepishly, almost like the shy delivery boy he had once been, and with an air of uncertainty, as if he had never been in the gallery before and we had never had our friendly chats. I offered him a drink and was grateful when he accepted, for I was impossibly nervous myself, having no idea how to begin the conversation. I poured us each a bracing shot of whisky. We clinked glasses. I toasted him, "Salud." It went down warm with a sting. I took his jacket. Close up, I was shocked to see how broad and round his shoulders were, sitting atop a weighty trunk whose nipples made little delicate points upon his pectorals. I poured myself another shot and almost immediately had the bright idea to simply open up the portfolio drawers and begin to show him some things he would not have seen since his elevation to waitering inside the Athena.

But as I was bent over to my task, I sensed Nikos closer beside me. I looked up to see him standing quite near, one hand with an empty glass, the other provocatively perched upon his private parts as he said, "Is good. You like."

I felt the color rush to my cheeks; I stood up tall to face him squarely. He had escalated the steps of our encounter precipitously, for I had not been expecting to get to this point either so abruptly or by him taking matters, so to speak, in hand. I had forecast at least another few weeks of sidelong glances and innuendo, a test of old abilities which had on my side lain dormant since those early days when *I* was the object of snare. Nikos had by his simplicity gotten somewhat crudely to the point, and I felt it my duty to be shocked, however much I was privately pleased.

"Why did your uncle Theo say you were to come here?" I asked with an edge of annoyance.

"Oh, he say you maybe have job for me. I think you maybe want Nikos to take off clothes."

He was impertinent. My heart sang with joy.

"But . . . surely, you are in love with Mademoiselle Melina! Everyone knows this."

He stepped in even closer and put his hand to my breast.

"Is no reason not to like man like you. I must be satisfy many ways, many times. Am young, no?"

Indeed he was. I was exhausted before the night was over, and he was yet ready for more. Whatever my qualms, they diminished in the playful roughhousing to which Nikos subjected me, mixed with an astonishing tenderness that nearly broke my heart it was so genuine.

So began my shameless affair with Nikos, who visited me after hours a couple of nights a week. But it was not so simple a thing to take a young man like Nikos to bed, for his understanding of our relations did indeed include a commercial aspect. It was my guess that he was looking to bring his own dowry to Mademoiselle Melina, who needed none herself. Perhaps he saw me as a means to achieve his ends with her. I was not unwitting in this matter, only unpracticed. I had never before picked up a hustler, nor ever suggested a favor in exchange for a bedmate, and with Nikos this took on a particular coloration.

He was for one thing remarkably free in his sexual principles. He stood on no "masculine" ceremony and would as likely lie on his back hugging his knees to his chest to permit my entry as insist gruffly on my sucking him off with the authority of a roughneck at a truck stop. And yet he delighted in affection and ribald laughter, enjoying tickles and sweet caresses as a puppy who wags his tail and licks your face. Still, he made known some internal hierarchy he held in the value of his favors by the manner of payment he would suggest as night made way for day. After our first encounter, when he made familiar with the storage racks and chose a Stieglitz picture of Georgia O'Keeffe's hands and breasts, I had to explain that he might choose from what I personally owned, but not from the gallery's stock. If, as eventually transpired, he was short for cash, he would say that his rent was due and could I help him out. I soon sensed that for the thrill of fucking him my own inventories might be well depleted; mutual masturbation was less painful to my purse. Least injurious to my accounts was accepting his pummeling, for here I think he felt that I, Mr. Stefan, was doing him honor. He would don the requisite condom as if performing a sacred ritual.

Although there was in these particulars what might be thought an unseemly measure of calculation, the fact was that we neither of us ever forced upon the other an act distasteful to our dignity, nor weighed a scale of sacrifices one against the other. Surely from a mercantile standpoint, Nikos was making out like the proverbial bandit, but I parted with a few drawings, prints, and photographs, and a bit of cash, secure in the belief that an ill-educated young man who chose as well as he did had an aesthetic sensibility that was educable. Indeed, I dissuaded Nikos several times from an inferior choice, not with an explanation of market values or likely resale opportunities, but by explaining technical finesse, formal inventiveness, and the significance of a particular work in the arc of an artist's career. Nikos had, I soon found, an excellent eye.

One quiet morning at work, however, I was startled to find Mademoiselle Melina touring my exhibition space. It happened we were alone; my assistant had called in late, so I was forced to keep alert out front—there had been several recent thefts in galleries along Fifty-seventh Street, Madison Avenue, and downtown in SoHo. Thus, my precaution gave me the opportunity to view Mademoiselle Melina stroll my two modest gallery rooms, where the blond laminate floors and peach walls set off the frames of a first show by a photographer too young to be known but too socially well placed to be ignored. When she passed the threshold into the far room, I wandered idly from behind the reception desk to keep her in my line of sight, but was embarrassed to find she stood staring back from the doorway as if waiting for me to appear.

"It seems we have an interest in common," she said by way of introduction.

I made no answer but merely cocked an eyebrow.

"Come, come, let us not be coy. He tells me you have been very good to him. I am glad of it."

There seemed no need to confirm or deny anything. I was content to let her speak as she did, seeing that I was dealing with someone from that cosmopolitan milieu whose codes of behavior I had spent the whole of my youth studying. I had learned their rituals; she and I understood one another.

She had meanwhile walked to my door to make her parting, but as she pulled at the knob, I felt impelled by her high bearing and unusual raw beauty to let down my guard.

"What will you do? He is in love with you."

She turned half round and offered me a look that was neither smile nor grimace. It was like an acknowledgment, nothing more, and then she was gone.

It was not the first time I realized that in the short weeks of my affair with Nikos, I had done nothing to discourage his affections for this woman. She had never come up in our conversation except for that once at the start. Perhaps I'd been wary to mention her for fear of finally assuming the role his uncle Theo had asked of me: the sage counsel who speaks about hard realities and holds romance at bay. Yet I was sure that what I said was true; Nikos loved Mademoiselle Melina, because his earnest efforts to improve his lot were the mark of a man proving his ardor. He hoped to show her he was worthy.

Now, her brief visit forced my hand. So when next Nikos was

in my bed, I mentioned Mademoiselle Melina's appearance in the gallery, though only to say that she happened by to see the current exhibition.

"I must cut her out my heart. She will never have me," he said with remarkable bitterness.

"Have you asked?"

"Is not necessary. Is not for her to say no . . . but will never say yes."

"She is a woman of great wealth," I replied. "She has a child. She will look to marry someone of her own . . . status. Do you understand, Nikos?"

He looked at me then with very hurt eyes, then hugged himself to me and whispered into my chest, "I am not your status, but does not make you ashamed—like my uncle Theo say she will be."

I thought of the dinner parties and auctions to which I would never have brought Nikos, venues where the cultivated made witty talk in front of each other and snide comment behind each other's backs. Perhaps in summertime he would be a smashing success on the beaches at Fire Island or the Hamptons, though he would be uncomfortable in the company of gay gossip mongers where he would be made to feel stupid, though extravagantly prized, while I would be envied and betrayed by people who called themselves friends. No, I was not ashamed of Nikos, but his confidence in me only made it worse, for I had done nothing to earn it. We had never even walked out on the street together in daylight.

I was resolved then to end the affair, to spare us both the embarrassment of discovering that I was nowhere as noble as he would believe.

"You must find a girl—or a boy—your own age," I said. "You must look for your happiness with someone who is at the same place in life as you are."

He looked up at me wide-eyed; then quickly the expression on his face curled sour.

"You don't want Nikos no more? Okay. I leave now. You are just like her. I am not enough good for you, eh? Okay, I go. First, you show me the Englishman drawings. You know. I take maybe one, maybe two. You say many weeks ago you let me choose. Okay, so today I choose."

He had by then jumped out of bed and hastily pushed himself into his clothes, his immodest genital display mocking me with its plump bounce. I wrapped myself in my silk bathrobe, then quietly pulled open the slim sliding drawer where I stored the David Hockney etchings I'd bought many years earlier. He picked two splendid etchings from the *Rake's Progress* series and waited testily as I carefully wrapped them for him to transport by hand wherever he was next headed. My hands shook and tears welled in my eyes, but I composed myself so he should not see.

About six weeks went by during which I avoided going into the coffee shop or even ordering food from the Athena. I was naturally concerned about Nikos, but believed that a certain time must lapse before we could begin to communicate again on a fresh basis.

Then, near the time I thought I should make a first attempt at rapprochement, I found myself absently turning on the TV after work as I was preparing a simple dinner. On the news I found live coverage of a hostage crisis taking place in New York City: the announcer described an intense drama where traffic was rerouted, police helicopters flew overhead, and federal agents were on the scene. I paid this little mind. I removed the wax paper from the thawed chicken breast I was about to season—in New York City, a disaster crosstown or in another borough can seem as foreign as a bombing in Beirut—but then I heard sirens wailing and the rotary whir of a chopper outside my window in the early evening sky. Suddenly, I was alarmed to think that the siege was actually near. No sooner did I turn up the volume than the announcer said, ". . . a young Greek immigrant, Nikos Strapoudopolos, who federal authorities say is suspected of several recent thefts of art works from major New York galleries. Mr. Strapoudopolos is reported to have attempted selling rare Roman coins and several drawings to authorities operating a sting operation in the heart of New York City's thriving art world." Simultaneous with these last words a grainy photo of Nikos was flashed, followed by a cut to footage shot from a telephoto lens: Nikos, through the windows of the Athena Galleria, could be seen, fuzzily, holding a woman in one arm while pointing a gun at a group of customers seated at the counter like ducks in a row.

I felt suddenly nauseous. My bathroom seemed to loom a vast

distance away. I reeled my way to it, hung my head as I sank to my knees, then threw up into the toilet. It took a moment for me to get my bearings. I splashed cold water on my face, tidied myself quickly, and raced out the front door. No sooner did I reach Madison Avenue than the evidence of some calamity was at hand. A block north two policemen were redirecting traffic east toward Park and Lexington Avenues. Beyond them I could see that the rest of the avenue remained clear of traffic until, just south of the Athena, a vast mobilization of police cars and TV vans jammed the street. A bullhorn was blaring, though from my short distance its message was blurred. I quickened my step, eventually breaking out into a run.

As I neared the scene, the crush of gawkers was thick but silent. It was a curious crowd, full mostly of stylish preppies out for the spring evening and proper Upper East Siders finishing purchases for dinner or returning from a day at the brokerage firm or bank. There were even a few couples who seemed to be on their way to some swank benefit or opening a short walk away, but, having found themselves caught by dramatic circumstance, were taking in the scene as if their little black cocktail dresses and tuxedos were the prelude for this very event. Someone, a client I think, suddenly called out my name in greeting, but I was in a panic and was determined to reach the front of the crowd near the police barricades. Instead of turning around, I wormed through the press of bodies and reached the front.

"I've got to speak to the man inside!" I shouted. "Please! I can help!"

A young cop approached and asked me for specifics, including my driver's license. He seemed not at all concerned that the seconds and minutes were ticking by. Meanwhile, though I could not take proper measure of my surroundings, I heard a voice through a police bullhorn repeating phrases like, "You won't be hurt. Just give yourself up. We'll talk this out. Just give yourself up. You don't want to hurt anybody." I tried to compose myself, sensing that the rookie would need assurances that he wasn't being taken for a fool. But it was hard to contain my emotions; my urging him to "please hurry" only prompted him to slow his pace as he looked back and forth between my license photo and my worried face.

At last he escorted me to a higher-ranking officer, Detective

Moran, who asked how I knew Mr. Strapoudopolos. I described myself as a longstanding patron of the Athena who had recently been teaching the young waiter something of the art trade. At this, the officer, solidly built but silver-haired, raised an eyebrow and asked if Nikos spoke English.

"That fellow ain't spoken nothing but Greek to us since we made contact. Say, you know a dame name is Melissa something?"

"Melina. Mademoiselle Melina."

"Yeah, that's it. Seems he's got it in for her, near's I can tell. And Theo. You know who they are?"

"Theo's his uncle. Mademoiselle Melina is . . . the woman he's in love with."

I was not immediately put through to Nikos on Detective Moran's cellular phone. Moran was not satisfied by my credentials until finally persuaded that I might be able to get Nikos to put his uncle Theo on the phone; that I was even aware of the family relations, and could back them up with specifics about where everyone lived, seemed to offer Detective Moran some comfort. He himself had made little progress. I was warned to make no commitments about the criminal outcome of Nikos's actions, but I should assure him that if he gave himself up without hurting anyone, then he would be "helped" with whatever problems he faced.

Nikos himself answered and I shouted, "It's me, Mr. Stefan!"

I could hear muffled cries beside him as he shouted, "Shut up!" to his frightened audience of hostages.

"Is who? Goddamn police! Get police away! No talk now! Get . . . !"

"Nikos! It's me! Mr. Stefan! Listen to me! Let me help you! Please! I will pay for a lawyer. You need help."

There was a long pause on the other end. I waited this out while Detective Moran stared at me as if hoping I would offer an immediate assessment. I turned my back to him, then felt his large presence close in on me. Apparently, I was not to be granted a private audience with the suspect.

"What you want you son of bitch?!" Nikos shouted into the phone.

"I will explain to everyone that the art you had I gave you, that you stole nothing. That I gave you the drawings and photographs for friendship."

"I steal nothing! You tell fucking uncle I steal nothing. He say I cheat from him cash register. Why? I tell you—don't move! NO, YOU DON'T MOVE OR I SHOOT YOU!" Behind his command I could hear women screaming. There was another long pause; then he spoke again into the phone. "He say I steal. You know why? Because I charge Mademoiselle three dollar, not five, for burger deluxe, mash no fries! So he find out every day I no charge her full price what she eat!"

"Nikos, Nikos, listen. I will make Theo understand. Okay?" but then I let out a nervous laugh, for it struck me as perversely funny that of all the women in the world who did not need discount prices, Mademoiselle Melina was the one.

"Why you laugh? You think Nikos funny!"

"No, no. Just . . . Mademoiselle Melina is a very rich woman, Nikos. She did not need such favors from you. Why ever did you cut her price? Theo must have added his receipts and—"

"*Why?* WHY? Stupid! You stupid man! Because I fuck with her! I fuck with her! Tell him! TELL HIM! FILTHY BITCH, TELL HIM!"

He was screaming so loud that Detective Moran's eyes stared as he heard the screeching coming through the phone. Nikos continued in this vein until a weak female voice came on the line, saying, wearily, "Who?"

I could hear Nikos in the background angrily explain it was Mr. Stefan. And he continued to scream his instructions, and then she screamed back in terrible fear, "No! No! Don't shoot me! No!" and he responded, "TELL HIM I FUCK WITH YOU!"

I could hear her whimper, pathetic as a dog thrashed for a domestic infraction. But then her hoarse, gasping breath came on the line.

"It's . . . true. Yes. He was . . . my lover."

This was not good enough. Nikos demanded the exact words, ordering her as a master his slave.

"Yes. He . . . fucked me."

"How many times?" Nikos persisted in the background, a prompter delivering the star her cues.

"Many times. Yes. Many, many times."

Suddenly, I could tell the phone changed hands.

"You hear! Many times! You see, stupid Mr. Stefan. When I

am not with you, I am with her! Many times. Many, many. I fuck with her . . . and she give me things much more money than what you give. From many, many ages old. And she give me cunt, this rich woman, you see?"

"Stop, Nikos. You are—"

"Yes, I stop. Goodbye. Tell police go away, now."

"Please, no! Nikos, put on Theo. Let me talk to Theo. I promise I will explain to him. I promise. Please."

I was astonished by the sound of my own whining plea. I had reverted to childhood, that place we are sometimes ashamed to remember is the house where we still live.

"Mr. Stefan? Is Theo."

"What happened, Theo? How did this all start? Who's in there? How many people?"

I heard Moran mumble "Good, good" under his breath.

"Is no good, Mr. Stefan. He say they give him back the coins or he gonna kill her. Help soon, Mr. Stefan, or somebody get killed."

Then I could hear Nikos shouting a string of Greek words that in their staccato delivery I took for obscenities. Then the line went dead, but I shouted out "Theo!" repeatedly as if I couldn't believe the silence on the other end. At last I handed the phone to Detective Moran, who looked at me with a pained expression.

And then, just as silence had become familiar once again, there was the unmistakable sound of a gun going off, and police I hadn't even realized were so near materialized from the vaporous film of the early spring evening and stormed the entry of the Athena Galleria. The window's front glass shattered. From within emerged piercing screams and wails while the commanding voices of a score of police shouted a volley of orders. Lay down. Don't move. Stop now. Hands over heads. Lay down. Stop. Don't fucking move!

And when it was all over, Nikos Strapoudopolos was stopped by a gunshot wound sustained, it was said, as he thought to kill Mademoiselle Melina; his uncle Theo, equally determined, had interceded to save her life.

When the hostages emerged, Melina and Theo were last, ashen-faced and shaking. Melina wore a teal-colored Chanel, but her springlike attire was in marked contrast to her stricken face.

She collapsed in the gutter as they bore Nikos out to a waiting ambulance. He would be declared dead on arrival.

New York magazine soon wrote an account of the entire episode in which they reported conflicting accounts of how Nikos got shot. One hostage claimed Nikos killed himself; another believed Theo was not wrestling away the gun, merely redirecting it back upon Nikos. The official police report settled nothing, but neither Theo nor Melina was ever charged.

From the article, however, I learned that Theo had weeks earlier fired Nikos because he continually undercharged his own favored customers, Mademoiselle Melina chief among them. The sums of money were negligible. Nikos had not in the least profited personally. It was the principle that rubbed Theo raw. This set Nikos off on an abrupt attempt to convert to cash what art he had amassed from Mademoiselle Melina and myself.

Melina and I were painted as worldly sophisticates who took advantage of a simple young man; the government's sting operation was derided for its bad execution. Strapoudopolos, after all, had stolen nothing, but merely tried to sell what had come into his possession for "in-kind services," they smirked. The feds were in fact no closer to solving the spate of thefts in the art world than they were before initiating their little scam.

Meanwhile, Theo came to despise me for admitting that the photographs and drawings Nikos had tried to sell were tokens of my affection. To Theo I did not have to explain that I had slept with his nephew, but neither did he wish me to announce this to the world. Theo in his years in America had become his own kind of cosmopolitan.

Needless to say, my business suffered following my portrayal as a vampire/seducer. I have since been forced to go into private dealing. I thought of leaving the city. I was ashamed to face up to my portion in this nightmare while everyone I knew looked on. But then I received a short letter from Brandon. He had seen me weeks before on the television news as the report showed me trying to get through to Nikos in the coffee shop. Brandon had read the *New York* magazine piece. I was not a villain, he said. I was a dumb-shit middle-aged homo with a late taste for rough trade. He thought I might need a friend and wanted to see me. We have reconciled—on a new basis, to be sure. Brandon has had me move from the neighborhood of the Athena to join him in Murray Hill. The Athena, meanwhile, has "closed for repair," though I wonder.

What no one knew, except for Theo and Kris and Old Jimmy and the rest of Nikos's family, was that Mademoiselle Melina paid for Nikos's body to be flown back to Greece, and I paid for the simple monument that marks the sight of his burial. And now we, Mademoiselle Melina and I, we must live with ourselves.

A TOUR OF THE COLLECTION

REGINALD HARRIS

The Powell Library is quite small. It's not even half as large as the city's Museum of Art, the Martin Gallery, or any of the other art spaces in town. But they often have good shows there, great ones at times, making up in quality for what they lack in size. And the Powell certainly has the most attractive space. Set on perfectly polished marble floors edged with hand-waxed parquet, the exhibit hall is a shining rectangle of light beneath six wrought-iron-encased floors of perfectly shelved first editions and world, local, and family histories. Centuries of gleanings from far-flung continents have been brought to the Powell to be catalogued, analyzed, stored, and preserved. Directly over the main hall, the gilt-edged skylight circles a blue-white dome of sky like a halo. It is a glorious place, often rented out for parties and dances, book signings and receptions. Novelists and historians have haunted the library's collection for months, years even, mining it for material for their works.

An African-American Miscellany

Selections from the Collection

I pick up a brochure from the mirrorlike oak table just inside the door as I walk in. As usual, there is no one else here viewing the exhibit. Easily overlooked because it seems to be just another brownstone on its historic, formerly residential street, people walk past the Powell every day without knowing what treasures lie inside. Then again, the middle of the day in the middle of the week is not exactly prime museum-going time for most people, either. But it suits me fine. I don't like a lot of people pushing and shoving, forcing me to rush through something meant to be taken in leisurely and savored.

But that's not exactly true, is it? I am not alone. There is always a guard. This one glances at me as I walk in, curious about how a young man can afford not to be working on a Wednesday, spending the day at a museum. I don't think I look particularly dangerous in my polo shirt and khakis, and could, after all, afford to pay the entrance fee to get this far. I don't seem a threat to him or the collection. He wanders to a neutral corner to eye me occasionally as I peer into the series of glass cases, making sure I don't lose my mind suddenly, smashing them and trying to run off with their precious cargo. I wonder if the fact that we're both Black makes any difference in the level of attention I get from him, whether our shared skin and my short dreads makes me less of a danger—or more. To be honest, it really doesn't matter to me one way or the other what this rent-a-cop thinks. I ignore him as I always do and move on to the exhibit.

Visions of Africa

A Journey to the Capital of the Mandingoes—The Revelations of an African Trader: "This colorful account of slaving adventures in West Africa may be fact, fiction, or a mixture of both. The narrative was prepared to expose the American involvement in the outlawed slave trade and protest the growing effort of its supporters to reopen it."

I look down into the first case, containing early European views of the "Dark Continent." Maps with vast empty spaces marked "Unknown" or "Here Be Dragons." Printed on surprisingly well-preserved paper, a nineteenth-century woodcut depicts a slave market on the west coast of Africa: A white man haggles with a trader over the price of the slave sprawled upon his back beneath his knee. A second white peers into the slave's open mouth, checking for sores or missing teeth, while yet a third leans back casually, pen at the ready to record the sale. The clerk seems anxious to move on to the next item so they can get out of the oppressive afternoon heat. It's a simple transaction, like inspecting a cow, a sack of sugar, not a person. They're savages, anyway, not human—it's best not to even think of them that way. His eye ignores the curving bullwhip in the background, high over a group of manacled, bare-breasted women being pulled away from their wailing infants, just as the ship in the distance (Is it the *Estrella*? The *Jesús*? Maybe *Esperanza* or *Mercy* made this trip) floats quietly before a deceptively calm Atlantic horizon, tightly packed with stacked and shackled cargo hidden from our view.

A year or so ago I would never have come here, would not have been interested in looking at this kind of thing. Certainly Brad would never have brought me here, nor been at all pleased if I'd suggested it.

"All that slavery stuff is over, Michael, all in the past. It was a hundred years ago—no one wants to hear about that anymore. Why even bring it up?" He'd look at me and smile a little half-smile, blue-green eyes crinkling under his wire-framed glasses, then lean over to kiss me. "Of course, if you *really* want to go . . ." he'd begin, but by then I would have already started shaking my head to erase the thought from both our minds.

We met in a bar, of course. There was nothing special about it, just another weekend evening. I was tired of looking at the same faces, ignoring the same old lines. The Black guys at Lypton's all bored me—not that I was interested in them then, anyway. Half seemed on their way either to or from visits to probation officers. All were hard and beat-up looking, and incapable of carrying on an intelligent conversation, or even of speaking in complete sentences. When I'd tell them I worked with computers ("No, I don't repair them. I'm a systems analyst"), at most I'd get a blank stare and mention of word processing or some children's game. I was interested in someone who could talk to me intelligently, who could do something for me, who didn't need me to help him out because he didn't have a job, was still living with his mother, had some daughter somewhere to take care of. Someone whose skin was far lighter than mine was.

I don't even remember what Brad said to me that night. Does it matter? He spoke; I smiled. He made me laugh; I was lonely.

He flattered me, commenting on my looks. I allowed myself to be flattered and commended him on his. We left together. What more is there to say? I cross the glossy marble floor of the library, flickering from the sun's rays coolly filtering through the skylight as if we were underwater, and move on to the next case.

African-American Lives in Their Own Words

Of Sunlight and Shadows: Sketches and Reminiscences of My Life. The True and Authentic Narrative of the Wondrous Dealings of the Lord with the Slave Tom Marin. The Life, Labours, and Uncommon Suffering of G. L., a Coloured Man.

The narrative of *my* life? It's the same old one of Hardworking Single Mother, abandoned by Some Bastard Who Got Her Pregnant. The Evil Stepfather entering the picture when I was four, calm at first, genuinely loving, later turning into a pendulum swinging without warning between poles of silence and rage. The solace of television, and schoolwork, despite the terrors of the place itself, running home from that enormous granite building, haunted by the taunts of "nerd," "punk," "four-eyes," and "faggot."

Rescued from middle school by Mr. Havers, on a multi-culti fishing expedition deep in waters he'd rather not be in. Tandy Prep for Boys looked more like a park than a high school: the well-kept lawns and ball fields, old buildings modeled on Oxford, a dream rather than reality. The students and faculty were so comfortable with their money, access to anything, the instant gratification of their every whim, that even thinking about their position in society was impossible. Even the other Black students there—not us scholarships kids, with our cheap ties knotted too big and petrochemical loafers much too shiny next to the scuffed leather of our classmate's real ones, but the others, the doctors' kids, the lawyers' kids, the children of the ones who'd made it—even they seemed to fit in. Less than one generation from my own street, some of them acted as though they were related to the Prince of Wales, not second cousins to Princess Washington from the Heights. Most behaved just like their peers, crashing cars and having them replaced by their parents, or sneaking off for beer and blow jobs during eighth period, few questions asked. They treated us just as badly as the white kids, worse in some cases. A few would even speak to the grounds crew and maintenance people before they said a word to us, as if a simple hello would turn us into albatrosses around their new-moneyed necks. A few became blazingly radical, "Super Nigger," there to push The Man to be more inclusive. It was all so funny—they'd never last ten minutes down by the projects where I grew up, but knew all about the plight of "those people" from books, TV, newspapers, or the tinted windows of their parents' BMWs.

The Prestige Southern College was no better, more of the same, only larger, with a smaller range of skin colors. Somehow I scraped together enough money dressing in the brightly colored smock of a drone at the 24-7 convenience store at night, and working at the school during the summers, to make it. I didn't have to return home often. Just enough to keep an eye on Moms and whatever man she was with that month (Stepdad long since lost to the criminal justice system) and maintain my supply for the only really lucrative job I had—small-time dealer of better weed than the homegrown that the white kids could manage to coax from the sandy native soil.

Us charity cases were saved thanks to our weird genetic quirk. We managed to be smart enough to rise above the expected curriculum of Fast Food, AFDC, and Prison taught in the public schools. We remained silent, afraid of being discovered, thrown out because we really didn't belong. Every grade felt tainted somehow, not really ours but another part of the scholarship rules. Some of us played ball, carrying the school on our backs or chests, to the joy of screaming alumni, swigging bourbon and collecting bets from their cross-state rivals as we made the winning home run/basket/touchdown.

Others—okay, *me*—*were* nerds and accepted it, spending our time studying harder, staying in the then-primitive computer lab or library with the other outcasts: the white nerds more comfortable with machines than with people. They later became the toast of virtual nations, inventing essential software and paving the Information Superhighway, eventually fawned over by the very people who used to abuse them. Then there were the Jews at our WASP temple of learning, barely tolerated for their money, "included" by the school by the brief mention

of "Judeo" as a prefix for the description of the Traditions We
Uphold Here, but called "pushy" and "big-nosed kikes" just
barely behind their backs not only by students but by parents
and faculty as well. Finally came the queers, the faggots, the
boys who couldn't throw or catch, the ones too weak or
"queeny" to be thought destined to turn into "real men" later,
self-selected for isolation as much as forced into it out of fear
of an inadvertent slip when talking of their dream lovers, or a
too lingering look at swimmers or soccer or lacrosse players in
the showers after their own games of tennis, volleyball, or running track.

We were all there in the library's carrels, the study rooms, the
lab, reading, working problems, planning our smart-boy revenge
on them all for pushing us out to the edges. We dreamed of the
day when They at forty, fifty—the kids rebelling, second wife
already gone, the boss yelling, wondering where They'd gone
wrong, why They had never made it beyond mid-level in the
corporation's hierarchical chart, what They had done to find
themselves living in a $200,000 tomb—They would see us,
happy with our lab coats, thick glasses, books, keyboards, brilliant wives, lovers, fuck buddies, few fiercely held long-term
friends, and finally They'd envy us for a change. The pain They
had forced onto us had made us think of ourselves as more than
just the prestige job and corner office They'd never give us anyway. We knew who, not "What," we were. When we hit a wall,
we could find a way to go over it, under it, around it while They
would just smack into it and break. All their money, prestige,
family connections were as fragile as eggshells when They faced
even a small part of the world They had constructed for us, but
never imagined that They would have to deal with themselves.

In back of our dreams, however, we still longed for their ease,
their grace. We wanted to know what it was like to be certain
from birth that we'd grow up to run the world. To feel deep in
our bones that we'd be welcome anywhere, anytime. Anywhere,
that is, except in our old neighborhoods, which we didn't want
to fit into anyway. So if one of them smiled at us, or made friends
with us, we hated them, we loathed them—we wanted them, we
wanted to be them. Some part of us knew that despite all our
learning and studying, we were destined to remain in their eyes
nothing more than fragile documents whose only meaning came

from how they used us, living ink relieving the suffocating blankness of their lives' empty pages.

Blackness & Whiteness

Thoughts on the Colonization of Free Blacks to Africa. Old Crip's Trip to the Centennial, a Negro Farce. B. Williams Smidgens of Burnt Cork: A Collection of Minstrel Gags, Stories, Monologues, & Etc., with Free Bar of Wash-Up Soap to All Subscribers— Quick-Change Cleanser from Black to White Instantly!

Brad was not the first white guy I'd gone out with, of course. There had been others—tricks and one-night stands, some guys in college where we were all trying to figure out who and what we were by what felt good to us and by what family, friends, and classmates would tolerate. A few quiet, furtive things at home, both of us afraid of being discovered; sneaking in and out of trailers before their families came home to find not only a Man, but a Black One, in their favorite son's bed. Being warned about the blond hair sticking from my collar by a co-worker, who assumed it was a woman's but was still concerned, not sure whether to be angry or ask for sordid details. The one long relationship with Andy, ending when he met someone closer to his idea of a "Real Black Man"—someone younger, broader, darker, who worked in the kitchens at his hospital all day, gold chains and sweat dripping from his neck, a plastic bag on his head. Someone who looked good on his arm and wouldn't mind the constant passes from his friends, a quiet one, unlike Mr. "Why Can't You Be Nice to Don? And Must You Always Have an Opinion on *Every*thing" me.

And Black guys too, Latinos, but just for quickie sex, one-time blow jobs as a substitute for my hands, or a fast fuck in the alley after the bars had closed and no one else was available. Yes, I did blame Antoine for stealing Andy from me—"Black Monkey Motherfucker," I called him far too many times behind his back as the men he now called friends giggled—and not Andy for dumping me.

Still, no one before Brad seemed genuinely interested in relationships. I didn't care whether they did or not. Then I moved to this new city, far from home. The men here were different;

they had to be. I thought they were after different things. There was no hiding here. We were no longer relegated to groping in dark corners. Men were almost too open with their interests. Surely here there had to be someone who'd like me for my mind as well as my perhaps too-skinny body. And so I went to bars, exchanged my glasses for contacts, and spent a little time at the gym, mainly in the pool, but also pretending to work out. I again got used to swimming alone both at work and after hours, the only dark face in an all-white sea.

My first nights were spent clinging to some guy who'd brought me home, making dark furrows through cornsilk. My arms crossed their pale chests in a bandolier's X of bullets. Cold hands, phosphorescent in the moonlight, turned into ghostly gloves on the mute-eyed mahogany table of my chest. I liked the way white guys looked and tasted and smelled—almost invariably like that soap that's supposed to be so completely pure.

Soon, however, the knife-edge of Desire would always dull and rust away. The dailiness of an actual relationship would grind us down to nothing. I never seemed enough for these men. I always found them looking intensely at other dark men when we were together, already contemplating my replacement as if I were a part in some machine, destined to wear out. Or they wanted me to be "Blacker"somehow, just as Andy had, "cooler," wishing I would give up my love of serious, "difficult" music and art for rap or basketball. Because street slang doesn't fit well in my mouth, I heard more than once, "What kind of Black man are you?" Not just from whites. Blacks, too, thought I "sounded white," while I raved about a new book or recording I'd purchased. They'd look at me strangely. All thought I was little more than a white man with an incredible, permanent tan. Maybe they were right.

The few Black friends I had I'd known since high school or college. I felt tentative around other Blacks, afraid to meet their gaze. My friends were like me, had similar histories, would not judge me for who I was attracted to. They, too, usually entered restaurants with some white man on their arm, or stood around in clubs, last to be served by the bartender, ready to throw themselves at the first pale face to glance in their direction. Even so, they were barely tolerated by my dates, who would stand to the side as my friends and I talked, frozen that I dared speak to another Black man in front of them. When my friends left, these white men would fold themselves around me like a fog. Later my friends would tell me how these same guys would try to pick them up when I'd gone to the bathroom and left the two of them alone. It became obvious to me that for most of the men I went out with, no matter how much they proclaimed their love, once I left the room I was just another Disposable Nigger to them, exactly like all the rest.

If you don't call them, they'll show up on your doorstep, that's what I noticed. It's okay for them to play hard to get, or not to call when you've asked them to. But for you to ignore them, to dare suggest that maybe they are not the suns around which your life revolves, that is sacrilege. It drives them crazy. You must call them, just *must*! Of course, once you do, the power shifts back to them to call you back or not. With them everything's a game, to see who's in control.

Brad didn't play that way. He called me first. Then I called him, and he quickly returned my call. We had common interests, his computer graphics work a perfect melding of my workday and after-hours interests. We could talk to each other about software, art, design—real things, and not just the usual pabulum that passes for conversation. He also tried to sweep me off my feet, which was nice. Phone calls, flowers, romantic dinner dates, the works. Never had anyone devoted so much time and attention to me.

Yet even with Brad, something seemed slightly off. I hesitated after seven months when he suggested we move in together, finally saying no. By then things seemed to have changed between us. We would go places together, do things with each other, but increasingly they became his places, his things. He'd follow my suggestions seemingly under duress, if he went at all. Was it that he knew no Black men he hadn't slept with at some point that disturbed me? Black men who, if I were not with Brad or someone else white, would act as if I were a complete stranger? Maybe it bothered me that he could not understand my dislike for his best friend and his original prints by that famous white photographer—all those dark Black male bodies in perfect classical poses, nightstick-thick penises hanging from the flies of cheap suits. "That's art," he'd say to me. "Look at the composition. . . . And it's worth a *hell* of a lot of money, too," he'd add, whispering under his breath. I would just stare.

Once I managed to convince him to go with me to an African-American photography show at the city's Museum of Art. He didn't want to, of course, complaining about the work he needed to do, a free-floating pain rippling through his back. I took him anyway. I was fascinated by the well-attended show, which ranged from the early years of the camera to the present. Some figures seemed to be alive under the emulsion. The artistry of some early untrained photographers and the daring subject matter and compositions of contemporary artists surprised me. Brad could only complain. "They should have used a different lens here," he'd say. "The framing of the woman in this one is off." The only thing he found to approve of was that many of the men photographed were attractive. I said nothing, making a mental note never to bring him to anything like this again.

We turned a corner and entered another gallery. Off to the left were two couples, Black and white. To the casual eye they looked like two husbands and wives, friends or neighbors enjoying the show. But we recognized who they were. The women were lovers, as were the men. The women we had often seen out in clubs. The Black man was a local TV newsman, quietly active in the community, not completely open about his life, but not locked at home hiding, either. The white guy with them had to be his much-talked-about but seldom-seen lover. All four were crowded around a photograph of a family group; fifteen people of various ages arrayed across someone's front porch. The women pointed to various people in the shot, commenting on the faces, wondering about their lives. Someone said something about the clothes and they all laughed, shaking their heads at how anyone managed to survive wearing the requisite high collars, long sleeves, and bustles of their day.

As we approached them, they all turned to look at us. They smiled, we smiled, Brad said hello. The women and the white guy said hello, moving on to the next photo. The newsman smiled at us, then looked at me for a moment before saying, "What's up, brother? How're you doing?" and moving off to join his partner.

Brad watched him leave, glancing at me as the newsman casually put a hand on his lover's forearm. Then he leaned in to look at the photograph that had held their attention. Brad glanced around it, coughed slightly, and moved away. I stood looking at the quartet as they made their way to the next gallery, feeling a slight ache, the women's fingers brushing against each other as they turned the corner. I glanced at Brad. "I'm not feeling well," I said. "Let's go." He was more than happy to comply.

Slavery & Anti-Slavery

The Voice of Blood—Observations on a Guinea Voyage, in a Series of Letters. Scriptural Researches into the Licitness of the Trade in Slaves. Injured Humanity, Being a Representation of What the Unhappy Children of Africa Have Endured.

On the last night Brad and I were together, we went to a bar with another interracial couple. To me, Davis and Jay seemed to be constantly performing. They were so affectionate, overflowing with kisses and ass grabbing, that it seemed unreal, for everyone else's benefit but not their own. If their relationship really were that secure, I thought, they wouldn't need to paw all over each other in front of people the way they did.

I hadn't particularly wanted to go out that night and had started knocking back Cuba Libres early. It was a strange night for everyone. Even the usually light-drinking Brad was also getting drunk trying to keep up with me. "It'll be hard to get him moving in the morning," Davis whispered to me. I nodded. And Lypton's was not a particularly great place, either—dark, too small, and quickly overcrowded, with a long bar along one side opposite the small stage and even smaller dance floor, a pool table near the entrance to the bathrooms.

It was a Saturday, the night the bar featured "exotic dancers." They were usually not much. Three or four Black guys, mouthing the words and gyrating to the latest ballads and Urban Contemporary slow jams, eventually peeling out of their baggy clothing down to G-strings with exaggerated baskets in front. There was no way any of these guys could be as well hung as their otherwise skimpy costumes made them appear, but that seemed to be part of the act. They would dance on the postage-stamp-sized stage for one number, then come down to pass among the men gathered in the bar, rubbing against those who seemed most interested and likely to part with a dollar for their efforts. I never gave them anything, not even my attention. They knew it and avoided me. They usually avoided all four of us, knowing all their twisting and grinding would be in vain.

The dancers were not quite hustlers, but were not quite *not* hustlers either. They inhabited some gray area in between, doing whatever it took to make a few bucks. The story they liked to tell was that they were "really straight." They may have been not at all effeminate, with deep voices and strong hands incapable of giving a snap or twirling. But I seriously doubted that there was a "straight" man on the planet who, for any amount of money, let alone the few measly dollars they got from the crowd there, would allow another man to grope him the way these dancers did. But the thought of a straight man wriggling for them, available to fulfill a fantasy, sent chills down many spines.

Most of the guys in the bar that night were Black. Lypton's was one of the few Black bars in the city, surprising since African-Americans make up the majority of the population. But the owner was white, as were the bartenders, so it wasn't all that Black. It was just one of the few places that allowed Blacks in large numbers to congregate, not trying to slow the gradual darkening of the bar by asking for multiple pieces of identification, or by suddenly replacing the dance floor and R&B or House Music DJ with pool tables and "High N-R-G Nights," as had happened elsewhere.

A quarter of the men in the place were white. It was a major hangout for those that were interested in Blacks, and they usually came on to just about anyone, whether these men were interested in them or not. The white guys just assumed that if you were in the bar, you were interested in them. If you responded even slightly to any of the white guys, all who were single and many who weren't would try to say something to you or offer to buy a drink. If you didn't respond, or only talked to other Blacks, they would stare at you, seething, still interested, but for the most part leaving you alone.

The four of us stood near the end of the bar, waiting for the show to start. To the right of us was another white guy we all knew. He was groping two well-dressed Black guys I hadn't seen before—perhaps they were from out of town. I could see the blunt outlines of the erections he'd worked up in both their pants, and overheard him repeat the same phrases every ten minutes: "That would be so nice. To share that with you. If it's all right with you. I'd like to do that." One of the Black guys glanced at me, an omnivorous look of contempt on his face.

What did we talk about that night? Who knows—who cares? The same things: Davis's job. Brad's new client. Jay was telling someone about how he met Davis after his being "straight for twenty years" and was now happier than he'd ever been before, even during his brief marriage. He punctuated the story by throwing his tongue down Davis's throat and proclaiming to all within earshot how much joy Davis's thick Black penis still gave him after eight years together. I said nothing, apparently the only one embarrassed by this revelation.

The announcer stepped onto the stage and the show began. He was famously dreadful, speaking with a thick local accent. His rap was meant to entice and inspire us, but it came out barely intelligible. It amazed me that no one had told him not to hold the microphone so close to his mouth, so he would not distort his voice even more. Most likely no one cared that much about what he had to say.

The first dancer was fair, muscular, with no body fat. He knew all the latest moves, exaggerating the pelvic thrusts and hip swings in his dancing for the crowd's somewhat unappreciative benefit. He made a good deal of money on stage anyway, and even more when moving through the crowd.

"Everybody must be horny tonight," Davis said, shaking his head.

"I know I am," Jay stage-whispered, licking Davis's ear.

"Why someone would pay for *that* is beyond me," Davis continued.

Brad said, "Me too."

The second dancer came to the stage. He was thicker than the first, a football or baseball player to the first guy's Average Joe. His moves were not as sharp as the first dancer's, but he compensated for his lack of style with muscle display and by impressively clenching and unclenching his large behind.

When the third dancer came out, I could not tell whether it was someone new or the first dancer again. Looking more closely, I saw it was someone new, taller than the first dancer but in other ways very similar. He did nothing special, and nothing for me. I used his appearance as an opportunity to go to the bathroom.

I *drank* too much, I thought, leaning my swirling forehead against the cool tile over the urinal. Brad, who really could not drink, had also had too much. I really needed to take him home and go on to my place and get some sleep.

"And now, ladies and gentlemen, something different for you this evening," the announcer called as I left the bathroom. I looked around and indeed there were a few women in the crowd. "Just arrived from the Capital—Enigma!"

"I'm surprised he can pronounce 'Enigma,' " someone behind me said.

"Just try to get either one of them to spell it," Brad said as I returned to him. Everyone laughed. I smiled slightly as he put an unsteady arm around my waist.

Enigma was the darkest dancer of the night. His skin was nearly blue-black, and he moved and looked as though he might actually have been a serious dancer in his other life. He wore a half hood over his face, black leather covering him from the top of his head to just under his nose. The hood's eye slits made him look almost Asian, but the full lips under its edge were pure African. He held a small whip in his hand, running its tendrils up and down the arm of his black silk shirt. The music started and he turned his back to the audience, sticking out a small, tightly leather-covered rear, and proceeded to beat himself lightly with the whip. Enigma slid down to the floor, legs splaying out to either side in a split, then quickly fell forward and began humping the stage. Someone behind me gasped, then coughed.

I looked around. Brad was blinking behind his glasses, brow furrowed, trying to clear his vision. Jay again had his tongue down Davis's throat, but both their eyes were open. They twisted to follow Enigma's movements on stage. The trio to the side of us was also enthralled by the performance, an identical look of lust on all three faces.

I looked back at the dance floor. Enigma had taken off his clothes and wore only a white silk G-string. His body was completely smooth, the firm muscles under his dark skin rippling like waves. He again turned his back to the audience, moving his hips to make his small, perfectly shaped tail roll in tempo with his music. He stuck the end of the whip between his legs from the front, causing the hard, knobbed end to protrude obscenely from beneath his crotch, just below where the glossy string bisected the two halves of his dark, moonlike ass.

I turned away, unable to breathe. The room seemed to swim slightly, and I thought I could hear the faint chirping of birds over the heavy beat of the music in the bar. I motioned to the bartender for another drink. Brad glanced at me, then turned back to watch the show. I suddenly felt hot, as if I were standing under a blazing sun, then very cold, dropped in frigid waters. I wiped my forehead with a tiny cocktail napkin and sipped my drink, trying not to see the end of the dancer's performance reflected by the mirror behind the bar.

"Enigma!" the announcer called. I turned around as the dancer left the stage to a rush of intense applause. Another song started and he began moving through the crowd, undulating and offering various men the opportunity to beat him, trying to attract some money. A few men, both Black and white, seemed genuinely interested in taking the whip. Others gave him a few dull slaps. Many just ignored him as he ground in front of them until he moved on.

Enigma danced in front of the trio next to us. The Black couple seemed interested, and one tried to reach for his wallet, but our white friend restrained him. He again placed his pale hand on their bulging crotches and shook his head at the dancer, who shrugged and moved away.

Then he approached the four of us. The other dancers obviously had not clued him in to us or else he would not have wasted his time. He gyrated in front of Brad. I couldn't tell whether or not Brad could even see him through all the alcohol he'd drunk. He just blinked even more rapidly than before until the dancer moved away. Davis and Jay had their arms around each other, so he didn't attempt anything with them. And so he came up to me, offering me the whip. I smiled slightly and shook my head. My eyes fell down his slim body, and I felt a stirring in my crotch. Looking away, I shook my head.

"You sure?" Enigma said, placing himself against me. "O. . . . Oh! I see *some*body's interested." His hand rubbed my growing erection.

Brad stared at me. Davis and Jay stared, too. I cleared my throat and pushed him away slightly. "No, really . . . really." My voice was cracking. "That's not . . . necessary. Thanks."

He moved from me, then turned back, eyes flashing behind the mask. Brad placed a hand on my shoulder.

"Damn." Enigma stared at me. "What? You gotta be *white* to get some money around here?" he said before moving on to another group of people.

Africa to the Americas

The Curious Adventures of Capt. Delano During an Expedition to the South. Reports of Messrs. Merwyn and Richmond, Delegated to Visit Various Sites, for the Purpose of Ascertaining the Advantages to Colored People by Migrating There. Trial of a Slave for the Crime of Obeah (Voo-Doo) and Murder.

"We're going home," Davis sighed, throwing an arm around Jay's neck. "We've seen more than enough." Brad and I hugged the two of them and they slowly made their way to the door. Brad pointed to the rear of the bar and headed unsteadily toward the bathroom, leaving me on my stool alone.

I put my glass down, not thirsty anymore, then looked around the bar. The trio beside us had left without my noticing them. Small clusters of mainly Black men stood around talking, laughing. A few whites remained hovering around the edges of the crowd, waiting to see who might become available to talk to. Two of the night's dancers had returned, almost unrecognizable in their street clothes. Enigma, however, was still next to nude, swerving in front of a plump older man with a full beard, a Black Santa Claus in his workshop, who stood in the corner near the pool table. The dancer got a dollar from him and gave him a peck on the cheek in return.

I walked over to him. "Did you say something to me?" I asked. Enigma peered at me from behind his mask and smiled slightly. He was taller by almost half a head than he seemed while dancing or moving in front of me. He offered me the whip. I took it as he turned around and gave him a couple of quick hits on his waiting butt.

"Mmm," he said. "That's more like it. I *thought* you might get into this." He smiled, then climbed onto the pool table and went down on all fours, offering me his G-stringed ass to do with as I pleased.

"You say something to me?" I repeated. I drew my arm back

and brought the whip down forcefully against his left cheek. The dancer jumped, moaned, and wriggled his ass for more. I dribbled the long black fingers of the strap down the crack between his cheeks, then lashed him violently again on the right side. Again Enigma moaned, and looked back at me, smiling. He blew me a kiss, then lay spread-eagled on the green felt, his fingers and feet grasping at the corner holes, waiting for another assault.

I slipped two wrinkled dollars under the white silk of his G-string and began going back and forth from right to left, alternately whipping and caressing him with the lash. I imagined the two of us were in some secluded place playing this game all alone. "If you've got something to say to me, then say it, boy," I growled at him, slapping his cheeks. "Speak up!" To me, this was a game—I was acting a part. Enigma, however, seemed quite serious. He wiggled his dark butt gratefully in counterpoint to the lashings of the whip.

The sound of the leather moving through the air suddenly grew louder, from a soft rush to a whistle. The bar seemed incredibly hot. I was surprised by how excited I had become, an erection straining in my jeans. The sounds of the other bar patrons slid away. There was only me and this dark young man, jumping and squealing under my repeated beatings, looking back, saying, "I've been bad, I've been bad, Daddy," over and over. "I need to be punished—punish me for bein' so bad."

Brad came up behind me, breaking the spell. "You . . . *like* that?" he asked, disbelieving. "That's weird. I never knew. . . ." He stared at the young dancer, whose wiggling slowed as my slaps drizzled to a stop.

"*He* sure seems to like it, though," Brad said quietly, his eyes glazed from alcohol and imagination. "You do too, don't you?" he said, cupping his hand over my crotch. "Damn, you're hard as a rock." He paused, leaving his hand where it was, then squeezed me.

Brad leaned in to whisper in my ear. "You want me to see what he's doing later? Bring him home? I'd love to watch you two guys go at it. Maybe even get in between you." His voice went lower, furtive. "I've always wanted to, you know? Two Black guys? That would be so hot."

I looked up. Every Black man in the bar was watching us. No one was openly staring, but I could feel their eyes on me. This is some trial, some test I must pass or fail for them, I thought, and I don't even know what the questions are, or have a clue as to how I'm supposed to answer. The skin all over my body was crawling, shriveling as if I were shedding. I looked down at my hands and caught a glimpse of alabaster.

"Want me to hold him down for you?" Brad asked. "Here, let me hold him down." He moved to the other end of the pool table, stuffed a dollar into Enigma's mouth, and clamped his hands around the dancer's wrists, holding them to the felt. Brad looked up at me, eager, grinning. "Go ahead, baby," he said. "Let him have it. Then let me get a couplea good licks in, too."

Skin ran off me as if I were melting. The flashing lights of the bar had shifted. Again I felt myself to be outdoors, in dappled sunlight. Everything seemed strange, yet very familiar. The felt of the pool table had turned into soft grass; the smoke of cigarettes changed into aromatics curling from a smokehouse behind me. There was a stagnant river to my right. In front of me, Young Master Bradley held down a recalcitrant Negro buck whose back already showed the scars of his previous transgressions. Patrollers and owners from nearby plantations were gathered around to witness the ritual. And I, the Overseer, long bullwhip in my pale hand, was keen to mete out his punishment. But I was also a fraud. I whipped the slave forcefully, beating out his uppity nature—but was also lashing at the brown undertone of my Creole forebears from Louisiana and the Islands in my own skin.

"*Traitor!*" someone said. I looked to my left around the bar. The three of us were being spectacularly ignored by the Black patrons. The few whites remaining had crowded around us, urging me on. I searched for where the voice might have come from. Every lip looked sealed.

"*Traitor!*" I heard again. I looked in the other direction. No one, nothing, just the small stage the dancers had writhed on, the covered windows to the street. "*Traitor,*" the voice said again. "*You're nothing but a fucking traitor!*" I looked around once more, but there was no one who could have said it. The voice was coming from inside me.

I dropped the whip and pushed my way through the crowd. The whites all felt they had to touch me as I went by them, their fingers reaching out as if to pull my skin off, like tearing strips of tobacco from a leaf. The repeating sound of *"Traitor!"* was driving me mad. Brad called my name, but I could barely hear him as I rushed away. The Black patrons turned from me as I went by them and out the door. I was grateful for that. One look from any of them then would have killed me.

I burst through the doors and rushed down the street toward my car. Leaning against the wall of the apartment building next to where we'd parked, I put my head in my hands and began to cry. Soon I was facing the wall on my knees, bawling my eyes out. "What have I done, what have I done?" I said between sobs, *"Traitor!"* slowly fading from my head. My skin was still crawling, flaking off me. My body ached all over as if I had been in a fight. I had never been in such intense pain before in my life. I felt like I had somehow betrayed every Black man in that bar (*"Traitor!"*). For the first time, that actually mattered to me.

Brad came running down the street toward me, weaving. I really didn't want to see him and curled myself up into a ball, hoping he'd go right past me.

"What's the matter, Michael? Are you all right?" Brad asked, standing over me. He was winded and put his hands on his knees to catch his breath. He held out his hands to me. I pulled away. I couldn't stand the thought of his touch on me.

"Are you sick, baby? You want me to take you home?" He tried to lean down on his haunches but wound up flopping onto his butt on the sidewalk. He reached out his arms to hold me.

"Don't touch me—don't fucking touch me!" I said, standing up quickly, knocking his hands away. I moved a few steps farther down the street.

"But . . . what's wrong?" Brad struggled to his feet. "Is it what I said about that guy in there? I just brought that up because I thought it would be fun, that's all. Is that what's upset you?"

I turned and stared at him. He was again blinking rapidly behind his flashing glasses. "You don't understand, do you?" I yelled at him. "You have *no* idea what happened in there, what we were doing, what was *really* going on, do you? *Do* you?"

Brad's eyes crinkled and he began to cry. "I'm sorry. . . . I'm sorry. Don't be mad at me. I didn't mean anything." He took a step toward me and slipped, falling facedown onto the pavement. He began crying in earnest then, still repeating, "I'm sorry.

Don't be mad at me. Don't be mad at me," into the cold concrete.

"Oh, get up!" I said to him, exasperated. "Have some goddamned self-respect." I moved to him, hooking my hands under his armpits, and started to lift him to his feet.

Brad grabbed me around the waist when I'd gotten him to his knees. "Don't be mad at me—don't yell at me, please. I . . . I can't stand it when you yell at me," he muttered into my belt buckle.

"Okay, okay—I won't yell at you. Just get up, please, so we can get the fuck out of here, okay?"

"I'm sorry . . . I'm sorry," he kept repeating, rubbing his face into my crotch.

The movement of his head caused an involuntary response. Brad looked up at me. "Please?" he asked. "Can I please?" He began fumbling with the zipper of my jeans.

My nose crinkled in revulsion. "Oh, God! Get the fuck away from me!" I tried to push him away.

"Please," Brad said again, holding me tighter. One arm snaked around my waist, his right hand tugging my fly open and reaching inside. "You know how much I love it."

"Get OFF me, man!" I yelled, trying to push him from me. But it was too late. He had pulled my semierection from my pants and began to suck on it. I moaned involuntarily ("*Traitor!*"), then winced and again tried to move him away. I used both hands to push his insistently sucking mouth from me. Brad continued on, driving his face further into my crotch, trying desperately to swallow more of me.

I finally gave up and leaned back against the wall ("*Fucking traitor!*"). I started crying again, deeply ashamed of myself. I wasn't sure why—I was not the one on my knees, sucking dick on a public street. I looked up and down the empty sidewalk. No one was out at that hour, and anyone who might have been would more than likely have been coming from one of the gay bars in the area and, therefore, more turned on than repulsed by what they'd see.

I looked down through my tears at Brad. He seemed completely lost in working on me. There were tears in his eyes also, small drops visible through his slightly fogged glasses. He always enjoyed doing this with me, and this time he seemed especially eager, almost licking my skin off. I felt like vomiting and my erection deflated. Brad pulled me tighter to him, willing me back to life.

I thought again of the dancer in the bar. Enigma's eyes stared at me from under his hood. I longed to run my hands over his smooth body the way water ripples across flat stones in a river. I could whip him if he wanted me to, and pictured him jumping in pain and pleasure at my assaults. But I longed for us simply to explore each other's body, cartographers mapping out unknown territory. Removing his hood would reveal a young and beautiful face. I wanted to hold his dark head in my hands, kiss his high cheekbones and sloe eyes. We would share each other, his whip transformed into a cowtail switch, flicked from side to side to set the magic for the tale our bodies would tell.

Brad moaned and I looked down again as I filled his mouth. He seemed so pathetic there on the ground, desperate for my maleness. He would eat me alive if he could, I thought, strip off my skin and eat it in long strands like brown spaghetti. I had never realized how much I hated him.

"You like Black dick?" I asked. Brad moaned and again looked up at me, eyes glazed. "Then take it." Grabbing his head, I forced myself down his throat. He sputtered as I pushed into him. "You want this? Take it. TAKE it!" I jammed myself in and out of his slack-jawed mouth. I thought only of getting off and giving Brad exactly what he wanted.

Turning us both around, I put Brad's back to the wall and again began to assault his mouth. "Take it, take it!" I yelled at him. "You want Black so much, here, here—take me!" I pumped angrily into him, banging his head against the building. Brad looked up at me concerned, the pain clearing his head slightly. But he didn't stop sucking and, in fact, managed to pull his own shriveled penis from his pants and began stroking himself.

I could not have cared less about his pleasure and thought only of myself. Again I thought of Enigma, on his back this time, legs spread wide to welcome me. We were outdoors, no one around but the two of us. I lowered myself onto him and we kissed, his full lips moist and soft, strong arms and legs wrapping around me, hands gripping me firmly. The thought of him caused me to cry out and bang my head against the wall. I came into Brad's eagerly lapping mouth. Shuddering, I felt crushed (*"Traitor!"*), a used piece of paper being crumpled and tossed away.

I stepped away from Brad, stuffing myself back into my pants, disgusted and ashamed of what I'd done. I wanted to apologize to him but could not speak. Brad looked at me fuzzily—and smiled. "Wow," he said. He waved his semierect penis in my direction. "Now do me. Help me get off."

I didn't know whom I hated more at that moment, him or myself. I could no longer hold in my revulsion and turned and puked into the gutter. The night came rushing up in burning rivers of vomit. I dropped to my knees and heaved again, longing to turn my insides out, to get the sickness from inside me. Trying desperately to breathe in air, I began to cough, and got unsteadily to my feet. Brad had passed out, penis still in his hands, sweat and semen smeared across his face.

I felt ill again and started running through the dark streets. The light of false dawn began to crack the eastern sky. I ran away from Brad and my car, the bar, that neighborhood, everything, toward my own apartment, where I prayed I'd find the hottest water in the world to wash him and my shame and the night— all of it, everything, everything—from my body.

From St. Domingue to Haiti

Echoes of Harper's Ferry. Revolte Generale Des Negres— Massacre des Blancs. *The Historical Events of the Haytian Revolution and Subsequent Acts of That People Since Their Independence.*

The phone began to ring at six the next morning. I let it. I had no interest in anything anyone had to say at that hour. After getting up and showering, I made my way back downtown to my car. I got in it and drove out of the city. I wanted to get away from Brad and myself, from everything I had known so far. I had no idea who I was anymore. If I had ever known.

I drove and drove. At first I thought of heading to the mountains about an hour and a half north of town, to go up to a great height and survey the world, imagining my life spread out before me like the landscape. But I took a wrong turn somewhere and wound up heading in the opposite direction, toward the ocean. I didn't feel like turning around and starting over. Thinking one place would be just as good as the other, I just kept driving.

The day was gray and overcast. The sky hovered on the edge of rain. The usual beach traffic had been halved by the threat of showers. I drove to the farthest of the string of public beaches that dot the shoreline leading away from the city like a strand of pearls. It was usually the least populated even on good days, the dunes less well kept, the waters rougher and wilder than at the other stops along the coast. I parked in a nearly deserted lot and walked to the beach.

The green-gray ocean came in uneasily, groggy, rolling in irregular swells. I flopped down on the damp sand and stared out at the waters, then dropped my head into my hands. Images from the night before flashed through my head, whips and sunlight, Brad on his knees, Enigma staring at me through his mask. The taste of vomit and alcohol filled my mouth. The soft sound of the waves was like a whispering chorus of voices I could almost understand. They were trying to say something to me, and I leaned in closer to hear it. I was sure if only I could pay better attention, listen more carefully, I could hear exactly what they wanted to tell me. Getting up, I took off my shoes and socks and stepped into the water. Coldness shocked me, and I jumped back onto the sand.

I stared out at the empty waters. The rush of incoming waves was strangely calming. Again the rolling swells called to me. Putting my wallet and keys inside my shoes, I stripped off the T-shirt I'd thrown on at home and ran straight into the ocean, diving in without removing my jeans. The water was stunningly cold, as frigid as Death, and I started to swim. I hadn't been swimming in a long time. It felt good to stretch those muscles again. I leaned and stroked, turning my head at the proper angle to insure I was gulping air and not saltwater, trying to pull myself through the waters.

I imagined I was back in the YMCA pool at home, being taught by Mr. Perkins, hoping no one would notice how closely I hung on to his every instruction, drinking in his tight and lithe brown body with my eyes. It had been years since I'd thought about him and my thirteen-year-old's crush, and I was amazed that the memory came back so clearly. It must have been the water. Just as he taught me to, I pointed my feet while kicking, heading farther out, away from shore. I didn't know where I was going, had no real destination. I just wanted to swim away from land and everything on it.

Too soon I grew tired. My unused muscles began to ache. I cursed myself for coming out so far and wondered how I was ever going to return to shore. I stopped swimming and began to alternate between floating and treading water. My contacts, which I had passed out still wearing the night before, had somehow popped out, lost in the water. The shoreline seemed incredibly far away, unclear and hazy.

The wind picked up and it began to rain softly. The troughs and swells became larger and deeper, sometimes curling into fine strands, the whitecaps like a shock of hair falling at their tops. I took a deep breath and started to swim back. Strangely, I didn't feel alone in the wild expanse of water. At times it was as though I were swimming surrounded by figures rising from and returning to the ocean, generations of men, women, children, all ages, colors, and sizes, watching as I struggled toward the shore. The figures roiled up, looked at my labors for a moment, then returned to their wet silence.

The water became so choppy it was difficult to keep it from my mouth. I swallowed a gulp of saltwater. It burned in my throat, and I sputtered and coughed. I stopped again, bobbing with the waves. Somehow the shoreline did not seem to have gotten any closer. I realized I was too tired to swim any farther, too far out of practice to continue. I should call for help, but to whom? I wondered. The beach was probably still deserted. What hope for mercy could I expect in these empty waters? Perhaps the unseen stars or Jesus could help me. I understood then the real reason why I came here, my true destination: I was going to drown.

I stopped swimming, leaned back, and gave myself up to the waters. The swells rose up again, looking down at me and returning to the depths. I closed my eyes as the ocean wrapped me in its arms. I longed to dissolve, flesh, skin, eyes, hair, all running off me, and become one with it.

What does it feel like to drown? I thought. Once I stopped struggling, the waters felt soft and inviting, luxurious, delicious. I closed my eyes and wanted to breathe water. I gulped and swallowed the sharp, rancid-tasting sea. Rising to the surface, I had to spit it out, but was still determined to turn my lungs to gills. At first, the waves could not be counted on to cooperate, pulling me up as well as dragging me down. Soon enough, I was pushed deeper into the ocean's wet breast. I opened my eyes under the surface to stare into the murk, waiting for my life to flash before me as I'd always been told it would. Soon enough it did, sights and sounds and voices coming through the screen of dirty water, jumbled and mixed together, slowly melting into nothingness as I drifted leisurely into unconsciousness:

A blue-white dome. My broken tooth. The whoosh of a leather belt. How come he brought that skank white boy in here? You have to let the screen warm up first before you can see anything. Tomato soup for breakfast. A black mask peeling back to reveal my face. Get outta my way, you four-eyed faggot. Umm . . . kiss me. Burnt toast and milk. Vanilla, flax, cherry ice cream. It's gonna be hard to wake him in the morning. I ought to beat the living SHIT outta you! I love you—you is cute. Rum and Coke. I don't think of you as a nigger—*you're* not like those others. Humming, crying, screaming. I bet you don't get fucked, do you?—You're all man. I think the motherboard is shot. A birthday cake with lime green icing. Ooh, I *love* that show! How big is it? Running running running down the street. It's only a short interview, don't worry. Mama's boy, mama's boy! Suck you mama's tit-ties! Turn OFF that TV, damn it, and go to BED! Welcome to Tandy, young man. Sure, let's try, why not? Don't let the lights and cameras bother you. The sound of creaking wood. Just speak normally. Running across the beach into the water. When is your birthday again, sweetie? I always forget. Take UNIX in the Fall. *Pull* yourself though the water. An extended family portrait, a dozen people, everyone looks like me. Mr. Perkins, dripping wet. You have 39 e-mail messages. First time on TV? *Traitor!* A flickering screen. Let's do a check, okay? How are you doing, brother? *Fucking traitor.* How you doin', brother? I've always wanted to, you know? Brother, how ya doin'? Thank you, Ladies and Gentlemen—*Traitor!*—Good night! How ya doin', brother? How *you* doin' brother how're you doing brother and the screen goes dark brother howyadoin' how yadoin' brother howya do in brother brotherhowyadoin brotherhowyadoinbrother howyadoinbrotherhowyadoinbrother

African-American Thought & Action
Community & Culture

Minutes of the Atlanta Conferences for the Improvement of Free Peoples of Colour in the United States. A Vindication of the Capacity of the Negro Race for Self-Government, and Civilized Progress. An Interpretation of the New Negro.

"We're closing soon, Brotherman," the guard says to me. I jump and look at him dumbly. He stares at me for a moment and I nod. He moves off again, looking confused, back to whatever shadow he came from.

I woke up three hours later, coughing, on the beach. I must have been caught in a riptide heading in to shore after losing consciousness, not as far out as my nearsighted eyes had led me to believe. I don't remember being washed ashore like a piece of human driftwood. It was as if the water had just placed me back where I belonged, then gone on about its business.

I felt like hell—beaten, drained, hung over, managing somehow to be both depressed that I was unsuccessful at killing myself and glad to be alive. I had no idea where I was in relation to my clothes or the car, and wandered the empty beach for another hour before finding my things. I dropped onto the sand, wiping my salt-caked face with my T-shirt and looked out at the mute waters. They rolled on and on, stretching to forever. The tide had started to come in, depositing a grooved shell between my damp shoes. I grabbed it and my shoes and moved farther inland and fell asleep again at the dune break, exhausted, lost in a floating dream, holding the small thing tightly in my hand. That shell now hangs around my neck.

After a week of avoiding him, I apologized to Brad for what I'd done. We met in an outdoor restaurant, and I kept my sunglasses on the entire time. I didn't want to give him the pleasure of seeing my red eyes. He seemed more upset that I'd left him alone and exposed on the sidewalk than for nearly raping him. He also couldn't figure out why I was leaving him. I didn't tell him about what had happened to me in the bar, or about nearly drowning, knowing he would never understand any of it. No explanation I could give him of my dissatisfaction with our relationship seemed adequate. He could not believe that I just didn't love him anymore. That seemed impossible.

Soon afterward I began my historical researches. I started reading the works of historians and sociologists, and ancient myths. I have no illusions about ever being an expert on slavery, Black culture, or anything. I can only say I know more now than I did before. That may not be much, since I knew practically nothing before I began, but it is a start.

My personal life has not been as successful.

This is where the Happy Ending is supposed to be. I return to the bar and meet Enigma, whose name is Mark or John, Curtis or Brian. I rescue him from stripping, and we live happily ever after. I use electronic mail, or chat rooms, the Internet or personals ads, to meet others like myself. Or a new Black programmer is brought on board at the office, Byron this time, or Ron, Bernie or Tim, and we hit it off and begin seeing each other after work. Life is not this simple.

I shaved the sides of my hair and let the rest grow out, braiding it into the small crown of dreads that fringes my head now. After a while I started trying to date again, tentatively at first. I'm sure it must have seemed to some of those first men I met that I had just been released from a hospital or prison. I couldn't even let the first man I tried to have sex with after Brad—a Black man—give me a blow job. The feel of his lips on me made me jump with revulsion, as if I were back on that dark street again. I have dated, gone to dinner or drinks, had fun with some, been bored by others, slept with a few. I eventually even went back to Lypton's, very frightened, wary of anyone I'd known before, or who may have been in the bar on that night. But meeting people does not come easily to me. Meeting decent Black men seems especially difficult for some reason, but I keep trying. I can sense I am not alone on this particular voyage. I know that they are out there. After all, wounded though I am, *I'm* out here, aren't I?

I turn from the last display case and head for the door. The guard has moved to the front exit, looking out occasionally at the few passersby on the sidewalk. He glances at his watch. The library will close soon, and he'll be able to get on with the rest of his life. He pulls out a small penknife and begins to clean his fingernails. He's younger than I thought he was when I first came in. He's still older than I am, however, but not by much. I notice how snugly his uniform fits his body, molding his thick thighs, his curled biceps straining the short sleeves of his white shirt. He looks up at me and I glance away, not wanting him to notice that I've been looking at his body. As I draw closer to him, I look at him again, this time directly in the eye.

"Thanks, man," I say, as if he were directly responsible for the exhibit and not just guarding it.

"Take care, brother. Come back and see us again sometime," he says. I notice the name "Robertson" written on the gold nameplate on his shirt.

"Hey—we've got the same last name. You from around here?" I ask. "Maybe we're related."

The guard shakes his head. "No, I don't think so. I just moved here not too long ago from down South. I got no kin here. But then"—he nods toward the exhibit behind me—"maybe we are related. Born on the same plantation, y'know?"

"Yeah—Yeah! That could be true. Robertson family extended," I say, smiling. Then we both start to laugh, softly at first, then gradually louder. Our laughter dances across the polished floor and weaves its way between the display cases. The guard's laughter subsides, but somehow I can't stop myself. I keep laughing louder, barely able to control myself. The sound rises, floating up and up, until it bounces off the bright, clear skylight and comes filtering down again like a waterfall.

I move toward the door. I need air, need to leave and try to contain myself before my noise brings curators and librarians out from the closed and darkened stacks. I calm myself enough to shake the guard's hand.

"Well, you got family here now, cousin," I say, wiping away tears.

"Thanks, man," he says. "See you around."

I nod and walk out of the building. The day is bright and warm, cloudless. I squint in an attempt to adjust my eyes to the sudden light. I feel emptied, regenerated by our laughter after viewing the exhibit. I walk down the Powell's steps slowly, looking left and right, unsure of which direction to move in.

I get to the bottom of the stairs and glance both ways again.

The door above and behind me closes. The lock clicks. I breathe deeply and head toward the intersection to my left. I've never been this way before, I think, and wonder where the street will take me.

THE MARRIED MAN

ANDREW HOLLERAN

He didn't really have a type—certainly not the teenagers who
swarmed around him every day he went to work cleaning a high
school in Philadelphia. (He had begun his career at the school as
an English teacher, but after one year decided, as he put it to his
father, "I'd rather sweep up after the little shits than have to
teach them manners," and he signed on as a janitor instead.) He
preferred his peers, so he laughed when friends asked him if
working at the high school was not like sweeping floors in Paradise. His job might have been paradise for a pederast. He'd
found all his boyfriends among men his own age in the bars. The
students staying after school for sports were often beautiful, but
their raucous brutality reminded him of what he had hated about
adolescence, and it was with no repressed longing whatsoever
that he mopped up after their swim meets and basketball games.
There was only one student he ever fell for all those years, and
he got a crush on him around the time friends of his began dying
of AIDS, and he decided nothing was worth the risk of that. His
amatory career came to a halt, in fact, as abruptly as his academic one, when the youth he had a crush on at school came by to
see him one hot August afternoon after graduation. The boy was
now eighteen. They went up on the roof of the old apartment
building on Chestnut Street he lived in at the time and gazed at
the sunset over the Schuykill—but when the youth turned to
him, shyly offering himself, Luke realized it was out of the question: he knew he could do nothing that would even remotely

jeopardize the young man's health or future; and at the moment of refusing him—this person he'd been a little in love with since he was a sophomore—Luke realized he was going to stop having sex altogether. The next day he went to get tested. The result was negative.

He learned that giving up sex was like giving up sugar or red meat; the less you have of it, the less you want it. He could not extend this logic to cigarettes—but after stopping sex, he was amazed at how it ceased to bother him: the heretofore constant itch of lust. All those years spent looking for sex came to an end at a single stroke. Going to the 247 for a few beers after work was now a purely social experience. No games, no heartbreak, no tightening to the stomach, or avoiding of eyes; no grim competition, no tedium, no suspense, no disappointment, no drama, no tension. It was just a bar. Knowing he would sleep with no one, he was able to converse with his fellow patrons the way a straight man might—there was no subtext beneath the surface, no double entendres. He simply enjoyed the company, spoke to the handsomest man as easily as he did an old acquaintance, and went home to bed alone. Eventually the entire city changed that way. The ghetto itself was desexed—gay men going home from the gym, with their pumped muscles, looked to him like housewives who have just obtained a permanent at a hair salon. It was life outside the ghetto that began to seem erotic: the cashier at the Chinese restaurant, the 7-Eleven store, postmen, policemen, fathers with their kids sitting on their shoulders as they came down the sidewalk fresh from a baseball game. Riding home from work on the subway, he would stare at the veined hands of the graduate student reading a newspaper beside him while everyone swayed together through the dark tunnel toward Rittenhouse Square: a sight that was for him what a glimpse of women's ankles had been for men in Victorian times. From these fragments he could construct an entire body in his imagination. And that was all he wished to do. He was retired from the necessity of pursuit, unplugged from the electric current that ran beneath the surface of city life; a neutral observer, detached, nunlike, when he sat on a bench in Washington Square and watched the men go by. Sleeping with no one, pursuing nobody, they were all his. Not even pornography upset him. He put his collection of old *Mandate*s into the closet—the men in plaid shirts and hard hats—where they gathered dust, like toys that have been abandoned, and began turning his energy to other things: long visits to the art museum, books, researching his family's genealogy, antiques and movies.

He went to the latter more than ever, with his best friend, Pietro—a man his age who still taught school and lived with his Sicilian parents in the suburbs. Shortly after he took the test he asked Pietro not to tell him anything about his own sexual adventures; he didn't want to have to worry about him. He figured that Pietro knew everything he did, so there was no point in discussing it. Before, they had shared sexual confidences, though neither one had been a boaster. That made it easy for their new agreement to be observed. Luke said nothing when he noticed Pietro seemed to be dating only black men. He said nothing when even the black men disappeared—about their disappearance, or the considerable weight Pietro began to put on— because when that happened, he surmised Pietro too had given up sex, his sudden obesity a consequence of his having gone cold turkey. Finally, not only did Pietro give up cigarettes, become fat, and start watching television with Luke, there was one last conclusive sign that Pietro was now celibate—Pietro began talking dirty: proof, in Luke's eyes, that the lust which had been heretofore discharged in bed was now bubbling to the surface in other forms.

At first it was confined to the safety of Pietro's little sports car, where, even with the top down, they were not likely to be overheard by the crowd of men leaving the Spectrum after a hockey game; but it was on such occasions, pausing at a stop light to let pedestrians go by, that Pietro began to say, in a dark, sharp voice, things like: "That one's got a whopper. Bet he could smack your face with that thing. Bet it could break your jaw." The slightest flicker of a throat muscle was the only sign on Luke's porcelain-white, freckled face that he had heard. He told himself not to encourage or reprove him. He told himself it was gay small talk. It harmed no one in Pietro's car. When the occasions became more frequent, and the monologues longer and more lascivious, he still refrained from saying anything; he considered it a nervous tic that was the result of Pietro's giving up cigarettes too. (Luke could not imagine giving up sex *and* cigarettes.) Therefore he had no standing, he felt, to criticize Pietro's food consumption, or complain when Pietro, on the weekends, took him driving to Bucks County, ostensibly in search of antiques, and ogled men with their girlfriends and wives. He decided Pietro had focused his attention now on what he clearly could not get (heterosexual men), a form of safe sex if there ever was one. It was at least one response, Luke thought, to the problem—and it was a problem, giving up sex in the prime of life. Luke wasn't even sure sometimes why he had done it. "I wasn't very good at sex," he told Pietro one evening as they dined in their favorite restaurant. "I think you were much better at it than I was." Pietro dismissed the remark, but Luke suspected it was true; celibacy was easier for him than it was for his friend, since he had been growing less and less enamored of sex by the time he quit.

So he was patient and tolerant as Pietro's filthy panegyrics began to increase in intensity and occasion. Sitting in front of the television, he let Pietro go on about the genitals of every man who came on screen, including even the local Irish-American weatherman's "big, fat, juicy cock" as he delivered the statistics on a cold front moving down from Canada. "I bet they have to clear him before he goes on camera, his cock is so big and fat it makes a bulge—look, he dresses right, you can see it going all the way down his leg—I wonder what he does with that piece of salami," he would say as he tore at a fried chicken wing. "I bet his girlfriend can't even take it all the way, I bet if I phoned the studio and said I could, he'd call me right back, and tell me where to meet him, so I could take care of that big piece of Irish meat!" And Luke would silently serve the tea, light a cigarette, and go on watching the television as if his best friend had said nothing at all more unusual than "Looks like it's going to be cold next week." He began to think of it as he sat there listening to these graphic monologues as something like Tourette's syndrome: an uncontrollable stream of obscene language he simply should ignore as he stared straight ahead at the isobars and cold fronts being described by the man on screen on whom Pietro, his pudgy fingers gleaming with chicken fat as he continued to dismember a bird, was bestowing a penis of such enormity Pietro had to switch to Italian to describe it, until Luke, unable to stand any more, said, *"Basta!"*

In restaurants his patience was not so great when Pietro started in on the waiter only a few minutes after they had been seated, or the father dining with his wife and kids two booths away. Nor did he like it when Pietro poured forth in front of gay friends who came by to visit, especially ones Pietro hardly knew. Nothing was sacred: not *Hamlet* or *Schindler's List*. One night they were watching a documentary on raising polar bears from infancy—since giving up sex, they spent a lot of time watching TV—when Pietro said, in front of guests he had just met, as they watched the scientist holding the cub: "Look at his hands. Just look at the hands. Do you know what those hands are connected to? A piece of monster meat, with veins as big as the veins on the hands themselves. I wonder how he works in the lab, pressed against the counter like that—I'll bet he has an erection all the time. I'll bet he lets the polar bear play with it, I'll bet the polar bears suck him off because they think it's a bottle they can get milk from. That big Polack cock—you can tell from his hands, and nose. All Polack meat is thick, you know, very, very thick, they have the thickest cocks in Europe," till Luke had to turn and say: "Could you please shut up so I can hear what the man is saying?" and roll his eyes at his guests, while Pietro went on muttering in a lower voice, as he put grapes in his mouth, one by one, with fingers stained with Camembert.

Luke considered suggesting Pietro resume smoking, as if that—giving up nicotine on top of sex—had pushed him over the edge. But he did not. A certain deference to each other's privacy was one of the things that made their friendship work. Five years after Luke gave up sex completely, in fact, they both bought apartments on the same floor of an old renovated brewery north of the art museum—and they continued to spend most of their free time together going to restaurants, antique shows, renting movies on the weekends, even visiting Peru. One night, coming home late from work, Luke saw Pietro ushering a man out of their building whom he did not recognize; but he did not ask Pietro who it was—some respect for privacy, or desire not to know, kept him silent. Then, a month later, a Cuban friend who now lived in Fort Lauderdale but who came to Philadelphia several times a year to take part in a protocol for an experimental AIDS drug and stayed with Pietro, an old friend from teaching days, told Luke that their mutual friend was indeed still having sex; had been having sex with a married man from the suburbs for almost ten years now, a man who'd had a drinking problem but was sober now and who thought (because he'd once, while drunk, visited Pietro at Pietro's parents' house) that Pietro was married too (to his sister, who still lived with them). Pietro had gone along with the presumption; the apartment in Brewery Town, he told the married man, really belonged to Ramon, and he, Pietro, stayed there only occasionally while Ramon was in Florida.

"Stop!" said Luke. "I don't want to hear any more. I don't want to know a thing about it. That's enough!"

Ramon, delighted at having produced a reaction, continued to supply more details, but Luke started talking at the same time and finally got up and went into the kitchen. "Look," he told Ramon when Ramon followed him, "I am not going to worry about Pietro. His friends were also mine. They're all dead. We made an agreement that he wouldn't tell me anything about what he does sexually, and that's that." Ramon, his eyes sparkling, said: "Well, I can tell you the man has really got a big one, so we should be glad for our sister!" "That's enough," Luke said, and that was the last he heard of it.

One evening not long afterward, however, in late January, he came home from a movie and saw Pietro and the same man leaving the lobby together. He was about sixty, the same size and shape as Pietro—burly, overweight—and had a gray crewcut. Now he understood the reason Pietro said he could not go to dinner or the chamber music series at the Academy of Music on Tuesday nights: Pietro was with this man. He was astonished—that Pietro had been seeing this man all these years, right in their new building, to boot. Ten years was a long time to see anyone. That their sexual bond had not weakened by now was remarkable in itself. That the affair had only intensified Pietro's habit of talking dirty was too. Of course, the man might be the inspiration for that. Even more important, if the man was married, and having sex only with Pietro, besides his wife, it was quite possible that what they were doing was totally safe. Pietro was therefore having a pleasure that he, Luke, had given up for over a decade. (Perhaps he was depriving himself unnecessarily, he thought; perhaps he had been too cautious, too draconian.) Still, when Pietro came over to watch a movie, when they went out to dinner or to shop for antiques, he said nothing; he was not supposed to know—about Pietro, at least.

In recent years, however, the years of his celibacy, he had begun relishing the stories which other friends who were still tricking told him on the telephone. People liked talking about what had happened to them, he realized, and that included sex. He was now the confidant of three or four people who were still going to bars, rest stops, library toilets, parks. He loved hearing the details of their sexual adventures. It was part of his celibacy; the pleasures of the nonparticipant. He often played several of them over in his mind the way he smoked a cigarette; months after someone had ceased to mention Roy or John, he would ask him again about Roy's skin, or how he had come, or what John had done in the threesome his friend had had the night before New Year's. He was the repository of other people's ongoing sexual diaries; they phoned him the next day and recounted what had happened in detail. Still, he could not ask Pietro what the married man was like, much less what they did in bed together, how it had evolved over the years, the dimensions and shape of his penis, as he might with another friend. It would have violated their agreement. Now, however, he found himself scanning the cars in the little parking lot outside their building when he came home, looking for any vehicles that weren't usually there, glancing down the hall in Pietro's direction when he left the elevator, hoping, when he walked through the lobby, he might see them saying goodbye, or just coming in. And sometimes, as he sat watching a movie with Pietro beside him, eating marzipan, getting fatter as he tossed the candy animals down his gullet, he would find his mind wandering from the film to the questions he might ask Pietro if only he would allow himself to. Or at night, home reading a book, he would lift his eyes from the page and stare blankly at the wall, wondering if at that moment Pietro and the married man from Devon were down the hall in bed; and when Pietro sat beside him spouting obscene paeans to the penis of the weatherman, he began wondering if Pietro was recalling the penis he'd had a few nights ago, and everything being attributed to the skinny Irish meteorologist with the big Adam's apple was in fact nothing more than a description of the married man.

At first he didn't really envy Pietro at all. He thought: *Oh, he's still doing that. He couldn't quite give it up.* But the fact that he had narrowed it down to one person, and one person only, he did find enviable: sex within a context of monogamy and safety, sex that was ongoing, personal, intimate, domestic—the sort of sex Luke had always been looking for all the years he went out, when he settled instead for ten minutes in a bush behind the art museum, standing up, or an hour with a trick who did not call back. His own sex life had been inferior to Pietro's; Pietro had usually "seen" people for much longer periods of time. Luke wasn't sure why this was but it was. Luke's last boyfriend had broken up with him amiably in 1980, the difference in their education and background too great; since then it had all been tricking, and tricking after a while had ceased to appeal to him. His crush on the senior at school was based partly on the fact that he was an ideal, not a possibility, and when the young man came to see him that evening as the latter, the fear of infecting someone on the verge of adult life was only half the reason he refused to respond. The realization that he would not endanger this young man at the outset of his career—believing then that no test could be entirely reliable—was in some ways just a pretext.

Now, like some underground river that breaks out into the sunlight, his erotic imagination reappeared again, and he began fixating on the inspiration for Pietro's streams of obscene rhetoric in the aisles of grocery stores, movie theaters, subway cars, the Art Museum, even churches. He had never been a size queen when he was sexually active. Once, in the 247, a man had come over, glowered at him for several minutes, and then asked, "Are you in the Plus Nine Club?" and Luke had replied in an icy tone, "No. Are you in the Social Register?" It was a famous story in the bar. Pietro, on the other hand, *was* a snob: He had a large penis himself and, exactly like someone in the Social Register, which was what it amounted to in homosexual life, would only have sex with people similarly distinguished. Now that these were off-limits Pietro had turned to more conventional objects for his powers of discrimination: art, food, Italian accents, neighborhoods and houses. There was something admirably rigorous about Pietro's standards: what made him a teacher whose classes parents fought to get their children into—that he demanded, for example, perfect pronunciation from his students and nothing else—was what made him bestow, as they drove around Bucks County in search of the perfect andiron or salt cellar, huge dicks on all the men he found attractive, or likely to have one (because of their hands, ears, noses, height), like some monarch creating peerages. In fact, on such fall days in the little sports car, in a brisk wind that blew his long, curly black hair straight back along with the silk scarves around his neck, Pietro's full and ruddy face, when he turned to Luke to praise some jogger, looked to Luke exactly like Bernini's bust of Louis XIV—sated and concupiscent—and he laughed at himself for ever believing someone so in love with the refinements of life and all its physical pleasures could have given up the very summit of both: sex.

Yet he could not imagine Pietro with the married man at this point—Pietro was so plump, the image summoned up was distasteful. He himself, however, had kept his figure. It was one of the things he was proud of. No gut, no butt, not even love handles; for some reason—metabolism, no doubt—he was skinny, and always had been; his body at fifty-four was virtually what it had been at thirty-four, except for the hair on his back, which he had Pietro shave for him when he got sick of seeing it on his shoulders. (That was the simplest index of their friendship, he thought: of their original circle, they were the only ones left alive to shave each other's back.) Now when he shaved Pietro's he realized he was preparing him for the married man. One night he handed the razor to Pietro and asked him to return the favor. "Going out?" said Pietro. "After all these years?" In fact he was merely thinking of the married man.

He was thinking of him often now as he sat at home; it made more sense to him to reduce the world to one single sexual object, if he was going to have sexual feelings at all. He had certainly seen enough of the disadvantages of the chase; even now, when friends called him up after a night at the bars, he listened to the brief summations of the defects of their tricks (inevitable in middle age, it seemed) the way a car mechanic listens to customers describe their engine knocks. It was somehow more romantic, civilized, intimate when he thought of himself and the married man. He even liked the fact that the married man was nondescript. He saw him one night in the Chinese restaurant down the block in a booth, drinking tea while Pietro stuffed himself with noodles and sesame sauce; he wore a trench coat, and a tie askew; he had a thatch of gray hair that grew low on his forehead still, bags under his eyes, jowls, a mournful look, and glasses held together with a paper clip. The hands holding the white cup were quite thick. Luke imagined himself allowing the married man to trace the lineaments of his own face with his big, thick hands; he imagined nuzzling against them, of finally taking them in his mouth, while he sat there in bed, feeding them to him digit by digit—those stand-ins for the penis, the enormous penis which sat, still untasted, still untouched, between his legs. Would the pubic hair be gray or dark? Would he be able to get a full erection? Of course. He'd been screwing Pietro for ten years. He was sober now. He was that most erotic of objects—a completely average, ordinary man.

This was the most erotic thing in life in Luke's eyes: the idea that behind the facade of the average, the everyday, the plain, there often was wonder. Like the houses of the rich in Bogotá where Luke, in the course of that long education which had come down to his pushing a broom through the halls of a high school, had lived one summer as an exchange student behind high drab walls on which there was no sign of what was within; and then, when the dull door was opened, one stepped inside— to Paradise. A garden, lawns, trees, courtyard, fountains and mansion. It was a Moorish idea that Paradise was hidden, enclosed, unseen by the world. Often he walked the streets of the Italian neighborhood to get olive oil or cheese or bread, along the long plain red facade of the row houses, and wondered what beauty was inside. He had no interest anymore in the muscular beauty who sat parked in a convertible on Delancey Place allowing himself to be admired. He preferred the nondescript fellow shuffling down Spruce Street who imagined no one would look at him. Glasses, ill-fitting clothes, responsibility for a cluster of shrill children, a tired businessman on the streetcar, excited him more; until this avatar of the ordinary, this supremely nondescript being, came into his life—the married man, eating soup with his big white hands and tired eyes.

Everything began to induce a daydream now, not just Pietro's paeans to the penis whenever they went anywhere together or sat home listening to the weather forecast. A picture book of Roman ruins, a photograph of the giant hand from a lost statue of Constantine, forefinger raised, made him think of the married man one afternoon—feeding him his blunt fingers one by one till he put all five into his mouth, each one the penis the man still had not given him, keeping it back with the confidence, the reserve, of a man who knows his will give pleasure; and as the married man stood shyly before him in his soiled trench coat and askew tie, a slight, sardonic smile on his lips as he witnessed Luke's increasing appetite, the frank, ravenous sucking on his thick, fat fingers, Luke finally released his own penis from his pants and began stroking it in anticipation of the moment when he would unzip, with shaky hand, the zipper that guarded the tremendous thing, which was not even hard when it was freed. It was at moments like these—finally going down onto his knees, finally taking the massive head in his mouth—that the phone would ring, or there would be a knock on the door, and he would open it and find Pietro saying to him: "Darling, they're showing our favorite episode of *Are You Being Served?* tonight—the question is, should we order Chinese or Mexican food?"

Then, once Pietro was gone, Luke would subside back into his reverie. Sometimes he imagined them in his bedroom, in bed, and there he wasn't sure what happened; sometimes he was reversing the hierarchy of penis size and giving the married man a surprise by penetrating him. That was what most married men wanted, in his experience: the one thing they could not do with their wives. Other times it was the married man who took charge, removed his penis from Luke's slobbering mouth, lifted his legs and began carefully and slowly to insert the blunt instrument into Luke's rectum, which produced a series of cries ("I can't! I can't!") till finally, ignoring them, the penis found its entrance and Luke felt a searing pain shoot through him, till he recalled the blessed paradox—that it was easier to absorb a large penis than a small one, because the large one overwhelmed, obliterated the sphincter's resistance, made refusal foolish, whereas a small or average cock it was possible to fight with, and because the very idea of this enormous schlong entering him dissolved resistance, was itself the ultimate aphrodisiac that made muscle relaxers and lubricants unnecessary.

These sessions in his imagination became preferable to television. He sat home with the set turned off as snow fell past the windows. Once the married man had to call his wife to tell her he was snowbound. They then took a shower together that steamed up the bathroom mirrors, and he lay in his arms afterward, warm and clean and tired, watching the snow drift past the tall window that overlooked the brick wall of the loading dock behind. When the married man left, Luke was so sore, so sated, he slept for a very long time and awoke only when the phone rang and he heard the married man say he was thinking about him and could he come back on Wednesday? In other words, an affair that went perfectly—that's what he imagined as he sat there in his chair with the book on Roman ruins lying on his lap, where it had fallen from his fingers. Even though imaginary, the affair was so pleasing he began doing situps at night. He took out a pair of old faded jeans that made his butt look good—the ones he had worn to the bar, even after he stopped having sex, out of vanity. He did flys with five-pound weights. He shaved off his mustache, mottled with gray. He shaved his chest and stomach, and finally pubic hair, to make his penis look larger.

Then, to his surprise, without a word of explanation Pietro joined him at the chamber-music concert on Tuesday night in the Academy of Music and let Luke know that he was available for dinner or a movie every night but Friday, when he went to his parents' in the suburbs. This change could have only one meaning, Luke decided: he had dropped the married man. The last obstacle—loyalty to his friend—was now removed. When Pietro called one Friday night to ask Luke to see if he'd left his checkbook in the dining room—the two of them had keys to each other's apartment—Luke took the opportunity to peruse his friend's address book on the table by his bed. Ramon— amused by Luke's stubborn refusal to hear anything about Pietro's private life—had told him that the married man was named David Kucinski. In the book he had two numbers, one of them at the University of Pennsylvania. He called the next day and learned he was a professor of Oriental literature, went to Penn that afternoon and got the course guide listing classes, lectures, times, and showed up for his Tuesday lecture on Masterpieces of Literature in Japan, in a small classroom on the second floor of Franklin Hall, where he sat in the last row behind about forty undergraduates. It was eleven in the morning; he did not have to be at work till three. He enjoyed the lecture on *The Tale of Genji*. He waited till all the students who went up to the podium to ask questions afterward—something he himself used to do—had left, and then he stood up and detained the professor on his way out with a question about translators.

It was strange seeing him close-up. The married man was

obviously a man who had boozed—with bags under his watery blue eyes, and a delicate network of veins visible on his cheeks, and jowls. There were moles near his eyes. His blunt fingers were white with chalk. He put them to his forehead, then his chin, as he deliberated his answer and the door closed behind the last of the other students, leaving the two of them alone in the dim, musty room. A clock on the wall ticked as loudly as Luke's heart. He was so nervous he began licking his lips. The married man finally began to look at him as if he understood the question was not the point, even as he answered it in his slow, rich, dissolute voice, till finally he stopped and Luke, squeezing his own crotch, said hoarsely: "Look. I have another question. Do you want a blow job?" The professor's face hardly altered. The room was so quiet, and so dim. There was no danger to him at all: Luke was obviously too old to be a legal problem; he had never seen him before. He said: "It depends. I have a small requirement in these matters, and I hope I won't offend you if I ask first if, by any chance, you are hung." Then the married man reached forward and squeezed Luke's crotch. There was nothing there but shriveled, unused, terrified flesh.

"Some other time," the professor said with a faint, sad smile. "I have another class to teach right now. All the best," and he opened the heavy door and went out. Luke stood there staring blankly at a bust of Benjamin Franklin, in shock, for five minutes, the placid, smiling visage of the Founding Father of no help whatsoever, and then went downstairs, so ashamed his face stung, and his eyes watered, when he walked out into the wintry morning. Around him the bare trees shook in the wind, the sun danced on the surface of the puddles in the walk, the students in their coats and scarves all looked to him indescribably hopeful and handsome. He felt alive again. There is nothing quite like rejection, he thought as he walked toward the bus stop, there is nothing quite like losing one game to make you try again. He felt like a baby who's just been slapped into life by the doctor's hand. He realized he had no choice now; he would have to go back to having sex.

GRACE UNDER LASHES

AARON JASON
(FOR EVAN)

to the tune of "Walking in the Rain,"
sung by Grace Jones

Walking down the street, kicking cans,
Twinky says we must be more aggressive than usual.
"Joshua, sweetie, the age of bitchy drag queens is over, and we'll see enough of those old things tonight. So we have to be *totally* better than bitchy. We have to be . . . you know, that word everyone uses these days . . . *empowered!*"

The two of us head to a lesbian bar for the birthday party of some semifamous local drag queen. Our invitation came second-hand, as no one invited us. In short, we're crashing.

Twinky practices empowerment by lashing out at everything: he kicks at trashcans and blue recycling bins, orange men-at-work cones, haggard tennis shoes, bag-wrapped whiskey bottles, anything not glued or bubblegummed down to the sidewalk. Pedestrians dance out of our way, but whether from the urban garbage flying at their knees or from our appearance it's hard to say.

I carry a transparent plastic handbag filled with my essentials: Wet and Wild lipstick, Ritz crackers, aerosol cheese, rhinestone sunglasses, stray tampons, a disposable Kodak, a gold Bible (placed by the Gideons). A clear shower cap covers the curlers Elmer's-glued to my head, and I wear my best Bea Arthur muumuu of green terry cloth that's like a hundred sizes too big

and smells faintly of wet mothballs, a dead giveaway I bought it
secondhand. Twinky sports a cottony wig he made from white
bedspread stuffing. It's crazy on his head, three feet wide, teased
out like an Afro. His face is titanium white, his lips and cheeks
and eyes varying shades of hot pink and periwinkle. He wears
scuffed saddle shoes, svelte stonewashed jeans with provocative
rips, and a matching half-shirt cut off just above his pierced
navel. Elf-thin, smelling of baby powder and vanilla, with his
tight clothes and white wig, Twinky looks like some enchanted
Q-tip come to life.

We get looks from the Saturday night crowd, looks that
Twinky invites. He skips down Castro Street with a sprightly
step, his tapered fingers spread behind him like tailfeathers.
When someone gives him a particularly offensive scowl, he yells,
"Like, what are you gawking at? We're just getting back from
Bible study, my God!" I plod along in my Reeboks (spray-
painted green) and keep up as best I can—not easy while nego-
tiating the bulky muumuu. People stare at me as well. Can they
smell the mothballs? Smell the secondhandedness? Trying not to
think about it, I point a shaky finger and reply, "God's gonna
getchya!"

The worst comes from the other queens, not ones in drag but
the twenty- and thirtysomething men in their Gap button-
downs and those pristine yellow work boots, the men who sport
pierced left ears and GQ hairstyles. Full of contempt and embarrassment, their superior glances scream, "Why do you have to be
that way?" I want to smack them with my big plastic bag and
read them up and down the way Twinky does.

But I don't.

I hesitate, look over to him. "Are you sure we should be doing
this? I mean, bad enough we weren't invited, but what if it's black
tie or something? And I reek like the Salvation Army."

"That's Salvation *Armani*."

"I'm serious. Why are we doing this again?"

"Sweetie, you've never looked better. And I'm so sure there's
no drag dress code."

Before I can argue, potential trouble approaches: those easily
provocable Lower Haightniks with their baggy shorts, bleached
hair in dreads, pierced noses and eyebrows. Twinky flies over,
throws a handful of glitter in the air above himself, and spins a

graceful gossamer swirl as the sparkle cascades on and around him. Covered in colorful dust from wig to toe, Twinky gives them an innocent grin, then flits off.

I'm more careful. Wispy and fast, Twinky could sprint to safety despite his huge white wig and saddle shoes. As for me, ever try running from vicious skateboarders dressed like Maude?

Looking at the billboard,

We come to a Hugo Boss advertisement at a bus stop, a six-foot-tall poster of some model who could be Kate Moss's brother: rumpled black sweatshirt, tousled hair, gaunt cheeks, hungry eyes, an expression as blank as a starter pistol. Twinky runs up to the two-dimensional model and plants hot-pink kisses on his starved face.

"My God." Twinky swoons around to face me. "I've *got* to have him." A mischievous eyebrow rises. "We'll come back after the party, break the glass, and rescue him. He *needs* me."

"He needs a sandwich."

"Oh, shut up. Let's set him free!"

"Don't you think we should do it during the week or early in the morning when there aren't so many cops or witnesses?" What I mean is, when we're not in drag."

"Joshua, sweetie, nobody's gonna stop us. You forget we're *empowered* drag queens. And like, my God, what *are* witnesses gonna say? But you know, it *would* be fun to get arrested, huh? Hauled into the big house! Can they make us take our wigs and makeup off for the mug shots? You know, with the Bill of Rights and everything? I totally forgot my cold cream. They *must* keep some at San Francisco police stations for drag queen arrests. Whattaya think?"

"I think you're crazy."

"Perrrrfect," he growls in his best Eartha Kitt. He draws a lipstick from his minor arsenal and poises it before the model. "*That's* what I'm supposed to be."

We leave Mr. Hugo Boss behind with TWINKY LOVES YOU scrawled across his face in Jungle Red and sparkling from a handful of Twinky's "glamour dust."

Summing up the people, checking out the race,
Immediately let in despite the line halfway round the block, we push our way up the stairs to the dark, crowded bar. Twinky stops. In the darkness his glittered white face glows phosphorescent, his pink lips and eyes set alight with an eerie will-o'-the-wisp fire. He gives the bar a slow once-over, his fluorescent eyebrows come together over his glittered lashes and nose, his narrow ears perk up despite the earrings (Christmas tree balls) that stretch down his lobes. In ten seconds' time he surveys the bar like a nocturnal cat.

"Not pretty, sweetie. Chinos and polos *everywhere*, and *uch!* Designer Imposters fragrances. *Definite* bridge-and-tunnelers tonight."

I check out the crowd, which is easy enough since when we entered all eyes turned toward Twinky who is pinker than a Jayne Mansfield wet dream. Even though we're in what is normally a lesbian bar, on weekends the men outnumber the women, and I notice very few of the latter. For some reason I had hoped that more lesbians would make me more comfortable. But no. A predominantly conservative crowd of men surrounds us, the same types we saw on the street. Here, however, their faces register freakshow amusement instead of disgust. They lean on each other's shoulders, giggle and smirk like high school jocks, and drink suburban beers found at any 7-Eleven: Coors, Budweiser, Michelob, Heineken.

"You're right, Twinky. It's not pretty."
"I know. Perrrrfect!"

Doing what I'm doing, feeling out of place,
I'm still relatively new at drag, only been at it for about a year. Twinky, on the other hand, has been doing it for five, since he was thirteen and saw *The Rocky Horror Picture Show.*

I envy his ease. In drag, he moves with a courage that belies his eighteen years, and it's times like these I don't think of him as four years younger.

As for me, the chilly draft up my thighs still annoys the hell out of me, and my chest constantly burns from the depilatory cream. Heels in a woman's 16 are impossible to find (hence the Reeboks), and I'm just not comfortable with my wallet and keys in a purse and not safely close to my body in a pants pocket.

Twinky points toward the back of the bar, where Mylar balloons bounce up against the ceiling, and the light reflects off sequins and lamé and lips and eyelids. The suburban queers divide us from a garden of teased bouffants, human hair beehives, and lace-front falls.

"Come on, sweetie." Twinky heads toward the party; the crowd parts for him like a biblical miracle.

I hesitate. Alone without Twinky and very aware of my curlers and tampons and Bible, I look at the suburban men, the Log Cabin Club queens who stare with their amused eyes and whispers. No turning back now, I'm pixie-led by Twinky. Adjusting the sides of my shower cap, my hands side blinders, I follow in his wake. "Whither thou goest, I will go. . . ."

Walking, walking in the rain,
When Twinky and I prepare ourselves at his place, the choice of music is crucial.

"No show tunes, no ABBA, no Judy Minnelli or whatever," Twinky declares. "We're a new breed of drag queen, sweetie. Only Grace Jones for us, because as you well know, not all great drag queens are men." Grace's androgynous voice reverberates throughout Twinky's tiny studio. He sets his CD player to loop that one song, "Walking in the Rain." It plays for an hour while we dress, and because of that, it drones in my head for the rest of the evening.

"Oh, and *definitely* Saint Susan." Twinky silences Grace and reverently puts in the soundtrack to *The Rocky Horror Picture Show.* "Oh, Susan, you're *totally* the reason I'm a drag queen."

How he worships Susan Sarandon rather than the more decadent characters from the movie always surprises me.

Unlike Twinky, who can throw himself together in minutes, I require a good two hours. My damn lashes take forever. I try and try but I can never quite lay them on straight, and I reapply and reapply, which only spreads glue everywhere, and inevitably I end up with sealed lids like the Envious in Purgatory, whose eyes are sewn closed with wire.

I squirm at anything having to do with eyes. At seven, I witnessed cataract surgery on *That's Incredible!*: metal instruments poked into naked eyes, removed cloudy lenses, and replaced them with the callous ease of changing a tire, and made all the worse by Cathy Lee Crosby's awestruck narration. I've been squeamish ever since by eyes crossed or rolled up, sickened by elementary school kids who folded back their lids, or friends removing contacts. I can't use eyedrops to save my life.

I'm inspired to get my lashes right one day. As a child, I watched my grandmother with her Carmen Miranda lashes thick as palm fronds. At the end of a day, a towel turbaned around her head like Liz Taylor, she donned a cashmere robe and sat at her burled walnut vanity. She gracefully peeled off each lash, the eyelid stretched in protest.

And me: blinded by lashes in Twinky's bathroom, my frantic hands sticky with glue.

"Sweetie, sweetie, cut the flailing! A little *grace* if you will. You must have grace in the most hopeless desperate situations. Act like everything that happens is totally meant to happen."

For all of Twinky's erratic energy, his elfin fingers are gentle, meticulous as they remove each lash and rub the excess glue from my eyes.

"I'm just nervous. I mean, look at what I'm wearing. What's everyone going to think when I waltz in dressed like Mrs. Roper?" As Twinky delicately re-lays a lash across my lid, I open my eye.

"Keep it closed, I'm not done. Sweetie, you're gonna look great. Besides, don't worry about what you wear. That's like, so secondary."

"Really?"

"Yes, really. The drag queen makes the outfit, not the other way around."

"I guess so. But still, why are we crashing this party again?"

"Of course I'm right, no, don't squint! Just relax. There. Now I've got to get myself together," and he jaunts off.

Feeling like a woman, looking like a man,

I never wanted Bette Davis eyes, just her eyebrows. And although mine are still in the thickly arched, Jane Russell stage, the thinner they get, the more I think the guys at the gym are growing wise. I struggle there enough without being recognized as a drag queen.

I hate the gym, don't know why I haven't quit. I hardly ever go, and when I do, those fatless bodies, perfectly toned like

International Male models, just discourage me. I arrive in my DON'T LAUGH IT'S PAID FOR T-shirt and leave after half an hour. When I first joined, everyone gave me those encouraging looks of "Don't worry, we all start somewhere, you'll see results soon." But I have yet to see any. And when I started doing drag, boy, did *those* looks change.

What have they noticed? What causes that distance they put between themselves and me on the stretching mat? Or those whispers in the locker room that end abruptly as I enter? Why do I constantly find myself alone by the free weights, the Nautilus machines, the water fountain, even during peak hours? Is it indeed my severely tweezed, ever-archening brows? Or telltale chest stubble grown in from the weekend? Perhaps an unnatural darkness around my eyes, a smudge of shadow, a streak of liner my cold cream missed. Or maybe a bit of eyelash glue, like jellied semen, caught in my natural lashes. In my reluctant hurry to the gym that morning, did I overlook an eyelash accidentally stuck to the back of my green sweatshirt, the lash that bats goodbye in my rush to flee?

Whistling in the darkness, shining in the night,
As we make our way toward the birthday party at the back of the bar, Twinky gets the usual responses from the nondrag crowd, the whistles, the construction-worker catcalls, the propositions.

"Hey, you're looking pretty hot, nice pink pants!"

"Hey, come party over here with us!"

"Hey, check out the wig!"

Twinky primps his cotton hair and announces to his audience, "If you wanna get anywhere with me, sweeties, you're gonna have to buy us cocktails!" And they do. As we pass through the crowd, fresh drinks are handed to us like Dixie cups of water to marathon runners. Some of the men shove folded bits of paper into Twinky's face. He stuffs them casually into his saddle shoes.

Drag for Twinky is all the more reason to pursue conquests, secure free cocktails, make friends, make dates, turn tricks. Once home at the end of a drag evening, he'll count his purseful of crumpled business cards and phone numbers scribbled on napkins and gum wrappers, count and organize them like a kid would his Halloween candy, or a leprechaun his gold.

I respect this about Twinky, his ability to attract drinks and phone numbers and flirt shamelessly. Even in drag his tightly muscled body shows through, lithe as a reed, ethereal, gracefully sylphlike. And no amount of makeup can conceal his big eyes that charm men wild when the morning light sets the brown aglow. Twinky's drag extroverts him, and I envy how it accentuates his natural beauty, how it brings him to life, down from the screen into the dark theater like Jeff Daniels, a Pink Rose of Cairo.

On the other hand, I stand back, one eye on the door, the other still glancing about for lesbians. Nervous, I watch Twinky like a chaperoning mother. My role. It's much darker in this part of the bar than where the drag queens gather. But this is Twinky's element, the darkness, the night.

The men call to me as well.

"Those are some pretty nice rollers!"

"Shoot a couch for that dress?"

"Estelle Getty with ya?"

I sip my cocktail and follow.

Come in all you jesters, enter all you fools,

Wigs turn, high heels step back, appalled faces leer. I notice the famous ones: Hellena Handbasket, Mina Vaginitis, Speedie Sedgwick, Ida March, Edie Puss, Gloryhole Steinem, and every Anita from Anita Mann to Anita Fixx to Anita Rush. Their makeup is flawless, clearly long hours spent at MAC counters throughout the city. Not a follicle shakes loose from the platinum bobs and brunet pageboys sprayed up into concrete perfection. These queens flock and preen like Fabergé peacocks in their shimmering cocktail dresses, their Academy Award couture, their faux Bob Mackies, Gaultiers, Lacroix, split legged or strapless, lamé, sequins, rhinestones, ermine, fox, mink, some fake, others perhaps not, it's hard to tell in the darkness. I feel like Alice in the garden of talking flowers. Tall stalks—waving gracefully, fully bloomed and meticulously pruned—look down their powdered noses at me: the little green weed in curlers.

Three notoriously evil queens size us up immediately. Tammy Pawn, Maxine Padd, and Stacy Free. The Three Menstrual Furies.

"*What* is girlfriend wearing?"

"Oh, honey, the neighborhood is goin'."

"I jus' knew this shoulda been a private party."

"Put it in a bad wig and some cheapola makeup and it thinks it's in drag."

"More like *dragged*, honey, *through* the alley, okaaay?"

"I hear whatchya sayin'."

"*MM*-HM."

Twinky takes one look at the assembled queens, a Cheshire Cat grin splits his sparkled titanium face, his pink lips blaze ever more iridescent. "Perfect!" he battlecries as he charges into the queens, his tailfeather fingers spread, his white puffball wig a toadstool in the overgrown garden. A glamour dust trail hangs in the air.

Sit down, no no,

"Greetings there, young thing in curlers," comes a slow drawl from the smoky shadows to my left, with throaty r's and Gloria Swanson over-enunciation. On a barstool sits a large figure in an antebellum dress, red with black trim like the one Bette Davis wore in *Jezebel*. A fat arm beckons me over with the sluggish strength of a termite queen, bloated, immobile, yet powerful in her colony.

The other drag queens turn their backs to me as they focus on Twinky within their nest and block my view of him. So I approach the big queen like I'm about to have a dangerous audience with Marlon Brando. As my eyes adjust to the shadows, I notice this drag queen is considerably older than the rest, at least sixty or so. All the makeup in the world can't hide a chin doubled with age; purple crumbs of shadow fall from the crevices around the eyes; powder gathers in the tiny canyons around the mouth; a tiara of lusterless rhinestones is lost in the thick Scarlett O'Hara curls that frame the sagging face. She looks me over with flared eyes, an effort, perhaps, to keep those heavy lids up. Sitting there in the shadows with all the younger drag queens dancing and carrying on and ignoring her, she reminds me of a deposed empress.

"Sit down, young thing in curlers." The Empress waves a plump hand at a nearby barstool. I almost curtsy, but I catch myself and quickly sit, not knowing what to say.

"Do you not know who I am?" she asks nonchalantly.

"No, were . . ." I almost ask, "Were you once a performer, someone big?" But I imagine her bulk leaping at me, long nails at my throat as she declares, "I'VE ALWAYS BEEN BIG! IT'S THE *DRAG QUEENS* THAT GOT SMALL!" I continue: "Sorry, I've only lived here for about two years."

"Neveryoumind, neveryoumind." The Empress reaches for what looks like a Blue Moon, and unlike most drag queens, who sip their drinks through dainty red straws, the Empress swigs directly from the glass; smears of dark purple line the rim like margarita salt. She chews an ice cube. "Far before your time, far before the time of many around here. Nowadays, I *am* my own milieu. But neveryoumind." She sucks in a deep breath. "What summons you here on this stormy night?"

"Well, we," remembering our *secondhand* invitation, "well, my friend was invited and dragged me along. And what do you mean 'stormy night'? The weather seemed nice on the way—"

"Give it time, give it time. In this dreary little hamlet of ours, fickle Madame Weather changes her mind with the flutter of her false eyelash. And is it not nasty business when she catches one of our ilk unawares?"

Discussing the weather with a drunk drag queen as old as my grandmother makes me uncomfortable. But then again, what else have I to do? Enter the nest of those serpents with their scaly sequins and shimmery lamé skins, their nails sharpened fangs, their words venomous bites? Not as strong as Twinky, I couldn't survive. At least here I can relax and pretend to be social. The Empress seems harmless enough. "Well, I suppose when that fog comes in—"

"Neveryoumind, neveryoumind the weather. I must say I envy you. Coming here. *Un*invited." The word trills in the back of her throat a second too long. With a snap of her fingers, I imagine the Empress could summon those drag queens. They'd swoop in on me, a pack of dragon ladies, blind me with their glinting rhinestones and beguiling sequins, lash me down, tear my green muumuu to shreds with their Lee Press-on talons, kick me out naked onto Castro Street, where my makeup would bleed from rain predicted by the Empress.

I sputter to defend myself. "This is a public bar, you know, and there's—"

"Now now. Do not let us bunch our bloomers. I said I *envied* you." She slurps the Blue Moon and takes another deep breath. "What brings *you* here?"

I'm Alice again, this time before the Caterpillar on the mush-room, the incessant questioning, the languid and sleepy "Who are *you?*"s. What does she want? I look over my shoulder for Twinky, though I see no trace of his white or pink among the dragons. But the smoke above them sparkles: Twinky must have tossed a handful of his glamour dust. Uh oh. He can usually take care of himself, but rarely without starting trouble. I'll engage the Empress. "Shall I say I don't know why I'm here, so then *you* can tell me?"

"Ahhh, young thing in curlers." She rises a bit from her impe-rial slouch. "I am pleased to hear your bathing cap is not too constricting." The Empress nods a single, satisfied nod, then swigs the Blue Moon. "Every once in a while they call me to *their* little events, their balls, their pageants. Brush the dust and webs off me, their mascot, their ceremonial security blanket. Rouse me from my bed, from my waller of mothballs so I may sit in all my finery and lashings, like . . . like some senile grandmother picked up from the rest home on Thanksgiving so she can waste the evening away, ignored by her so-called loved ones because they are too scared to disturb her and would not know what to say even if they did." Her voice drops an octave, "I despise those too scared to disturb."

The mention of mothballs unnerves me. But I think of my own grandmother, how she no longer wears her Carmen Miranda lashes or cashmere robes, how she avoids our family dinners to sit in her big empty house with "Aunt Pearl," her live-in nurse. I look down at my handbag, at my Ritz crackers, my Bible. "Well, I hope I'm not disturbing you."

"Certainly not, certainly not. As a matter of fact, you are the first to wish me happy birthday."

"But I . . . uh . . . oh. Happy birthday."

"Why, thank you." The Empress downs the Blue Moon and leans further back into the shadows; she shakes the glass of ice. "I come from an older time, when it was not unchic to croon Andrews Sisters songs to sailors and perverts. A time when one *earned* one's drag, one *did* something." She finishes off her Blue Moon. "What, young thing in curlers, do *you* do?"

"Well, to be perfectly honest, I don't *do* anything. And to be even more honest"— I look down at my spray-painted Reeboks—"I'm not particularly pretty tonight, either."

"Am I not sensing a touch of unease from beneath your green?"

"Well, it seemed like a fun idea at the time. Actually, it was the pink . . . my friend's idea to be a little outrageous tonight. But all those *looks* we got, and everyone here is so beautiful, even my friend in his ripped jeans. I wish I could look like some of these others. And other times I just don't think all this drag, this outfit even, is me."

"Nonsense."

"What do you mean?"

"Drag was made for the queen, not the queen for drag."

"Really?"

"Yes, of course really," her tone went from interrogation to concern. "*That* is the difference between a drag queen and a . . . well, between a drag queen and this charade that surrounds and chokes us."

The Empress slams down her glass, then lunges off her barstool from the shadows. Her unsteady hands close around mine like a Venus flytrap; one of them is chilly from holding the glass. Heavy from either her curls or her Blue Moons or both, her head sways a bit, but her eyes deadlock onto mine. "Young thing in curlers, I wish I had something to offer, some trinket, something deeply moving yet incredibly wise to say. I wish I could espouse some scant bit of fortune cookie wisdom, before I vanish. Forever."

"Why, thank you, I guess I—"

"Alas, I have nothing to offer. Nothing." She lets go of my hands and slumps back. A tiara stone glints in the shadows. "Kindly remove your eyes from my tiara! I shall be buried with both it *and* my lashes."

"I'm sorry, I—"

"Do *not* feel sorry for me! I have thrown stones in my day, tossed a brick or two!"

"So, I should throw a brick?"

"No, my dear, not just that." Her hands flare open as though casting a spell. "Bigger!"

"So what *are* you saying to do?"

"*Do?*" Her brow furrows; powder swirls off her face into the smoky air. "My dear young thing in curlers," she says, shaking her head at me with a squint, as though she didn't understand why *I* didn't understand, "you have already done more than you know."

I am completely confused by this stubborn old Taurus. Is she drunk? Nuts? Both? "I don't get it. What do you—"

"Neveryoumind, neveryoumind," the Empress huffs. She heaves herself back onto her barstool and leans against the wall. "Do not trouble yourself too much. Do not trouble." Her fatted hand flicks at me in dismissal. Not a sparkle from her tiara, she takes a deep breath, props her elbow on the bar, rests her head on her fist, closes her eyes. "But speaking of trouble"— her words are controlled and nonplussed, as sleepy as when she first addressed me—"I see your young friend courts a stoning of his own."

Coming to conclusions, button up your lip,

Twinky's white head bobs up and down in the garden of wigs as he deftly swivels his way toward the edge, one of the Three Furies from earlier in close pursuit. Maxine Padd: a demonic Lucille Ball in her fifties polka-dot dress and Technicolor red hair. She holds aloft a Zippo lighter like an Olympic torch. "Lemme at that thang! I *know* she wasn't talking 'bout my hair, 'cause if she was, she gon' lose hers *real fast!*"

The Empress is gone. Scanning around, I see the back of her immense, farthingaled hips retreat into the crowd of suburban beers. She bounces toward the exit with unexpected pep. The shadows swallow her up.

Twinky dances his way out, grinning like a red-handed imp. Tammy and Stacy hold back Maxine.

Twinky breaks from the queens and skips over to me.

"Joshua, sweetie, *there* you are. Whatcha doin'?"

"Uh, Twinky, what's going on?"

"Nothing. Whattaya mean?"

"*Twinky?*"

"Well, that snotty Miss Whatever just lashed out at me about my hair. And I like, couldn't let *that* go. I'm empowered, remember? So I read her the riot act!"

A blood-clotting Barbara Steele scream peals from the drag queens. "LEMME AT 'ER! LEMME AT THAT PINK BITCH!"

"I think we'd better go, Twinky."

"Oh, come on. Like, the fun's just starting."

I pull Twinky toward the exit.

Walking, walking in the rain,

The Empress was right.

Twinky and I emerge onto the wet sidewalk, where rain beats down in angry bullets. I search vainly for the Empress, but she probably caught a cab.

Twinky and I walk slowly. Without umbrellas, we're drenched in seconds, but we can't do a thing about it so there's no reason to rush. My shower cap keeps my scalp dry, and my clear plastic handbag protects my crackers, tampons, and Bible. The rainwater actually soothes my chest, still burnt and itchy from the depilatory cream.

The rain slows Twinky. I would expect him to break into his Gene Kelly, leap off the curb, twirl around lightposts, dance with make-believe parasols and fairies. But no. He walks a calm, graceless strut beside me.

"So were you talking to somebody at the party, or what?" Twinky asks. The rain washes away the glamour dust that had covered him in sparkle, and soaks his white wig, which now droops like a wet perm. He reaches up and squeezes out the water, which makes it look even worse, shrunken like used cotton balls squashed together.

"Just some queen."

As the rain washes away my mothball odor, tiny hailstones begin falling from the sky, crashing down, bouncing around and on us and the sidewalk like millions of spilled rhinestones.

"Sure is shitty weather, huh?" Twinky asks, a shiver in his voice.

"I kind of expected it."

"Really?"

"No, not *really*. But I'm acting as though I did."

Twinky stops; white cotton mush hangs in his eyes. We're only a few paces from the Hugo Boss ad at the bus stop, but Twinky doesn't notice. He looks down at the sidewalk and grinds melting stones with the toe of his saddle shoe. "Sorry if I ruined your night. I guess I sorta screwed up, huh?"

"No, you didn't ruin it at all."

"Really?"

"Yes, *really*. Remember, you were empowered."

Twinky looks up at me, a smile brightens his rainstreaked face with his eye makeup running as if he's been crying.

THE STRAIT

ALEX JEFFERS

My parents were not waiting for me when, bewildered, I pushed through the glass doors from Customs. I had flown British Air, changing planes in London; every time flight attendants or captain mentioned our destination they mispronounced it. Even as the jet descended into Turkish air space I heard no announcements in my native language, only overheard it from an excited child some rows ahead and across the aisle. Then, in the airport named for the father of my country, within ten minutes I saw three portraits of Atatürk. The signs too I recognized with a start as if I'd never thought about it before—not simply the language, the alphabet, but the typefaces: unornamented, graceless, sans-serif styles that seemed to rebel against a perfumed memory of Arabic calligraphy. Turkish smells and sounds and voices overswept me. Even the air on my tongue (I stood openmouthed, breathless) tasted indefinably, indisputably Turkish.

My parents had not come to meet me. Shifting the weight of the flight bag on my shoulder, hefting my suitcase, I peered around the international terminal. Everywhere families reunited with glad cries and eager embraces. There were ornamental kiosks displaying huge backlit photos: Aya Sofya, Topkapı Sarayı, the Covered Bazaar, the Bosporus Bridge. There was music in the background, muffled, tanbur and voice, the melancholy baritone singing Osmanlıca verses I could make no sense of. There were jandarmalar in uniform, the same uniform I had worn for my national service; men and women and children in stylish

Western attire and a few women in handsome long coats wearing scarves that hid their hair and pinned tightly under their chins, mustachioed men in drab, shiny suits, their collarless shirts buttoned to the neck, skullcaps clinging to cropped scalps. Nowhere was there a single member of my family. Stern Atatürk in fleecy black kalpak like a bandit or başıbozuk glowered at me unwelcomingly.

I followed the signs to a rank of telephones, then remembered I'd need a jeton and looked about for a vendor, then remembered I had only dollars and a few British pounds in my wallet. The prospect of dealing with currency exchange—discovering just how much value the currency had lost—was more than I could face. Then I heard my name, then I recognized a voice that made my throat ache with its familiarity, then his arms were around me, squeezing out my breath, then I was weeping on my brother's shoulder.

"I'm late," Mehmet was saying as he slapped my back with open palms, "I'm sorry, traffic's a nightmare, were you worried? What a welcome, to arrive and find nobody to greet you. Welcome back, Ziyacık, welcome home."

"Say all of that all over again," I said in English, unsteadily, "in Turkish."

Instead, holding me a little away and gazing into my eyes, he said, in Turkish, "Why are you crying?"—enough to set me off again.

Smiling through my tears, I clutched him harder. "Selamünaleyküm, kardeşim."

"Aleykümselam, sevgili kardeşim." Tender, he kissed my cheeks, licking up the tears, his mustache tickling. "I am very happy to see you."

I pounded his shoulder. My cheeks ached from smiling. "Mehmet," I said, "it's really you."

"Of course it's me. But who are you?" He cocked his chin. "I think you must be a tourist from America. May I show you a lovely carpet, efendi? Very cheap. Your grandmother will not like this at all." The edges of his thumbs scraped through my goatee, and then he pinched my earlobes. The punctures were new, not fully healed, the gold posts heavy. I flinched. "Please tell me you don't have ugly tattoos as well," he added.

I drew away, shrugged the strap of the flight bag off my shoulder, let it slide to the floor. "Not where Grandmother's likely to see them, anyway," I muttered sourly. "Where is everybody, Mehmet? I expected the whole family."

Mehmet bent to take up my bags and the leather knapsack he had set down before accosting me, bulky with books. "I had to come into town anyway, do some research at the university library this morning, so I told them not to bother. The women are all crazed anyway, preparing your welcome feast." He kept his face turned deliberately away. "Your little brothers were very angry, but I couldn't keep an eye on them all day and Sacide wouldn't hear of their coming all this way on their own."

I couldn't think why my sister should make that decision, should claim authority over Veli and İzzet. Sacide did tend toward bossiness, yet in my experience only exerted her will on Melek, too independent and tomboyish for her liking. The boys were boys, little men, and so far as Sacide had anything to do with them she indulged them. Her way of rebelling against our parents was to cultivate traditions and attitudes they scorned. The elder of my sisters, I had worried before I left for America, promised to become a woman I could not like. Shaking my head as if I were an American, I said, "Take me home, please, Mehmet."

The first two taxi drivers Mehmet asked to carry us to Emirgan politely refused him: it was too far, efendim, too late in the day, they would never find a fare back into the city. Before he could offer to pay double fare, I asked the third, "Sirkeci?" The man agreed happily, tossed my bags into the trunk, beamed as I urged Mehmet into the backseat. "I want to take the ferry," I told my brother. "I want to stand out on deck drinking tea and watch the shore lights go by. I saw too many motorways and ring roads in Massachusetts."

"It will take much longer," Mehmet grumbled, "traffic through the city will be horrible," but he acceded to my whim.

Once we were clear of the airport, traffic into Stambul was not all that heavy. At the end of the working day, everyone was heading out, not in. The driver naturally chose the traditional touristic route, through the old land walls at the Cannon Gate and along Divan Yolu, the imperial way, toward Sarayı Burnu. After dark, I saw little to tell me this was İstanbul rather than any other city in the world, despite absence of high rises and proliferation of neon signs. Not that I knew so many cities. It was none of the lamp nights so the grand mosques were not illuminated, no strings of white bulbs netting together their minarets, nor was it high tourist season with son et lumière at Sultanahmet. I leaned against my brother, my head on his shoulder, holding his warm, solid hand against my thigh. "I'll call from Sirkeci," he said. "İzzet and Veli can come down to the ferry landing, help carry your bags up the hill."

"Sacide will allow that?"

"She's not that bad."

"There's something you're not telling me, Mehmet."

His grip on my hand tightened for a moment but he said nothing. Along Divan Yolu we would pass below the hilltop campus of Istanbul University, which I might have attended in a different life, if I hadn't gone to Ege in İzmir, or Ankara, or Mehmet's own alma mater, Boğaziçi, on the heights above Bebek a little way up the Bosporus. But I had chosen to go, and our parents chose to send me, to the United States, where I was out of their sight and my family out of mine.

It seemed that I was wide awake though very tired—I had been traveling for many hours. I could grasp no notion of the day or the hour. It seemed that Mehmet and I had been riding in the backseat of an İstanbul taxi for as long as I could remember, as if I had never left. There was nothing we needed to say for we knew everything about each other, everything there was to know. Yawning, I leaned harder against my brother.

Glancing forward, I caught the eye of the driver in his rearview mirror, gazing back on us with disinterested approval or affection. A string of blue plastic prayer beads dangled from the mirror's stem. An American cabbie, I knew, seeing us cuddled together like kittens in his backseat, would take us for a pair of homosexuals and be disgusted or enraged. He would be half wrong, but also half right. I had not told my brother this thing about myself. I didn't know how. I didn't know how he could understand me—I had not understood myself before I left Turkey, and here, back again, it seemed improbable, incomprehensible. There were no words, there was no precedent.

The driver turned his head and, in the mirror, I saw more of his face. In repose, his features fell into sternness but the signs of good humor were as clear as one could wish, the brackets around his wide mouth and wider mustache, the squint lines about his deeply set eyes. He had not shaved today and his stubble was salted with white, though the mustache was as black and glossy as if it had been doctored with shoe polish. The collar of his shirt was grubby and the knit watchcap pulled low made his ears stick out. He looked back to the mirror, found me observing him, and smiled quickly—as fast as if it were reflex but really, I thought, with calculation. "Where are you coming from, efendim?" he asked.

"From America. I'm at university there."

His broad grin said how fine it was that a young man should attend university—in the United States, no less—and I loved him for his thoughtless charity. "Ah," he said, "New York? Or California?"

"Boston. North of New York."

"Yes," he said, "I know Boston"—but clearly it was a pity I hadn't known enough to choose Manhattan or Los Angeles, as if I were to pick provincial Ankara over eternal İstanbul—although, really, it was the other way around, as far as I could tell. "I've driven many Americans. It must be very strange for you, efendim—they are a peculiar people."

Not nearly so peculiar as they find me, I might have said. "I am very happy to be home, amcam."

Shutting his eyes briefly, he dropped his chin in agreement and murmured, "Maşallah," closing our little conversation with natural grace. Still, when they opened again and after he had checked the street, his eyes sought out my reflection again in the mirror. I smiled to show that, unlike an American, I was not offended or perturbed by his staring at me, and squeezed my dozy brother's hand. Mehmet grumbled unintelligibly.

The taxi swung left, dodging and honking, onto the avenue that would take us to the ferry terminal on the bank of the Golden Horn. Once the driver had regained mastery of steering wheel and clutch, he applied his authority to the accelerator and his eyes wandered to the mirror again. On the advice of one of my Harvard professors, an Iranian, I had lately been reading classical Arabic and Farsi poetry. The English translations of Abū Nuwās, Fārid, Ghazzālī, 'Irāqī, and the others struck me as either overworked or underdone—I have not much patience for poetry in any case. Overall, I found it more rewarding to read around than in the poets' works, commentary rather than text. Still, some of their phrases, images, concepts stayed with me, and although I doubted the taxi driver was any kind of Sufi or mystic, there was in his gaze, the persistence of his gaze, something that made me think of the nazar of the poets: that gazing upon the face of the beloved, a stare more active than reactive although it was seldom carried further (in the poem, at any rate), that might stand in for—represent—witnessing the glory of God. Often enough, more often than not, the beloved so contemplated was a boy of perfect beauty.

I was no boy, if that short and small, nor beardless, nor were my eyes black and languishing but dangerously blue. Perhaps the driver was no more than perplexed by my earrings and goatee, Western fashions not yet widely adopted by Turks, however Westernized. Perhaps I was fascinating by way of being ugly—perhaps he had no thought of wishing to fuck my tender, boyish ass.

The truth was I could not now look on his handsome, weathered face, the full lip below bushy mustache, the intent, liquid eyes, without imagining it. The truth was I relished the image of myself prone below him and his prick standing up big and proud and eager before he pushed it in, then the flexing of his buttocks and lean flanks as he took his pleasure. I sat back more firmly in my seat and gingerly moved Mehmet's hand from my thigh to his knee. The truth was, however sympathetic he might seem, however gentled by lovesickness or exalted sentiment, I would not trust a Turk to fuck me. I would very happily suck him off or myself fuck him, for he was good looking, gave every evidence of being sweet tempered, and I could trust myself to keep his pleasure as much in mind as my own, but the contrary was not to be hoped for.

I lowered my eyes and for the rest of the short ride to Sirkeci, though continuing to feel the driver's eyes on me, concentrated on imagining myself as Turkish and manly as could be. When the taxi pulled over to the curb I was ready, roused my brother from his stupor, fetched my bags from the trunk without the driver's aid. After Mehmet paid and tipped him, I added an American five-dollar bill, for which he thanked me effusively. Then my brother and I entered the terminal, where I begged a few thousand lira from him to buy tea at the café and he went to check the schedule, purchase our tickets, phone the house in its suburb up the strait.

Waiting, I gazed out the café windows over the Bosporus, busy with shipping even at night. The lights of tankers and freighters and ferries appeared as hasty cousins of the distant lamps of Üsküdar in Asia—as if the ships were an early, motile, individual, aquatic life stage of those great reefs of stone, concrete, steel, glass on either bank. In Boston, the Charles was a placid pond, enclosed, ruffled at most by racing sculls, while the town turned its back on the harbor that had given it birth, hiding the amniotic waters behind a screen of skyscrapers. My city lives and dies with the Bosporus; in Turkish we call it simply the Strait of İstanbul, but *boğaz* means also *throat*: sucking sustenance, life force. When Fatih Sultan Mehmet built his fortress at Rumeli Hisarı, twin and complement to his grandfather Beyazit Yıldırım's Anadolu Hisarı in Asia, he said that he had with that stroke cut the throat of Byzantium.

"Ayfer will come by for tea tomorrow, I think, or the next day," Mehmet said, "to meet you." He leaned against the rail, leaning out and peering upstream into the head wind, toward the Black Sea. His words whipped past me, gone as soon as uttered.

"Your fiancée?" I could not get used to the idea that he was to be married. My mother had announced the engagement in a letter only a few weeks before. Mehmet himself, in his twice-weekly e-mails, had said nothing until I asked. "Not tonight?"

"Tonight's just family."

"Uncles and aunts and cousins?"

"Possibly. Probably a few. İsmet and Rebekah and little Süleyman—İsmet never misses a party. Besides, you're his favorite nephew."

"He's my favorite uncle. He's like you, only not so serious." I squeezed my brother's shoulder, pulling him back from the brink. "I can't help but adore him."

Mehmet snorted. "He's an idiot. Charming, I'll grant you, but a fool. What you and Rebekah see in him I don't understand. He just got fired again."

"Oh, dear."

Looking about for a place to set down his empty tea glass,

Mehmet avoided my eyes. "Not to worry," he said. "Baba will save his ass again."

"He ought to stop fooling himself. Rebekah does a much better job of supporting them than he ever could. She enjoys her work."

Mehmet laughed, a little eruption in his unfathomable mood. Neither of us need bother saying that İsmet would sooner castrate himself and feed his only son to rats than allow his wife—his American wife—so to shame herself. Shameful enough she worked at all. He had never dared admit to his parents that Rebekah had insisted Süleyman, son of a Jewish mother, born in the United States, was a Jew and must have a proper bris. The boy was seven now. Soon enough, his Turkish grandmother would start to lay plans for his sünnet, his Muslim circumcision ceremony, and what would İsmet say then? Süleyman's American grandparents called him Solly.

"Will I like her?" I asked abruptly.

"Who?" Mehmet flinched, still not looking at me. "Rebekah?"

"Ayfer. My future sister."

"Ziya, please, you have to decide that for yourself. Does it matter? It all happened so fast, I don't know anymore how much *I* like her."

When I took the glass from him, Mehmet crossed his arms over his chest, hunched his shoulders. Both my hands were encumbered: I could not embrace my brother. "What's wrong, Mehmetciğim? Tell me what's bothering you. Is it Ayfer?"

"I'm cold." He shuddered elaborately. "It's going to rain—or snow. I'm cold and very tired, Ziya. Let's go in." He turned away.

I followed him. In the main cabin of the ferry were prosperous bureaucrats and businessmen going home for the evening, young people heading for expensive shoreline restaurants. They drank tea or rakı or water, nibbled at toasted nuts, smoked fragrant cigarettes, read their newspapers, magazines, books, listened to the music of their Walkmans, talked, talked, talked. We found seats that were not particularly private but not in the middle of anyone's conversation, arranged our baggage about us. Across the way, two business-suited men in adjacent seats argued politics. The one who despised the prime minister stroked the back of his friend's hand, gentle, as he counted off his points.

"I'm so tired," Mehmet said, leaning back and closing his eyes.

"Aren't you tired, Ziya?" He spoke in English, as we tended to do in a crowd.

"I slept on the plane. Anyway, you're forgetting, I'm eight hours earlier than you, for me it's mid-morning."

"I don't think I've slept for a week. Baba wants to start work in March. I can't seem to pull it together and he can't apply for the permits till I finish."

"Mehmet," I said, "I don't know what you're talking about."

He sighed. "The Bodrum house."

"Oh." My brother was an architect. I didn't know how good his designs were, none had yet been realized—I believed him to be brilliant, but I was his brother. For years, in his mind, on paper, latterly on the monitor of a personal computer, he had been building, tearing down, rebuilding a summer residence for a seaside resort. It was plain—it was made plain—that he intended to demolish our old summer residence in the Aegean resort of Bodrum, a nondescript structure that couldn't be said to possess even a naïve vernacular charm, and make something splendid. "In March?" I asked. I had never brought myself to believe the possibility.

"He wants it finished by June."

That's not enough time, I wanted to say. "Why?"

Mehmet's lips tightened, his eyes began to widen, for an instant he appeared to be about to panic but covered his mouth and coughed thickly instead. I leaned forward. He waved me back, peremptory. "I'm getting married in June," he said after another moment. "Baba and Ana say they want to give us the house. There has to be a house for them to give." He pressed his skull against the back of the seat, lifting his chin. "Of course, we can't live there, I have to be based in the city, Ayfer's work is here, but they keep saying it."

A moment before, "we" had meant my brother and myself—or, stretched to its broadest compass, our family. I stared at my hands. "I thought you were working up a place for them to retire."

"I want a drink." Rising to his feet, Mehmet looked down at me. "Stay here, I'll be right back." As he edged behind, he paused to pat my head, ruffle my hair. "I'm going down for three or five days next week. Would you like to come with me?"

"Of course. I'd love to."

"Ziya." His two hands held my head still, rigid. He spoke in Turkish and I had somehow to translate the little sentence to make sense of it. "Ana's ill." Holding my head, still, he bent to press his cheek against my skull. "That's what's wrong. She wanted to tell you herself. I can't. . . . I am a poor actor."

"That's why you're getting married," I said dully, but he had released me and gone.

I stared for some minutes at my feet in their American black canvas sneakers, lolling unconsidered at the ends of legs clad in American blue denim. The jeans were Levi's, from San Francisco, a city that people who had seen both told me resembled İstanbul. My coat, too, bore an American label, if it had been tailored in Hong Kong. I could not return to my home without carrying the United States on my back. Anyone who saw me would take me for a foreigner. In all my family only my mother and I had blue eyes. Even my undershorts were American—my stylish haircut, my facial hair, my earrings. The four words that ran through my mind were English, pronounced in a broad Massachusetts accent: My mother is dying.

"What is it you're doing?"

I raised my eyes. The man peering at me held a cigarette between forefinger and thumb, squinted through its smoke. "What are you doing?" he asked again.

I thought that I had never seen him before, but he had used informal address as if we were friends. My hands, I realized, were fumbling at the post through my right earlobe. I lowered them to my lap. I had not been able to remove the tight backing; the lobe would be inflamed, the gold shining more brightly in contrast, and I should swab it with disinfectant for who knew what agents of contagion my hands had encountered.

"You don't know me, do you, Ziya," the young man was saying. He took a long drag on his cigarette. "Well, I'm sure I've changed as much as you—I recognized your brother first." He smiled pleasantly as the smoke cleared from around his face. "Cem," he said, as if such a common name should distinguish himself from any other Cem I might have known.

In fact it did. "Cem Arslanoğlu?" I asked and his smile broadened. He had been a boy when I knew him at school, as had I, though he was a year the elder, a year ahead. "You are well?" I asked, taking refuge in formality. I didn't know what to make of him, standing there and genially smiling, smoking. I noted that he was nicely dressed, affluent and informal, clean shaven and barbered. I noted that he wore a plain silver band on his left ring finger. In school he had tried to look like an American; now his models appeared to be European—French or Italian.

"Indeed, indeed. And yourself? I heard you had gone to the United States." Taking a last drag, he looked about for a place to stub out his cigarette, choosing finally the only reasonable choice, the ashtray on the table before me. "May I join you for a moment?"

"Of course."

I looked away as he took a seat, twisting my hands in my lap. His parents and mine were acquainted. In school I had admired him, as small boys are prone to admire larger, for he was tall and broad and handsome, and friendly as only those with no doubts at all can afford to be; he was an athlete and, though not much of a scholar, academically competent. Literally translated, his surname meant *son of the lion*, as if a grandfather had expected just this descendant. One afternoon, inexplicably, Cem had invited me to his house to watch an American movie on his new VCR; his elder brother had brought the tape back from the States, he said, so it was neither dubbed nor subtitled and, he implied with naïve calculation, we might consider watching it an adjunct to our language studies.

Cem's family lived in a luxurious, Western-style apartment on the heights above the Asian shore, near the bridge. The brothers—they were the only children—each had his own room, his own TV and VCR. There was nowhere to sit in Cem's bedroom except on his big bed, reclining side by side in a mound of soft pillows. The movie was inane, slow moving, unexciting. I did not notice at what point Cem's arm lodged in my lower back, when he urged me to lean against his shoulder. I must have dozed off, because it was dim in the room after he closed the blinds and climbed back onto the bed, rocking it. Helping me to sit up and lean against him again, Cem said, "Perhaps this one won't put you to sleep." He lit a cigarette and turned his attention to the screen. I did not notice all at once that he had removed all his clothing except his underpants.

"What was it you were doing?" the grown-up Cem asked again, startling me when I looked to find him fully clothed, lighting another cigarette, ourselves sitting at our ease in the upper lounge of a Bosporus ferry. The second video had been an American pornographic production—heterosexual, needless to say, if featuring a preliminary lesbian entanglement that puzzled and then revolted me. Before I made out much more about the male performer than that he found the women's antics exciting, I had been coaxed out of my own clothes and was unable to see the screen. Cem did not remove his underpants to fuck me, only pulled the elastic down under his balls, as if baring his buttocks might open the possibility of my using them as he used mine.

"I was trying to take out my earrings," I muttered. My reasons had become confused.

Cem smiled amiably. He indicated my luggage and asked, "You're returning from the States?"

"Just for the winter vacation."

"And how long till you come home for good?"

"Three and a half years more as an undergraduate." I shook my head, a gesture that felt immediately wrong, for we were speaking Turkish. "Then I might stay on for a graduate degree." The possibility had not before occurred to me.

"Here's your brother," Cem said, rising to his feet.

Bearing a small tray, Mehmet made his way toward us. I rose to take it from him, saying, "Mehmet, do you remember my friend Cem?" On the tray were two glasses of water-clear liquid, a plastic bottle of water, a dish on which four grape-leaf dolmalar floated in a puddle of green oil, a bowl of shelled nuts. I set it down on the table.

"Not very well, I'm afraid," Mehmet allowed with an apologetic grimace. He shook the hand offered him, politely murmuring, "Merhaba."

Graceful, Cem indicated we should sit. "Why don't we get together one evening while you're home, Ziya?" he said. "I'll give you a call. When do you go back to the States?"

"Mid-January."

"I'll give you a call," he said again. Then, as he turned to leave us, he added, "The earrings suit you. Keep them."

"What was that about?" asked Mehmet. He had poured a little water into one of the glasses, clouding the rakı; as he swirled the glass, the fluid became opaque, milky, the pearly color of a dense Bosporus fog.

I looked after Cem. Already he had disappeared, submerged himself in a group of similarly well turned-out young men. "I was trying to take out my earrings."

"Well, that might be best." Mehmet's tone was thoughtful, judicious. He took a small sip of his rakı. "Baba's likely to think America's turned you effeminate. Sit down, Ziya. Drink. Eat. We'll be home soon."

I sat. I poured water into the rakı Mehmet had brought me, ate a dolma that seemed not as good as those I could get at either of the Turkish restaurants in Boston. "They're not healed yet. I can't take them out, they'd infect."

"Whatever you say." Mehmet blinked mildly. "Why are we speaking Turkish?" he asked, returning to our second language. "I didn't like the way he looked at you."

"Cem?"

"As if he wanted—you know, as if you were a woman in a short skirt, a tourist woman from America or Europe."

"As if he wanted to fuck me?" I took a breath, held it for a moment. "He did once."

Mehmet waved my confession away. "He was the one? But that was long ago, boys fooling around." We were grown up now, he was saying, Cem and I—I was a man, I had hair on my face, it was inappropriate, perverse, for Cem to find me desirable. Still, Mehmet eyed me narrowly a moment longer, taking in again and reconsidering his younger brother's earrings and club-goer's goatee. It is practically an article of faith in Turkey that a man should want his ass never to be penetrated simply because he will find the experience too pleasurable to resist again. Like the needle in the vein, the prick in the rectum—that first sublime rush—leads to abject addiction. Not that ultimate consequences were likely to dissuade the average Turk from taking his opportunity: it wasn't *his* ass, his manhood, in question—though it might well be his cousin's, his nephew's, his brother's. No eldest son, naturally, would ever submit, though it was very nearly expected of the younger. I wondered suddenly, appallingly, if Mehmet had yet had Ayfer, or anybody else, woman or boy or prostitute—if he were a virgin.

"Tell me about Ana," I said.

*   *   *

Ours was a proper Ottoman house, living quarters above, arranged around the başoda, or reception room. My mother rose from the divan under the shuttered windows when, trailing my three brothers, I came up the stairs. Crossing the başoda, house slippers silent on carpet, I stepped up into the wide, shallow, windowed alcove, low divans hugging its three walls. She was not alone—several other women sat at their ease with glasses of tea or wine, and I was aware of having bypassed my father, uncles, men I could not be bothered to recognize—but it was to my mother alone I went and my mother who held out her hands, saying, "Merhaba, Ziya. Welcome home."

She did not appear as frail as Mehmet had led me to fear. When I stepped back from kissing her hands, the startling beauty of her hairstyle might have brought me to comment if I were greeting her after a separation of a few hours only—a trip to the beauty parlor in Nişantaşı. There was no mistaking it for her own hair, nor had I known her to be so expert with cosmetics. "Ana," I said, my voice rough. "Anacığım."

Calmly, she kissed my cheeks. "Say hello to your grandmother, dear."

I turned to my father's mother, who, legs precisely crossed, sat erect on the edge of the divan and did not rise. Her black suit and the pearls at her throat displayed how well she valued her grandson, while a severe expression revealed her disapproval. Kneeling, I took the tiny hand she offered. She flinched a little ostentatiously when my mustache brushed the papery skin, but after I touched her hand to my brow she pushed the fingers into my hair, stroked it. "It is good to see you, torunum. Please, to please an old lady, will you shave in the morning?"

"Of course, Nine, whatever you wish." I looked up. She smiled. "May I keep the mustache?"

Her chin moved slightly. "If you must."

I lowered my eyes. "And your husband's mother, Nine?"

"She is well—very old, but well. Asleep now. You may greet her tomorrow."

Then there was no help for it but to stand and face my father's sister and his brothers' wives, then my mother's sisters-in-law, each exclaiming falsely I was the handsomest, cleverest boy in the family and how had I found America and was it a shock to come home and (I had reached Rebekah and, beside her, small and sleepy and well behaved, Süleyman) did I even recognize my handsome little cousin, how he had grown up in my absence! Grinning fondly, Rebekah would not allow me to kiss her hands but insisted on embracing me, saying, "We have so much to talk about." Süleyman stared at me wide eyed, shook my hand with unnerving dignity that splintered into laughter when I took him around the waist and threw him over my shoulder.

Carrying him, I stepped down into the main area of the başoda and across the richly figured carpet to the end of the room that the men had claimed—that stood in now for the selamlık of a still more traditional house. Nevertheless, all the men being related to all the women, they should have been welcomed into the haremlik, where they would recline on divans and the women serve them. I handed still giggling Süleyman off to his father and turned to my own.

It was my little brothers who had grown up—they were nearly as tall as I, no great feat, and though I recognized them at a distance, identical twins being unusual, up close they seemed nearly to have become men—and my father who had changed. It was he you would take, on first impression, to be ill. His hair had gone completely gray and the new, short, youthful cut did not flatter. He had lost weight. When he smiled the pouchy skin under his eyes wrinkled, when he lowered his chin the slack flesh under his jaw showed how loose it was. "Babam," I murmured, prepared to salute him with proper filial respect, but he threw his arms around me and simply held me for a long moment. A tear fell from his cheek to my neck and slid coolly past my collarbone. He smelled of the lemon cologne bus conductors sprinkle on passengers' hands.

Holding me still about the shoulders, he displayed me to my uncles and male cousins, saying, "Look at my son the American!" The complex pride in his voice distressed me so that I could only mumble, "Merhaba," in the face of all these smiles, affectionate or considering or mocking. Süleyman's father, my mother's brother, who had spent far more time in the United States than I and picked up the mannerism there, winked at me.

"Sacide!" my father called. "Bring your brother something to drink. What will you have, Ziya? Bourbon? Vodka?"

I had been to parties in Cambridge and Boston where men and women mingled easily and the young felt free to argue with their elders. This was Turkey, a Turkish family, and the younger women, my sisters and their cousins, were on the far side of the room, together, apart. Sacide broke free of the group and came toward us across the great expanse of carpet. Her hands were empty, her eyes lowered behind severe spectacles. She wore a plain blouse, a plainer skirt, her beautiful chestnut hair was drawn tightly back into a schoolgirl's braid—she looked at once younger and older than nineteen and I imagined her leaving the house to go to classes, scrubbed face framed as stiffly by a scarf as any Catholic nun's by her starched coif. Behind her, peering across the room from among her cousins and smiling happily for me, Melek in T-shirt and dungarees looked more as I thought a teenage girl should.

"Kardeşim," Sacide said in a low voice without raising her eyes, "what may I do for you?"

"You may kiss your brother," my father said, impatient, "and say hello and welcome home, and get him something to drink."

Flushing a little, Sacide lifted her eyes to my face for only a moment.

"Sacide," I said—it seemed suddenly impossible to call her in turn *kardeş*, sibling. "It's good to see you. You have been well?" Formally, I kissed her warm cheeks without touching her in any other way. "How is *your* first year of college going?" Without the masculine obligation of national service, my sister had begun college in the same month as I. Sacide had expressed no desire to go abroad or even so far away as Ankara or İzmir, likewise scorned Boğaziçi, an American school before it was nationalized. Although it was a third-rate degree factory, conservative and restless, İstanbul University was where the friends from her Koran study group were going. "There is food, I believe," I went on in the face of her disapproving silence, "as well as drink?"

"I will bring it."

"I will come with you—you needn't serve me, Sacide."

After I had greeted my other sister and my girl cousins, when I had a plate of little delicacies and a glass of sour-cherry juice in hand, I was compelled to sit in state as if I were a vezir granting audience to supplicants, in the honored corner of the enclosed balcony above the garden. The men came to me a few at a time and I have no recollection of what I might have said to any of

them. I never had a chance to speak with my mother. Little
Süleyman with his own glass of juice sat beside me, eating from
my plate, until İsmet and Rebekah came to say it was past his
bedtime and they must leave. My little brothers, too, said good
night, and soon after, glancing across the width of the başoda, I
saw that my mother and grandmother both had vanished. My
father and his brothers were arguing cheerfully. Dayı Mustafa,
İsmet's elder brother, talked to me about the hac he had planned
for himself and his wife for the upcoming pilgrimage season. It
seemed I was to add my voice to the chorus attempting to per-
suade his sister and her husband also to go to Mecca and Med-
ina. The words were not spoken but I understood that it would
be my mother's last chance to visit the holy places.

Mehmet had been at my side for some time, quiet. When he
slumped against me and uttered a small snore, Mustafa frowned
and I looked at my watch. It said four o'clock—Boston time. I
could not somehow work out whether it was P.M. or A.M., but I
knew it was not, in Emirgan, noon, and I yawned.

Mustafa shook Mehmet's knee, rousing him, said, "Show your
brother to his bed, nephew. He's tired."

For a very long while I couldn't fall asleep, though my brothers' slow breathing and their warmth nearby comforted me.
Before sleeping themselves, Veli and İzzet had set out fresh pyjamas for Mehmet and me, taken our quilts from the cupboard
inset above the bed platform and spread them out. The boys did
not stir at all when we came in. Mehmet was so groggy he could
hardly unbutton his shirt. I helped him to undress, but when I
tried to help him with his underpants he became sleepily petulant, pushed me aside, and, forgetting his pyjamas, clambered
onto the platform, burrowed into his quilts.

After putting on my own pyjamas, I tidied our clothes away,
then for a few moments simply gazed at my three brothers.
Under his quilts, Mehmet was no more than a long hump, not
even his head showing. The twins lay on their sides, close
together, back to back, sleeping sweetly. Between them and our
elder brother on the broad platform lay my own bedding, and I
wondered how long it had taken them to become accustomed to
my absence, to fill that space. In my dorm at Harvard the very
presence of my roommate annoyed me, and there we had sepa-

rate beds: I wondered how long it would take me to become accustomed again to sleeping among my brothers.

I looked around the room. While I was away İzzet or Veli had tacked up a new poster celebrating their favorite of the İstanbul soccer teams, and I thought a few of Mehmet's renderings pinned to the walls were new; otherwise everything was the same. I glanced at the computer on the long counter: the keyboard was laid out in Turkish fashion, including the letters my American computer lacked but lacking *q, w,* and *x*—although I recalled (a physical memory in the tendons of my hands) the sequences of keystrokes that would call up the foreign characters. Still, I doubted I could touch-type on it. There was a lush volume on Turkish interior design, the text in English and French; there were my younger brothers' mathematics and science and history textbooks, a volume of *The Lord of the Rings* in English, purloined from my bookcase, a slim volume, in Turkish, of Koranic exegesis for youngsters.

There was a blueprint spread out on the inclined part of the desk, its curling ends anchored with scraps of masking tape, annotated with corrections and recalculations in Mehmet's hand. It took me a few minutes' peering to work out that it represented the main floor of the new Bodrum house, an odd melding of Western and traditional Ottoman floor plans that I could not bring together in my head, make three dimensional, raise walls from, walk through. I turned out the lamp.

In darkness, I looked out through a chink in the shutters. The narrow, cobbled street below was palely lit by the moon—the earlier clouds had fled across the strait into Anatolia. In the face of the house across the way a tall, shuttered window showed a horizontal grid of flickering blue light where someone was watching TV. Down the hill where the streets were wider and not closed to traffic, doubtless there was traffic, waterside and meydanı cafés and bars and clubs surely did a certain amount of late-night business even in winter. Turning away, I walked across the room, snuggled into bed between Mehmet and—was it İzzet or Veli? In the dark, I couldn't tell.

"Don't," I said, waking, but didn't at once pull away from my brother's grasp, the defining fact of his hard-on pressed against my pyjama-clad buttocks, the rocking motion of his hips as he rubbed it up and back, up and back. His hot breath smelled of stale rakı and the bristles of his mustache tickled my neck. My own prick, too, was hard—it was morning, I was waking up. "Don't."

"What?" he mumbled sleepily, continuing, not stopping. "It's good. It feels good, doesn't it? I've never hurt you."

"Mehmet!" Shouldering him away, I rolled over, leaned above him, held him down. "Mehmet," I whispered, my voice hard in my throat, "do you do that to my brothers?"

He blinked, coming awake, saw who it was holding him down. "Ziya?"

I pressed my weight into my forearm, into his chest, near his throat. "Do you fuck my brothers, Mehmet?" I wanted to shout, to hit him. "*I've never hurt you*, you said—you've never touched *me*. Was it my brothers?"

"You're hurting me, Ziya," he said, puzzled.

"I'll do more than hurt you—" Enraged, I reached down with my free hand, past the stiff cylinder of the prick trapped against his belly by tight underpants, and tightly grasped his balls, squeezed them together. A shudder rolled through him, and from the abject horror of his expression I knew no one had ever knowingly touched him there.

"Ziya, please!"

"Quietly." I pulled at his testicles, pushing them down between thighs that moved insensibly apart, knowing that that and the slow friction of my arm against his penis would terrify him. "Quietly, Mehmet, they're still sleeping. Is that what you do when I'm gone, pig, fuck my brothers?"

"No!" He tried to take a breath but I pushed more weight into his chest. "No, of course not, I've never put it in, that might hurt them—just what—Ziya, please. . . ."

His cheeks were blotchy, his eyes staring, tearing. When I let up a little, he gasped, then snorted, and mucus came from his nose. "You've never put it in them *yet*," I said, maintaining enough pressure on his chest that he couldn't get up without a struggle and continuing to tug at his balls and rub my forearm against his prick. "You will never touch them again *at all*, do you understand?"

"They didn't ask me to stop," he protested faintly. "I didn't hurt them."

I gave him a particularly sharp tug. "Do you understand what I'll do to you?"

"Don't!"

"How could they ask you to stop? Did you *ask* to start? They're just children, they knew nothing—you're their big brother, they love you, how could they ask you to stop?"

Weary and despairing of the argument—for he was *my* big brother, too, and I loved him—of the threats and the violence, I took my arm from his chest and pushed his underpants down and put my mouth on his cock. It was a good size. I had never seen Mehmet's penis hard and didn't look at it now, only licked it and sucked at it, fondled it with one hand while the other played more gently with his balls. I brought him off quickly, and after my brother's bitter semen had flooded into my mouth, down my throat, I sat up, gazed down into his scared eyes, and deliberately licked my lips. "The next time you need that," I said, "go looking for someone who can say yes as well as no, or take care of yourself."

Veli and İzzet were still sleeping innocently. I got down from the bed platform and went to the bathroom, where, despising myself, I took care of myself, then showered and, using Mehmet's razor and a steady hand, shaved off my mustache and goatee. When I returned to the bedroom he had gone without putting away his bedding.

The boys woke while I was dressing, both at once as they always had. İzzet said, "Ziya!"

"You're really here!" shouted Veli.

"We didn't dream it!"

Tousled and frisky as puppies—big puppies with no notion of the damage they could cause—they leapt on me, and I hugged them to me as if I'd never let them go.

My mother stayed late in bed, and when my father left for the office he said she'd asked for me to come say good morning. "Where's Mehmet?" he asked.

The boys and Melek and I were breakfasting in the gallery off the başoda, shutters open wide and the frost-burned garden below us. Melek had been shocked, pleased when I came down to the kitchen to help. Now she hovered over the cezve on a small brazier and was able to hand our father a little cup of sweet coffee as we spoke.

"He went out early, didn't say where, or when he'd be back."

"Far too early to be visiting Ayfer—I hope!" My father grinned and tossed his chin. "Well, if you see him, tell him I need something to show the permit board by Wednesday next. Good-bye, my dears, till this evening." He turned to leave, but then turned back. "Ziya, you look much better without the fuzz on your face, thank you. Now, about these—" He tugged at one earlobe.

"Babacığım," said Melek, "he's a grown man, let him be. I've seen pictures—in America everyone has earrings, respectable fathers your age, boys as young as the twins. . . ."

Veli hooted with delight.

"Not a thought of it, either of you," my father said sternly, waving as he went down the stairs.

"Thank you, Melek."

Flushed with pleasure at what passed for a victory, Melek grinned. "Sacide Hanım would *not* stop talking about how America had corrupted you. I wish you'd kept the goatee too."

İzzet was stroking his chin, reached to feel his brother's. "*We'll* grow them—"

"—as soon as we can!"

"But no earrings till you're twenty-one," I warned.

"Didn't it hurt," they asked together, "when the needle went in?"

"Of course not." Melek's ears, too, were pierced.

"Whose bodies are covered with soccer bruises? But I'll tell you what did hurt." I leaned in conspiratorially. "Do you want to see my tattoo?"

All three gasped with gratifying shock.

"Promise not to tell any of the grown-ups." Unbuttoning my shirt, I pulled it open at the collar and turned in my seat to show them. The tattoo was innocuous, really, scarcely three centimeters across in red and black inks on my right shoulder blade, the tuğra of Sultan Mahmud II, the great reformer and a man I admired nearly as much for the blazing masculine beauty revealed in official portraits as for his attempting to turn the flow of history. The needles had been sharp, the work delicate at that scale, and the artist had said afterward that of course there were more nerve endings close to the bone than in muscle, if he'd put it on my biceps or chest it would have hurt considerably less, and I could have looked at it myself without a pair of mirrors.

İzzet and Veli naturally wanted to touch it and I let them, shivering under their cool fingertips—the memory of the tattoo man's hands was too recent—but Melek sobered. "You should go see Ana," she said. "Ask her if she'd like me to bring her some breakfast."

"You're right, okay." Standing up, I buttoned my shirt and tugged it straight on my shoulders. I pulled Veli's head against my thigh because he was close enough, and then I went upstairs.

My parents' rooms were on the third floor. They were not the grandest in the house—those had been the domain of İbrahim Bey, my great-grandfather, who had bought the property in the last inglorious days of the empire, and were divided now between his widow and daughter-in-law. My mother's room overlooked the street, not the garden, but it was just high enough that one could almost imagine seeing over the roof of the house opposite and down the hill to a gunmetal dazzle off the Bosporus. I knocked on the door. My mother's voice invited me to enter.

The shutters were still closed, heavy drapes pulled across as well, and only one lamp was on, a dim standard some distance from the big Western-style bed. I could make out that she was there, leaning up against pillows at the headboard, and I saw that someone was with her. "Ana? Günaydın, Ana."

"Good morning, Ziya dear," she said in English, her voice quite strong, the precise accents of her London girls' school clearer than I remembered. "Go along now, Sacide, your brother and I have much to talk about. Thank you, we'll be fine."

"Ana," I ventured, "Melek asked if you'd like her to bring you breakfast."

In Turkish, stubborn, Sacide said, "I'll go right down and bring it up."

"You will not, daughter, and you will please me by exercising the language I have tried very hard to teach you. Quite soon I will get out of bed, come downstairs, and then we can discuss breakfast."

"Yes, Mother," said Sacide submissively enough, but as we approached each other, one going, one coming, her lips were tight and she glared at me as if I were one of Şeytan's trickiest and most loathsome minions. I could not imagine what I had ever done—what I could ever do—to inspire such a look from anyone. It made me feel ill and very small. Smaller when I thought that Mehmet, whom I loved and admired, caught out at something not much out of the ordinary, might have seen such hatred in my eyes. I missed part of what my mother was saying.

". . . so kind to me, and yet she makes me impatient. I fear I don't like your sister very much, Ziya."

"She's grown more rigid, more stubborn." I felt uneasy saying this.

"She has. She has persuasive friends whose ideas I don't approve of at all. But it would go against everything I believe to forbid her to see them. If I could."

"If you were *your* mother you could have sent her to a British boarding school."

My mother laughed for me, a gift, and now I had come close enough to see her in the dusk. She had set aside the hairstyle of the night before, and, it seemed, the hair, wore a kind of turban that appeared to be a blue that would set off her—or my—eyes. Her skin was pale, chalky, but the cheeks flushed. "We have nothing more to say about your sister, a righteous zealot someone must be proud of, I'm sure. Let me look at you." She paused, blinked. Her eyes were very large, liquid, the pupils dilated. "Oh, bloody hell. This *coddling* is making me blind. Ziya, please open the curtains and let in some light. If it's too bright for my wretched eyes"—she laughed again, shortly—"I shall simply put on my extremely expensive sunglasses and imagine I'm Princess Grace of Monaco."

"Ana," I said before I went to the windows, "Mehmet told me."

She sighed gently. "I counted on it. It was cowardly of me not to meet your plane, and vain, but I wanted to welcome you with the serenity and composure of—of Princess Grace, to be at my best, such as it is, and I'm afraid I can't manage it in a crowd."

"You were splendid—"

"I was a mask on a stick. Imagine if you hadn't been warned. Go! Open the curtains!"

As I went, reluctant, she said, "We will dispose of the whole subject now. I'm bored with it. You know, considering how much I smoked, I would have expected it to be the lungs, but it's one of those completely pointless female reproductive cancers." Her voice was brisk, dispassionate, horrifying. "Genetic, apparently—

it killed my grandmother and two of my aunts. Your sisters will have to be wary. It's in Rebekah's family too—God grant she bears no daughters. At any rate, it was caught too late, they cut out of me all those parts a son doesn't care to know about, but the wretched thing had already metastasized. . . . Such a beautiful word, *metastasize*." She pronounced it with relish, repeated it. "Spread: short and to the point."

"Ana," I said, heartsick, unable to look back at her. "When did you know?"

"It's not interesting, Ziya. I wish to talk about you."

The curtains smelled of many years' dust. I drew them wide and pulled open the jigsawed shutters. Thin winter sunlight dazed me, though it was all reflection, no substance, the sun being above the wide eaves.

Behind me, my mother said, "One of the drugs makes me sensitive to light, but really there's no substitute. Come here. Let me look at you."

Scared of what she would see, I hesitated, crimping the fabric of one curtain in my fist, until she said again, "Come."

I could not be as courageous as my mother, whose given name, Alev, means *flame* and who had always dyed her hair to rival her name, who lay there burning so that I could nearly see the heat. The flame would consume all, burn out, leave ash but no coal. I couldn't weep, so I made my lips smile and went to her.

"You did listen to that silly woman," she said lightly, squinting at me. "I was afraid you would. Well, you're still my handsome son and I suppose you can grow it back anytime. You must remember, Ziya, that your grandmother is made happy when her men defy her in small things. Now"—she let the tension around her eyes slip, let her weight settle into the pillows—"tell me about America, about Harvard. How it must have changed since I lived in Radcliffe Quad."

"There are men there now, too, it's just two of the Houses, nobody really wants to live there because it's so far away. Radcliffe doesn't really exist anymore. They call it the Invisible College."

"And yet every year they ask me for money. You know, it's strange, but I truly think, back then, İstanbul was a better place to be a woman. It was much less terrible here for me to want to become a doctor."

I sank down by the bed, resting my arm on the mattress, my head on my arm. "That's why you came back," I said, wanting her to tell me a story.

"Oh, no. I'm sure I should have got a better medical education in Boston. I was set on Harvard Medical."

"Then why?"

Her hand touched my hair. "You know why, Ziya."

"Tell me."

She was silent a moment, then expelled the breath in her throat with a small sound. "My mother and your father are making inquiries about a suitable girl for you, Ziya, now that your elder brother's future is settled. Your father especially needs to feel certain you'll return from America. For myself, I'm not at all sure that you should. I think I've raised—what did they call it in those English fairy tales you used to love? A changeling. That's where we're different, you see, dear. I could be content after leaving the American I thought I loved, could come home and marry your father and grow fond of him." Her hand found mine, patted it. "Poor Harry. He said once that he would convert to Islam if it would please my family, learn Turkish and bring me home. We could never have been happy." Continuing to stroke my hand, she turned it over and grasped it firmly, nearly enough to cause me pain. Her voice was low. "You see, Ziya, I came to understand Harry later. He could not have been happy with any woman."

It was late. Mehmet had not come home all day, but he had called and told Melek that he was at the university, would not return for dinner. In the early afternoon my little brothers and I went out for a walk through the streets of Emirgan and down to the waterfront; as we climbed back up the hill, flurries of snow began to fall. Veli and İzzet walked at my sides, each holding one of my hands. When they happened to mention Mehmet there was no horror in their voices, no overtones but admiration, affection. Back at the house, we found all the women, even my nodding, benign great-grandmother, drinking tea and talking with a young woman I didn't know: Ayfer, my brother's fiancée.

It was late. Everyone had gone to bed, but I had stayed up with a book, saying I was still on Boston time—I would only lie awake and restless, disturbing the boys. I had found a bottle of white wine, domestic but drinkable. If I leaned back against the shuttered windows I felt the cold from outside, but inside it was warm and I sat in the corner of the divan, legs outstretched and my feet bare. The book did not hold my attention and I set it aside gratefully when I heard a noise from below—a key in the lock, the street door opening and closing, winter boots on the stone floor of the entryway as Mehmet crossed it to the bench where he would sit to take them off.

"Is it still snowing?" I asked as he came up the stairs.

He looked up, startled, eyes wide and smile forced, almost hidden under his mustache. "Snow? Did it snow? It rained a little, I think."

"I thought you'd go to the apartment, stay in the city tonight." Reaching down to the floor beside the divan, I grasped the bottle of Çankaya white by the neck and held it up. "Get yourself a glass," I said.

Soon he was seated not very near me on the divan and I had poured wine into his glass and more into mine. I smelled cigarette smoke on his clothes, on his breath. He drank half the wine in his glass at one go, then held it in one hand, stem between his fingers, globe cradled in his palm. "I went to Galata," he said, his voice slow, thick. "I got drunk first. It was a terrible place. It was dirty and it smelled. There were Germans and Japanese, very happy and excited. The Germans argued over the blond woman, was she really blond, really a woman, but the youngest of them went with her. The woman I went with called herself Sevinç—I didn't ask her, she told me. She was pretty. The room stank of perfume. There were stains on the bed, I didn't like to think what they were. She seemed shy of taking off her clothes but I suppose she was just acting. I told her I didn't want to fuck her and she said what did I want, then. Your mouth, I said—I didn't know the words. Well, then, lie back, open your trousers, she said, let me try. It was horrible. It scared me. *You* scared me, Ziya. She—Sevinç—she apologized, said it wasn't her special skill, men who wanted that usually asked for one of the boys, didn't I want to fuck her instead. How could you do that to me, Ziya?" Raising eyes that were black with moisture, unhappy, puzzled, Mehmet swallowed. "You're not like that."

I hardened my heart—not a figure of speech available to me in the language we were using, but still I felt the chill, solid lump in my chest. "I'm exactly like that, Mehmet, except I want the other man to make love to me as well."

He dropped his head again, unready to be forgiven if I were ready to do it.

"You're not a man who'd screw his twelve-year-old brothers, I thought."

"It's not that way," he muttered. He gulped at his wine. "It's play. They play like that together, İzzet and Veli. That's how it started. I woke up one morning, they were doing that, Veli humping İzzet—it made me excited. They didn't mind when I joined in. But I didn't—I would never hurt them, Ziya."

I took a sip of my own wine, astringent as semen. I could imagine it all too easily. Continuing to stare implacably at Mehmet, his head still bent, I said nothing. Ripples ran through the wine in his glass with the trembling of his hand.

"Even when they asked, I didn't even want them to see it . . . my prick." He lifted his glass as if to drink, but only gazed into it.

"Who did this to you?" he asked abruptly. "Who made you like this, Ziya? What you did—it was horrible."

"What if I hadn't wanted to hurt you and scare you and make you stop? If it was a man I wanted, who wanted me, it could be splendid." I wanted him to understand. "It's not that what you did might make them effeminate, make them crave being fucked so they grow up stunted. It's that they have no say. It's that you're fourteen years older and they're just kids."

Turning his face away, Mehmet drank from his glass.

"Mehmet, kardeşim, I haven't changed." Suddenly I had understood what it was I had done. My hands trembled and I wanted to snap the stem of my glass between them, to strike out with the sharp, slivery fragments—to cut something. I couldn't balance it out: had I preserved my little brothers, those big, happy boys, from abuse, or had I poisoned my elder brother's regard for me when I made him come in my mouth, when I swallowed it? Careful, I reached out and set the glass on the low table before me; glass rang against hammered brass. I stood up. "I'm going to bed."

"Wait." The one short English word. I remembered that I had read that word before I ever had to say it, when I was five or six.

Somehow I already knew its homonym, *weight*, and it never occurred to me they might be pronounced the same: I had made it rhyme with *white*. "Wight!" I called to my big brother, showing off, chasing after him as fast as I could on my little-boy legs, "wight for me, Mehmet, I want to play." Wait, he said. Weight.

THE DEATH OF JACKIE KENNEDY

GREG JOHNSON

Thomas Jefferson Sadler came out of the closet in 1993, a few months before his father died. It shouldn't have surprised him that his mother insisted on connecting the two events, pointing out that only a month after Thom sprang his awful news on the family, Thom's father began experiencing vertigo and uncharacteristic mood swings and eerie, intermittent headaches at the base of his skull. He was soon diagnosed with a malignant brain tumor and given six months to live. It was Lucille who kept using the word "sprang," as though Thom, for all his twenty-nine years, had been craftily saving up this piece of ugly information, waiting for the moment when it might bring the most sorrow and disorder to the family.

In fact, Thom had wanted to tell his parents throughout his twenties—he had come out to himself in high school; to his sister, Abby, the night before he went off to college—but his mother's volatile temperament and his own disinclination to make waves had kept him quiet. He'd chafed at the sense of confinement, the awkwardness and dishonesty of the old-fashioned "double life" that had never suited him and was now out of sync with the times. Clinton was president, gay movies were box-office hits, the talk shows Lucille watched religiously every morning decried homophobia with a shrill self-righteousness that Thom found almost unpleasant. Yet he'd lingered in the closet, hesitating. Two years earlier he'd vowed that he'd come out before his thirtieth birthday—which then had seemed comfortably distant—and when he'd finally told his parents, almost matter-of-factly, on the Sunday after Thanksgiving, as they were digesting their leftover turkey and dressing out in the den, it certainly couldn't be said that he "sprang" from the closet. If anything, he later felt that he'd come tiptoeing, or creeping, or even crawling out.

They were watching a Falcons game, and during a commercial Thom had reached shakily for the remote control and pressed the Mute button. "Mother? Daddy?" he'd said. His parents sat on their overstuffed floral-print sofa, and from the other side of the room Thom felt as though he were gazing at them across the Sahara. He and Abby were sitting together, on a loveseat that matched the sofa; afraid he might chicken out, he hadn't told his sister today was the day, but it was obvious that she knew. He felt her body stiffen, seeming to retreat to her side of the loveseat.

From their usual positions on the sofa, Thom's parents stared at him: his lanky father half sitting, half reclining, his head propped by cushions, Lucille prim and erect on the other end. Lucille had paused in her crocheting, a hobby that soothed her nerves. "Yes, honey?" she said blankly. Thom's father had offered the same polite, unreadable look he gave to anyone who requested his attention; he'd worked as a loan officer at a downtown bank for more than thirty years. Then five or six seconds passed—easily the longest silence Thom had ever lived through—and then, in a creaky, closeted voice, he told them.

It was over before the commercial had ended. (He would never forget: a Budweiser ad featuring male athletes flanked by bosomy blond models, three or four women for each man.) There was another silence, and Thom wondered whether he should press the Mute button again: whether they might simply continue watching football, as though nothing had happened.

His mother's reaction was predictable enough. She stood, white-faced; fled into the kitchen; returned immediately and dropped onto the sofa; burst into tears. She denied ("You're confused, that's all"); she took the blame ("I was too young when I had you, and I was a smoker then, too"); she sent the blame boomeranging back at him ("You're enjoying this, aren't you—ruining our holiday weekend like this. In fact, ruining it for the rest of our lives. Our turkey day will never be the same, Thomas

Sadler!"). At this last, all too characteristic remark, Thom's sister—who had sat quietly beside him through all this, staring into her lap—gave a brief, sputtering laugh.

Lucille gaped in horror. "Abigail!"

"I'm sorry, Mom," Abby said quickly, putting a contrite expression on her face, "I didn't mean to laugh. It's just the way you phrased it—"

"I should have known!" Lucille cried, her round blue eyes bubbling again with tears. "The two of you have always sided against me—*always*. Why, I wouldn't be surprised if you'd put your brother up to this!"

Thom took a deep breath. "Mother," he said gently, "that really doesn't make a lot of sense."

Lucille didn't hear. "You've always enjoyed tormenting me, you two!"

They knew better than to contradict her. It was always best to let her rave, let her get everything out of her system. What affected Thom far more keenly than Lucille's histrionics was his father's reaction. As Thom delivered the news, his father had bravely maintained the open, nonjudgmental facial expression he must have used every day at the bank. Thom might have been some shirtless teenager with a pierced nose and electric blue hair, brashly requesting a million-dollar loan to launch his career as a rock star; the reserved Southern gentleman in George Sadler forbade so much as a creased brow or a dubious shake of his head. Yet Thom had glimpsed something in his father's gray, placid gaze: a clouding of the eyes, a look of closure that put Thom in mind of a bank vault, its massive gray steel door soundlessly and irrevocably sliding shut.

Before Lucille, gape-mouthed in shock after Thom's announcement, had uttered a word, his father had said quietly, "Thanks for telling us, son," his lips forming a brief, rueful smile. Then Lucille had started in, and for the next few minutes Thom's father had stared silently at the silent TV set. The game had been scoreless but Thom, his own eyes grazing the screen, noted that Detroit had just scored a touchdown. Atlanta was losing.

Shortly after New Year's his father fell ill, and Thom started spending more time around the house. His parents had bought their place in 1965, the year after Thom was born, and until he left for college it was the only home he knew. A comfortable four-bedroom ranch in Sherwood Forest, an in-town neighborhood that had become unexpectedly trendy in the late eighties and nineties, his parents' house was one of the few that had not changed hands, suffered a "sparkling renovation," and been resold for an unbelievable sum. Thom's father had often insisted he would never sell; he remodeled only as needed—an updated kitchen when Thom was a teenager, a new roof several years later—and he liked to remark that when he left this house, it would be feet first. Driving slowly through the neighborhood during his frequent visits that winter, Thom endured sudden throes of nostalgia. As a boy, he'd loved the storied names of the neighborhood streets—Little John Trail, Lady Marian Lane, Friar Tuck Road—and had raced with his friends along the untrafficked pavement and through the flat, enormous lawns that were never quite so green these days (or so it seemed) as in his boyhood memories. When he was seven or eight he had played Robin Hood to his sister's Maid Marian, loping ecstatically among the towering backyard oaks and pines on a stick horse (made by his father at his basement worktable), wearing a green chintz cape his mother had fashioned from leftover drapery fabric. As an adult, he seldom saw kids playing outside: most of the renovated places were bought by affluent, childless couples or gay men. The elaborately landscaped front lawns were now dotted with placards warning of security systems, and the lawns themselves were tended not by white-legged dads jauntily riding their mowers but by professional crews arriving in large trailer-trucks with three or four men who cut, clipped, trimmed, blew, and departed after less than an hour.

Lucille sometimes complained that she no longer knew her neighbors and that maintaining the house was too exhausting—she had steadfastly refused to hire cleaning help, hating the idea of "strangers in the house"—but on the two or three occasions when Thom had suggested his parents might consider a condo, she had shrieked in disbelief. "Why, those are nothing more than glorified apartments—we might as well just move to an old folks' home as buy one of those little cubbyholes!" Then she would point out they were still a *family*, after all, and Thom was welcome to move back home any time it suited him. "Your sister seems to like it here," Lucille would say, airily. "You haven't seen *her* moving off by herself." Lucille had complained that when Thom went to college, he'd chosen Mercer only as an excuse to move out of the house. There were plenty of good schools right here in Atlanta, after all; he could have gone to Emory, as Abby had done. For once, Lucille's paranoid suspicions were correct, but of course Thom knew better than to tell his mother that, and after moving back to the city four years later, he'd evaded her petulant queries: What was the point of renting an apartment, instead of reclaiming his perfectly good boyhood room? He did intend to *visit* his family once in a while, didn't he, since he lived just a few miles away? Though Thom came to dinner every Sunday night and often stopped by on weekdays, his visits were never frequent enough or long enough to suit Lucille. Vague sarcasm had become her primary means of holding the feet of her prodigal son to the fire. "Guess we're not as fascinating as your Virginia-Highland friends," she would say, following him to the front door. His father and Abby would smile at him, shaking their heads. "Thanks for granting us an audience!" Lucille would call out, as he hurried down the sidewalk to his car.

Once his father had become bedridden, however, Lucille had grown strangely silent. Thom visited every day for several hours, giving Abby a breather so she could have a date or study in the university library, and at times his mother sent him long, sad-eyed looks that seemed to suggest—if only for a moment—some measure of gratitude. Throughout January and February his father's condition slowly worsened, though in their mother's presence Thom and Abby maintained the fiction that he might eventually recover. Their family doctor, along with a neurologist colleague, had conferred with all four of them and told them the truth, but within days Lucille behaved as if the meeting had never taken place. "He'll be fine, they've just been working him too hard down at the bank," she would say, nodding. "It's a stress reaction, I think—another week or two of rest and he'll be good as new. Don't you think so, Abby? Thom?" Her children nodded, not knowing what else to do. Sometimes Lucille sat with her husband in the master bedroom, watching her talk shows and providing him with a running commentary as though he knew what she was saying, but she spent most of the day in the den and kitchen, following her usual routine while Thom or Abby tended to their father.

Not surprisingly, neither of his parents had referred again to their son's announcement a few months earlier. After Lucille's fit of lamenting and lambasting had gone on for half an hour, Thom's father had given her a quick, sharp look, said, "That's enough, Loo," and turned back to the football game. That was all it took. Within minutes his mother, too, had gotten absorbed in the game, perching on the edge of her seat and squealing excitedly whenever the Falcons were close to scoring. Thom later supposed that he shouldn't have made the announcement in the first place. Like certain of his friends, he should have allowed the matter to remain an open but undiscussed fact of his life, like a wart on his nose that no one in a good Southern family would be rude enough to mention. Even Lucille, with her limitless capacity for denying the obvious, had years ago stopped inquiring whether Thom was "dating anyone," or thinking about "settling down"; and when he'd moved in with Geoff in the spring of 1988, and began bringing him along to family dinners, she behaved with the same effusive, almost hysterical politeness a mother often adopts toward her son's unacknowledged lover.

In private, though, her complaints about her children—she hauled them both into the same net, as usual—grew equally shrill. Outside their mother's earshot, Thom and Abby coped with the stress of their father's illness by reverting to the nicknames—John-John and Caro—they'd used during their teenage years. They were teenagers, in fact, when Lucille last compared them unfavorably to the Kennedy siblings; but whenever their mother exulted over Caroline's fruitful marriage ("Such a distinguished, handsome hubby she's got, and those adorable kids, and look, now she's written a book, too!") or John's good looks ("Isn't he the most gorgeous young man you've ever seen? No wonder he goes out with movie stars"), they felt the sting of inadequacy no less keenly.

About a year earlier, at the dinner table, Thom had dared to joke about the Kennedy children. "He might be handsome," he'd said, winking across the table at Abby, "but I guess he isn't brilliant. How many times did he flunk the bar exam?"

"He passed it the third time!" Lucille protested. "Those tests are hard, I'll bet."

(Thom particularly enjoyed this little dig: when he'd gotten his real estate license, his mother had not even congratulated him. "Real estate?" she'd said, wrinkling her nose, the night he'd announced his career plans. "Oh, honey, you can do much better than *that*.")

"And poor Caroline," Thom went on, as Abby lifted one palm to her mouth and pretended to cough. "She didn't exactly inherit Jackie's looks, did she?"

"Why, she's a lovely young woman!" Lucille cried. "Always so well groomed and polite. You should have seen her on *Good Morning, America* last week, talking about her book. What a lovely hairstyle she had!"

Abby's hand drifted toward her own thin, rather styleless auburn hair, her fist clenched slightly as though prepared to pull out a handful.

"I guess you could say she's *cute*," Thom said, with an air of magnanimous allowance. "Or maybe your word is better, Mom. 'Well-groomed' is good. Very tactful."

"Well, compared to Amy Carter or Chelsea Clinton, Caroline Kennedy is practically Garbo," Lucille said smugly.

Thom and Abby both laughed in surprise.

"Score one for Mom," Abby had told her brother.

Flushed with victory, Lucille had added: "And I know a young man who'd be lucky to find someone just like her." She fixed her cool, triumphant gaze somewhere beyond Thom's shoulder, as though willing Caroline's twin to materialize behind him.

That had been the moment—he had just turned twenty eight—when Thom had made the vow to come out before he was thirty. He'd longed to say, "Oh no, Mom, I'd much rather find someone like John-John," but had to bite his lip instead. He supposed it was just as well. The very notion of a gay John-John would have fallen upon Lucille's world-view like the A-bomb.

Nowadays Thom and Abby contented themselves with private jokes, Thom murmuring in his sister's ear, "You're looking very *well-groomed* this evening, Caro," when she came downstairs after primping for one of her dates, or Abby catching Thom when he'd paused before the oval mahogany-framed mirror in the foyer: "Don't worry, John-John, you're still the sexiest man alive," she said smartly, passing by. They seized whatever scant opportunities for humor came their way, falling easily into the

teasing banter of their adolescence, as if their father were laboring at one of his woodworking projects downstairs—a bluebird
house for Lucille, another bookshelf for the Civil War collection
he kept in the den—instead of vegetating in his bed; as if their
mother were handling all this with maturity and good humor
instead of alternating between outright denial and the occasional
outburst of self-pitying emotion that were rendering a painful
situation almost unbearable. One night in early February, as the
three of them were sitting over a quick meal Abby had whipped
together—roast chicken, baked potatoes, a Caesar salad—
Lucille suddenly dropped her fork.

"You know, your father is three years younger than I am," she
announced, tears welling in her eyes.

"We know that, Mom," Thom said, trying to keep an edge of
impatience from his voice. Abby had already shot him a pleading
look.

"I always assumed he'd outlive *me*," Lucille went on. "I wasn't
going to be like your Grandmother Allan, stuck off by herself in
a nursing home with a hundred other old widows. My husband
was young and strong, and he never got sick. Do you children
remember his *ever* being sick, when you were growing up?"

Thom remembered a couple of times, but there was no point
in mentioning them.

"Just try not to upset yourself," he said.

"I wasn't supposed to end up all alone!" his mother cried. "I'd
have my husband, and I'd be surrounded by grandchildren, too."
She cast quick, accusing looks at both Thom and Abby. "I was
going to have a happy old age—I *always* thought that. I never
worried about it, not for one minute."

Thom longed to point out that *always* believing something
hardly made it so, but at that moment Lucille put both palms
over her face and began to sob.

Variations of this scene had recurred throughout the winter. It
was usually Abby who took their mother in hand, gentling her
into an easy chair in the den, providing little comforts—a cup of
hot cocoa, a box of tissues, a new magazine or catalogue that had
arrived in the mail—and murmuring close to Lucille's ear until
their mother's sobs gave way to intermittent sniffles and finally
to a semblance of calm. For his part, Thom would clear the
dishes or do other chores that normally fell to Abby, instructing

himself that he really should visit more often, that his sister should not bear the larger burden of caring for their parents simply because she lived at home while Thom, as Lucille would put it, had absconded. He would like nothing more, of course, than to abscond altogether, but that fantasy occasioned a massive sense of guilt that in turn lent an anxious compulsiveness to his almost daily visits. After showing a listing in Midtown or Buckhead, Thom would drop by the house on his way back to the office, chatting with the male attendant—a nursing student at Emory—who tended their father from ten to four, feeding him lunch and changing his bed linens and taking him for brief, clumsy walks through the house and, when the weather was warm enough, around the backyard. Outside, their father often stopped and sat for a while (so touchingly, to Thom) in the wooden bench he'd made himself, overlooking the small garden he'd tended for almost three decades, now a sad-looking mass of desiccated yellow pansies that no one had the heart to replace. It was the nursing student, Jason, a tall, freckled boy in his mid-twenties with crew-cut reddish hair (meeting him the first day, Thom had noticed with a brief, familiar pang that he wore a wedding ring) who had informed him briskly of a recent change in the routine of his father's care.

They'd just emerged from the bedroom, late one afternoon, after standing for a while at the foot of his father's bed, watching as he nodded off during the five o'clock news. In the hall, Jason had touched Thom's forearm.

"Were you aware that your dad is incontinent? Your sister—she seemed to think you didn't know."

At first, Thom had thought he'd said "incompetent," and he simply stared. "What do you mean?"

"He's been holding it pretty well, waiting till I led him to the bathroom, but yesterday I got here and the bed was completely soaked. I told your sister, and she put a supply of Depends in the linen closet. So in the evenings, you guys will have to change him."

Thom gaped in horror.

"It's really not that big a deal," Jason said awkwardly, glancing away. "You'll get used to it, and he's pretty good about helping. Number two is what's tough, of course. But it's just what you'd do—" Jason stopped himself, embarrassed.

"Go ahead," Thom said. "It's all right."

"I just meant—it's the same as with a baby. You got any kids?"

That night, Thom had told Abby that he'd try to handle the diapering on his own; if an accident happened after he left for the evening, he'd be glad to come back. Abby looked guilty but grateful. "Thanks," she said. "I haven't had to do it, yet. Mom did it the first night, and then Jason. . . ."

"You shouldn't have to do that," Thom said gallantly, wondering if Abby had ever glimpsed their father's nakedness when they were kids. Thom, of course, had accompanied him into the men's changing room at the beach, and a couple of times had blundered into the bathroom as his father was emerging from the shower. But he doubted that Abby had suffered such an encounter, just as he'd never encountered Lucille, even as a small boy, in anything more revealing than a bra and panties, glimpsed once or twice when her bathrobe had fallen open. The thought of seeing anything more now chilled his blood.

"Really, don't worry—I'll take care of that. You shouldn't have to deal with that."

"Thanks," Abby said, trying to smile it off. "I can make sure we don't run out of diapers, at least."

"Don't worry," Thom said again, his voice strained with a sudden, wrenching emotion he couldn't have named. "I'll protect you from that."

But he was wrong. Two days later, they took their father for his bimonthly visit—along with Jason, who shared with Thom the task of maneuvering his father in and out of the car, the elevator, the examining room—and after the exam the neurologist had left their father with Jason and had herded Thom, Abby, and Lucille into his office for yet another brief, predictable conference. The doctor, a slender, silver-haired man in his fifties who kept his eyes trained on Lucille, probably because Lucille insisted on staring up at the ceiling, delivered the usual bleak news and even bleaker prognosis in a smooth, sibilant voice that always made Thom feel drowsy. The tumor grew steadily larger, Dr. Jansen said; there was nothing that could be done, or should be done; it was only a matter of months, or possibly weeks; his functions would continue to deteriorate, but he could certainly stay at home; if they could no longer deal with him at home, he could certainly recommend an appropriate facility; though there was nothing to be done, they were welcome to call him if they had any questions or concerns. At least there was no pain, no discomfort of any kind, and he hoped they took consolation in that. . . . Thom nodded, trying to pay attention. Trying to stay awake. During their first couple of conferences the doctor had brought X rays along, but since no one showed much interest, he now came to the meetings emptyhanded. After asking if they had any questions—and they didn't—he'd herded them back out again, and Thom and Jason maneuvered Thom's father back inside the car.

"I know he's a little better this week than last week," Lucille said from the backseat, as Thom slowly drove them home. "All their fancy tests don't show it, maybe, but I can tell."

Thom and Abby stayed silent, but Jason said agreeably, "You never know, Mrs. Sadler. Sometimes the docs know less than we do."

Later that night, after Jason went home, they all sat in the den, watching one of those dismal TV movies Lucille loved. Lindsay Wagner kept getting beaten up by her husband, and spent most of the movie gazing at her own bruised, sad-eyed face in the bathroom mirror, or holding a telephone and listening with a bruised, sad-eyed expression while her mother or her best friend urged her to leave. "But I . . ." Lindsay kept saying. "But I can't . . ." Thom tried to follow the plot but his attention kept straying to his father, whom he and Abby had helped into his recliner, as they often did after their father had enjoyed what Lucille called a "good day." For her, a good day meant that her husband had seemed to recognize her, or had put together a few words that Lucille could interpret as a coherent thought and thus a sign of improvement. "He asked for the newspaper!" she'd announced one afternoon, the moment Thom opened the front door, but in the bedroom Thom saw that the paper lay askew across his father's lap, parts of it fallen to the floor. His facial expression never changed: the kindly, pale-gray gaze (Thom's fondest image of the man his father had been) had turned glassy and faraway, his well-chiseled Sadler mouth dragged downward on one side so that the left shoulder of his pajama shirt was often wet with drool. Now, watching his father, Thom imagined him performing a duet with Lindsay Wagner, saying "But I . . . But I can't . . ." though Thom doubted his father felt any such frustration or, in fact, felt anything at all.

Around ten-thirty, Thom stretched his arms and said, "Well, we'd better get Dad into bed, don't you think? Then I need to be shoving off."

Lucille looked over, blinking. "What? Don't you want to see how it turns out?" She bent toward her husband's reclining form, speaking a bit more loudly as though he were merely hard of hearing. "You want to finish the movie, don't you, George?" She was nodding vigorously. "Look, his eyes are glued to that screen."

Abby and Thom sat side by side on the big, cushiony sofa their mother had reupholstered, along with the loveseat, about once a year. Now it was a bright pink-and-green floral that pestered the edges of Thom's vision and clashed energetically with the blue velour Barcaloungers in which his parents sat. He felt something on his knee: a little pat from Abby's slender, ringless hand.

"Another half hour won't hurt," she murmured. "You can go if you want. Mom and I can get him into bed."

"Oh, that's all right. I'll stay," Thom said quickly. He gave a vague smile and shrug, aimed at placating his mother. After he'd suggested he might leave, a commercial had come on and Lucille had sat there scowling as though he'd uttered an obscenity. When the movie resumed she turned back eagerly to Lindsay Wagner, who now sat in a courtroom looking bruised and sad-eyed in front of a sympathetic black woman judge, and Thom exhaled slowly. For some reason he'd been holding his breath.

When the movie ended, Thom and Abby rose at the same moment and approached their father; his eyelids were drooping, but he hadn't yet dozed off.

"Ready for bed, Daddy?" Abby said gently.

Lucille had stayed in her chair. "You're leaving already?" she asked Thom. "Don't you want to watch the eleven o'clock news?"

Thom and Abby had become adept at handling their father. Each would cup a hand under one hip, and as they lifted him— one of them calling out a cheery "Alley-oop!"—their father would put his arms around his children's shoulders and help pull himself to a standing position. But this time, as soon as they reached down for him, both drew back their hands. Their father had wet the chair, soaking through his pajamas and bathrobe; Thom saw a dark, circular stain on the seat cushion. For a moment he was rendered mute, but Abby said quickly: "Sorry, Daddy, I shouldn't have kept refilling your lemonade." Then, trying to make a joke: "One glass is your limit."

No one laughed. Thom remembered that during the movie Abby had topped off their father's glass several times. Dipping his head toward a straw and drinking was one of the few tasks he could still perform on his own.

Now Lucille had risen, but she hung back a step or two, peering over Abby's shoulder.

"You mean he's wet himself? Out *here?*"

"It's okay, Mom," Abby said. "Thom and I can handle it."

"But George, if you needed to—" Though tact wasn't Lucille's strong point, she stopped herself, staring helplessly down at her husband. To Thom's relief, his father didn't look even slightly uncomfortable or embarrassed. With the same mild, amiable expression as always, he gazed up at his wife and children as if happy to see them hovering there but not quite sure what they wanted.

As usual, it was Abby who took the situation in hand. She urged Lucille back into her chair, suggesting she watch the news while they got Daddy into bed. "Okay, you ready?" Abby asked Thom, and again they reached down, this time grasping his waist instead of his hip, hauling him upward with a louder and cheerier "Alley-oop!" than usual. For some reason, Thom laughed. His father, one arm hooked around Thom's neck, looked vaguely at his son, his own smile broadening. His lips parted as though to speak, then closed again. Hobbling, Thom and Abby crossed the den with their father, whose step seemed to grow weaker and more halting each day; before long, Thom knew, he and Jason would have to carry him. Tonight they got him down the hall and into their parents' bedroom without much trouble, Abby murmuring gently into their father's ear as they negotiated each new turn. When they reached the bed, Abby told Thom, "Hold him there for a sec, okay?" and then she hurried into the bathroom and emerged seconds later with a stack of towels. She unfolded them deftly, placed them on the bed, and with Thom's help they lowered their father to a sitting position, plumping the two pillows between his back and the headboard.

Abby straightened and said, "Okay, now we've got to undress him."

"Honey, that's all right," Thom said quickly. "I can do it. Or Mom can help me, if I can't."

Abby bent to Thom's ear, whispering. "Mom's had enough— she sort of broke down today, before you got here. I don't think she can handle much more."

Thom glanced anxiously down at his father, but his eyelids had begun drooping again; clearly, he couldn't hear them, and even if he could hear, he probably didn't comprehend. It had been weeks since his father had seemed to understand a word Thom said to him, and more than two months since he'd uttered his own last words.

Thom took a deep breath. "Okay, then."

They undressed him slowly and with a surprising skill, as if they'd been doing this all their lives. They unhooked the old burgundy-flannel bathrobe from his feebly lifted arms, and with a nurse's efficiency Abby unbuttoned his pajama top and slipped it off his narrow, sloping shoulders. Folding up the robe, Thom smelled the sharp odor of urine, and now he gazed at his father's body: the thin, sunken chest, the mottled chalk-white flesh hanging loosely from his arms and stomach. Abby had taken one of the towels and dabbed her father's belly and groin; matter-of-factly she undid the pajama bottoms and swiftly pulled them along the length of his pale, near-hairless legs. Feeling helpless and incompetent next to her, Thom watched as Abby swabbed and prodded their father's body with the towel, her hair hanging down as she worked so that Thom couldn't see her face. Yet he sensed her determined, almost grim absorption in her task.

Their father endured all this with his affable half-smile, apparently feeling no sense of indignity or shame, only a kind of patient and childlike befuddlement. Abby finished cleaning him up—she daubed his penis and scrotum without hesitation, with her same efficient thoroughness, while Thom stood there holding his breath—then went to the linen closet and returned with a clean diaper.

"Should we take him to the bathroom first?" Thom asked. "Maybe he needs to go again."

Now she did hesitate. "You think so?"

"Well, all that lemonade . . ." Thom smiled wryly. "What's that expression? If life hands you lemons . . ."

Abby's hand flew to her mouth, a gesture Thom remembered

from their teenage years. She and Thom were always laughing at "inappropriate times," according to Lucille. Thom was glad their mother had stayed in the den, since he and Abby were now giggling uncontrollably.

"And if life hands you lemonade," Abby got out, "then you make water. Right, Daddy?"

Smiling, their naked father looked back and forth between his two laughing children as if eager to share the joke.

Thom and Abby lifted him from the bed and helped him to the bathroom, each supporting him on one side, giving way to a new spurt of giggling at every misstep. When they reached the toilet, their father urinated like an obedient child, and after helping him back into bed they arranged and fastened his diaper, eased his limbs into clean pajamas, adjusted his pillows and blankets. Their urgent need to laugh had vanished as quickly as it came, but also gone were the awkwardness and discomforting melancholy Thom had felt a few minutes before. The moment their father's head touched the pillow, his eyes had closed and his mouth had fallen ajar. He was sleeping peacefully. Thom and Abby kissed his forehead and went to the doorway. Like fond young parents, they glanced back at the bed and, assured that all was well, put out the light and quietly shut the door.

As the doctors had predicted, George Sadler deteriorated slowly. March passed, and April; by the middle of May, he was semi-comatose but still at home, attended in these last days by several home-care nurses, middle-aged women who came and went in regular shifts. As usual, it was Abby who arranged everything, did the hiring, spoke with the doctors and pharmacists and insurance people. When Thom asked what had happened to Jason, she'd merely shrugged. "Quit," she said. Thom felt disappointed and oddly hurt but hadn't pressed his sister for details. Dropping by the house several times each day, he spoke politely to the various nurses but couldn't keep their names straight, much less their constantly changing schedules. For Thom, the only real constant was his father, lying motionless in bed, surrounded on all sides by flower arrangements sent by his friends from church and from the bank. Making his way toward the bed, Thom felt himself struggling through the oversweet stench of the roses, gladioli, and chrysanthemums that multiplied daily around the bed, their sensual and riotous life seeming to crowd out his father's, like bright and unruly children. Or so Thom imagined, feeling a vague sickness to his stomach that he blamed on the flowers. He'd have liked to take them all outside and toss them into the dumpster.

Sitting quietly next to the bed while his father slept, Thom kept pushing away his recurrent sense of déjà vu: for all the rituals of the sickbed, the pragmatic details surrounding fatal illness, and even his emotions were essentially the same as during Geoff's final bout with AIDS. This troubled him. His father and Geoff were sharply divergent personalities, they bore relationships to Thom that were completely dissimilar, so how could his emotions be the same? The anxiety, the fear of coming grief, the anger and helplessness and even the self-pity, which he allowed its full, harrowing force—how could they be the same? Certainly the illness itself was different, though Geoff had finally died of a brain disease, too, a raging viral infection that proceeded with such merciful swiftness that he'd lived only a few days in the twilight state Thom's father had inhabited now for months. Geoff had been hospitalized once with a case of pneumocystis so virulent he almost choked to death, and once with a stomach virus that had ravaged his entire system. So, on that Friday in spring 1989 when he'd complained of a dull but persistent headache, they hadn't thought much about it. In his logical, decisive way, Geoff had decided to wait until Monday before calling his doctor; he'd begun to feel that he bothered her too often, complaining of ailments that turned out to be minor or even—it *was* possible—imaginary. Thom's lover had a CPA's methodical, almost grave tendency to figure the odds and act accordingly, distrusting mere impulse, and as usual, Thom had kidded him: "I thought you had no imagination. I thought you were proud of that." Geoff had performed one of his dry smiles; then he leaned across—they were sitting on the den sofa—and gave Thom a peck on the cheek. "But I can't discount the possibility," he said. He cupped his hands and raised them, doing his dead-on impression of President Bush. "That wouldn't be prudent. *Wouldn't be prudent.*"

Thom laughed, but by Saturday night Geoff's headache had reached migraine proportions and Thom had called the doctor himself. On Sunday, in his hospital bed, Geoff complained that his vision was wavering—"It's like I'm seeing you through water"—and that night he developed a fever that reached 104, causing even the eminently sane Geoff to talk out of his head. Or so Thom had thought. "I need the Baxter file, the Baxter file," Geoff kept saying, raising up on one elbow with a wild, unfocused look in Thom's direction. Geoff died two days later, but it was months before Thom accidentally learned, in a conversation with one of Geoff's co-workers, that the "Baxter file" was one of Geoff's most important and problematic business accounts. Geoff had fallen sick and died in early April, in the raging heart of tax season.

The shell-shocked aftermath of Geoff's death: a period of numbed, thoughtless routine during which Thom showed and sold houses during the day, watched television and saw his friends after work, and visited his parents and Abby on weekends, imagining he'd stumbled accidentally into someone else's life and didn't quite know what he was doing. The pain he took in small doses (alone at night, or driving in his car), like a bottle of hateful medicine he must sip and sip over months, years, until every drop was gone. As time passed, he chided himself for not having "come out"—the phrase had a superficial ring, during such grief—when Geoff was alive, but when he'd told his parents about the pneumonia, and the viruses, he hadn't spoken the word *AIDS* and neither had they. He knew they must be worried about his own health, and when Abby had asked quietly, one afternoon when they were driving somewhere together, if he'd been "tested," he'd needed only to say, "Yeah, I'm negative," to know that she'd pass along the good news and that the subject need never be mentioned again. At the funeral, Lucille had embraced Geoff's mother tearfully, and Thom's father had shaken Geoff's father's hand for a long, solemn moment, as befitted this wordless and puzzled bond between two men whose sons had loved one another. And that was all.

During his father's last days, Thom spent almost all his free time with Abby and Lucille, doing what he could to help care for his father. The nurses did most of the grunt work, but he could see that his mother and sister needed moral support. These days Abby was looking drawn, pale, underfed; the spring semester was ending and she was trying to write seminar papers on George Eliot and on Saussurean linguistics in the midst of her father's dying. Both she and Thom were worried about their mother, who did indeed seem to be breaking down, though in an unexpectedly quiet way. After her husband became incontinent, Lucille began sleeping in the guest room, and during the day she escaped almost wholly into television, not even entering their father's room for days at a time, frowning briefly whenever one of the nurses passed through the den on her way to the kitchen, as though the woman were a stranger wandered in from the street. When Abby and Thom discussed their father's condition over dinner, careful to make only encouraging remarks—that he seemed to be resting more comfortably, or that he'd gained a little weight—Lucille did not even bother to accuse her children of lying, though plainly they were. After dinner, they sat with her in the den and watched more television, one program after another, the sitcoms and cop shows and TV movies all passing before their glazed, undiscriminating vision like a version of life itself they accepted gratefully, since they were not included.

One night they sat watching a hospital drama, in which emergency-room doctors and nurses rushed around with the ceaseless frantic motion of an ant colony busily working its few square inches of earth, when the program was interrupted to report some "breaking news." Lucille had been laboring over a newspaper crossword puzzle, but now she stopped, frowning at the screen. Thom and Abby glanced at one another, alarmed. Thom had seen an article in today's newspaper and had shown it to Abby, who had quietly crumpled the page and thrown it away. They knew the article would upset Lucille. But now they watched helplessly as Tom Brokaw, in deep and mournful tones, announced "the impending death of Jacqueline Kennedy Onassis, in her Manhattan apartment." According to family sources, the end was "very near." Immediately Thom suspected that Mrs. Onassis was receiving euthanasia, though the television report did not hint at that. Neither had the newspaper article, which had announced that all treatment had been suspended and that the former first lady was "gravely ill." Last week, Thom had seen a tabloid newspaper his mother had brought home from Kroger's, its front page showing a frail-looking Jackie on the arm of her male companion, walking through Central Park, and of course there had been earlier articles in the daily paper; but Thom and Abby had known better than to mention the stories to Lucille. As usual, a tacit silence had reigned in the house, making their lives still bearable day by day, hour by hour, but now Tom Brokaw had ruined all that.

Thom glanced fearfully at his mother, who had slumped a little in her chair. Although Lucille, unlike Abby, had looked remarkably the same throughout their recent ordeal, keeping her hairdresser's appointment every Friday and seldom missing a meal, Thom saw now that her face had paled, making her look suddenly much older, grayer. Her facial muscles seemed to sag. Although the news bulletin had ended and the hospital show had resumed, she'd kept her pale bluish eyes fixed on the television set.

"Mom, are you okay?" Abby asked.

Lucille didn't answer. She stared at the set, unblinking.

Thom fell dully, unaccountably angry. "There's no point in getting upset, you know," he said. "We have our own troubles."

His mother said nothing, as though he and Abby were beneath her notice. Thom had the helpless idea that if Caroline and John-John were in this situation, they'd know exactly what to do. Kennedys always knew, didn't they? They *acted*. They wouldn't have sat here gaping, their hearts pounding queerly.

Now Tom Brokaw reappeared on the screen. God out of a machine, Thom thought. *Save us.* In a reverential, inhumanly deep voice, he reported that Jacqueline Kennedy Onassis had, as expected, died. The family would issue a statement in the morning, he told them, and the funeral arrangements would be announced. There was no further information at the moment, but yes, Jackie Kennedy was dead. Please stay tuned for further details. Good night.

The hospital drama resumed. Not knowing what else to do, Thom grabbed the remote control and flicked off the set.

Lucille stood, her eyes a little wild. Her look reminded Thom of something, but he couldn't remember what. The unfinished crossword puzzle his mother had clutched in her lap fell to the floor.

"Mom?" Abby said, sitting forward anxiously. "Are you—"

"I'm going," Lucille announced. She looked briefly at each of her children, as though daring them to argue. "I'm *going*."

"That's a good idea, Mother," Thom said. "It's been a tough day. I'll make you some hot chocolate, I'll bring it back when it's—"

But Lucille had stalked back toward the bedroom, not listening. Abby sat there next to Thom, shaking her head. She didn't look at him, either.

"That's not what she meant, Thom," Abby said, in an older sister's gentle, explanatory tone. "Going to bed—that's not what she meant at all."

What his mother had meant, evidently, was that she was going to Jackie Kennedy's funeral. She stayed up late in the guest room, packing and repacking her overnight bag, making reservations for her hotel accommodations and her flight to New York. Thom and Abby took turns venturing into her room, trying to reason with her, to insist that she get a good night's sleep before making any further plans. At first Lucille ignored them, and then she became hostile. "You don't understand, *you!*" she said to Thom, the last time he'd tried. He stood in the doorway, staring dully. What did she mean, *you?* Her tone was accusatory, almost hateful. Who was *you*, anyway? But of course there was no point in asking.

He escaped to the den and told Abby he had given up. The earliest flight reservation their mother had been able to secure was for eleven o'clock tomorrow; if she still wanted to visit the Kennedys in the morning, he would drive her to the airport himself. Abby told him to calm down. He'd been sitting perched on the edge of the sofa, methodically cracking the knuckles of one hand, then the other—a habit from his teenage years. He heard the echo of his voice and knew he must have sounded like a teenager. He hadn't felt this jumpy and out-of-sorts in years, and his sister's standing there in the middle of the room with her air of saintly forbearance didn't help.

"Thanks so much, Caroline," he said. "I'll certainly try."

"Good," she said, then turned and left the room.

It was official, he thought. Everybody was mad at everybody. He went back to check on his father, expecting to find Abby in there, but evidently she'd retreated to her own room. The nurse, a crabby-looking woman in her fifties who was Thom's least favorite of the three, glanced up briefly from the dark corner of the room where she always sat with a paperback romance novel, a portable reading light clipped to the cover. He'd never seen her do much of anything. Thom stood for a minute next to the bed, gazing at his father's comatose form with a pang of something like envy. No anger for him, and no pain, either. He'd already reached the end of his journey, Thom thought, and now lay here with his usual patience and quietness, simply waiting for his body to catch up.

The next morning, Thom came back before ten o'clock, fully expecting to cooperate with his mother's lunatic wishes. Instinctively he always went first to the kitchen, where he found Abby preparing a tray of sliced cantaloupe, frosted pastries, a cup of cinnamon-scented tea. Their mother's favorites.

"I talked her into spending the day in bed," Abby said, a bit shortly. She hadn't quite met his eyes.

"Look, I'm sorry I snapped at you last night." Thom leaned back against the counter, his palms turned upward in a gesture of appeal. "It's starting to get to me, I guess," he said, but he couldn't have said what "it" was, exactly.

A brief pause, and then she looked at him. She'd pulled her hair back and tied it carelessly on one side, but a few limp reddish strands had escaped, hanging along her slender throat; her normally clear, fine skin had a grayish pallor, and there were tiny purplish crescents beneath her eyes. She'd thrown on a wrinkled plaid blouse and denim skirt, and Thom felt shamefacedly fresh and well-groomed in his starched khakis and polo shirt, the scent of his cologne and hair gel filling the room.

"Well," she said, smiling slightly. "I guess I forgive you."

"Honey," he murmured. "You're the one who needs a day in bed."

Abby rolled her eyes in her old, girlish way, reassuring him. "Sure. Like I have time for that."

He offered to help, and after she returned from Lucille's room with the empty tray—Thom still didn't dare to go in there—and hurried off to put some last touches on one of her seminar papers, Thom cleaned up the kitchen and then made a to-do list for the rest of the day. The yard needed mowing, and last night he'd noticed a stack of unopened bills on his mother's little rolltop desk in the den; he could sort through those, write out the checks, and have Abby take them in for Lucille's signature. Then he'd go to Kroger's and do the food shopping. He added a few more items to the list, aware that he'd begun feeling better. The list looked so neat and orderly; it would guide him through the day. But before starting the first chore he went back to check on his father.

The room was dark and close-smelling, all the blinds drawn. To Thom's surprise, his father was sitting up, propped by pillows, glancing around the room with the mechanical alertness of a bird. His sleep-mussed whitish hair and purse-lipped mouth seemed oddly birdlike, too, and Thom approached the bed slowly, not wanting to startle him. "Hey, Daddy," he said. On the other side of the bed, the day nurse—a stocky, unsmiling woman whose thick glasses cruelly magnified her dark, popping eyes—stood fiddling with some items on a tray table. Napkins and straws; some plastic spoons and forks; a cup of sweet tea, another of plain water; a container of ready-made pudding. She lifted the foil wrapper off the pudding and reached for a spoon. Neither she nor Thom's father had even acknowledged his presence. The nurse kept her dark gaze lowered, and his father's glance flitted about the room in that mechanical, birdlike way.

"Why don't you take a break," Thom said. "I can feed him." He joined the nurse on the other side of the bed; she hesitated a moment, then handed him the pudding and the spoon. "Just a tiny bit with each spoonful," she said. "Otherwise he'll spit it out." Her huge eyes blinked behind her glasses, seeming to focus just past his shoulder. She said, "I guess I should check on your mother. Abby said she isn't feeling well." "She's fine, she's just resting," Thom said quickly. "Why don't you take an hour off. Go have some lunch." The nurse looked slightly offended. "He'll probably eat a third of that, if you're lucky," she said. "We'll, I'll be back," she said, hesitating. Finally she left the room.

Despite the constant movement of his father's head Thom managed, little by little, to feed him. He held out the white plastic spoon with its dab of vanilla pudding, his hand trembling, and his father's head would swivel briefly in that direction, his lips parted vaguely, like a communicant's, just enough for Thom to slip the spoon inside. His father's stubbled jaws made a chewing motion, and Thom was ready with a napkin, touching at the tiny spots of pudding that oozed from each side of his father's mouth. Then he put down the napkin and took up the spoon again. A kind of rhythm was established, soothing Thom's nerves. Clearly his father no longer had the capacity to recognize him or anyone, but somehow that didn't matter. Thom felt how his shoulders and arms had relaxed, as though someone had massaged them. That sharp little pain at the back of his neck that always throbbed in times of stress had gone away. He took deep, slow breaths, in rhythm with his father's feeding. The surrounding room was so dim and quiet, Thom thought, they might have been anywhere—disembodied, out of time. Thom's eyes had grown moist; they stung pleasantly. He dabbed at them with the same pudding-stained napkin he'd used for his father. That's when he heard the ruckus starting up, somewhere behind him: his mother, followed by the nurse and a bewildered-looking Abby, had blundered into the room.

"What are you doing?" Lucille cried. She'd just woken up, Thom saw. Her eyes were puffy and her dark-tinted reddish hair stood in angry tufts about her head. "Mrs. Phillips is supposed to do that."

Lucille grabbed the pudding cup and spoon out of Thom's hand and dropped them onto the tray.

She stood there, breathing fast. Abby and the nurse looked too shocked to speak, and Thom himself had nothing to say. Did his mother want him to wait here, docile on the edge of the bed, while she screamed at him? Did she still want him to drive her to the airport, so she could catch the plane for Jackie Kennedy's funeral? Whatever she wanted, he thought calmly, he would oblige.

Now she looked shamefaced; she went to the opposite side of the bed and fiddled with the blanket, bunching it around her husband's waist.

She said, "You can't feed him too much—the doctor told us that. He throws up all the time, just like a little baby. . . ." Her face had started to crumple.

"It's just some pudding, Mother," Thom said. "He seems to like it." He added, "He seems happy, in fact."

He glanced at his father who was, indeed, happily oblivious to the scene playing out before him.

Lucille had put the tips of her fingers against her forehead, in an attitude of woe. Tears slid freely out both sides of her eyes, but when she looked up, her voice was amazingly steady and her eyes held a strong, malevolent glare.

"What do *you* know about it? Happy? You think he's happy? Are *you* happy now, Thomas Sadler? Are you?"

"Mommy, stop it." Abby had stepped forward and clamped one arm around her mother's shoulders. "Be quiet," she said sternly. "There's no point in blaming Thom."

But Lucille kept glaring at him—there *was* a point, and she would not relinquish it—while Thom stared back with his new calmness, which must have struck the others as defiance, or simple indifference.

"*Are* you happy?" Lucille repeated. "Are you?"

Thom stood, sighing. He gave Abby a rueful smile. He was always doing this—leaving his sister to clean up. "Guess I'd better shove off," he said, to no one in particular.

And no one answered. The nurse looked around at all of them, her huge eyes like blurry dark wounds behind her glasses.

"Should I feed him the rest of that pudding?" she asked.

And so it happened that Thomas Jefferson Sadler did not attend his own father's funeral. The morning after his mother's outburst, Abby called him at 7:12; he would always remember the time, for he'd awakened to the shrilling phone, and the blaring red numerals on his digital clock had burned the moment into his memory. Abby told her brother in a subdued, almost apologetic voice that their father had died in his sleep.

Thom blinked, staring at the clock. Now it was 7:13. "Okay, I'll be right over."

"Thom?" Abby said. She sounded very afraid. "Thom, could you wait a little while . . . ?"

That's when he knew: Lucille had decided to blame him. After an awkward pause, Abby acknowledged that his mother, for the moment, had forbidden him the house, but she added quickly that Lucille was being "irrational," that she would certainly "come around." But Abby's voice held little conviction: its fearful, girlish apprehension was something else he would never forget.

They talked for a few more minutes, and Thom insisted that he could make phone calls, at least, so that Abby could cope with Lucille. "Oh, Thom, thanks so much," Abby breathed out. "That's a great idea."

Another long, awkward silence. Thom felt the question hovering between them. "*You* don't blame me, do you? Abby?"

But he didn't dare ask. He didn't want the answer.

So Thom made phone calls: the parish priest, the funeral home, a handful of far-flung relatives around the country. Only to Father Coughlin—a bluff, barrel-chested man he'd met a few times and disliked—did Thom mention that he might not be attending the funeral. Family conflicts, he muttered. The priest said that he'd spoken to Lucille often in the past few months and that he understood. He seemed eager to get off the phone. "You understand? You understand what?" Thom didn't ask.

"During the eulogy, I could say that you're indisposed," Father Coughlin said awkwardly.

"Thanks," Thom said, feeling a sudden pang of sympathy for the priest. "That's probably for the best."

Early on the morning of the funeral, which was scheduled for two o'clock, Thom slipped into the funeral home shortly after the doors opened at nine. He'd hurried into the same jeans and pullover he'd worn yesterday; he hadn't bathed or shaved. Although Lucille had not "come around," Abby told Thom that an early-morning visit would be safe: she and Lucille had stayed with the body fairly late the night before, receiving a steady stream of visitors. Whenever anyone had inquired after Thom, Abby reported, Lucille told them Thom was "indisposed" and then pointedly changed the subject. Earlier in the day, Lucille and Father Coughlin had conferred.

Now a sleepy-looking man appeared in the dim, high-ceilinged hall and stared at Thom, blinking. "Sadler?" Thom said. The man gestured quickly to a door on his left and wandered off. Thom went inside. He saw the opened visitor's book with its long list of signatures, but of course he didn't sign. The casket was opened and his father, dressed in one of his gray banker's suits, looked no different from the sleeping man Thom had watched over frequently these past few weeks. Standing here, Thom felt a little sleepy, himself. The night before, he'd drifted off while watching one of the endless documentaries about the Kennedy family that had been broadcast since Jackie Kennedy's death the previous week. The familiar clips from JFK's funeral had been replayed, and Thom had stared balefully at Jackie in her black veil, holding her children's hands. Caroline and little John-John, in their tailored woolen coats. He'd seen the film countless times, of course, but despite his exhaustion he forced himself to watch it again, his eyes burning as that little boy, urged gently by his mother, stepped forward the moment his father's coffin passed by. Thom had felt his eyes glaze over when the scene shifted, or had a commercial come on?—he couldn't remember. And this morning, raffish and inconsequent above his own father, he felt that same drowsiness, almost a numbness, spreading through him like a drug. He waited a minute or two before knowing that he couldn't shed a proper tear, much less imagine some noble gesture, his belated version of that tiny, perfect salute.

BIOGRAPHY

KEVIN KILLIAN

I'm walking down California Street to meet a man and tell him about my father's life. The famous San Francisco twins are on the corner at Leavenworth, waving to a cable-car load of cheering fans. Today the famous twins are dressed in cream-colored flannel coats and cherry-colored hats. They're about sixty, I guess, and everyone knows them because they're on TV all the time, and they're in the credits of that movie *9 to 5*? It's supposed to be good luck when you see them. On Polk I pass by a guy who calls me by my name, "Dan," he goes, "want a white zombie?" But I don't know him and I walk on by as he pleads with me, "Dan! Danny! Come back!" I'm kind of a cold person and it shows.

My father, Ralph Isham, was rich for one reason, and famous for another. Now he's dead, and more famous than ever. But I have trouble with the facts, which is maybe why I feel so isolated. Kit says I'm ridiculous. "What's money, after all? Only a tool. With a tool in hand, you can build what you want." I'm the only child of a rich man, and a famous man. Now he's dead, and it's January and I have an appointment with Jacob Lowery, my father's biographer. I'm going to tell him nothing about my father's life. Kit sits at the kitchen table, a study in concentration and grim silence.

"I like Jacob," I say.

I want to go—but I don't know if I really want to go or not.

"But I don't like him," I continue. I talk a blue streak. Kit says nothing. He's heard this soliloquy before. Jacob Lowery teaches at City College in New York and he's writing a biography of the great poet Ralph Isham. But Kit remains silent, scissors flashing. He's cutting up pictures of my father's face to paste on squares of cardboard to use in a demo.

Kit's in ACT UP and so am I, I guess. I mean, he's really in it and I'm just this cold kind of asshole. Sometimes I say to him, Why, why, *why all this activism*, it's not like either of us has HIV! He just stares me down, his dark eyes cold with Old Testament fire.

And I'm like, Daniel, in the lions' den. . . .

"Lowery's a leech," Kit says. I'm stoned. Pictures of leeches crawl across my mind. Not that I've ever seen a leech. Kit's never seen a leech either. They're far different creatures from the anthropomorphic insect we have in mind. "Sucking and parasiting off your father. If I were you, I'd avoid him like the plague. He's straight, too, right?"

"Yep." Onto the cardboard he rolls the paste, with his big red hand, thumb extended like a hitchhiker's. My father left my mother before I was born, and I didn't get to meet him until I was twelve. He was living with a boy called Skip then, and Skip was sixteen. That didn't last long. I kept seeing my father once a year at summer and every summer there was a different boy. One year he and I were the same age. After that I was one year, two years, three years older than my father's other boy.

That was some years back, but we never were close. I was like this damaged product, a sensitive plant. Ever since my father got on TV and said he had HIV and called President Reagan a killer, everyone expected us to get close again, but I didn't. And then when he died they said, *You must feel bad.*

Kit says my father's become a symbol. Before I was born, my father had been interested enough to set up the trust fund upon which, whether I like it or not, the both of us depend. "He was very big," Kit says. "A superstar." He presses down on my father's haggard face with his big red hands; paste squeezes out from all corners, like slugs from under a log.

"In his own little world."

My stomach's tied up in knots. Two pieces of toast pop up out of the toaster, burnt black.

"You're a leech too," I add.

"It's my nature," he mildly remonstrates. "Daddy, buy me another toaster? This one's like something Clive Barker dreamt up."

"Leech," I say. Like all my words this is meant as a joke, but a joke that hides something pretty hideous. Kit should have known: I can't discuss Jacob Lowery without considering the subject of the leech and—broadening it.

"You sound bitter," Kit says. He's painting a big pink triangle across each of my father's eyes.

"And you say—what right have I to be bitter?"

"No, you've got every right to. I hate all these heterosexual guys coming in, rereading our experience back to us," he says, almost by rote, as though he were David Halperin or some other queer theorist, David Halperin in front of the blackboard on a bad day, broken chalk, hangover, problems at home or whatever. "Break free of straight male discourse! Break the stupid lunch date with Jacob Lowery."

"A leech on my bank account, leech on my face—a leech on my cock in the middle of the night."

"You couldn't ask for a clearer picture," he says thinly, "of our meaningful relationship. Leech, huh."

He knows I'm just worried about meeting Jacob Lowery; he knows that I'm only taking out on him that which can't, under present conditions, be taken out on anyone else. Nevertheless Kit sags a little. Down. Defeated.

I try to console him but he knows our estrangement goes deeper than tears. "Don't talk about leeches," he cries.

"I was just kidding," I say.

"Oh yeah," Kit says, "and I'm Melanie Griffith."

"I love you," I tell him. "And your toast is delicious, Miss Griffith."

"It is not, it sucks." He's sulking now. Of course he is.

"I could eat a whole loaf's worth," I say.

"Then buy me a fucking toaster," Kit says.

"Hey," I say. Suddenly my chair's next to his. These tawdry little tin lawn chairs we'd seen on Mission Street and made away with at a yard sale. The two chairs adjacent, now, and me rubbing Kit's face with a linen napkin. "Hey, Kit."

The linen—stained, greenish, a hand-me-down gift from my mother—feels cool and absorbent on his wet face. Kit stares into his placard and it seems to fail him. It isn't at all what he had meant it to be.

The kitchen is warm; traces of gray smoke cling to the toaster's damp sides. From my hands he leaps, the linen napkin cast aside. He'd meant, he declares, absolutely nothing of what he'd said. Nothing by anything that came out of his mouth. Didn't mean to have said it. Just came out. I shrug and relapse, leave him to go to the bedroom and smoke some more pot. He sits there straightening his files on my father's death from A to Z. The smell of paste now pervasive, and him muttering how the white cultural hegemony of biography rests upon a discursive formation in which the homosexual must be posted always as the most radically other, and I'm rolling my eyes, like, you'd think *he* wasn't white.

And after I'm way stoned, this moody heap on the bed, I get the munchies, bad. I want to go out, maybe bite someone. As I leave the house, Kit calls after me melodramatically: "Go to the white man, Pocahontas! Save our people!" I'm walking downtown, down California Street, getting ready to bite. Interview with a *vampire, huh?*

I get to Kendall's a little past noon. Never having been there, I don't know what kind of place to expect, so I'm wearing this ugly wool suit, no tie, hoping that I won't be admitted. I look like a street person. Well, not exactly, but I'm unshaven. Unfortunately, Jacob has outguessed me and this isn't the four-star restaurant he prefers but something more plebeian.

"Can I help you?"

"I was supposed to meet someone here," I say nervously. There's a hole or tear in the side seam of the suit pants, and through it I scratch my taut, tense skin. "But maybe I have the wrong place? Is Professor Lowery here?"

"Sure he is. Won't you come this way?"

The waiter holds out his arm as though he expects me to take it; but I prefer to follow him at a discreet distance. The walls of the restaurant sport thirties paintings by Maxfield Parrish, yet there's a smell from the kitchen as though a million Asian workers are expecting their daily ration of tofu. It isn't very crowded for lunch. Here, the waiters wear earrings and their hair's much longer than mine. Jacob is sitting at a table by himself, drinking from a glass filled with a red liquid. Jacob is forty-five or so, and I've known him for years. But I don't like him.

That is, I like him but I don't like him.

"Hi there, Danny," Jacob says. Jacob has worn a beard ever since I first met him, and today the beard seems newly trimmed or chopped so that it's acquired the texture and color of a pine cone. It makes him look fierce and mercenary. I'm not sure whether or not to give the headwaiter a tip.

"Come back in ten minutes, Sammy," Jacob says. "Sit down, Dan."

I pull out a chair and sit down, as Jacob had asked. The chair's made of willow. Will it hold me? I sit down gingerly. "What's happening, my man?"

"I've been hanging in there," he says. "Do you want a drink?"

"No," I say. "I'm on the wagon."

Not even a tremor of emotion passes through the beard.

"Okay then." Against the side of the table stands Jacob's large attaché case. In it, I suspect, is the ticking tape recorder I know and dread of old. It's Jacob's way of life: everywhere he goes he carries a tape recorder to help him in his biography of my father. Even when I was a boy and lived with my father Jacob was always there with his taping equipment—only then it was big and cumbersome, like a funerary urn. These new cassette things you could put in your mouth and swallow if you were careless and forgot they were there. "We're being bugged," I say, pointing to Jacob's attaché case and faking paranoia. "Watch what you say."

"It's for my ears only."

"And for the ears of your readers. That is, if you ever get this book off its ass."

"Oh, I'm writing it," promises Jacob.

"I also want to tell you," I say, "that I don't think you're the appropriate person to be writing my father's life story. I know you knew him and everything, and you've probably interviewed like one zillion people, but Jacob—"

The waiter sidles by again. "This young man will have a beer after all. A Heineken?"

"A Budweiser," I contradict. "I hope they have more than tofu here."

"Hamburgers?" the waiter interposes.

"Wasn't talking to you, asshole."

"Oh, man, I'm hurting," the waiter says sincerely. "Here's what, I'll get you your beer right away."

"Sammy," Jacob says, nodding almost imperceptibly; and Sammy takes off heading for an unmarked door. Jacob swivels to me and asks, "Now what were you saying? I'm not appropriate?"

"You're not gay," I remind him. "I doubt you ever sucked a cock in your life." This is something I firmly believe. I used to want him to come to my room in the big house on Long Island and suck mine, why wouldn't he, was all he cared about a poet's life?

"Why are you so uptight? I mean—even with the hired help?"

"I don't mean to be," I say.

Jacob lowers the baby bottle and looks, for the first clear time, into my eyes. "The tape is off," he says gently. "Why? Because I want you to relieve yourself."

Sounds like taking a leak. I can't listen to him. Suddenly it's all too much. Jacob notices and makes me look at a menu while I regain some composure.

"What's a white zombie, anyhow?"

Jacob taps the menu, knowingly.

"Amphetamine," he whispers. "Ah, here's your beer."

"Thank you," I say meekly to the waiter. "Sorry I called you an asshole."

The waiter is beatific; he's stoned too, his brown eyes rings of root beer and bliss. He raises his hands in an Arabic gesture and proclaims, "Oh, we're all assholes; assholes of Allah. Our lives are the holy ordure of Allah." Then he bows away and back into the unmarked door and disappears before I can do more than blink.

"When was the last time you saw Ralph Isham?" Jacob asks.

"Gee, I don't remember," I say.

"Bullshit," Jacob says, with scorn. His scorn however is such a kindly thing that I feel patronized. A little boy again. When I met Jacob, I *was* a little boy. Jacob was the first one I'd told about having wet dreams; I'd asked Jacob what they meant, how bad for you are they? And Jacob responded to me. Even though a child, I had known response's flavor. And then all the nights I used to wait for him to come to my door and say, It's not him, it's you, tell me your life story, Danny.

"You I haven't forgotten," I say. "Sometimes at night before I go to bed I say prayers, like my mother taught me. I say, 'God bless Uncle Jacob' like a kid."

This is flattery, guaranteed to please, and Jacob, even with his beard, isn't Solomon: he's susceptible as the next guy. He grins, and I relax. "I think I got a Christmas card from him, two years ago," I say, "postmarked Venice."

"He was reading at the Festival there."

"It was in English," I say. "And I got an enormous check."

"He loved you," Jacob says. But shit, that's just what Jacob always says!

The restaurant's crowding up now, and I feel uncomfortable explaining to Jacob exactly what I mean, with people pushing at my long elbows to pass behind me on their way to the john.

"Sure he loved me, but that's so bourgeois."

Jacob leers.

"It is," I insist. "Don't come over so man-to-man with me now, Jake. . . . You did a great job of it years ago, but that's all over now. Oh, fuck. Forget it. I mean forget how I feel. How's— well. I don't even know his name. Who was the new kid?"

"What do you mean?"

"When my dad died, he was with someone, right?" I drop my fork. "He picked them up and dropped them a year later once they turned sixteen. So who was it?"

Possibly Jacob's tongue-tied out of confusion. So I say to forget that, too. "It's not that I'm interested. I was just making polite conversation. Forget it."

"It was Thomas Reynolds."

I'm shocked and show it. Jacob nods.

"Hamburger for my friend here," Sammy insinuates. "Béarnaise for the professor. All as you like it?"

"We'll buzz you," I threaten, and the waiter shrinks away. "Thomas Reynolds! He must be so old by now!"

"I think he's twenty-seven," Jacob says apologetically.

"I seem to have misplaced my fork," I reply.

"He is twenty-seven, in fact."

"I didn't know that—Daddy—could get it up with someone over twenty. That's all. I thought he liked them young."

"Twenty-seven is young," Jacob pointed out. But twenty-seven isn't the same thing, we both know, as the eternal fifteen which Ralph Isham had spent so many years pursuing. Last time

I saw my father was four years before, at the Long Island beach house, and the boy's name had been Glen. "I wish I was still twenty-seven."

"Oh, no you don't. Y'know, I do remember Thomas Reynolds. If it's the same one. He came to give my father and Glen—cooking lessons. Don't tell me they were still together. What a freak thing to happen. Maybe Daddy was in love."

And somehow the thought of my father in love pains me, since for years I've been attached to a picture—a picture of Ralph continually unhappy, continually in a rush from boy to boy to boy, solely because he couldn't have—say custody of—the boy: myself: Danny. I'm like this dog in the manger, but there it is: another dirty secret on the table with the Béarnaise. I trust Jacob to work it out: who other? He's writing the book—we're only his characters.

Jacob makes haste to assuage the hurt. "Not in love," he says soothingly. Years ago he'd put Band-Aids on my scraped knees. For years his reddish beard and his big brown eyes, the deep color of Coca-Cola, were dependable markers in my father's screwy house. "Not in love. Maybe he depended on Thomas. It wasn't love."

"Good."

"Whatever love is."

"Yeah, sure. And say, did the two of them still fuck?"

"You're too loud," Jacob whispers, "for this restaurant!"

"Oh, what do I care about loud," I say. "All I care about is—" I stop because it's so unpleasant.

"Is what?"

In front of me the unmarked door opens. "Is me," say I hoarsely. "Is me."

And the door swings shut. "Many, many people care about you," Jacob says. "Your father had quite an entourage," Jacob reminds me. "You know most of them. They all miss you. George lives in Provincetown now, most of the year. Lorna's in New York—you know, she married Herman Zygote?"

"That must be fun," I snort.

"And Ronnie Verel is doing very well on MTV and everywhere else." Jacob is determined, I know, to glide along unruffled, a swan on Swan Lake. There isn't much that can faze Jacob Lowery anymore. Once he'd been shocked by Ralph Isham and his "entourage"—Lorna had had to drag him into it by the balls. Now it's his second skin; now, Jacob's unflappable as Clifton Webb. He sits urbanely eating, one hand protecting his beard from the sauce Béarnaise, and I want to spatter him with—

What can I do? All I have is a voice to undo the folded lie. Trouble is, what had once been folded had long since been undone, by my father's own blatant, unquenchable drive for personal publicity—everyone in the Western world knew all about Ralph Isham who had eyes to read or ears to hear.

And no one cares anymore. "I hate him," I say. "You know what it's like—to be his son?"

"I've tried, over the years, to make it out."

"In a zillion years you couldn't know. You're so obtuse. Know what's the worst?"

"That your father was a great artist?"

"Shit on that. Know what the worst is, Jake?"

"That he wanted, more than anything else, to be on speaking terms with you."

"What would you say if I told you he tried to fuck me?"

Jacob raises an eyebrow. "Was that the worst?"

In a panic, I feel my determination beginning to fade. I'll be iron again someday, but not today. Not anymore. "No, that's not the worst—but isn't that bad enough?"

"Bad enough for whom?"

"For anyone! Big Shot wondered why I didn't come round scratching anymore. To see him. To see George and Lorna and Ronnie and all them—well, they can kiss my ass in living color. His love life and his poetry and his peace marches and trips to Hanoi and Havana and Prague and Woodstock and shit on that—"

Fumbling, I begin again. Jacob hasn't stirred except to sip at his beer. I flash that probably the old tape recorder is on under the table. Suddenly I feel like reaching under the table and grabbing Jacob's cock and yanking on it.

Instead I try breaking up the hamburger and putting different parts of it on different parts of the plate. Silent. Jacob asks me a number of pointed questions trying to flesh out his biography.

So what happens next is Kit arrives unexpectedly. He's wearing this determined look I know well. "Where are the truffles?"

he says. "I thought you'd be having truffles over Ralph Isham's dead body."

"It's a pleasure to meet you," Jacob says politely. He snaps his fingers to try to summon the waiter.

"You didn't have to come," I tell Kit. Against the side of the table Kit leans this big enormous sign he's been carrying like this was Calvary instead of Kendall's.

"Oh yes I did," he says.

He doesn't add why. He's building up to some kind of scene. "It's an issue of representation," he tells Jacob. "We're tired of hearing our life stories told—distorted—by straights."

Jacob protests. He knew Ralph Isham intimately, he says. Okay, not "intimately," but he was there at the Berkeley Poetry Conference, when Isham gave a ten-hour reading on acid; he was there at the march on the Pentagon when Isham chained himself to the steps; he was there when John and Yoko put the music to Isham's poem.

"You've never sucked a cock in your life," Kit says.

"Gee, that sounds so familiar," Jacob says. "Gee, where have I heard that before?"

"I told him how we feel," I say to Kit in this weak little voice—Marge Simpson's voice.

Jacob goes to me, "Is he doing your talking for you now?"

Kit says, "Are you doing Ralph Isham's talking for him?"

My hand falls under the table and feels for the machine. I switch it on and speak clearly into the centerpiece of white flowers.

"Testing—testing. This is Danny Isham speaking."

Jacob starts to argue with Kit. They're both happier arguing. Kit says that his ACT UP sign is the sum total of Isham's life. Jacob says that my father's death was only one signifier in a lifetime of signs. That Kit is trying to turn a human being into a symbol for political purposes. Kit says that when the virus entered my father's body his accomplishments and his "humanness" receded in importance. Jacob says that's reductive. Kit reiterates that no straight man can understand the dimensions of the AIDS crisis. Jacob brings out my father's fat *Collected Poems* and demands to know if Kit thinks his goddamn poster is worth more than a whole life's work in art—wagging the book before him like a sword. "This is action," Kit says, as the poster sways from side to side and my father's face bobs over the restaurant like a pink balloon. "And that book's poetry."

I want to say that no, he didn't really ever try to fuck me. I just wanted to make the biography more about me, by adding a little lie, into these wheels I shall throw a wrench.

"How's the lunch, gentlemen?"

"Bring us more beer," I tell the waiter. "And some truffles."

And Jacob says easily, "You can't stop this biography," which shows you how much Jacob knows.

"Yeah, maybe not," Kit says, "but we can stop AIDS."

"I'm not standing in your way," Jacob says.

"Now *that's* reductive," Kit fires back. When he says we can stop AIDS if we put our backs into it, sometimes I believe him. I guess he's right that first we'd have to mow down a whole bunch of assholes like Jacob who have these other priorities. I look at the fat book and think, that work destroyed my life, that work fucked up my dad's life too. I'm confused. Things have come to a standstill at the other end of the table. Jacob says he'll wear a pink triangle if that's what Kit wants. "Yeah," Kit says, "because it doesn't mean anything to you. Let me tell you a story, guy, about our friend here. About Danny Isham. I want to tell you about how I met him, what he was like then."

"Ah, don't," I say.

"Say, Dan, I met this friend of yours on the way over. Tall dude, with red glasses? And he said he had some pills for you. Here. Take 'em and weep." He undoes a button on his knapsack and throws a handful onto the table.

"Why are you being such a bastard?" I say. How I wish I was stoned. God, do those pills look good.

"Because you're waffling on this," Kit replies. "You're like Clinton you waffle so much. Look at this guy, he's out to take you for everything you got. He's out to smear your life for the delectation of the Book-of-the-Month Club, the Movie of the Week. He's stealing our history."

But he's sincere, I say.

"And what's 'sincere'?" he snaps. "Why are you privileging *sincerity*, for Christ's sake? This isn't like a primary, Dan, this is war, and whose side do you think *he's* on? You think he cares about AIDS? Huh?"

"I don't know," I go. "I thought he did. I mean, in general."

"Prove I don't," Jacob says calmly. "This is America, you're innocent till proven guilty."

Kit's dark eyes, trained on me like bullets, won't budge. "In general," he repeats, a disdainful echo. How am I supposed to prove, one way or another, how this average straight Joe Schmoe feels about AIDS—or gay life—or anything else? I touch his arm—as I used to touch him when I needed him, when I needed a force to come between me and my father, and in the touch an idea comes to me. "What time is it?" I ask Jacob Lowery, and he shakes his sleeve the way straight men do, to show off his watch.

With both hands I grab his forearm and raise it to my mouth. Chomp. He howls and I look down briefly, my bite across the tight flesh of his arm. The blood welling up.

Then I find out how he feels about AIDS. His nostrils flare like a tortured horse. The dazed, scared eyes of cattle before a storm. He's sputtering and gasping, as though a coronary were right outside the door. "Are you *inflected?*" He can hardly get the words out. This must be his worst nightmare. "No, I am not *infected,*" I say. "You say inflected, I say infected."

Jacob stands up, knocking over a dessert plate. A ring of cream clings to the fabric of his thigh. He's summoning the waiter, making desperate motions for a cellphone. "Call the ambulance, 911!" he shouts. "I've been bitten bad!" He's drooling on his pine-cone beard, and little pricks of blood are on his wrist, four or five drops of blood in discrete planes, and now he's waving his hand like—like this bearded mad fag out of *Priscilla, Queen of the Desert.*

Sammy sidles up with the check and a cellphone. "What's the goddamn number?" Jacob's yelling. "Son of a bitch!"

"9-1-1," Kit says. "How quickly they forget, once they've been *inflected.*"

"Like father, like son," Jacob says, punching the digits. "If you fucking cocksuckers've given me fucking AIDS I'll—"

"Oh, Jacob," I say. His eyes, those liquid pools of Coca-Cola, have frozen now, into icy brown buggy lenses. "Let's call the whole thing off." I sign the check myself and move out of the restaurant only, of course, two big cops stop me and Kit at the door and we're busted.

As Kit and I walk out of the Hall of Justice he keeps looking at me. I guess I'm forgiven. I'm out on bail, that embarrasses me, but Kit says, well, *I've* been out on bail a dozen times, twenty-five times. When we reach the cable-car track he stops me, he says, "We're all on remand." He pretends I still have Jacob's blood on my mouth, wipes it off with his thumb. "They'd like to make us all criminals, don't let them fool you."

"What's going to happen?"

"And you," he says, "were ready to give up all your integrity for a book of goddamn poetry!" We stand there facing the same direction, and below us the city spreads out at sunset, a lovely bowl of shade and yellow light. Ready to give it all up. The sounds of traffic, faint, seabirds. What was I giving up? "The way his arm felt in my mouth," I said, "I liked. Kind of."

"Well, what's so terrible about that?"

"I used to love him," I confess. "He was like this big brother, father kind of guy to me."

Kit and I walk a few steps. He sings that old song about, *oh well, I used to love her, but it's all over now. . . .*

GRAFFITI

CHRISTOPHER LORD

Almost two years after he moved into the rowhouse Harmon Weydon bought a new car. After some consideration he realized that the stress of the longer commute would be lessened by having a car that provided greater comfort and required little or no maintenance. He took test drives, studied brochures, even watched a video for one particular model. At last he chose a Japanese luxury sedan, pearl white with dove gray leather appointments and an audiophile-level compact disc system, an indulgence of almost embarrassing proportions. His final yielding, after six months of deliberations, satisfied a deeply felt need for economic independence and self-worth.

Because it was still nearly dark during his commute to and from work, Weydon did not notice the message on the wall until Saturday. As he walked back from the neighborhood video store after returning the foreign film he had rented the evening before, Weydon stopped in front of his walkway. Fifty feet away from the cluster of rowhouses was a commercial building that completed the block and faced the busier cross street. Across the building's side wall, in bright kelly green spray paint, the words CONSUME OR DIE were printed at eye level. The message, an exhortation really, was large enough to read easily from a distance. It rippled slightly, as if the author, or artist, had tired during its execution.

It had not been there the previous weekend when he swept the decaying leaves from his driveway. No, this had occurred during the week, the same week he had driven home his new car for the first time. His face flushed. He looked behind him at the windows of the neighbors' rowhouses, and across the street. This message could not be for him, about him, or bear any reference to him, his car, his house, or his first editions.

The late-winter morning air pricked at his lungs as he attempted to breathe calmly. What kind of politics was this? Weydon pondered the sophistication required for such a creation, knowing that he was intellectualizing his emotions, stifling his sense of embarrassment, trying to stop the pounding of his heart.

He went inside his house. It had a long narrow entry with a deep ruby Persian runner that led toward a nook containing his first major art acquisition, a large sapphire blown vase that he showcased with a gallery spot installed in a recess in the ceiling. He told people that he had decorated his combination living/dining area with the assistance of a designer, but the more complex answer was that he had resisted most of her efforts because of his own more formal and simple demands. He had overcome her objections to the linen fabric, the monochrome window treatments and paint, ultimately owing to her tastes only the topaz chintz pillows on the sofa and the cushions on the dining room chairs. The other colors in the room were the jewel tones of the jade marble tiles surrounding the fireplace and the rich amethyst of a glass bowl that sat in the sun's path across the glass and chrome coffee table. Above him in the cathedral ceiling skylights let in the murky gray of the morning with light enough to reflect off the tangerine fused-glass frame holding James's picture, an enlargement of the snapshot taken that previous summer at the lake.

He went into the kitchen and started to heat some water for tea, murmuring the message under his breath: Consume or die. Of course. Now it became clear; the error was his. Eat or die— not an ironic indictment of his lifestyle or a supercilious command but a truism, banal, childish, a smear across a wall.

The thought made him hungry. He would call George and suggest a meeting at Cafe Olé for a cappuccino and a scone.

But George, when he arrived much later than promised and only after Weydon had already finished his coffee and was considering another, had little interest in the no-longer-cryptic scrawl.

"Hoodlums," he drawled, daubing his chin after sitting down and taking a bite of his chocolate croissant. "Not to worry, my dear. If someone doesn't sponge it off you should move. It could have been worse, you know. Some well-meaning homosexual could have covered the wall with Laura Ashley wallpaper. Or worse yet—a Wyland mural. Now wouldn't that be frightening—waking up some morning and having one of those anthropomorphic whales staring down at you like some Fitzgeraldian nightmare image of God."

As he returned from Cafe Olé that morning, and then each day thereafter for a while, Weydon made a special point of noticing CONSUME OR DIE, even when he had to slow down as he neared the driveway to peer through the darkening sky and strain to see the message on the wall. At night from his study Weydon watched couples from the nearby rowhouses walking with strollers, or dogs, or both; Generation X-ers in their loose-fitting, often colorless clothing; individuals walking with purpose; homeless people with their shopping carts and uncombed hair. He could not see any of these people as the perpetrators of such an act of vandalism.

He began to notice markings associated with gang activity as he commuted to work. On buildings near his office, closer to the inner city, he saw spray-painted signals, gibberish mostly, not even words—in one case "vort2" and "grbzze" painted across a billboard near his freeway off-ramp. What did these territorial markings signify? Some had been executed with a perverse artistic flair, even when the canvas was as mundane as a storefront wall or a freeway underpass. Regularly he found new evidence of these scrawls on windows, on the corrugated sides of the warehouses in the industrial park, on buildings in the commercial district.

When Weydon asked George whether he, too, had noticed the territorial markings, George simply harrumphed, "Would you have them use their scent glands instead, my dear?"

At the office Weydon received sympathy for what he called his "neighborhood crime." For the last five years he had been the director of public relations for his company, the corporate spokesman who gave quotes to the newspaper and occasionally appeared on the local evening news when his company's position on a civic matter was required. And while the salary for this position was generous, he had never felt economic freedom until he had made the decision to move to the bigger city and commute to the office fifty miles away. What he had characterized to colleagues as a refinancing decision had been only the visible manifestation of a profound, if incomplete, reordering of priorities.

The move had transformed Weydon's life from one of rigid adherence to defined social conventions into one more naturally following the contours of his orientation. He had made the superficial changes represented by a greater freedom of dress and an increased permissiveness in spending. While Weydon acknowledged several influences, James was at the top of the list. If Weydon had not begun to build a relationship with another man he would not have done the soul searching nor have completed the therapy that put him reasonably at peace with the person he knew he had always been. And only in the last two years, with the arrival of James as his life partner, had Weydon begun to feel any degree of freedom.

None of the past melted away—the college nervous breakdown, his mother's death from emphysema the week he and Sheila had filed for divorce, the awkwardness of gay dating—but it began to make sense when James came along and, as Weydon had said to him on more than one occasion, "completed my life." A few years younger, James was an attorney on the partnership track and was occasionally away—as was true now, with a products liability case that had returned him to New York after one week in the city with Weydon. They still maintained separate living accommodations but, more and more when he wasn't away on business, James was moving in shirt by shirt, a progression that Weydon found reassuring. George's only concern—and he was a good enough friend to mention it only occasionally—was that Weydon preserved too much of the mystery of his private life while at the office.

One night several weeks later, when the novelty of the message on the wall had faded, Weydon parked his car in the garage after returning late from work. It was darker than usual. The streetlights that lined his block were the halogen type that shut themselves off intermittently and the one directly in front of his house, the one nearest the mailbox, was dark. Weydon walked toward the community mailbox that served the six rowhouses in his block. He placed one hand on the top of the box as he negotiated the keyed box front with his other hand. As he looked up again the streetlight flared on. The unexpected blackness on the top of the box, normally a muted silver, caused him to jerk his hand back as if a spider had touched him. What he saw, however, was not a spider, but a spidery marking in black spray paint that in the harsh light and slightly foggy air appeared to read "jool." The sight was unpleasant and confusing. Weydon walked quickly inside, locking and bolting the door behind him.

This new untranslatable marking was only twenty feet from his front door. Was this a warning to other gang members, or perhaps a signal to the owners of these urban-renewal dwellings that their lives were not as comfortable as they might seem? These stylized letters somehow not letters, this word not quite a word, this more intimate location, had sinister implications. This mark was new; it could only have been painted the night before after Weydon had returned home. What had he been doing while the vandal had been outside? Sleeping, perhaps reading, the light from his study assisting the man, or boy, who had done it?

He slept poorly that night. He had been expecting a call from James but instead had received only an internet message. James was back in New York. "Much love," the screen had said, "am too busy to call just now. I'm eating a potsticker for you." The rest as always was implied in the easy familiarity, the unsaid caring, the spare, uninflected messages that, at a time like this, were poor substitutes for reassurance and protection.

George was not much more supportive, even when Weydon described over the phone the mysterious "jool" marking, its location, the proximity to his own individual mailbox. "My dear," he intoned, "it's far less threatening than any of those 'Free Angela Davis' proclamations you see on the freeway tunnels."

Weydon attempted a laugh. "So seventies of you, George. But this was done right in front of my door."

George was not convinced of any encroaching doom. "And when you found a shopping cart and litter on the side of your house, didn't you feel threatened by the menace of the homeless?"

"That was different, somehow," Weydon said. "The only things those people left behind were cigarette butts."

"And, mysteriously, eggshells," George added.

Over the next few days Weydon saw gang markings everywhere. It was as if his sense of awareness had been heightened, his level of consciousness now attuned to this demimonde that coexisted with his urban environment. He made an attempt to notice everything. But the strain of taking so much in when he felt so full of impressions, facades, responsibilities, already, was more than he could sustain. As weeks went by he realized that he had relaxed his vigilance to a more normal level.

He was only marginally and temporarily reengaged when one Saturday he noticed that someone had repainted the mailbox, making the mysterious "jool" virtually invisible beneath new, heavily silvered paint. Weydon ran his finger along the line of script as he remembered it, as if feeling a scar.

Several Sundays later the weather cleared and, since James was away again in New York, Weydon spent the morning handwashing his car. Its curved white surfaces glinted in the sun, almost hovering above the ground like a giant freshwater pearl, smooth and soothing to his touch. Road grime loosened from the interstices of the wheel covers, and Weydon rubbed them until he could see no traces of tar, dirt, or streaks. More than the glass or the first editions, the car had become his favorite possession—it cradled him in leather as he drove to and from the office each day mentally unraveling corporate problems, crafting language for public pronouncements with subtle flair.

The afternoon was perfect for driving to the city park in the hills and luxuriating on the grass in the sun. Even George agreed and had come along, bringing a picnic basket filled with pasta salads and iced tea. Although it was sunny the air was brisk, and so Weydon had brought a sweater, which he wore tied by the sleeves around his neck. He was surprised that the park was almost deserted. Except for a Jeep, a station wagon, and two motorcycles, the parking lot was empty. A few teenagers on bicycles and skateboards congregated at the far end of the parking lot, their occasional laughter punctuating the air. They appeared to watch with detachment as Weydon and George unloaded their items from the trunk. George carried the picnic basket, leaving Weydon the blanket and portable stereo. Weydon looked at the teenagers once more as he set the car alarm, then followed George over the top of the hill.

Stretched out on the blanket, they ate lunch in the full sun, then began reading to the background sounds of the birds in the park and a Mozart violin concerto.

Weydon did not know how long he had been asleep, but when he awoke the trees cast long shadows across the blanket where he and George had been dozing. Weydon shivered in the now cooler air.

"Wake up, George," he said. "We should be leaving."

George awoke with a start. "Hmmm . . . it must have been the poppies."

They gathered up their belongings and descended the hill. Weydon could see his car, now alone in the parking lot. As they walked nearer, he quickened his pace. He started sprinting and dropped the blanket and his book. When George caught up, Weydon was standing silently beside the car, his head bent and in shadow.

The white surface of the car, dull in the near twilight, was cut harshly across the hood and the driver's side with bright red streaks. QUEER was painted in large narrow letters on the hood, stretching from the window-washer ducts nearly to the front. On the driver's side, FAGGOT spread across both doors. The letters were large and blocked, except for the second G, which seemed an afterthought, for it rode above the others, done by a different hand.

"Oh, my dear," George said, after a silence.

Blinking, Weydon walked slowly around the car, taking in each square inch. The crimson letters were sharp except for several places where the paint had run.

"Those delinquents on bikes," George said. "They must have done it."

"It doesn't matter, really, does it?" Weydon asked, his voice thick. "The car is ruined." George was silent. "Ruined," Weydon repeated, after a long pause, "by teenagers who don't even know how these words feel."

George now stood by the driver's door. "Or how to spell."

Weydon was trembling, and sat on the grass in front of the car, his face averted. These words he read so frequently in magazine articles, overheard in fey conversations at parties, stung with the recollection of how they had sounded when he was a teenager so unlike those who, with little thought but meanness, had damaged his car. He took a deep breath.

"I can't drive," he said.

"Of course not," George said. "I'll take care of it."

"After dark. Let's just wait until it gets dark."

"You can have it redone. No one will know."

"I'll know," Weydon whispered, lowering his head. George came over and sat down beside him, spreading out the blanket on the grass. Weydon moved toward George and put his head against George's shoulder. "Nothing like this has happened since high school, when a girl asked me in senior year why I wasn't in gym class. 'Oh,' she said, 'you must be a fag, then,' in such a light manner. . . ." His voice trailed off as he recalled the image.

"I have some experience here," George replied. "Unlike you, I am absolutely sure there has been no doubt about my orientation since I was five and told my mother I wanted to grow up to be Auntie Mame."

"James and I talk about these things from time to time. Not this exactly, but the way the past creeps up on you." He paused. "You know, besides you, George, I don't know many gay men. I mean, I slept with a few after the divorce and before I met James."

"Yes, my dear. I remember the horrible tales, particularly the one about the underemployed carpenter with the interesting dental work."

"And then I met James, really before I was expecting something to happen, before I believed that men could have a lasting relationship with depth. I spent most of my energy on James; I didn't take the time to come to terms with where I'd been. Coming out to others seemed unnecessary, since I was coming out to myself. Finding in myself the capacity to care, to extend—to love—another man. I didn't go backwards because I was going deeper. That seemed to be enough."

Weydon knew that George's friendship—when George was so inclined—was best demonstrated in the unencumbered conversation when the issues were serious, an endless dialogue parsing every point, examining every nuance of feeling or thought. He recalled the virtually endless discussions a year ago of his mixed emotions about coming out at work, and George's patience as Weydon played out variation after variation involving which person he would tell first and what the response might be. Weydon had first told Cindy, a manager in another division of the company. She had waited, she said, for him to disclose the strategic piece that had been missing since he had stopped talking about his divorce. Finally he supplied it, the shape of which she had already discerned. "People know," she said. "And they don't know. If they think about it at all." The rehearsals, the months of planning, had come down to that. Later, Weydon had told two other women friends with whom he had socialized regularly before he had met James, and then he had stopped.

George held out his hand silently; Weydon gave him the keys and got in on the passenger side. The car was cold, the leather seats strange and stiff. As George drove, Weydon did not look to see whether the drivers who passed were staring at the car.

After George left him with a kiss on the forehead, Weydon sat in his study. He heard muffled steps and laughter as people walked in front of his house. He had turned on his reading lamp but then turned it off and sat in the dark. When the phone rang, he let the machine pick it up. It was George, who left the name of his auto body shop. Weydon considered calling James but decided not to—he was not yet ready to talk.

This was the kind of event his father had feared when Weydon, at the age of thirty-eight, came out to him. James had been in his life for more than a year, and Weydon could no longer talk about his "friend" without feeling guilty. "What about your job?" his father asked first, then "What about gay bashing?" Only after the shock had worn off had his father asked about AIDS. He told his father he was not worried about work, although at that time he had not come out to anyone. He was not worried about gay bashing, since he and James seldom went to the bars. And his father did not have to worry about Weydon's health—he and James were fine.

Weydon realized that he was experiencing memories, ideas, feelings, in a random, haphazard order. His demeanor was the product of years of self-effacement. Minimizing differences was his goal, his way of accommodating the sense of shame, awkwardness, and confusion he had experienced from his adolescence forward, even when it meant he had to lessen the force of his intellect in order to blend in. He still avoided certain obvious gay "types," in spite of George's criticism; he had refused that first turbulent year after the divorce to attend, let alone march in, the gay pride parade. At some deep level he had known all along that refinancing was never the true force behind the decision to move, behind the incomplete truths told at the office, behind stories about his lawyer "friend," behind some of the control he experienced when he chose, or did not choose, to commission another piece of glass. Even his coming out to co-workers had been incomplete, stopped at the very moment it had become something less than absolutely safe, stopped before someone out of either anger or disgust could ask him a personal question or make a moral judgment about sexual practices or "lifestyles." He had never forced himself to move forward, and after a certain amount of progress he had allowed inertia to take over.

The next morning Weydon sent a message over the internet that he had personal business to take care of and would not be in the office until the next day. He called the auto body shop, explained the general problem, and made an appointment to leave the car.

It was light out, and traffic sounded brisk. He got into the car and backed it out onto his street. The car felt foreign to him; he considered driving back home and asking George to take the car in for him. He breathed deeply. No, that would be foolish, weak. He focused on the road, trying not to look either directly at the hood of the car or at drivers as they approached or passed. After a drive that seemed much longer than the distance traveled he pulled into the open garage door of the shop. A technician waited as he stopped the car and got out. The technician looked carefully at the car, not at Weydon.

"We can match that paint—no problem. Should take two days. We don't have loaners."

"I've arranged to have a rental agency drop off a car for me. It should be here soon," he said, without inflection.

"Don't see too many like this," the technician said, finding a silence even with the burr of sanders in the background.

"That, at least, is fortunate," Weydon responded, realizing a second later that the technician was referring to the car itself, not the vandalism.

He signed a form that the technician held at arm's length on a clipboard. He turned around to take another look at the words, scanning each letter, its form, location, size, color and thickness. He walked to the front and peered at the hood, tracing the Q with his index finger, noting the texture of the paint where it covered completely and where, in other areas, the red appeared pink as the white underneath bled through. At this distance, his eyes close to the paint itself, these words seemed less threatening, somehow less personal, the words disintegrating into letters, the letters into smears of color, the colors into meaninglessness.

"Mr. Weydon, we'll call you when it's ready," the technician said, causing Weydon to stand up, his back stiff from leaning over. Weydon noted that the technician was at least fifteen years his junior, possibly twenty. He went into the office to wait.

The rental arrived ten minutes later, driven by a handsome young man in a navy blazer and knitted tie. He was tall, his hair close-cropped and thick with gel. He wore a small gold ring in one ear. He opened the passenger door for Weydon, explaining that they would drive back to the agency and complete the rental agreement.

"It's a shame someone would do that to such a beautiful car," he said, looking directly into Weydon's eyes.

Weydon was momentarily distracted by a combination of the man's beauty and his own embarrassment. He felt old. Weydon looked down at a small pin on the man's lapel spelling out the word PRIDE in multicolored enameled letters. He returned his gaze to the young man's face, now realizing he had seen him before, one of the more beautiful faces he had seen that last time he, James, George, and a few others had gone slumming at the newest bar, with Weydon reluctantly enticed onto the postage-stamp dance floor to gyrate away with no particular partner. This young man had been nearby, bathed in the glow of the tawdry lights and, Weydon remembered, had smiled as they bumped together in the crowd.

"Yes," Weydon said, after a moment. He held the glance of the young man.

"My name's Zach," the young man said, looking away and turning the car into the street.

"Harmon," Weydon replied in monotone.

"You're not out, are you?"

At first the question struck him as impertinent. It presumed several things, things that Weydon did not want to acknowledge might be visible even to an observant, knowledgeable, or intuitive person. Everything about Zach bespoke a different kind of life, unencumbered by artifice or confusion.

Weydon thought a moment, then answered. "To myself—yes. A few others. I don't hide anything."

"But you don't reveal, either, do you?" Zach smiled, showing bright, straight teeth, then looked back to his driving. "It's not my business, really. I'm sorry."

"It's okay," Weydon said after a pause. "I'm upset about this damage. I don't understand it. I don't understand the hate. It's as if I had been physically struck."

The young man's white smile dimmed. "The car isn't damaged. It will look like new when it's repainted. It's not at all the same as being struck."

Weydon's face flushed with embarrassment. "Now it's my turn to say I'm sorry." Weydon looked at the young man's cheekbones, his forehead, his chin, searching for scars.

"No problem."

"It must be different for people your age. I see so many of them—openly gay, holding hands in public, not just at the parade or in Provincetown or Palm Springs. Even here."

"Somebody has to be first, I suppose."

"I support the causes, I give to the charities. . . ."

"You sound like one of the hillside fags talking. Justifying your silence behind Victorian gazing-ball gardens and Tiffany lampshades."

The indictment stung. Weydon considered for a moment how to respond. For some reason he was not offended. He knew some of these "hillside fags," at least by sight, and had always seen himself as a very different sort.

"Are you an activist?"

"No," Zach said. "Just aware of who I am."

They arrived at the rental agency and went inside. Zach helped Weydon complete the paperwork on the car.

"Mr. Weydon—Harmon," he said, handing Weydon the keys, "thanks for choosing our company. I'll see you again on Wednesday. Bring the car back here and I'll give you a lift to the body shop."

"Thanks, Zach," Weydon replied.

"Good luck."

Weydon drove home cautiously, the rental car having harder steering and an unfamiliar feel. He called the office for messages, trying to make himself believe that this was just another telecommuting day, something he did when he needed to concentrate. He sat on the couch in the living room working on press releases for a few minutes, then realized he had lost his focus on the work. He called George but got the voice mail and hung up without leaving a message. James would call tonight. He would tell James everything.

Pouring through the skylights and windows, the sun glinted off the coffee table and other glass objects in the room. The beveled glass of the chandelier over the dining room table cast elongated rainbows on the silver plush carpet.

Weydon walked over to where the refracted light shone on the carpet and sat on the floor. He first moved a finger, then his hand, then his wrist, into the light until the warm transparent bands appeared to conform to the contours of his forearm. He looked separately at each band—pink, orange, yellow, green, blue, violet. Weydon closed his eyes and saw in his mind each band as wide as a door and himself floating slowly through one after another. Opening his eyes and looking ahead, he moved his face completely into the bands of color and waited for them to leave an imprint, some kind of permanent mark.

SWEET THING

KEITH McDERMOTT
(FOR FRANK ARCURI)

Frankie had nothing to do. He sat on his porch singing to himself, "Ca-ca-ca-crazy, Crazy Canazie," and with a twig began digging out the caulking that his father had used to repair the porch steps. He jabbed and jabbed at it, surprised to find that it was soft and easy to dislodge. Then the sound of a car made him stop. He threw his stick off to the side of the steps and brushed the loose putty away with his hand. His father was installing a tub in Belpre and would not be back until dark; still, Frankie sat up straight and placed his folded hands in his lap, in his best I-didn't-do-it posture.

Out of the corner of his eye he saw Mrs. Woody's green Fairlane driving down the block. He held his breath as she passed in front of the house, her gloved hands on the steering wheel. She was looking straight ahead, but he knew that she had seen him and he held his pose until he heard her turn into her driveway two houses down. Mrs. Woody had spotted him peeing along the side of the house last summer and had told his mother.

What to do today? "Ca-ca-ca-crazy, Crazy Canazie, you're the ca-ca-ca-crazy girl that I adore." The thought of Crazy Canazie as either adorable or girlish made him stop and scrunch his face up like a prune.

Mrs. Canazie was an old woman who lived three blocks away in a rundown house between two empty lots. It was assumed that she had once been married, since a middle-aged man said to be her son stopped by and hacked through the weeded lots when the neighbors complained too often. The house itself would have looked abandoned except that Mrs. Canazie had nailed sheets and torn quilts to the eaves of the porch, shrouding it in layers of dirty linen. Sometimes at night, her shadowy figure could be seen, larger than life, projected onto the sheets by a Coleman lantern. Frankie had never seen her himself, but some of his friends claimed that she came out with the full moon to paint white patches on two oak trees that grew in her yard.

Of course, someone must have seen her. She must get groceries, but Frankie wasn't even allowed on her block since the "Halloween episode." That was how his mother referred to last Halloween, when he and some of his friends had made up the Crazy Canazie song, and sung it as loud as they could in front of her house, to lure her beyond the cocooned porch. However, neighbors had alerted the police to their devilry, and Frankie and his friends had been rounded up and taken to the police station, where they had to be picked up by their parents.

He had felt badly about that night, not for the whipping he'd gotten from his father, or having been caught by the police—he was used to adults overreacting—but for the cruelty of his act. He felt a shame much worse than anything his parents could kindle, and it came from an awareness that he had, in his unkindness, behaved like someone else—like fat Tommy Woodruff, for instance, who knocked the books from his arms while they waited for the school bus, or like his father, who called Mr. Johnson, the gardener for most of the neighborhood, a nigger.

Frankie left the step and went into the house, letting the bang of the screen door erase the song from his mind. He pulled himself up the stairs like a man suffering from heat exhaustion and stood on the second-floor landing, wondering which of the rooms might offer some amusement. He walked quickly past his own room and placed his hand on the doorknob of the guest room. His father always laughed when he heard it called that, and cited it as another example of his mom's "airs," perhaps because they hadn't had any guests since his grandma died two years ago.

Frankie turned the handle without opening the door. If he went in, he couldn't touch anything, and if he touched something he had to remember exactly where it went, because the guest room was off limits for him, on the assumption that he would untidy it, or disturb Nana's things. As he released the doorknob, he spoke aloud a line from an imaginary courtroom drama: "I never even opened the door."

His parents' bedroom, while not strictly off limits, was a there's-nothing-in-there-for-you room. He walked backwards across the carpeted floor, feeling like footprints were less incriminating on their way out. He went past the dresser, whose drawers he'd already been through that morning, around the bed, into the adjoining bathroom, and into the shower. He closed the glass door behind him and felt a rush of pleasure as the opaque light seemed to shift from dark to light and back to dark again. A dull film covered every surface: the blue tiles, the door of pebbled glass.

Frankie had never been allowed in the shower. It was for adults—"You might fall and crack your head." He'd always used the tub in the big bathroom. He dragged a finger across a tile and made a shiny smudge, like an archaeologist in an Egyptian tomb might disturb centuries-old dust, and reminded himself to add this spot to his list of cover-ups, wondering if it would involve scrubbing down the whole shower, or cleaning the entire bathroom, or the second floor. . . .

To end this line of thinking, Frankie reached out and gave the cold-water handle a sharp twist. Water shot through the nozzle; he barely had time to scream before he was soaked to the skin. He laughed and hopped in surprise and quickly turned off the water. The sound of his laughter made him feel bold even as he realized that the sodden clothes would take major steps to conceal. In his fortified mood, he stripped the wet things off and pulled out of his soggy sneakers.

He opened the glass door to let the air dry him; that way, he would not have to use one of his parents' good towels or track water across their carpet. The clothes, for the moment, could be left on the shower floor. When most of the drips seemed to be dry, he left the shower and tiptoed back into the bedroom.

He froze when he saw his reflection in the full-length mirror on his mother's closet door. The sight of himself naked, crossing the room like a thief, made him laugh out loud again. He opened the door and scanned his mother's neatly arranged clothes: shoeboxes and hats on the shelf above; dresses, skirts, and blouses on pink-cushioned hangers below; neat rows of shoes on the closet floor.

Without thinking, he crouched down and reached toward the back of the closet, pulling a dark leather case out by its handle. His mother's Avon sample case. He hadn't thought of it in months, the whole summer in fact, not since his mother had refused to do any more door-to-door sales work (the way she had sneered the words "door-to-door" at his father had made him think of the neighbors who kept a chicken coop in their backyard). He'd forgotten about the case in those agonizing, jobless weeks when his mother was home constantly, assigning him countless chores in cheerless parts of the house—the basement, the garage—before she got the job in Culpepper as a receptionist in a company that made rock bits for drilling tools.

He didn't bother opening the case now. He could tell by its weight that the Avon products were still there, the brushes and combs held to a laminated black centerpiece by elastic bands, the jars and tubes of cosmetics on the lower layer, and beneath each toiletry, words printed in gold like an invitation to an exclusive event: "Enter the World of Great Grooming: 50% Natural, 50% Nylon, 100% Luxury."

Frankie shut the closet door to look at himself; with the case in his hand he looked like a naked businessman on his way to work. He shifted his weight to one foot, lifting the other heel slightly, and brought his fingers to the base of his throat, throwing himself into a mock-girlish pose. Then he rang an imaginary doorbell and whispered in a soft, flutey voice, "Ding-dong, Avon calling," mouthing the words with a pouty expression like Marilyn Monroe.

The idea of going to someone's door, Mrs. Woody's for instance, and appearing on the front stoop naked made Frankie smile and cup an imaginary breast in his free hand. To make the illusion even more comical, he went back into the closet and got a pair of his mother's high-heel shoes and a large yellow sun hat he had never seen her wear. He put them on. Once again, he checked the result in the mirror, this time turning his back to it and looking seductively over his shoulder.

The shoes, though awkward to balance in, were not a bad fit. The hat was too much. He took it off, threw it on the bed, and began to thumb through the hangered clothes. After passing up a number of skirts and blouses as too difficult to match, he pulled out a lightweight summer dress in yellow cotton with a thin matching belt and, before his courage failed him, slipped it off the hanger and over his head.

He tilted his head from side to side and pushed one shoulder dramatically forward. It looked good. Still, there were adjustments to be made. He pulled the waist of the dress up to meet his own and cinched the belt tightly to keep the straps from falling down his arms. He threw his shoulders back and pushed his chest forward.

Now the black heels were wrong. He dashed into the closet and grabbed his mother's sandals tooled in bleached leather. The effect of these with the yellow dress made him suddenly aware of what his mother meant when she spoke of *taste*—even though she most often used the word to describe others in whom she found it lacking.

Frankie picked up the Avon case again. This time he was touched by the image of a frail young woman carrying a too-large case. His fingertips returned to the base of his throat, endowing the earlier gesture with genuine feeling. The sight thrilled him—until he focused on his head and face. The close crewcut he was made to wear in the hot months ruined the effect of the dress and sandals. And he had never seen his face as ugly before. Now, as he pulled his lips back, his huge front teeth looked grotesque in his small twelve-year-old face, and he seemed to lack eyelashes and eyebrows altogether. Well, he thought, I can certainly change that.

As he ran into the bathroom, Frankie marveled that even his thinking sounded different in the yellow dress and bleached sandals. He pulled open a drawer full of cosmetics and felt a pang of love for his mother, remembering how she looked when she dressed up in her black dress, high heels, and gold hoop earrings which he'd heard a neighbor say only she could bring off. Frankie wondered if he, too, could bring them off, but decided they wouldn't go with the sandals.

He applied color to his mouth, then blotted the greasy lipstick on a piece of toilet paper as he had seen his mother do. The sable eyebrows, when he had drawn them, seemed a bit severe, but he liked the arch he'd given them, making him look interested, as if his eyes were saying "Oh?" and "Is that so?" Eyelashes, he reasoned, were too difficult.

Now for the hair. He went to a drawer where he knew his

mother's scarfs were kept and pulled out a red-and-orange one that seemed to complement the dress; he knotted it under his chin. The effect was disappointing. He didn't know exactly why it looked wrong, but he remembered his mother commenting on women who wore scarfs over hair curlers. "Taste," he said aloud, and pulled the scarf from his head. He took the sun hat he'd rejected earlier and tried it on. It still gave him a slightly dressed-for-church look, but at least it matched the dress.

I wonder, Frankie thought as he backed away from the mirror, if you didn't know me and I wasn't too close . . . ? He studied himself from across the room. Or if you were old or crazy . . . He picked up the Avon case. "Mrs. Canazie, may I interest you in our ultimate moisturizer?" Well, it's something to do today, he reasoned gamely as he left the room, flap, flap, flapping in the sandals.

Frankie paused at the top of the stairs. To get the three blocks to Mrs. Canazie's house in broad daylight without being recognized was a nearly unimaginable job. He remembered his father's advice—break the problem to be solved into smaller, more manageable tasks—and rejected it for a method of his own.

When Frankie was faced with an unpleasant chore, he often relinquished his power to an object at hand, endowing it with temporary control of his mind and body. For instance, he hated mowing the lawn, but didn't mind letting the "magic mower" do the work while he trailed behind thinking of other things. This method was less successful with some problems—he once gave his "magic pencil" the power to complete a math quiz, with disastrous results—but in problems requiring a more physical approach, the method worked well.

The sandals, he thought, my magic sandals. I'll let them take me to Mrs. Canazie's—and I won't think at all, he added as an image of wet clothes on blue tile intruded upon his memory.

The sandals began moving one in front of the other, carrying him down the stairs. They didn't take him out the front door as he assumed they might, but turned and headed through the kitchen, where Frankie had just enough time to remind himself that he hadn't eaten the lunch his mother had left for him. Brilliant, he thought, the back way.

The sandals guided him out the back door, through the yard and into the alley that ran behind the house. Each block had an alley separating the rows of houses, garages, and backyards, used mainly to put out or pick up garbage. One of the older boys had set up a basketball hoop, but Frankie knew he'd hear the ball bouncing against the gravel if anyone was out playing. No one saw him.

Up ahead was the first street to be crossed; he clutched the handle of the case as he heard the sound of a lawnmower close by. It's in a yard on another block, he thought optimistically, but as he neared the intersection where the alley met the cross street, he saw Mr. Johnson mowing the corner lot. "Merciful Mother of Jesus, save me," Frankie incanted, hoping that the call to another source of power would not offend his footwear. Onward they took him, and a slight sucking sound now seemed to accompany the flapping as his sweating feet clung to the flat soles of the sandals.

Frankie had crossed the street when Mr. Johnson saw him, and though he didn't dare turn, he could tell from the idling of the engine that the old gardener had stopped pushing the mower. He switched the case to his other hand as if it might shield him from sight, and tilted his head so that the brim of the sun hat hid his face. He was nearly past the house and into the next alley when he heard a long low whistle sail over the whir of the lawn-mower.

If Mr. Johnson intended any irony, Frankie didn't catch it. He simply felt ashamed, coupled with the sudden realization that he wasn't wearing any underwear. He began to run through the alley. The case, which seemed to gain in weight and volume, slapped painfully against his leg. He ran all the way to the end, stopping just short of the next street, behind a row of bushes.

Looking behind him, he was surprised to see that no one was following. He had had such a sensation of running away—not only from Mr. Johnson, but from the entire neighborhood. How did I stop? he asked himself. The sandals are no longer moving me. Because I stopped trusting them, he reasoned. I ran.

Mrs. Canazie's house was the last one on the next block, but Frankie felt no will to move. "Taste," he muttered. The word did nothing to eliminate the nasty feeling of fear that lay in his stomach where his lunch should have been.

He shoved the Avon case between two bushes and tried to back in beside it. The space was small, forcing him to squat down and fold his arms around his knees. His bare bottom touched the earth; the sensation shocked him and caused him to wrap the dress around his legs and fall forward. As he did so, his knees caught in the fabric and the delicate stitching gave at the waist.

He got up and inspected the finger-length rip, and saw wet circular patches darken the thin yellow material under the arms. He'd ruined the dress.

The day, which had seemed so endless when he sat on the porch steps, was racing to its conclusion. His mother would discover the ripped, stained dress, her closet and drawers ransacked, the shower desecrated. That, however, was nothing compared to what he was doing now. If only he could trade this present crime for an earlier one—the putty on the porch steps. That was surely worse, being in his father's domain, along with misplaced tools and breaking the basement window, crimes for which he'd been severely punished in the past. If he admitted to digging the putty out of the steps with a twig, with the full intention of undoing all his father's work . . . But something of this magnitude—going out in his mother's clothes and stealing her Avon case—would never be ignored. His mother would tell his father when he got home, in a foul mood from installing tubs, "workin' like a nigger" all day.

The thought of his father made Frankie tremble and begin to sniffle as he stood by the bushes. His father hated him to cry— "Crying is for girls." But he couldn't hold back the little sobbing noises that came up from his throat. Then the tears began; the sun dress lent him a frailty that permitted, even encouraged, them.

He let his head fall forward and clasped his thin arms with his hands, hugging himself and saying over and over, "Poor thing, poor, poor, sweet thing." It was a phrase he'd made up to console himself. After he'd been punished, he'd lie in bed and imagine running far away from home and climbing into the back of a station wagon parked in the driveway of a big house. There he'd fall asleep until he was awakened by the station wagon's owners, a beautiful, childless couple who would take him into their arms and croon, "Poor thing, poor, poor, sweet thing." The words consoled him now, even though he could not conjure the kind couple in daylight. He was comforted by the disembodied voice and heard the cooling words instruct him.

"Dry your eyes, poor thing. Pick up the case, poor, poor thing. You can do it, sweet thing."

But here the magic voice stopped, just as the sandals had, and he waited in vain for the next command. What should I do, he wondered, looking about him for a new source of power: a bush, a discarded bottle cap, a neighbor's cat sleeping on a back porch, the hot summer air. Nothing would answer him, or contradict what he felt must be true: that everything he'd ever done was some form of disobedience, and that dressing up like this and going out had broken a special code that was beyond his understanding, but for which he would be severely punished.

Frankie wished he were still sitting on the porch steps singing "Ca-ca-ca-crazy, Crazy Canazie. . . ." That's it, he thought. That's when it started. I said her name, and after that everything I did led me here. And he understood: His own clothes would never have let him come. It no longer mattered if he was caught. He was doing this for them too, his mother and his father, and for the whole neighborhood.

He began walking, and this time the flap, flap, flap of the sandals seemed to be trying to keep pace with him. The Avon case swung rhythmically at his side. He crossed the street. Instead of taking the alley, he flap-flapped onto the hot pavement of the sidewalk, putting his free hand up to steady the sun hat.

Someone opened a screen door down the block. Frankie recognized little Emily Pryor, who was three grades below him in school. She had seen him too, and was slowly crossing her lawn toward him. He didn't bother to try to hide behind the hat. When he was nearly in front of her, he snapped his head in her direction and shouted, "I'm not wearing any underwear!"

Little Emily stopped walking, stared open-mouthed at Frankie, then screamed and ran for the house. "I'm going to tell my mama!" she warned him over her shoulder before she was safely behind the screen door. Frankie quickened his pace.

Mrs. Canazie's house stood between its two untended lots. As Frankie reached the first lot he noticed the weathered blotches of paint randomly decorating the two oak trees. He stood at the edge of the yard with its knee-high weeds and looked toward the porch draped with gray sheets and wounded quilts, their batting exposed. They had been crudely nailed to the eaves, forming a tentlike structure against the sagging frame of the house.

"Mrs. Canazie," he called from the sidewalk, "it's Avon calling."

He began to wade through the weeds, remembering that it was rumored she buried broken glass and rusty metal in the yard to discourage trespassing. He imagined his feet bleeding in the bleached sandals as he mounted the crumbling steps and knocked ineffectively on a hanging sheet.

"Mrs. Canazie?"

The sound of a screen door opening down the street—Emily's mama?—made Frankie push the sheet aside and step behind it onto the porch. The wooden floor gave slightly under his feet. He reached his hand out to balance himself and saw that to his right, about two feet away, the boards had given completely, leaving an enormous hole, as if something huge had dropped through the floor, into the darkness beneath the porch. The left side was intact, but more difficult to interpret. Light filtered in through the linen walls, giving Frankie the same feeling he'd had in the shower, but here the light seemed to be all around him.

On this side of the porch, the house had been covered in bits of silvery metal rectangles—tin cans that had been cut, flattened, and nailed to the wooden siding and up onto the ceiling. Frankie stepped closer. He saw himself divide in the reflective surface: a boy's ear in one silver rectangle, over a pair of red woman's lips in another, a pair of masculine eyes beneath the penciled arch of a single eyebrow. He turned from this asymmetrical version of himself and called again for the old lady.

"Mrs. Canazie?"

The front door had been removed from its hinges and things tied with varying lengths of string and yarn were fixed to the top of the doorjamb: a toy soldier, a pine cone, a tarnished spoon; objects found underneath a couch pillow or in a schoolboy's pocket. A miniature execution staged by the eccentric old lady? But where was she? Frankie pushed aside the web of string and yarn and entered the dark front hall.

The structure of the house seemed to be like his own. Stairs to the second floor ascended in front of him, and behind that closed door at the end of the hall would be the kitchen. He tiptoed partway down until he heard a shuffle of feet; suddenly a silver line illuminated the bottom of the door.

"Please, Mrs. Canazie, I'm sorry about Halloween."

The door opened. A figure stood in a rectangle of hazy light.

The old lady extended the palm of her hand toward Frankie, as if she were trying to shield him from her sight.

"Please"—he knelt on the floor and put the Avon case down in front of him—"I just wanted to say . . . I'm really sorry— about . . . I'm just so sorry."

He thought the woman tried to say something, but it didn't sound like words, only a low, croaky moan.

He pushed the case toward her. "I brought these for you. They're ultimate . . . one hundred percent." Then he jumped up and ran, pushing his way through the stringed curtain, across the porch, through the wall of sheets and out into the sunlight. As he crossed the dense lawn, the image of the old lady with her hand outstretched came back to him. Only this time, she seemed to beckon him. He heard her kind old voice calling him back: "Sweet thing, sweet, sweet thing."

FRANKIE'S WEDDING

ERNEST McLEOD

Frankie and Cynthia stood with the justice of the peace in the dappled shade of a maple tree in Frankie's backyard; gathered in a circle around them were seventy-five or so friends and family members. It was the last Saturday of August, a sunny day, not too humid. A tent had been stretched over a portion of the yard; white balloons decorated its periphery and beneath it were rented card tables draped with paper tablecloths. Streamers had been wound around the posts of the back porch. Suspended from the porch roof was a meticulously painted wood sign saying: HAPPY TRAILS FRANKIE & CYNTHIA!

Frankie's house was not much, but the view was lovely: pastures and woodlands to the east and north, mountains to the west, to the south the rooftops of the small Vermont city in which Frankie had grown up. It was a pleasant spot for a gathering, and Frankie and Cynthia made an attractive couple. She wore an elegant ivory-colored dress that was lacy at the top and fell just below the knee. Her long auburn hair was sprinkled with baby's breath. In her slightly trembling hands, she held a bouquet of daisies picked by Jennifer, one of Frankie's two children from his first marriage. Frankie was wearing cowboy boots, jeans (pressed for the occasion), a white shirt, a string tie of silver and jade, and a sky blue jacket embellished with rhinestone horseshoes and a line of fringe across the chest. It was the type of outfit only someone like Frankie could carry off.

There were many who said the marriage wouldn't last. Bets on its duration had been placed, and two years was the most anyone had given it. Cynthia had been through one divorce; Frankie two. They ran into each other, literally, outside a bar in Jackson Hole, Wyoming. Either Frankie's gigantic red convertible collided with Cynthia's horse trailer or vice versa, depending on whose side of the story you chose to believe. Cynthia was on her way to New England (her family, though from New Jersey, spent their summers on Lake Champlain) after leaving her rancher husband in Idaho; Frankie was clearing his head out west in the aftermath of his second divorce. After the police reports were completed, they discovered they had much in common: they both appreciated Vermont summers, bluegrass music, and dancing in honky-tonks that had seen better years. They both hated traveling alone. During the many days it took to repair their vehicles, they went out a few times, and, when that worked out, shared a motel room. By the time they reached Vermont together, they were in love. From the start it had been a stormy relationship.

Snapping a photograph as the ring was slipped onto Cynthia's finger and again when his brother kissed the bride, Ethan didn't think about whether the marriage was a good idea. They looked like they were in love. They looked beautiful. They looked completely happy. In his almost twenty-one years, he had never felt like they looked. Ethan watched Frankie's smile illuminate his handsome face and Cynthia's bouquet held against his fancy jacket and their lips meeting and then Frankie calling for the party to begin and everyone rushing up to congratulate them and he was awed by the ease with which they accepted all the attention. Had he been in their shoes his discomfort would have been as vivid as Frankie's coat. While the rest of his family joined the well-wishers, Ethan held back and, to occupy himself, focused his camera on the distant horizon. He knew that he should go and kiss Cynthia's cheek and slap Frankie on the back as the other guests were doing, but he couldn't quite force himself to move.

Finally, he pivoted on his heels and saw Star and Chestnut, Cynthia's horses, watching the spectacle from the edge of the pasture with hopeful curiosity. He was about to take their picture when his viewfinder was filled by a large, pale, smiling face topped by a shock of raspberry-colored hair. The hair had caught his attention before the ceremony and his mother, Beverly, had whispered that it belonged to Cynthia's sister Darnelle. "What possesses people to do that sort of thing?" she had said, noting not only the hair but the gold rings that pierced the side of Darnelle's nose and one eyebrow.

"Hi, I'm Darnelle," the young woman confirmed, extending her hand. "You must be Ethan. I've heard a lot about you."

He couldn't imagine what. The only thing he had heard about her was that she was, according to Cynthia, the black sheep of the family. Appropriately, she was dressed in a loose pantsuit that was entirely black. A red rose with part of its stem attached was pinned to her lapel; above it was a wordless button stamped with a pink triangle.

"Pleased to meet you," Ethan said. He wondered why she had so boldly come over to him.

"I hope we get to talk," Darnelle said. She scanned the crowd and frowned. "I tried to get my girlfriend to come, but she thinks the institution of marriage is a crock of shit. Personally, I wouldn't mind a Cuisinart and a tax break, but I'm supposed to be radical, so don't tell anyone. Frankie looks like he's rehearsing for the Grand Ole Opry."

"We're very different," Ethan explained, glancing down at his tan chinos and unpatterned maroon vest. This woman bothered him. Why was she telling him about her girlfriend? He imagined she was the type who went around marching in parades, screaming that she was a lesbian as if the whole world had to know. Unconsciously, he slipped his fingers into his vest pocket and felt the small, rumpled square of paper he had carried with him all summer. It was a letter to his parents explaining that he was not the person they expected. Though he generally hated getting his picture taken (Frankie was the only photogenic one in the family), he was relieved when his conversation with Darnelle was interrupted by Frankie's call for group photographs.

Cynthia's family squeezed tightly together and wrapped their arms around one another's waists and shoulders. Although Darnelle was indeed a startling contrast to her sisters (they were all clad in flowery dresses and had hair colors more or less found in nature), no one appeared alarmed by her. A few of the children were intrigued by the rings on her face.

After many photographs had been taken of Cynthia's family

and then Frankie and Cynthia alone, Frankie said, "And now for the reluctant Matthews clan."

Ethan surrendered his camera to Cynthia's sister Theresa, and the Matthews clan stood with their arms at their sides.

"Closer, closer!" ordered Theresa. "What are you wearing? Invisible armor?"

Cynthia smirked and nodded her head.

Frankie, standing at the center of the group and smiling broadly, stretched his arms wide and pulled his parents toward him. "They don't want to be captured flanking their wayward son."

"Oh, stop," said Beverly.

While the buffet was being set, people clustered at the bar. Frankie and his father and the JP were at the head of the line. Frankie's friend Hammer—who like Frankie was a part-time DJ at WKMA, the local country music station—was serving as bartender. Frankie himself still did a little bartending as manager and part-owner of a nightclub and sports bar downtown.

"She looked pretty as a picture," Frank Sr. said, handing Frankie a rum and Coke and accepting a scotch and water for himself and a glass of white wine for Beverly.

"She sure did," Hammer said. "But it's all downhill after today. Know what I mean?"

"What do *you* know?" Paul, the JP, said. "You still live at home with your mother." Though they had all graduated from high school together, Paul and Hammer were paunchy and red-faced and looked far older than Frankie.

Frankie said, "Yeah, Hammer buddy, sometimes we gotta wonder who launches your torpedo, if you know what *I* mean. Hey, Batman, what can I get you?"

Several places back in line but within the range of conversation, Ethan answered, "A beer, I guess." From the time he was a kid, he had always disliked Hammer, whose real name was Armand. Beverly referred to him as "*that* Armand Choquette," as if, God forbid, there were several others.

"Two," Darnelle hollered. She had been asking Ethan about his summer. He could think of no explanation for his existence that didn't sound pathetic. Most of his time had been spent obsessing about the things he wasn't doing: he wasn't in Europe breathing in foreign languages or scrawling ideas onto napkins at outdoor cafés; he wasn't hiking through the desert with all his possessions on his back; he wasn't doing an internship for a glossy magazine in New York; he wasn't having sex.

Frankie handed Darnelle and Ethan their beers. "Sign looks great, Batman. I'm glad you two have become acquainted."

Ethan glanced in the direction of the porch. He had spent a lot of time on the sign. Frankie had wanted it to be permanent, not Magic Markers on cardboard. "Like a saloon sign," he had said. The "Happy Trails" struck Ethan now as hopelessly corny, but it did look pretty good with its old-fashioned letters, and Frankie did seem to like it.

"Should be 'Happy Trials'!" Hammer shouted from the bar. A few titters erupted in the crowd.

Frankie good-naturedly gave him the finger and said he was going to circulate among the other guests.

"Why does he call you Batman?" Darnelle inquired, thankfully abandoning the topic of summer accomplishments.

Ethan blushed and responded as quietly as possible, "When I was little I used to run through the house with a plastic Batman cape over my pajamas. Frankie latched on to it for some reason. He usually says, 'Hey, Batman, where's Robin?' It's very embarrassing."

"Oh, I can just see you. How cute! I bet they were the kind with the little feet."

Ethan turned even more crimson and admitted that they were.

"You must really be the baby," she said.

Ethan nodded. "The mistake." He said this in spite of the fact that his parents always insisted otherwise. "Frankie left for college when I was something like four, and Margaret's ten years older than me, so I sort of don't remember them." Actually, he held many clear memories from that time: Frankie's car—an old taxicab painted black—on its side in the neighbor's rock garden, Margaret wrapping her naturally curly hair around giant rollers in an attempt to straighten it, Frankie's girlfriend saying, "Shit, it's your little brother," as Ethan opened the bedroom door. For many years after that he had tried to convince himself it was her body that entered his fantasies.

"I remember life with my siblings all too well," Darnelle said. "Four sisters. The prima donnas and me. Actually it was like

Cyndie was Diana Ross, the others were the Supremes, and I was Janis Joplin trying to be a Supreme. Or something. Anyway, what was it like growing up in small-town Vermont?"

"Boring," Ethan said, sensing Darnelle was fishing for something. "You know that old Talking Heads song, 'Heaven.' I grew up in heaven."

"Ethan, take some cold meat," Beverly said. She inspected a spoonful of Nana Rose's potato salad and put it back, declaring it drowned in mayonnaise. Giving up smoking had caused her to become nutritionally obsessed.

"Take some cold meat?" Ethan said incredulously. Over the summer he had been forced into the habit of repeating his mother's more ludicrous statements in the form of a question. "How many times do I have to tell you I'm a vegetarian now?" His parents seemed unable to absorb this simple fact. "It's not like there's nothing else to eat," he mumbled, regarding the innumerable pasta salads which crammed the buffet table.

"I'm sorry, I forgot," Beverly said. "You know what this summer's been like."

Ethan knew all too well. In June his father had had a gall bladder attack, necessitating surgery. In July Margaret's family had been in a bad car accident on their way home from seeing the fireworks. (Miraculously, they had escaped with only minor injuries.) Then, at the beginning of August, after many traumatic debates, it was decided that Molly, the family dog, would have to be put to sleep. All summer long he had waited for the perfect moment to come out to his parents, but it had never arrived.

Beverly exclaimed, "Doesn't that look beautiful!" to Cynthia's mother, Sylvia, who was in the midst of making room for a carved-out watermelon filled with melon balls and strawberries. Sylvia responded that Beverly's dress was stunning.

Beverly brushed aside the compliment and said that it was old. "I looked everywhere and couldn't find a thing I liked."

Ethan watched his mother smile and listened to her lie. The fact was that she had defiantly not bought a new dress because, in her words, the whole wedding was "a farce."

"And all of your daughters look lovely," Beverly continued.

Sylvia sighed and shook her head. "Believe me, I have not

encouraged one of my daughters to hang jewelry from her face or dye her hair fuchsia. She used to have beautiful long blond hair." Looking at Ethan, she commented that it was nice to see that all young people did not find it necessary to make a statement.

Darnelle appeared on the porch and patted her mother's head. "What are you saying about me?"

Sylvia shooed her daughter's hands off her hairdo and said, "I was saying that you used to have beautiful long blond hair."

Darnelle picked a strawberry from the watermelon and ate it. "Mom, I hate to break it to you, but I never had beautiful long blond hair. I was born like this." She laughed and took another strawberry.

Beverly continued to smile, but Ethan imagined the checklist of objections scrolling through her head as she observed Darnelle. The moment they stepped away from the table, she made a *tsk-tsk* noise and said, "Did you see the way she picked up the fruit with her fingers?"

Because the plastic champagne glasses did not allow for the more traditional means of calling for a kiss, people began pounding their fists on the tables. Frankie and Cynthia put down their forks and stood up, brushing lips briefly. This polite gesture was met by a chorus of boos, so Frankie covered their faces with his cowboy hat and dipped Cynthia backwards with exaggerated passion. She batted her eyes and fanned herself in mock innocence when they returned to an upright position.

"Oh, for God's sake," said Beverly.

Frankie remained standing and announced: "I'd like to thank everybody for coming. I can't tell you how much it means to be surrounded by all the people you care about." He went on to specifically thank various friends and relatives for helping out and wound his way into an oratory about love and respect.

After a few minutes of sitting still for this rambling speech, the children wanted to abandon their meals and return to the sunshine. Their plates were littered with sun-dried tomatoes, black olives, capers, and other things they deplored. The Oriental Tofu Salad had been equally disliked by young and old. Flies soon became attracted to the smorgasbord of food, but the breeze seemed to completely avoid the oppressive blue shadow of the tent. The combination of alcohol and too much food caused everyone to become hot and drowsy; people longed to fall asleep on the grass but instead dabbed at their foreheads and took one more swallow of liquor.

Margaret's children, Cassie and Harper, wanted to visit the horses, thinking they'd be lonely all by themselves. "Come on, Eth," they begged, tugging at Ethan's sleeve. Frankie's kids, Ben and Jennifer, were already running toward the pasture.

Ethan was more than happy to escape. Beverly had just relayed a story about an entire planeload of people being stricken by food poisoning en route to Japan, and now she and Nana Rose were engaged in an argument about how long it takes mayonnaise to turn in August temperatures.

"A charming dinner topic," Margaret said, rolling her eyes.

"I don't understand all this fuss about food these days," Nana Rose said, calmly waving a wasp away from her bright white hair. "You've always been a worrywart, Beverly."

"Did it ever occur to you there's a lot in this world to worry about?" Beverly said, her mouth becoming a thin line. She looked to Frank Sr. for support. "I worry because I care."

Frank Sr. was searching through his pockets for a toothpick. "Did you hear about the plane crash in the Adirondacks? I guess the idiot thought the mountains grew there overnight."

Ethan wondered if his parents had a story of disaster for every situation in life. "Ready?" he asked Cassie and Harper, who were now busy making vomiting noises in response to the food-poisoning story.

The kids ran across the lawn and Ethan followed, walking. He was often shocked by how quickly his nieces and nephews were growing. Ben, Frankie's oldest, had recently shed his pudginess and was nearing puberty. Jennifer had just turned ten. Harper and Cassie weren't babies anymore. He had been a kid himself when they were born, the first uncle in his class. That and the fact that his parents had always been older than other parents, his siblings older than other siblings, made him feel as if his own childhood had been abbreviated. He remembered at an early age striving to be adult. Ironically, when he went away to college he suddenly felt young and naive. His new classmates had already declared their sexuality. They had had sex more times than they could count. They could make jokes about

AIDS and then ignore it. He reached for the letter in his pocket again. He knew the words by heart. In the days following the wedding there would be time. His parents might be able to hear it then.

Jennifer whistled, and Star and Chestnut galloped to the fence. Ethan lifted Cassie onto his shoulders and let her pat Chestnut's nose and feed him a carrot.

Ben acted disinterested in the horses. He suggested it would be fun to give them a bowl full of whiskey. "We did that to the dog once and she fell down the stairs," he said gleefully. "It was a fucking laugh riot."

Jennifer scornfully regarded her brother and caressed the flash of white between Star's eyes. Besides Cynthia, she was the only one he would let ride him.

"Can we give the horses whiskey?" Harper asked, seeking Ethan's approval. At five, he idolized Ben, but he was also an innately cautious little boy.

"No," Ethan said. "Picking on animals isn't funny." Harper was his favorite. Harper broke his heart. Earlier, in the buffet line, someone had dropped his plate and much of its contents had landed on Harper's blond head. Not surprisingly, he had burst into tears, but what struck Ethan was the look of guilt that had immediately swept over his face. Ethan recognized it so clearly he had to look away. He remembered being at a parade when he was about Harper's age and glancing down with horror to see horse manure splattered over his bare legs. Looking around at the clean legs of the other children, he had automatically assumed it was his punishment for being different.

"You're too heavy for me," Ethan said, returning Cassie to the ground.

"I bet I can bench-press more than you can," Ben boasted. "My stepdad lets me use his Soloflex." He rolled up his sleeve and flexed his biceps.

"I wouldn't be surprised if you could," Ethan said.

"Feel it," Ben said to Harper.

Harper was duly impressed. "Feel Ben's muscle, Eth."

"That's all right," Ethan said.

Jennifer took a lump of sugar from the pocket of her jumper and Star gently ate it from her palm; others who tried this risked being bitten. She said that she thought Chris, their stepfather, was an imbecile. "He and Ben lift weights and look at each other in the mirror. It's nauseating."

Ben rolled his sleeve back down. "We do not, you liar. At least he wears normal clothes and drives a normal car and isn't a druggie."

"He's queer," Jennifer said.

Ben spat into the grass. "If anyone's queer around here it's—"

"Me," Ethan felt like saying before Ben had the chance, but Ben didn't bother finishing his sentence. The unexpected turns in children's conversations made Ethan nervous. He didn't want to know that Ben preferred his other father to Frankie, he didn't want to hear them use the word "queer," he didn't want to feel intimidated by a twelve-year-old. He looked at Ben squarely and said, "Frankie is not a druggie."

From the tent, Margaret's husband, Bill, hollered that the cake was about to be cut.

Ben shrugged and said, "That ain't what I've heard."

Hammer said, "Hey, little Ether, how's it hanging?" a phrase that Ethan hadn't heard since he was about thirteen, the age at which he figured Hammer's mentality was stalled.

"I hope it's good," Margaret said. "Orange poppyseed. It might be a little weird." She and Ethan had relocated to the bar to get a better view.

Ethan focused his camera on the cake. It was a three-tiered affair with yellow roses around the circumference and the prototypical bride and groom on top. Frankie pointed to it and asked when Margaret and Bill had posed. He often referred to them as "Quintessential Yuppie Nerds" and considered Margaret something of a traitor for so entirely forsaking her party-girl days.

"Did you make it?" Ethan asked.

Margaret laughed. "Are you kidding? It's lucky I remembered to buy it."

Frankie took a sip from his drink and tipped his hat to the crowd. He didn't seem to be paying much attention to the cake.

"He better not try any funny business," Margaret said in a voice remarkably like Beverly's. "Cynthia will be pissed."

"I don't think he will," Ethan said, remembering Cynthia sternly warning Frankie about it when they were reviewing the wedding plans in his presence. Cynthia's warnings were not to be taken lightly.

"Ha!" said Hammer, fixing himself another drink. His red-rimmed eyes hinted that he had been taking full advantage of his proximity to the liquor. "I know Frankie."

Ethan snapped a picture as the bride and groom cautiously raised the slices of cake to each other's mouth and began to nibble. "So do I," he said. "He's my brother." There was a sprinkling of applause. He wanted to say, I told you so.

Then Hammer screamed, "Do it!" and Frankie did it.

Ethan closed his eyes. When he reopened them, Cynthia was wielding the cake knife and wiping a yellow rose from her cheekbone. Frankie shielded his crotch and pointed accusingly at Hammer.

"So, how much did we bet?" Hammer said, winking at Ethan.

"You're a creep," Ethan blurted out, surprising himself.

"No kidding," Hammer said. "But here, I'll pay *you* off just to show the kind of man I can be." He slid a beer in Ethan's direction. "Lighten up, my friend. You'll put wrinkles on that pretty brow."

Ethan walked away without the beer and returned to his parents' table.

"Now, why did he have to do that? That boy will never grow up," Beverly said. She took a bite of Frank Sr.'s cake and declared it very moist.

Nana Rose said she thought it was a little dry.

"She's never satisfied with anything," Beverly mumbled.

Nana Rose held up her empty plate. "I ate it, didn't I?"

The back door slammed as Cynthia went into the house and then again as Frankie followed her.

"At least none of our friends are here," Beverly said, taking the last bite of cake. "Frankie's crowd probably thinks this is all terrific. Margaret, *I* think the cake is very moist."

Darnelle approached their table with the guest book. Ethan had been watching her circulate, half admiring and half resenting the way she glided from table to table without appearing to notice that people accepted the book with a slight but noticeable hesitation. He couldn't imagine trying so consciously not to blend in.

"Autograph time, folks," Darnelle said. "Before World War Three breaks out."

Beverly apologized for Frankie's cake-cutting behavior.

"She'll get over it," Darnelle said. "Cyndie has always been partial to drama. Unlike myself, of course." She handed the guest book to Nana Rose and then to Frank Sr.

Frank Sr. scrawled his name illegibly and squinted at Darnelle's button.

Ethan knew what was coming and wanted to slide beneath the table. Instead, he picked up his camera and pointed the lens beyond the tent. Ben was giving Harper a piggyback ride, weaving across the yard and spinning him around. Cassie was dancing by herself; she twirled and lifted her dress above her head. The one man at the gathering Ethan found attractive was reclining against the trunk of the maple tree. His fiancée knelt down beside him and cupped her hand over his eyes. He smiled as she handed him a drink. The sun had lowered, and elongated shadows spilled across the grass.

"What's the pink triangle mean, Doreen?" Frank Sr. asked.

Darnelle passed the book to Beverly and matter-of-factly replied that it meant she was a lesbian. She went on to explain that the Nazis had used it to identify homosexuals during the Holocaust and that more recently it had been turned into a symbol of empowerment by the gay rights movement.

Frank Sr. nodded and said, "Hmmm. Is that so?"

Beverly halted in the middle of her signature. "Frank, I'm sure Darnelle would rather not stand here answering a hundred of your silly questions."

"I don't mind at all," Darnelle said.

Nana Rose suddenly recalled that there was a lesbian on one of her daytime programs, she couldn't remember which one, but anyway the girl had ended up meeting a handsome doctor named Brad and it was all forgotten.

"That's what I like about TV," Darnelle said. "Middle America's wish fulfillment in a box."

"Is that rayon?" Beverly interrupted, gesturing toward Darnelle's blouse. "It moves like rayon."

Darnelle said that in fact it was and placed the book in front of Ethan.

He pressed the shutter release and stammered, "Oh!" as if Darnelle's presence were a complete surprise.

"No aliases now," she quipped, handing him the pen.

*　　*　　*

Citronella candles were lighted at dusk to ward off the mosquitoes. Cynthia had not made an appearance since the cake cutting. Her absence had begun to inspire whispered speculations. Some of the older guests, including Nana Rose, had decided to make their getaway before the onslaught of bugs and loud music.

To avoid the Port-O-Let that had been stationed at the side of the house, Ethan went inside to use the bathroom. The door was locked, so he waited at the top of the stairs. There was a collage of photographs on the wall—pictures of Frankie with the kids, with friends, with Cynthia. In one photograph, his second wife was among the group of people posed in front of a ski lodge. An X had been drawn through her face.

"Hey, Batman, where's Robin?" Frankie said as he and Hammer emerged from the bathroom together. His eyes were very bright.

Hammer chuckled. "Should have joined us, Ether. Could have had a ménage du trois. You know what I mean?"

"What exactly do you mean?" Ethan felt like saying. He glanced again at Frankie's glassy eyes and thought of Ben's remark. He knew that several years ago Frankie did have some sort of drug problem, but he thought that was all in the past.

"Catch you later," Frankie said.

Ethan closed the door and snooped around a bit but found only prescription medicines. He remembered Frankie telling him once in an uncharacteristically fatherly tone: "The snow will mess up your life, Batman. Stay away from it or you'll ruin everything you touch."

When Ethan went downstairs again, he heard from behind a closed bedroom door Cynthia's tearful voice saying she couldn't believe he'd do that. Someone else said, "And what about the money? It's *your* savings."

Ethan crept quickly outside only to run into Frankie pontificating from the porch about the wonder of a sunset, pointing to the magenta streaks blazing across the western sky, declaring that his profound appreciation of the setting sun was perhaps the one constant in his tumultuous thirty-five-year history. He saw Ethan and forcefully gripped his shoulders. "Great sign, little bro. Terrific sign. Did I tell you that already? Fantastic sign." He didn't seem to want to let go.

"You told me," Ethan said, pulling out from beneath his brother's hands. It occurred to him that Beverly might be able to say, "I told you so," before the photographs were even developed.

Paul had taken over bartending duties. Hammer had set up the sound system and was acting as emcee. "We're beaming in from WKMA," he announced. "Why-don't-you Kiss My Ass, as my man Frankie lovingly refers to it."

Ethan went to the bar and ordered a triple scotch.

Paul raised an eyebrow. "Taking after your old man or your brother?"

Hammer announced a song for the newlyweds. "Where *is* the lovely bride? Maybe this will draw her out." Chuck Berry began singing "C'est la Vie," and Hammer sang along in an inappropriate key.

Frankie snaked his way through the dozen or so dancers, swiveling his hips wildly to the music.

Ethan took a gulp of scotch and tried not to choke as the liquor burned down his throat. He hated scotch. He thought back over the summer. Three more months of his life wasted. Days behind a cash register at the depressed mall, nights catatonic in front of the TV, punching the remote until dawn or tossing on top of soiled sheets, panicked that it would be this way forever. Most of his high school friends had drifted away. The time he spent with his parents was unbearable because it was false, but he remained silent. The letters he had written and shredded filled his wastebasket. He'd taken the scraps to the backyard one night and burned them all. *Dear Mom and Dad,* they all began, *For a long time now I have concealed who and what I am. I hope that what I'm about to tell you will not change your feelings. . . .* His counselor at college, the first person he had ever come out to, had told him to write the letter even if he didn't send it. "Carry it with you," she suggested, "then when the time comes to tell them, you'll know what you need to say." But the summer was almost over. He was leaving for school in four days and he hadn't talked to them, the one thing he had promised himself he would do. What good was the lousy letter now? Another year would pass and then another. Only hours earlier he had thought: after Frankie's wedding, when things calm down again. He had really decided to tell them. But things were not

going to calm down. He would be forced to keep quiet to protect them from further upset. "It's great you're so dependable,"
Frankie had said once as they coasted down Main Street in the
convertible. "I get all the room to fuck up."

Darnelle was trying to get Ben to dance with her. He stood
solemnly with his arms crossed and shook his head. His eyes
were on his father, who had left the crowd and was now dancing
by himself in the middle of the yard.

"Are you all right?" Beverly asked, waving her hand in front of
Ethan's face. "You look like you're in a trance. And what on earth
are you drinking?"

"I've had one beer all day," Ethan snapped.

Frank Sr. pointed in Darnelle's direction. She and Cassie and
Harper were shimmying down to the ground and back up again.
"You should have brought a date," he said. "There aren't many
prospects for you here."

Ethan watched as the attractive man escorted his tipsy fiancée
to their white sports car. He imagined her resting her head on
the man's shoulder as they drove home, the wedding just another
event in their busy social summer.

The screen door opened, and Cynthia stepped out onto the
porch. She had changed into jeans and a white blouse. Behind
her stood her mother and two of her sisters. None of them
looked happy.

Beverly looked at her watch. "Well, they haven't spoken to us
all day. Cynthia disappears for hours on end, and the last I saw
Frankie he was dancing like a madman—aren't they supposed to
be leaving on their honeymoon? But I *refuse* to get involved."

Hammer began chanting, "The lovely bride. Here comes the
lovely bride!" over the sounds of Chuck Berry singing about the
joys of life in the U.S.A.

"God, he is horrible!" Beverly said.

Frank Sr. took her arm. "Maybe we should be off, Mother.
Things are getting a little rowdy for us old folks."

"What is he doing!" Cynthia screamed suddenly. She stormed
down the steps and gazed past the tent, where Star burst into
view with Frankie sprawled haphazardly on his back.

Frankie shouted, "Look out!" one hand reaching for the cowboy hat, which had tilted down over his eyes, the other hand
grabbing desperately for Star's mane. The hat flew from his fin-

gertips and tumbled to the ground, spinning on its rim before coming to a rest near Ben's feet. Star snorted and reared back, veering left, then right, then lurching forward toward the sound-system table.

"Holy shit!" Hammer said. He ducked behind a speaker and sent the contents of his beer bottle trickling into the mechanisms of the tape deck. The dancers frantically parted, butting heads and elbows in the process.

Star halted for an instant, then jolted back and started in the direction of the driveway. Frankie's eyes were by this time squeezed firmly shut. Star's mane was no longer within his grasp as he slid quickly backwards towards the animal's muscular hindquarters.

"Oh, dear God," Beverly said. "He's going to break his neck. Frank, do something."

"What the hell am I supposed to do?" Frank replied, scratching his head.

Before anyone had time to do much, Star came to an abrupt and final stop, and Frankie was tossed off, landing facedown in the gravel. For a moment, nobody moved. Star craned his neck and looked down, letting out a short, seemingly satisfied whinny. Beverly put her hand to her forehead. Cynthia put her hands on her hips. Chuck Berry kept singing.

Then, all at once, several people rushed forward to check Frankie's condition. Star took off with a flourish toward the pasture. Ben hid his face in his sleeve and began to sob. He caught sight of his father's hat and planted his foot smack in the middle of it.

Frankie raised his head and stood up slowly. His chin was bloodied, and the knees of his jeans were missing. Cynthia said, "You fool! You complete ass," as she was helping him up.

"I'm okay, I'm okay," he insisted, trying to brush off his clothes. "I just slipped off. Fire it up! Keep the party going."

Hammer's mouth was still wide open. He was speechless for once. He wiped the top of the tape deck with his shirttail and put on a new song about heaven being just a sin away.

With the scotch adding a surreal layer of unbelievability to it all, Ethan had at first considered that what was happening couldn't be happening. Then he considered that Frankie had planned it all along as the final, ruining moment to his summer. Whatever he had to say would always seem tiny and inconsequential next to Frankie's actions. Without thinking about it, he pulled the square of paper from his pocket and held it in his hand. It was tattered from being folded and unfolded too many times. "I have something to give you," he said once and then repeated it more loudly.

"What?" his mother asked, watching as Cynthia went to search for Star and Paul led Frankie inside. "Frank, maybe we should go see if he's all right. Of all the stupid things to do." Frank was shaking his head. "Jesus H., what a day."

"Take this from me," Ethan pleaded, squeezing the letter into his mother's palm. "Take this with you."

She looked into his eyes and then at the square of paper in her hand. She looked at Frank Sr., who appeared confused. She opened her purse and slipped it between lipstick and tissues. "We'll see how he is and then we'll go," she said, clicking the metal clasp shut. She asked Ethan if he wanted to come with them. He shook his head no and said he'd walk home. His throat was dry as dust.

Most everyone had abandoned the party by the time Cynthia systematically took a razor blade to each of the white balloons bobbing in the breeze. It had taken a while to settle the children down after the horse episode, but they had finally been rounded up and convinced that it was time to leave. Ben had defiantly taken a beer from the bar and had started off toward the woods by himself when his stepfather arrived to pick them up; Jennifer called out, "Crybaby, crybaby!" Cynthia's family departed for their motel rooms in disgust; they had never liked Frankie and now were beyond pretending. Even the die-hard partiers said good-bye quickly when the balloon popping began. It was clear the time for revelry was over.

Frankie, cleaned up after his fall, returned to the porch and mournfully said, "Where did everybody go?" He picked up his crumpled hat and tried unsuccessfully to smooth it out. He went to Cynthia where she stood with the razor blade in her hand. She surrendered it without a fight. They waltzed round and round, across the yard and back again. Periodically she beat his back with her fists. "I know," he said. "I know."

Hammer held his hand to his heart. "My doubts have vanished," he exclaimed, looking skyward as if following them into thin air. "Here we have two people who deserve to be together. Know what I mean?" Looking genuinely touched, he began singing "Happy Trails" a cappella as he carelessly packed the sound system into his backseat.

Far into the night, when there was no one left and nothing else to do, Ethan and Darnelle began cleaning up—collecting the soggy plates and the half-filled cups that had been turned into ashtrays, stripping the stained and torn tablecloths, loading the mess into tall garbage bags. Darnelle stopped short when they arrived at the table which held the cake. All that remained of the bottom two tiers was a lopsided pile of crumbs and melted frosting, but the third tier sporting the bride and groom was mostly intact. "Amazing," Darnelle said. "The only unwrecked thing here." She backed away and pointed to the garbage bag. "You decide. Keep it or toss it?"

All through this time Ethan had wanted to talk, but he didn't know where to begin. He kept reaching into his pocket to confirm that it really was empty. The scotch had worn off. "Maybe they want to save it." He looked at the cake and then at Darnelle. Frankie had thanked him again for the sign before he and Cynthia had gone inside to bed. Ethan had been unable to meet his eyes; he looked tired and drunk and ugly, so different from the way he had looked under the maple at the start of the day.

"Ah, hell. Open the bag," Darnelle said.

It was then that Ethan told her what he had done. They left the cake where it was, and he explained that the next time his parents saw him they would know. He wanted Darnelle to say that he had done the right thing, but what she said was: "Frankie called me when Cyndie told him I was gay. He knows, Ethan. Maybe they do too."

Frankie knew. They all might know. Ethan tried to imagine it and couldn't yet.

"It's your turn," Darnelle said. She unpinned the drooping rose from her lapel and pinned it to Ethan's vest. She held his camera at arm's length. "Ready. To commemorate us." The flash lit a brief, brilliant circle around them.

The dark was fading as Ethan walked home. He knew he wouldn't sleep before the sun came up. The streets were quiet. There were lights in a couple of windows. A tabby cat emerged stealthily from tall grass with a mouse in its teeth and froze when it saw him. In the distance, a dog began barking. There were no lights in the windows of his parents' room as he crossed the lawn, but a fan whirred softly in one window, drawing in the cooler night air.

CALENDAR BOY

DAVID A. NEWMAN

It was Chicken Patty Tuesday. I was on patty four, including bun and gravy. My record was ten, which until recently was also our dorm record. I was thin, but I could chow. North Dining Hall had two edible foods: Jell-O and chicken patties. I looked around, noticing for the first time the lunch mumble was much quieter than the dinner roar. Everyone—the girl from Lewis Hall with purple hair, two oversized football players in mesh shorts at the black table, even Sullivan across from me—had their heads buried in the *Observer*, our thin and optimistic student newspaper.

CLASS OF '87: LARGEST, SMARTEST? a headline for a story about my freshman class caught my eye. I was one of eighteen hundred kids. Our male-to-female ratio was seven to three, ninety percent of us were Catholic and we averaged thirteen hundred on our SATs. I wasn't that smart. Or that Catholic.

"Lumber, listen to this." Sullivan wrinkled his paper down to look at me. " 'Do you have what it takes?' " he read in a high-pitched tone. " 'If so the women of Walsh Hall want you, yes you, for the second annual Men of Notre Dame calendar.' "

"Get serious." I popped the remaining chicken patty in my mouth and took a sip of Mountain Dew. "What page?"

"Personals. Page seven." Sullivan shook his head in a can-you-believe-it? gesture and I realized with a quiet shock who my new best friend of two weeks reminded me of: my father. Especially the wedding photo on my father's bureau. Something about the wiry frame and Adam's apple.

I found the calendar thing. It said to send a photo with name, year and major to L.L., room 140, Walsh Hall. "Who would actually go up for that?"

"You don't go up for it, Lumber." Sully tossed his *Observer* aside. "They pick you."

"Oh."

He reached for my Jell-O. "You mind?"

"Yes." I grabbed the parfait dish and downed the green Jell-O like a cold glass of milk.

A week later the personal was taped to my orange metal door along with my high school senior picture. "Not funny," I said to the empty hall as I tore it down, feeling my face get red. I unlocked my door, pretending I hadn't thought what I'd thought when I first saw it. That the women of Walsh Hall had put it there. For a second, I thought I'd been picked.

I looked at the picture now cupped in my palm. It was good. Too good. My face was fuller and tanner than the thin one I usually wore. My hair seemed lighter than its normal dark brown. I looked like the cocky older brother I was glad I didn't have, the kind of guy girls ask to their freshman dances. To the annoyance of Carpentcrelli, my shoe-and-belt-polishing ROTC roommate, I'd been getting a few of those calls. Quite a few. Because my too-good picture was in the Freshman Register, which like everything here, including me, was called something else: the Dogbook.

The Dogbook came with tuition. Every freshman had one full of their airbrushed senior pictures with names—JUSTIN CORBIN—and interests—TENNIS, STUDENT GOVERNMENT, TRAVEL—typed underneath. There was also a spot for a nick-name, which I mistakenly thought meant the nickname of your high school, so I put "LUMBERJACKS." Justin "Lumberjacks" Corbin. Nice. Chuck Pangborn on second floor thought the same thing and wrote down "PURPLE WAVE" and now all the guys sing it to him to the tune of "Purple Rain." I kind of hate it here.

"Check it out, guys. Think I can hit her?" Hendricks, Sully's new friend from baseball, dunked his dinner roll in milk and squeezed it into a round, wet lump.

I looked at his target: Wild Colleen the Dancing Machine

from Farley Hall. Colleen wore green terry-cloth shorts and a green striped tube top. In October. Three guys on my floor had slept with her. Including Sully. "Don't be stupid," I said softly.

"Christ, Lumber, lighten up." Sully narrowed his eyes at me. "We're freshmen, we're supposed to be—no, actually, we're obligated to be stupid."

"Is that why you put that thing on my door?"

"What thing?" Sullivan narrowed his eyes again, then elbowed Hendricks. "Five bucks says you miss."

"I was 8–0 last year with six complete games." Hendricks dunked the dinner roll back in the milk. "I don't miss."

I turned to Sully. "Daley said you did it."

"Did what?" Hughes asked Sully.

"Fuckifino." Sully shrugged.

"You know you did it." I gave Sully my incredulous look, which involved dropping my shoulders and rolling my eyes up. "Tell me you didn't do it."

"Tell me what it was I fucking did, Lumber, and I'll tell you if I did or didn't do it."

"Here's the windup"—Hendricks cocked his arm—"and the pitch!" He released the biscuitball and it flew in a high arch across the dining hall, cresting over the salad bar, descending dangerously close to the black table and finally hitting Colleen, who was by the soda machine, square on the left side of the head.

"Holy shit!" Sully smacked the table with his hand.

Colleen momentarily lost balance of her tray but righted herself as a large chunk of the roll ricocheted off her head and splatted against the wall behind her.

The dining-hall lady with the wig that made her look like George Washington waddled over. "You—you get out!"

We scrambled to our feet. Sully cradled two oversize peanut butter cookies in his sweatshirt as we ran, laughing, out the door.

*   *   *

October 14, 1983

Andrew J. Denton
Boston College
Cushing Hall, Room 219
Chestnut Hill, MA 02167

Dear Andrew,

So how's BC? Things here are green and pretty, just like the brochure (yawn). Kids here call themselves 'domers' because the Admin building has a golden dome with a statue of the Virgin Mary on top. Maybe they should call themselves Marys (ha!). Guess what I found when I was unpacking? Your Dartmouth T-shirt (actually, I stole it— psych!). I still can't believe we're not together in high school anymore. I keep picturing us cruising around in your Mustang listening to the Go-Go's. I'm trying to picture the new friends you've probably made but I can't. The one's I've made are nothing like you'd expect. I don't know if that's good or bad. Everybody here is very into football, just like my dad. Go Irish! (ha!). Well . . . I may not get the chance to mail this so I'm probably just writing to myself. Hi self. Bye.

Justin

I sat in a streamer-filled basement party room with REGINA MARIE NICKODEMUS, my formal date. Regina was what everyone called a "Smick Chick," meaning she went to SMC, St. Mary's College, the all-girls school across the highway from ND. Her interests included SAILING, DANCING and HEMINGWAY. I clasped my hands together and said, "You look different than your picture."

"I know." She raised her beer to her lips but didn't drink. "You don't."

"You think?" I scrunched up my face.

"If you need me to stroke your ego, Justin Lumberjacks Corbin, I will."

"No need," I lied.

Regina sipped her beer. I looked around. Girls with too many things in their hands—purses, drinks, roses—stood stiffly next to their well-scrubbed dates, trying to look comfortable. The reason St. Mary's girls were in our Dogbook was that Notre Dame used to be only men so they all married SMC Chicks. "My mom was a Smick Chick," Sully told me orientation weekend. "I plan on marrying one myself."

"Think if I'd put my high-school nickname in there." Regina lightly brushed my thigh with her hand. "Regina 'Bulldog' Nickodemus. That's attractive."

I smiled.

"Justin Lumberjacks Corbin," she said to no one in particular. "The truth is, you look better than your picture."

"Right." I shook my head.

"Jesus, you're insecure. A guy like you."

"I'm not. I'm just . . . not comfortable being judged by the way I look."

Regina finished her beer. "Why is it only really attractive people say that?" She grabbed my hand, pulling me onto the empty dance floor.

"White Wedding" by Billy Idol was playing. Regina looked me in the eyes as we danced, which finally convinced me. It hadn't occurred to me girls might find me attractive. I'd grown two inches and one shoe size over the summer, but those were changes you could measure.

"You're a good dancer," Regina said.

"No I'm not."

"Stop that." She faux-slapped my hand. "You wouldn't have gotten into Notre Dame if you weren't pretty special."

"You obviously haven't met the guys on my floor." I smiled.

We weren't really dancing anymore, just standing and shaking a little to the beat.

"If you're asking me over for a North Dining Hall feast, I accept."

"You like dancing, huh?" Something about Regina scared me. The way she seemed ten years older than me but didn't realize it.

She nodded, getting a little lost in the song.

"And sailing?"

She laughed. "I'm from Topeka. I've never sailed in my life and I despise Hemingway. My sister Melanie's a junior. She told me the Dogbook was a joke so I decided to have some fun, something this party is sorely lacking in, don't you think?"

After I dropped Regina off, I headed down the unlit pathway girls weren't supposed to take for fear of on-campus rape. I had five beers. Regina had seven. Halfway through number six she held out her hand, said "Get this," then belched letters *a* through *g* of the alphabet. The cemetery was on my right, married student housing on my left. Or the other way around. She liked me. She liked me. She kissed me, pulling my head closer with her right hand.

Girls liked me, Sully and the guys thought I was cool. I blew into the air, imitating Regina with her cigarette, hoping to see my breath, but it wasn't that cold yet. It was cool; I was cool. Be cool. I watched both sides for traffic, then crossed Highway 31. A Burger King billboard advertising both the Whopper and the Whaler was lit in the distance. I said both words out loud, which made me indescribably happy. I kept saying them faster and faster—whopperwhalerwhoppalater—like a helicopter taking off. When the path turned dark again I started to run.

I loved college. I hadn't touched a book. All I did every day was read *Rolling Stone* and listen to the Go-Go's. Over and over. I ran without making noise. I felt like calling Barry Anderson, the man who took my senior picture, and thanking him. Everyone thought I was the cocky older brother in the photo. Everyone thought I was "Lumber," but I knew I was something else. Something unformed and scared, and that night I made a decision to believe them and not me. I was the person in the picture, I was Lumber. I was drunk.

I jumped over a puddle and when I landed I heard my father's voice. "You're eighteen now." He was sitting in the driver's seat of our Seville and didn't turn to look at me. "We're not responsible for you anymore. What you make of yourself over the next four years is entirely up to you. No more funny business. Understand?" I nodded. "I didn't hear you, Justin." He flicked the right-turn signal as we neared Notre Dame Avenue. "I understand," I said, turning away from him and tracing the "ville" part of Seville on the dashboard until he said, "What did I tell you about smudges?"

When I got to the building that looked like Jiffy Pop popcorn

I stopped running. A group of guys were playing basketball on the lighted courts nearby. It was two in the morning. A skinny dude with a red T-shirt got hacked driving the lane, so he stopped, resting the ball on his hip. He noticed me in my sport coat.

"Hey, man!"

I looked over.

"Didya get any?"

I smiled and raised my head. The trees began to swirl. "Many!" I yelled, not sure what I was saying. I held my arms out wide. "I got many."

The next morning, instead of the alarm clock, the ringing phone woke me up. Carpenterelli was gone. It was light out. I turned off the fan I used to block out hallway noise and reached over the metal frame headboard for the phone, getting it on the fourth ring.

" 'Lo?"

"Um . . . hi. I'm trying to reach Justin Corbin."

"Regina?"

"Um, no. This is Lacy Lewis from Walsh Hall."

My heart pounded. Orientation weekend I had gone to the bookstore to get a soapdish because we have community bathrooms. On the way out, I held the door for this unbelievably pretty blond girl who was struggling with books and boxes: Lacy Lewis. Senior. Walsh Hall. Cheerleader. The first thing I told Sully when we met at Freshman Barbeque was that I knew—that I'd actually spoken to—*the* Lacy Lewis. He finished his beer and said, "No shit?" I still think it's why we became friends.

"Justin? Are you there?"

"Yeah . . . hi, Lacy. It's me. How are you?"

"Great, thanks. Listen, Justin, I'm calling with some pretty amazing news. We would like you to come in and interview for the Men of Notre Dame calendar."

My heart beat in my ears. "You're kidding."

"Of course not. Now, it's not official or anything, so don't get your hopes up, but we've narrowed it down to twenty guys; obviously we only get to pick twelve, so I can't make you any promises. . . ."

"Of course—I mean . . . I understand."

"Believe me, it's an honor to get this far. Especially for a freshman."

"Yeah, no, I'm. . . . How'd you guys get my picture?"

"We have our ways."

I nodded.

"Also, we posted notices on the doors of guys we wanted to encourage to enter. You were definitely supposed to get one."

"Actually, I did." I laughed. "I thought it was a joke."

"Now, why would a total cutie like you think it was a joke?"

"Listen to this," Sully set down his Coke and grabbed the *Observer* with both hands. " 'HESBURGH "JUST SAYS NO" TO GLAND. In a move that surprised no one, Notre Dame President Father Theodore Hesburgh disallowed any school funding or acknowledgment for the recently formed Gay and Lesbian Alliance of Notre Dame. The group, known as GLAND—' "

"Gland?!" Hughes put down his trapezoidal-shaped fish sandwich.

"Fucking butt plungers," said Hendricks.

"Butt plungers?" Sullivan laughed. "I never heard that one before."

"Keep reading," I said.

Sullivan nodded. " 'All we want,' said Kevin Agnostino, President of the fledgling group—"

"Agnostino's a poo jammer?" Hughes set down his milk. "He fucking lives on my floor!"

"Poo jammer?" Sully cracked up. "Where was I when they made these up?"

"Who's Agnostino?" I asked.

"That fairy on third who watches soap operas all day." Hendricks flipped through his paper. "What page?"

"He rearranged his class schedule around *All My Children*." Hughes picked his fish back up. "He's got a picture of Jenny and Greg on his door and a I-heart-GH bumper sticker."

"GH?" Sully looked confused. "Gay Homos?"

"*General Hospital*," Hughes said.

"What page, Sully?" Hendricks searched his paper.

"Three," Sully said. "Next to *The Far Side*."

Hendricks found the article, then held up his hand. "Listen to this shit. ' "All we want is to advertise our meeting times in the

Observer and on Campus Radio. Our goal is increased campus awareness and education. We are not seeking funding.' " "

"I know what he's seeking," Sully said, high-fiving Hughes.

"He lives in our dorm?" I asked.

"Not for long." Hendricks set down the paper and Hughes picked it up.

"I don't think I've ever seen him."

"Count your blessings, Lumber." Hughes pointed to the un-touched fish on my plate. "You want that?"

I shook my head.

"News flash, guys . . ." Hughes set my plate on top of his. "Lumber's lost his appetite."

All three stared at me, surprised.

"It's no big deal." I laughed. "I don't feel like eating." I shrugged. "I got a lot on my mind."

"Such as?" Sully actually looked concerned.

So did Hendricks and Hughes. I just sort of stared at them for a second. It was surprising how different they looked when they were quiet. Younger.

"We're your buds, man," Sully said. "If there's something eating you, you should tell us."

"Yeah." Hughes chased the fish with milk.

"Okay." I nodded. "Promise you won't freak out about this."

"About what?" Sully checked out a girl at the salad bar, then turned back to me.

"Um . . . you know that calendar? The Men of ND?" I took a sip of Mountain Dew. "It doesn't mean I'm in or anything, but they called—actually, Sully's woman, Lacy Lewis, called." I looked at Sully and raised my eyebrows. "She wants me to come in for an interview."

"Dude, this is huge!" Sully slapped me on the back.

"No it's not."

"Listen to Lumber!" Hughes looked at me with the widest smile I'd ever seen on him. "It's not like they called us."

"No kidding." Hendricks smiled. "How many guys are they talking to?"

"I don't know," I lied. "Like twenty."

"You're in the top twenty!" Sully held out his hand and I high-fived it. "That alone should get you laid until at least junior year."

I smiled a little.

Sully smiled a lot. "When's the interview?"

"Tuesday." I inhaled. "Shit! What the hell am I gonna wear?"

"Say no more, Lumber." Hughes stood up and grabbed his tray. "The boys are on it."

Lacy Lewis looked surprised when she opened the door. "I know you."

"Yeah," I nodded. "From the bookstore," I said. "I was the one with the soapdish."

"I remember. Come in." She led me to a chair by a large bay window. Sully had given me his tapered black pants, black socks and black shoes. Hughes tossed in a dark-green V-neck sweater and Hendricks handed over the pièce-de-résistance: a weathered brown bomber jacket. I wore Andrew's Dartmouth T-shirt underneath for luck. I had to admit I looked good. Sully even convinced me to put Spritz Forté in my hair and it ended up kind of cool and spiky-looking.

"I love your jacket," Lacy said as I slipped it off.

"Thanks." I sat down. "It's new."

"It doesn't look new." Lacy cleared pompons and magazines from the overstuffed sofa across from me. "I didn't recognize you from the picture."

"Is that good or bad?"

"Neither. I just . . . didn't know it was you." She curled up on the couch, scooching out of a patch of sunlight.

A large oriental rug covered the hardwood floor beneath my feet. A framed poster from *Fame* hung above her cluttered desk with a pair of ballet shoes taped next to it. "Great room." I motioned around with my eyes.

"Seniors get first pick."

I nodded. "You guys are . . . I mean your squad is really good. I watch you guys more than the game," I lied.

"With the team we have this year, who could blame you," she said, and we laughed, even though it wasn't funny. Lacy laughed a little longer, sighed, then said, "So tell me a little about yourself."

"Well, I'm a freshman, but I guess you already know that. I'm not sure what my major's gonna be. My dad wants me to go premed, but he and I don't usually—"

"Whoa, whoa, I'm not your academic advisor, Justin. We don't want to know about Justin the student, we want to know about Justin the person. What kind of things do you like to do? You know, like . . . what are your dreams?"

"My dreams?" I swallowed, wishing she'd offered something to drink. "Gosh. I don't know. I feel like this is one of my dreams right here."

"Meeting me?" She laughed.

"Well, yeah, that, and . . . I don't know. It sounds kind of pathetic."

"Not to me it doesn't." She leaned forward, holding me with her eyes. "The committee likes honesty."

I raised my eyebrows. "Well, then . . . to be honest, I wasn't all that, um, popular in high school. My best friend and I kind of had this reputation for being . . . we were sort of on the fringe. He goes to Boston College." I looked at the oriental rug, tracing the pattern with my eyes. "We're not really friends anymore."

Lacy watched me and nodded. "It's hard when friends grow apart."

"Yeah . . . no, but it's good. Anyway, I figured I would just blend into the background here. There's so many smart kids and athletes and everything."

"So you weren't expecting this."

"You can say that again."

"And you have no idea why we wanted to see you today?"

"Honestly no. I don't."

Lacy looked away. "Um . . . I'm—I'm not doing this anymore," she said to the closet door.

"Did I say something wrong?"

"No, Justin, it's not you." Lacy got up and started toward the door.

Behind it, someone whispered, "Open it, man!" Someone else laughed. Then closet door burst open and Sully and Hendricks and Hughes and Daley and Carpenterelli and one other guy I'd never even seen before fell onto the floor, howling with laughter. I laughed too; I didn't mean to—air just pushed out of my lungs and exploded into the room.

Lacy Lewis bit her finger. "I'm so sorry." She wouldn't look at me.

"Lumber, you're not pissed, are you?" Sully sat up, but then he doubled back over laughing, leaning on Hughes for support. "We totally had you."

I sat in the chair, hands pressed against the armrests, memorizing the rug as they scrambled to get up. I couldn't move. My skin burned.

"I feel like this is one of my dreams right here." Carpenterelli did a surprisingly good imitation of my voice.

Then Hendricks said, "Guys, he's pissed."

"Don't be that way, man." Hughes walked toward me but Lacy stopped him. "We wouldn't have done it if we didn't like you, Lumber."

"We're going to the dining hall." Sully motioned to the door with his head. "Come on."

"I'm not hungry." It came out soft, like when I tried to say hello when Lacy called.

It was quiet for a second. Hendricks picked up a pen from the desk. Hughes shrugged. Hendricks put the pen down. Then they started to leave, looking down. "Learn how to take a joke, man," Carpenterelli said, but Sully waved him off. They filed out quickly and quietly. Except Sully, who looked back at me still sitting in the chair. I stared at the *Fame* poster; the black guy was holding the white ballet girl in the air. Her back was arched. Sully finally walked away and Lacy quickly shut the door behind him.

"I am so, so sorry. I didn't know it was you. They told me you would think it was funny."

I stood up.

"No, Justin, don't go." Lacy touched me on the arm and for the first time I realized how incredibly short she was. "I really am on the calendar committee, and . . . I, I think you're great. Really, I do. Actually . . . I'd like to submit you for real." She smiled. "As a makeup."

I looked down and nodded. Then I moved slowly toward the door.

Lacy followed me, but not too close. "So you're not mad?"

"Why would a total cutie like me be mad over something like this?" I said and walked out of her room.

My friends had more money than me. I could tell by the fit of Sully's shoes and pants and the softness of Hughes's sweater. I walked past the lakes heading toward North Quad. A leaf fell and at the very last moment I lunged, caught it, then stuck it in Hendricks's coat pocket. There was something else in there. His wallet.

The basketball courts were empty. The path to St. Mary's was starting to get dark. Girls walked in pairs or clusters, checking behind them each time they heard my footsteps. The cemetery was blue and foggy. In the large lighted windows of married-student housing a woman was placing a baby into a highchair.

It was Chicken Patty Tuesday. Regina would be getting out of dance class. Sully and the gang would be loading up on patties, seeing if Hendricks could break his record of twelve. "But it's gotta have gravy and bun," Sully would say, "or it doesn't count."

Last time I walked this path I heard my father's voice, and now I heard it again. "Mr. Denton and I both agree it's for the best that you and Andrew are going to different schools." He was leaning against the front door of the Seville, wiping sweat off his forehead with a monogrammed handkerchief. It took us eight trips up three flights of stairs to unload my stuff. "I want to make sure you understand where we are on this, Justin. If you have any contact with him whatsoever, I'll stop paying your tuition. You'll be out of here faster than you can say 'Corbin Chevrolet' and you won't be able to come home. Your mother is with me on this. For once." My father watched the top of my head for ten seconds. I blinked and kicked at the gravel in the parking lot as he got in the car and whirred down the automatic window. "Make a clean start, son. No one knows you here."

Cars blew past as I reached Highway 31 and started walking toward the Burger King sign. A semi passed, then a station wagon. The next car, a tan two-toned Buick Skylark, pulled over and a man, balding and eager, reached across and opened the passenger door. "Where you heading?" He smiled as I ran up.

"East." I slid in and pulled the door shut with a thud.

THE GEOLOGY OF
SOUTHERN CALIFORNIA
AT BLACK'S BEACH

FELICE PICANO

Hang gliders dappled the sky as the T-Bird convertible ascended then flattened out onto the seashore plateau along Torrey Pines Road. Red and yellow, white and blue, purple and orange, the fragile little man/mechanisms seemed no bigger than dragon-flies levitating upon the strong Pacific ocean currents, gliding in slightly askew formation as though out of a child's illustration.

"That's Jonas Salk's Institute," Craig said from the backseat, still playing tour guide. "He's supposed to be working on a new vaccine," he added. "Keep going to the end. The parking lot's a right turn." Craig's voice, normally strained and even raspy, was even more tensed from having to yell.

The turnoff led past where the hang gliders were taking off. I turned to face them, watching a gang of people gather around one glider just landing. Did they simply run off the cliff to get going? Or were they lifted by currents from the rock ledge? The latter, I supposed.

The paleontologist in me couldn't help but notice the cliffs. The rock here looked pretty undistinguished, but California's geologic history was actually complex. These Southern Penin-sula ranges were defined Quaternary laid over a basement of Mid-Mesozoic rock, all part of what was known as the Nevadan Orogenic Belt, the earliest lifting of the western part of the continent when dinosaurs filled the land. Since then, under the influence of subducting plates and shifting masses, these coast-lines had risen and dropped many times, picking up fragments of various plates that had slowly moved north to become Alaska.

"Now remember," Craig poked me from behind, "no shilly-shallying! You must go directly down the cliff path! No matter how frightened you are!" He meant it to be a command, but the combination of Midwestern twang and childish whine undercut his authority.

"Cliffs don't frighten me," I said.

"Nothing frightens Roger," Mark said, as he lightly spun the steering wheel. He looked great behind the wheel of the T-Bird. For that matter, he looked great in any convertible in Southern California, his thick black hair riffling in the maritime breeze, his skin quickly tanning, tiny tension lines resolving from around his eyes. We'd been talking about moving out here, and this visit had been partly about him opening a San Diego office. Mark was staying with a law-school friend, Anita, a woman my age who'd returned to school after her children were grown. She was working in the attorney general's office but still open to the idea of joining a commercial practice, especially one as successful as Mark's.

"Yeah! Well maybe he's not frightened because he's never *seen* a cliff like this!" Craig insisted. "He'll be plenty frightened."

"I'm astigmatic," I explained. "All depths look shallower. That's why heights don't frighten me. I can't grasp how high they are."

Mark looked my way briefly, a smile hovering on his lips.

"We'll see! We'll see!" Craig warned darkly from behind us, not getting the joke. That evoked another tiny smile from Mark.

In truth, what I really wanted was to get into one of those hang gliders and rise, rise, rise above the earth, the sea, into the sky, and just soar away. How much could that cost? Fifty dollars? A hundred, tops? All I had to do was tell Mark to drive to where they were taking off.

"It'll be good to get more sun," Mark said. Although I'd just arrived in San Diego, he'd come five days earlier for the Bar Association Weekend. "The June Glooms," Diegans called the overcast, foggy weather, even though it was mid-May, the city's thousands of jacaranda trees just reaching bloom, littering the lawns and streets with pale purple blossoms. Mark had caught a bit of sun the first few days around the pool at the Del Coronado Hotel, where the conference was held, but since then the weather had been dismal. It was hard to know what to do. We had formed today's plans just last night at dinner, with the four of us—Craig, Mark, Anita, and I—down the Baja coast at that hacienda-turned-restaurant overlooking the channel islands near Ensenada. Craig had said he knew the most magnificent beach in the area. We'd go, he'd said, if the sun came out.

"People have fallen from that cliff," Craig went on, warning of dire consequences. "Miles Parker fell and almost died. He's got a metal plate in his head. His jaw was broken in three places and had to be rebuilt. A pacemaker had to be installed in his chest. . . ."

Mark would throw a fit if I said I wanted to hang glide. He silently worried all those days in the Caribbean as I'd found, put on, and tried out the snorkeling equipment. He grew tenser as I taught myself how to use it in the bayside house pool until I was certain I knew how to breathe right. I clumped along the deck in the big rubber fins down the ladder into that pale green bay water, where from the first instant that I arranged the face mask and breathing tube and put my head down and spread my arms and legs and floated, gently kicking, I knew this was what I wanted, what *I'd always wanted* to experience in the water. When I got out, Mark was in the deck chair right there on the quay— a first—wearing that worried face he couldn't shake. "You went so far! I could barely see you!" And even though I explained how safe it was, how easy, how I could see far off, every inch of water, enough to chivvy and chase a magenta-and-white octopus across the stark, barely vegetated limestone sea floor, I saw how worried Mark continued to be whenever I snorkeled, afraid that I'd be sliced by a barracuda, stung by a ray. No, hang gliding was definitely out.

Mark pulled the T-Bird to the end of the macadam at the post-and-wire guard rail. Craig leapt out, grabbing bags from the backseat.

"Ocean looks dirty," Mark said.

With less familiarity than I had of the West Coast, he was still surprised by how dark the sand was, how green steel rather than marine blue the Pacific usually looked.

"C'mon, Craig! Get off me!"

"You can't handle that! Let a real man carry it," Craig insisted. He'd grabbed me from behind and was trying to wrest the bag

away, then shouldered it and tossed his own, smaller bag at my
feet. "Once you get on the cliff's face, it'll drag you down."

Ever since I'd arrived at the airport, Craig had been doing
things like this, designed to show Mark how tall, strong, virile,
and manly he was. In short, how desirable. Which he undoubtedly was. Why else would I be out here?

Not that anything Craig did would make a bit of difference to
Mark, I knew. Except perhaps to the degree that it pleased or
annoyed me. (Nothing should *ever* annoy me.) But Craig didn't
know that. Despite how intelligent and well read he was, Craig
wasn't very observant of others. He tended to act almost entirely
out of a welter of instinct, exhibitionism, and petty revenge. All
of which made him unpredictable and thus a lot more attractive.

We headed to the break in the guard rail and protective
hedges and on to the path hewn into and down the cliff. It was
very high. Even with my astigmatism, I could see that the beach
lay quite far below. Suddenly across it ran the shadow of an
insect. I looked up behind myself: another hang glider had taken
off. It soared off into the distance.

"I knew you'd be scared the second you got here," Craig was
crowing. He'd already begun down the path, a makeshift steep
decline around boulders, between grass tussocks and through
sand patches. I followed. Mark brought up the rear.

At most points in the descent, I was so busy trying to hold on
and get around obstacles that I seldom looked around. This portion of vast uplands around La Jolla is of the late Miocene era,
sedimentary rock on top of and cut through by striated meta-
morphic and plutonic rock, the whole business known as the St.
Onofre Breccia. I had lectured often about how these high cliffs
were formed when the most recent part of this coast had risen,
relatively late geologically speaking, long after the dinosaurs
were fossils and the earth was undergoing repeated hard glacia-
tions. And thus, all this was, for me, a source of great interest. All
around I could make out a mass of indurated rock, gray wales,
shales, bedded cherts, and an occasional limestone lens or two. It
might have been a textbook diagram.

At one completely exposed turn-and-drop all-rock balcony
about a quarter of the way down the cliff, we were suddenly facing north, along the beach. Showing exactly how high up as well
as how vulnerable we were. I found it thrilling, so I remained

there while Craig went on, waiting for Mark to join me from behind so I could share the astonishing view with him.

He seemed upset: his normally cool demeanor jolted. I was about to say something about the rock, the stupendous view, when Mark reached a little shale shelf I was on and with a single glimpse realized where we were. His reaction was simply to turn away. "This the way?" he asked in a tight voice, gesturing down.

I went to where Mark was looking, where Craig had gone: a shallow sand slide between two outjuttings of rock, ending in a narrow sand pit. It looked like fun.

"Sure is! Follow me!" I started down, half sliding, while grabbing at the worn-smooth edges of rock on each side. When I landed with a thump in the little sand pit, Craig suddenly appeared from around the bend.

"What's taking you so long? At this rate, it'll take hours to climb down."

"Just go! Will you!" I gave him a little push. Then I looked up. Mark was where I'd just been, some ten feet above, sitting on the edge of the little shelf, his feet and bag hanging off to one side. He wasn't moving. "What's wrong?" I shouted up. Craig remained where he was. "Mark!" I shouted again.

"There's nothing to hold onto," Mark shouted back.

"Just slide down."

"I can't!"

"Sure you can. We both did it."

"I can't!" Mark repeated, and this time there was something else to the tone of his voice.

"I'm here. I'll catch you. You won't go anywhere."

"I can't!" he repeated and dragged himself up to his feet, slipped, quickly grabbed at some grass that instantly gave way, so that he had to scrabble at nearby rock, where he held on as though for dear life. "I'm going back," he shouted.

"What's wrong?" Craig asked me, annoyed.

"Are you sure?" I called up at Mark.

"If we go back up," Craig was saying, "we'll have to go around to the other parking lot and walk to the beach. That'll take a half hour."

"You go down. We'll take the long way and join you later."

"I've got to show you where the other parking lot is. You'll never find it on your own."

"Do what you want, Craig. I'm going back up," I said. "Mark! Wait for me!" I shouted, and began scrambling up the sand slide.

Mark was hunkered down where he'd grabbed on, looking all-in, panting, his bag at his feet.

"Let me take that," I said, grabbing his bigger bag, "I can cope with it," I said, chatting away, trying to ignore the obvious, that Mark looked pale, out of it.

"I can't do it!" he repeated. Then, "When I was a kid I used to have this nightmare of going off the edge of a cliff. I'd be holding onto tufts of grass, then sharp rock, then I'd slide off."

In all our fifteen years together, I'd never heard of the dream before.

"It's my fault we're here in the first place." I tried changing the subject. "If I weren't so determined not to let Stupid have the last word . . . I mean, this cliff *is* high, even to me, and it *is* scary, and . . ."

I don't know how much of it Mark even heard.

"And all of a sudden," Mark went on, "there I was! In the nightmare! Right in it!"

"Nightmare's over," I said. "We're going back up."

"I don't know if I can," he said.

I couldn't ever remember seeing Mark, or hearing him, like this.

"I'll be right behind you," I said. "You know me, I'm like a mountain goat. You almost have to be on this cliff. You'll have to flatten me completely to fall, and that's not going to be so easy. C'mon, now! Up!"

He stood up a little shakily, but with both hands free now of the bag, he had more to grip with and so a bit more confidence. He began climbing again, at first inch by inch, then picking up speed. I remained less than a foot behind him as he ascended, crowding him at times, touching him at all times, and so letting him know I was there. When we finally got over the fence, he went straight to the car, while I looked around.

Mark all but collapsed on the hood of the T-Bird. And so he wouldn't look strange, I did the same.

Although he was clearly nonplussed by this turn of events, Craig must have been embarrassed by what happened, maybe by the fact that it was Mark who had been daunted by the cliff and not me. Whatever the reason, Craig uncharacteristically didn't take advantage of the occasion with some comment, but instead decided to be sort of gracious.

"I'm sorry, guys," Mark said.

"The other way is a good path," Craig changed the subject brightly. "It's supposed to be one of the area's better nature trails."

A few minutes later, we all got into the T-Bird again. It wasn't a long drive along Torrey Pines Road to the cutoff that led to the other parking lot, and we would have easily found it without Craig, despite what he'd said. It wasn't as high as the previous parking lot, but while the ocean was visible, it was significantly further away. Craig said it would be about a half-hour walk from here to the water.

The trail turned out even better than Craig had said. I was already familiar with eastern shorelines, from the high sand cliffs of Truro on Cape Cod to the hardscrabble Florida islands. But this beach was high, solid, nothing at all like those nearly underwater fens and brakes I had trudged through as a teenager searching duckweed for amphibian life and its secrets. The dunes here were younger, of a coarser granulation and less regular hue. They lay heavily atop the questionable coastal soil they would eventually break down into, a first brush of icing on a crudely baked cake. The trail itself was cleverly constructed, mostly slatted wooden path or lightly fenced gravel, sometimes laid out between half-buried boards or semi-defining beachdrift, sometimes almost indistinguishable from its surroundings except that it was harder underfoot. You would think you'd gotten completely away from the path, only to suddenly arrive at a set of perfectly carpentered stairs rising to another set of wild-looking dunes.

"It's great!" I announced after a few minutes, and began pointing out the flora and fauna to Mark and Craig: the little habitats for tortoises and rabbits, the thin-leafed plants, thicker stemmed for better water collection, succulents I'd never seen before, or the odd appearance of certain more familiar plants in disguise: a very slender sarsaparilla tree, a sort of wild raspberry bush. The bird life was smaller and faster than on comparable East Coast shores, more colorful, more flickering.

"That's not" something or other, Craig would declare suddenly, with irritating certainty. Then we'd reach an area with names tagged on the fences and they would prove to be exactly what I'd said they were. Which annoyed Craig, so he'd ask, "Well, then, what's that?" pointing to some bush or reed, and before I could even suggest what it was, he'd declare, "Wrong!"

This game of egos-on-parade, which we'd gotten into since I'd arrived in San Diego, continued to draw us along the path, until we reached another set of stairs and a little deck that turned out to be the crest of the ridge as well as the halfway mark of the nature trail. Before us, the path swagged down widely, slalom-like, complete with angled side fences, apparently down to the water. It was beautifully done, and I turned to point it out to Mark. But he wasn't just a little behind us, as I'd assumed, but out of sight altogether.

Craig climbed onto the deck railing and from there quickly located Mark. He'd stopped and was seated on a bench in a little dale a few hundred feet behind us, or rather sprawled out, the way he'd been on the T-Bird's hood earlier, looking like an elderly pensioner stopping to catch his breath on one of those island benches in the middle of upper Broadway midway between Zabar's and home.

"Why didn't you tell me?" Craig demanded in that accusing tone of voice I'd come to know only since I'd arrived out here. In New York, a few months ago, Craig had been mellow, delightful; here he seemed angry all the time.

"Tell you what? What are you talking about?"

"Why didn't you tell me he . . ." Craig faltered. "You know! How bad he is!"

As Craig spoke, an electrical impulse raced up my spine and into my neck. Fear.

"What are you talking about? You heard Mark. He got upset coming down the cliff because it reminded him of a recurring nightmare he had as a kid."

"There's no cliff here," Craig pointed out the obvious. "And this isn't that long a walk. It isn't!" he insisted.

That electrical thread of fear tingled again.

"He's just worn out from what happened before!" I sounded defensive even to myself. "I'd be too!"

Craig wanted to say something else, but he didn't or couldn't bring himself to do it. Instead he shook his head and jumped down the stairs.

"If you . . ." I began and ended my threat, having to yell, as he was now out of range.

At the bench with Mark, Craig and I hunkered down, and I pulled out fresh fruit I had bought that morning. Naturally, when I threw away a plum pit, Craig questioned the environmental impact of my deed. I thought the soil too dry and too poor for peach or plum pits to take root. But Craig thought they might just take, and he had dire predictions for the destruction they would doubtless wreak on the delicate ecological balance around us. As usual, Mark watched the two of us argue without saying anything. Craig and I already had disputed at last night's dinner and this morning at breakfast: it was clearly part of whatever we had together. Mark could see that, and I could see amusement in his eyes. So at least we distracted him.

So much so that when we started up again, he joined us in a chorus of "Follow the Yellow Brick Road," which the trail a little bit resembled at that point. By the time we'd gotten up to the little deck and slalom-like fence area, Craig was ahead. It was pretty much all downhill from here, easier going. Ten minutes later, we reached another stairway that cut through cliffs to the beach.

"You must love this!" Mark often saw through my eyes.

As we descended, Craig was already rushing straight to the ocean, his shorts fluttering against muscled thighs, the red canvas backpack stretched over his shoulders glittering in the strong afternoon sun.

The lower cliffs that guarded the entire beach were only twelve to fourteen feet high, and much older geologically than the higher one, and they ran in a nearly unbroken line in either direction as far as I could see. As we walked along, more or less following Craig's lead, we would pass occasional undulations in the cliff face, forming little vertical caves where sand had collected in spots now just large enough for one person to lay down a beach towel. At other spots, sudden breaks occurred, forming arches where sediment had eroded, leaving the more durable ultramafic rock. At other points, even those had broken off eons before and fallen forward in the sand, where they lay glittering, their surfaces softly, inexorably abraded with every turn of the tide, making them ideally smooth now for basking mermen.

"Nice as it all is," I said, trying to tamp down my pleasure, "I still prefer that beach on Providenciales we found last time. And there wasn't a cliff in sight. Remember?"

"We'll go back," Mark said. "Around Thanksgiving."

"I hope so."

"This *is* what you wanted to see?"

"Sure is."

"Is it old enough?"

"Far older than the cliff we were on before. All this was laid down during the Middle Cretaceous. About a hundred and twenty million years ago. It was part of a primitive mountain range that didn't run north to south, like the Rockies or the present-day Coastal Ranges, but horizontally, directly under what's now the Sonora Desert into Nevada and Arizona. A thousand miles away you can probably find this exact pattern of sedimentary striation in some spot in the Grand Canyon."

Mark always followed what I was saying so easily, so eagerly, I never felt I was lecturing. Maybe that's one of the things we'd discovered about each other first, that we could teach each other without fear of being bored or, worse, of unbalancing our equality. He made me blush once when he told friends that I was the most intelligent speaker he knew. But it was Mark's own way with words, rather than his glamorous good looks, that had won me over when we'd first met.

Walking along the streets of Provincetown and the beaches of Cape Cod in 1975, that first summer we knew each other, Mark would ignore all the other Speedo-clad beauties vying for his attention, and instead sing to me the complete score to some barely known thirties or forties musical, Porter's *Nymph Errant* or Gershwin's *Let 'Em Eat Cake*. The first few times it happened, I expressed amazement: how did he know all that? Mark laid a hand on my shoulder casually, looking like one of those WASPy studs in a Ralph Lauren ad, and said, "I know my musicals inside out." It was one of the few times he'd ever boasted, and I was thrilled. Of course, someone coming upon us at that moment on Commercial Street in front of Spiritus Pizza might have easily assumed we were making love talk. And I guess in a way we were, since little else could have made me adore him as much as hearing what he loved.

"I found it! The spot!" Craig ran up to us. "There!" pointing down the beach.

"Where?" I asked.

"Just below those cliffs," Craig said, sparring at me so suddenly I almost dropped the bigger beach bag, before he rushed off again, his big feet splat-splatting the wet sand.

"I hope it's not too much further," Mark said, only half joking.

"Sto-op! Cra-ig! Don't!"

He'd just dumped a baseball-capful of cold Pacific water over my bare midriff. I leapt up and chased him into the ocean. At the water's edge, he stopped and doubled back on me, using his greater height and weight to throw me off balance into the swirling surf and then thrust handfuls of wet sand deep into my trunks. This proved to be incredibly annoying, and in addition, provided Craig with—if not the exact erotic stimulation he was looking for—then at least a gratifying substitute.

"Cra-ig! Sto-op!"

I managed to pull away from his grip. But he wasn't to be stopped so easily. For the next ten minutes he was at me constantly, after me, up and down the beach, until I heard myself squealing like a teenage girl, and then I figured out a way to trip him up and we were both rolling around in the surf, him unexpectedly so, soaking his walking shorts.

Chastened, he only made faint stabs at harassing me while I edged back to our towels. Mark was ostentatiously ignoring us, reading an oversized Somerset Maugham biography and listening to his portable CD player.

"Now I'm going to have to take these off and dry them!" Craig complained.

I would be washing sand out of my genitals all night because of his shenanigans. "Too bad! You should have known better than to come after me," I said, searching through the beach bag for my own book.

"Well, I'm not going to sit around naked here in front of everyone," he declared. He pointed behind us where the lower cliffs dropped into a half natural, half man-made stairway up, and where we had seen men dressed in only shorts and bathing suits standing about, striking poses: obviously the famous cruising area of Black's Beach. "I'll find a spot where I can be alone."

"Who's stopping you?" I let my disdain drip.

"Rat!" he said, without much heat.

"Dimwit!" I answered back, equally cool.

"I'd say more, except there's a third person here," Craig declared.

"He can't hear with those headphones on. And he doesn't care," I added. That, I knew, would really irritate Craig: the fact that Mark was so completely ignoring him despite all of Craig's efforts to get his attention.

Craig grunted something under his breath, grabbed his backpack off the sand, and went muttering off.

I settled onto the beach towel, covering myself with sunblock #30, then located my own paperback.

A few minutes later, Mark's CD ended. He dropped the book and looked around.

"Put some of this on my shoulder blades, will you?" I asked.

"Where did he go?"

"Up there." I gestured with my head.

"To cruise?"

"To dry off. And sulk."

"Why sulk?"

"Because you're ignoring him," I said.

"He's cute," Mark said, meaning that he thought Craig had a good body.

"He's cute," I admitted.

"But that mouth!" Mark laughed. "Anita really hated it! When I went to pick him up to come meet you at the airport, he wouldn't stop saying terrible things about straights. I thought I'd have to throw him out of the car."

"That's Craig's way of trying to impress you."

"Sure."

"No kidding. He's wondering what in hell he's doing sleeping with me now that he's seen you. He's wondering how to drop me and get in the sack with you."

"It's not going to happen."

"I know that. And Craig knows too. That's why he's sulking."

"You really pick 'em."

"What about you and the Christmas Child?" Mark's own

sometime boyfriend back in New York, nicknamed because of when and how he'd first appeared in Mark's life and because of his puerile temperament.

"He's no better," Mark admitted, then went into a long story involving the Child which ended with us both shaking our heads.

The sun was hot, the breeze off the water intermittent, all of it quite delicious. We lay on our towels enjoying.

"We have good luck with beaches," I said.

"I'll say! We seem to spend a lot of time together on them."

It was true. The long shorelines of Fire Island Pines, where we shared a house for a decade of summers; the more ragged, high-cliffed beaches of Truro, where we'd take a house each September; the Hamptons; the nude beach at San Gregorio in the Bay Area; Las Tunas whenever we were in L.A.; Jones Beach; Far Rockaway Beach; Gilgo. Our new favorites were on Turks and Caicos Islands. Mark's business partner owned a place, and we'd begun going there a few weeks at a time in the winter: wide white beaches, five shades of green-water Atlantic on the north, with a western shore only ten minutes from the house by boat, a strand so untouched we'd see no one, not a boat, not a footprint, all afternoon, and fish so unused to humans they'd bite your toes, while birds with markings unlike any I'd ever seen perched on our sunhats and pecked at the designs on our T-shirts and towels, thinking them edible. The east side was limestone, rocky inlets, half harbors, dreary fishing-dock areas. South was Sapodilla Bay, with languorous pale turquoise waters where I snorkeled; beachless, although the house was built on coral shelf perfect for sunning under papaya trees. We took boat rides with a local named Hammerhead Joe (he'd lift his shirt to show you the long knotted black scar from a shark he'd fought off) to nearby Shell Cay, Pine Cay, or to unnamed islets favored by plumed egrets, or populated by iguanas the size of Dalmatians.

"At least I have beaches to remember," Mark said in that suddenly dark tone of voice he'd used earlier on the cliff: this time it was laced through with something else: irony? bitterness?

I wasn't thinking when I replied, "I, for one, plan to go to the beach when I'm so old I'm doddering."

"Not me," Mark said. "You saw. I've lost all my strength."

What was he saying? Surely he didn't mean . . . ?

"It was your nightmare. You said . . ."

"At work I've got to take naps every afternoon," Mark interrupted. "I close the door and tell Cindy not to let calls through, and I put my feet up on the desk. Sometimes I curl up on the rug in front of my desk. Every afternoon. One, two hours."

"I didn't know that. Since when?"

"Every afternoon," he repeated. "It's started," he added in a smaller, less certain voice. "I know it. It's . . . started."

That electrical jolt rushed up my spine again.

"Anita noticed right away when I got out here," Mark went on. "And I don't mean she just noticed how much I'm sleeping since I got here. She . . . we always take photos of each other every time we're together. This time she wanted to wait till today. After I'd gotten more color, is the way she put it."

"Mark! You're not saying you're . . . ?" Symptomatic was the word.

"I'm saying it's started," Mark said flatly. Then, "Do you like him?"

The change of subject was so odd that for a second I thought Mark was going to say that Craig was symptomatic too.

"We have good sex and all," I said. "But I don't think it will develop into anything or that he'll move east to be with me. In fact, I'd say my being here these past few days has pointed that out."

Not what Mark wanted to hear. I remembered how much he'd encouraged me to get the air tickets, to reserve the room in the Balboa Park Inn. I'd thought because he'd wanted my company here.

"I'm not that disappointed," I began.

"Because I'd like to know that you have . . . you know, someone . . . you like."

He'd encouraged me to come out here and go after Craig following our hot little affair in Manhattan two months ago, because Mark wanted someone around after Mark was gone. This was too much.

"Look, maybe this is all just stress?" I tried. "All the work at the firm? The paper you had to deliver at the convention?"

"Maybe." Mark didn't want to argue. We never argued.

"Soon it will be summer. You'll hang out more. And in the fall we'll go back to the Caribbean. That always restores you."

He let me go on, looking at me in that fond way he had that he had for no one else in the world, no one, so I felt calmed again. The subject had been breached and we'd shoved it back.

We went back to reading and listening to music, sipping soft drinks. Above us, hang gliders in loose formation, blotting out the sun, speckled the sands with shadows.

Craig chose then to return, his shorts already dry.

"I did not have sex!" he declared, unasked.

"No doubt you were asked by scores," I said.

"It was sug-ges-ted," Craig said, suggestively, looking at where Mark lay, gorgeous on his towel. "But I told them some nasty older guy down here had at me so voraciously I had nothing left to give."

"Poor you!"

"Had at me night and day," he insisted. "You're burning!" he said, and used that as an excuse to turn me onto my stomach, straddle my hips, and seductively and thoroughly rub my entire back and legs with suntan lotion. When that had completely aroused me and failed to get Mark's attention, Craig climbed off, declared he had to wash the gook off, and headed for the water.

He decided to go for a walk. When he was too far to be seen, Mark sat up, put on a T-shirt. "Did you find what you were looking for?"

"The ammonite fossils? I haven't really looked."

"Let's look!" he said. I too put on a shirt, and we aimed toward the nearest cliff face, the direction opposite where Craig had gone.

The cliff was layered like a wedding cake. Actually many more times than that, but the strata were all clearly delineated.

"Hard to believe each layer is hundreds of years," Mark mused.

"More like thousands of years."

"And this green streak?"

"Believe it or not, that's aquatic life, algae and other early water plants. As they died they dropped to the surface and were squashed. The streak represents a time when this was all covered with water. Given these sediments below and above, I'd hazard it was a huge shallow lake for a couple of thousand years. Then land rose, emptied the water, and covered it with soil."

"Your fossils would be there?"

"If it were a branch of the ocean they should be. They were so common then. Far more common than fish or shellfish today. The ocean was thick with ammonites during the Mesozoic. They comprised ninety percent of sea life. Eighty percent of all the animal life on the planet. They were wiped out during the same great extinction that killed off the dinosaurs. You can see the line where it happened on the big cliff. It's known as the K-T boundary."

"A giant lake," Mark mused. "With its shoreline where? Out there somewhere?" pointing to the Pacific.

"Pretty far out, I'd guess. Then it became desert. But of course during that time this exact chunk of land wasn't here at thirty-two degrees north of the Equator. It was much further south. Somewhere off what's now Peru."

"Continental drift," he said. "Big plates moving slowly. When was that, about sixty million years ago?"

"Scientists call it deep time. Remember back in 1987, on my birthday, when we read about that star that went Nova in the Southern Hemisphere, the one in the Lesser Magellanic Cloud? That took place about the same time. Because it was so far away, it's taken all this time for the burst of light it caused to reach us. All this time for the light made in that huge explosion to stimulate our vision."

"Deep time." Mark was beginning to perspire. I moved us along a section of the cliff out of the sun. "Eighty percent of the animal life just vanished forever. . . . There must be shallow time too," he suddenly said. "The shallowest of all time." He laughed and turned and sat down on a little sand hill hidden by this bend of cliff. "That's *my* time."

"Mark."

"Go on looking. I want to think about eighty percent of all life vanishing forever and no one even noticing."

"They were noticed."

"You can't even find their fossils! And you're looking!"

There's a point in every young science major's life when you are suddenly faced with having to specialize. It's a fearful moment, and not only because it will undoubtedly shape the course of the remainder of your life. Certainly your career and earning capacity, and those you'll probably be working with and socializing with and in some cases even falling in love with. No, the real fear is that you've missed something essential, some moment during that decade-and-a-half of nature walks and difficult-to-explain-to-others experiments with planaria worms and dirt and matches and soot that all young scientists have experienced, some moment when—sitting in a shaft of sunlight, hidden in reeds, you watch an egg hatch, minuscule life emerge, kicking, clawing, scurrying—a moment that somehow you become aware of *must* happen. But in happening, will replace forever that other moment in which something else, somewhere else, equally directing in its potential, now *cannot* happen. There you are, choosing or having chosen for you: life—or once-life.

Then, and later in school when I had formally to do so, I decided on what-had-once-lived over what-was-now-alive, despite all indications that it was the wrong direction. Living nature—tadpoles and crickets and birds whose names you weren't sure of, what was soon to become known as ecology— that was the real future! I chose the past, although my favorite children's books were *Min of the Mississippi* and *Nature for Everyone*. Dragged by something inevitable that told me some things were so old, immeasurably old, I chose to become a paleobiologist instead of a botanist or ornithologist. My field is that paradox: dead life. Life encased in stone and slate and (if I'm very lucky) suspended in amber millions of years old. In choosing, I found I'd also chosen to study the rock and shale and petrified tree resin wherein dead life might be located. Old rock. Dead wood.

I took it as a challenge, and on those few occasions when I felt compelled to explain my choice, I always said it meant that from now on I'd continually sharpen my senses, go through life opening my eyes ever wider, forced to see in the least hints of fossilized ferncombs and feathertracks the possibility of something greater. And by extension, that in life in general I'd always have the details. Never miss what was right in front of me. I'd prided myself on that.

But in the past few months, I'd missed something crucial. The man who above all I loved in this life, whose love I'd come to take for granted, even while I never once took him for granted, had become symptomatic, and I had not seen it happen. Anita had seen it, although she'd told us last night she'd never met another person infected with HIV. Craig had seen it immediately, though he was the most egocentric of human beings. And I'd *not* seen it.

I did now, walking away from Mark, ostensibly to look for fossils I didn't expect to find. For the first time I completely felt Mark there behind me, knowing this consciousness of Mark would never go away again—until he himself did.

Stumbling forward, I thought I would cry. No, I'll wait until I get out of his line of sight, I told myself, behind that escarpment, where he can't see me.

I'd just reached it and looked back to check that I wasn't seen, when something huge and catlike leapt down at me.

"Gotcha!" Craig yelled as he dragged me down into the sand. He roared and pawed at me and in general acted like an animal. I don't know what got into me, since we always fought as equals, but this time I cringed away from him, and when he half came at me, I cringed again, cowered, shaking.

Craig could see how upset I was as I stumbled trying to get away from him, but he caught me and slid me against the cliff and held me there, held me tight, his front to my back, his larger, stronger arms over mine, his beard burning against my neck, letting me shake myself out, silently sob myself out. It was the longest that we'd been this close since we'd awakened that morning in the hotel bed together. After a while, he let go.

Mark was coming past us, on the way to our towels.

"I think it's time to go," Mark said. "What do you think?"

Even with all the rest, the walk back was still too much for Mark, and we waited with him while he caught his breath on the same bench where we had rested before. A few hours later, we drove him in the rented T-Bird to the airport to get his jet home. Much later, after dinner and more of our usual arguing, Craig and I went to bed together in my hotel room.

At first he was aloof. So I was too.

"He doesn't have long, you know," Craig said. He moved closer until he covered my body with his.

"I know."

Craig pinned me against the sheets.

"He's going to die soon."

He began to kiss me hard.

"Your beautiful lover is going to die."

He made love to me with complete wildness and total abandon and with the same unchecked ferocity he'd displayed on the beach. And I responded in kind, both of us acting unforgivably, saying unforgivable things to each other as we did, as though knowing it would be the last time ever.

SEX WITH TEENAGERS

BRIAN SLOAN

Exactly one year ago, I graduated from NYU's film school after completing an eight-minute film—*The Perfect Kiss*—for a mere $3,429. I won't bore with you the details. There's really not much to discuss about a film of that length. In fact, given the title, you could probably figure out the subject of this mini-masterpiece for yourself. Hah.

Despite its simplicity, though, *The Perfect Kiss* won the prestigious Dean's Award for Excellence in Filmmaking at the 53rd Annual NYU Film Festival. I'm convinced that it was so successfully received for one simple reason: it is short. People in this industry have notoriously short attention spans. However, I didn't make the film so short for that reason; I wasn't that cynical. Yet. I made it short because I could only afford to make an eight-minute film. Really.

The morning after the award, shortly after nine, my phone began to ring, and kept doing so for the next two weeks. Agents. Lawyers. Producers. D-girls. D-boys. Go-go boys (don't ask). I talked to them all. And roughly five minutes into each of these conversations, they all asked me the same question: "So, when are you moving to L.A.?"

I took this as a sign. On the third of June I left New York. I was twenty-three years old.

The main reason I went west so quickly was probably Charles P. Fleischer, the head of production at the Walt Disney Studios.

Charlie—as he was called by everyone, as if he were an executive version of Madonna—had been running production at the studio since the mid-1980s. It was Charlie who had saved the studio from itself. He pushed the studio to develop more "adult" films, films with bad language and questionable morals. At first, everyone said he was killing the essence of Disney, destroying its cache. But the minute his films started making more money than *Herbie the Love Bug's Hawaiian Holiday*, everyone stopped carping.

Since then, he's been a Hollywood colossus. One of those mythical gods who sprout up in this arid land every couple decades, like a gurgling spring to which people flock for nourishment. And jobs.

It was Charlie's persistent and convincing phone calls that finally got me to leave Manhattan. He didn't come out and say it—no one here comes out and says anything—but he just about promised me the world if I would only come to L.A. When I finally showed up at his office in the garish "Team Disney" building, the facade of which features ironically gargantuan friezes of the Seven Dwarfs, we hit it off right away. As it turned out, he had grown up on the Lower East Side in the early forties, in practically the same neighborhood I'd just moved out of. We had a great deal to talk about; Yonah Schimmel's bialys, the Sunday markets on Delancey Street, corned beef on rye at Katz's.

Despite my own reservations, Charlie saw a big future for me, one which he'd taken the liberty of planning without my input. It went something like this: I'd rack up a few good screenwriting credits, then onto some lower-end directing jobs on "programmers." Next up would be a classy drama with names, leading to several Oscar nominations and the power to create my own production company and, eventually, if all went according to plan, on some hi-tech day in the twenty-first century I would accomplish the ultimate in Hollywood success: synergy.

He spun a cloud of California dreams as I sat in his office that afternoon, looking out his seventh-floor window across the dusty brown fields where Old Yeller used to run. I could see why he'd become successful. He was one of those rare men who dream out loud and yet never manage to sound like a fool. Why? Because his dreams had an uncanny knack of always coming true. And it doesn't get more Disney than that.

An hour and a couple bottles of Evian later, Charlie had decided to set me up at the studio. Charlie would, in effect, be my godfather. I was a made man and then some. Squeezing my biceps, as I learned he was apt to do when excited, he told me that I was now a "Disney Man."

I was a little scared.

I stayed with a screenwriting classmate of mine in Venice for about a week as I looked for an apartment. I was interested in moving into West Hollywood; I'd heard that was the gay ghetto in this town that's not a town. But ghetto was the wrong word. West Hollywood was beautiful. Just like a movie. Wide streets with glowing green lawns, palm trees arching toward the sky, and gorgeously proportioned men who walked down Santa Monica Boulevard looking like they were on their way to audition for a porn film.

After a couple weeks, I found a decent apartment in the Fairfax section of West Hollywood. It was in a two-story stucco building that dated from the early 1940s. Despite the sexy guys walking down the streets, my building was no gay mecca. In fact, all four of the other tenants were Hasidics. For years, Fairfax had been a haven for Hasidics. I came to L.A. seeking glamour and gay heaven, but the neighborhood I ended up in felt almost like my old place in New York, on the Lower East Side. The major difference was that in Fairfax, I could look out my bedroom window and actually see sky. In fact, the sky was filled with sky. Very L.A.

Careerwise, things were going great. Charlie had provided me with my own office on the Burbank lot, and arranged a first-look deal for me at Touchstone. They told me to start work on a feature-length version of *The Perfect Kiss* and, as the deal indicates, they would get the first look at it when it was finished. That is what they told me to do. That is what I was being paid a sum of roughly fifty thousand dollars to do. Unfortunately, that is *not* what I did.

I ended up spending the majority of my time at the studio wandering around the lot, looking for locations from all my favorite Disney films: *The Apple Dumpling Gang* set up near the mountains; the house where *The Shaggy D.A.* lived; the garage where *Herbie the Love Bug* was born. It was during these self-guided tours that I realized something startling, something I'd never realized in four years of making films at NYU. Fact was, I didn't want to make movies. I just wanted to be in them. Be in their world. I wanted to inhabit movies in the most literal sense of the word. I wanted a life that was bigger than life—a life filled with grand passions, high comedy, writhing temptation.

And soon enough, this misbegotten desire would come true.

Charlie was a true patriot. An American Dream man. So the Fourth of July was by far his favorite holiday. Every year, he invited the A-list of Hollywood to his sprawling estate, nestled in the bottom of a canyon on about ten acres of land. Very expensive land.

At this point in my burgeoning career, I was on the temporary A-list, so there I was, standing around a large charcoal pit, lined up behind Mel Gibson and Meryl Streep for some barbecued chicken wings. But the real news was who was in line behind me. Initially, I thought he was an actor. It was something in the way he wore his sun-blonded hair in a casual but perfectly set flip. Yet, conversely, there was something less studied in the way he stood there, his hands nervously playing with a Chinette paper plate. He looked about sixteen years old.

"So . . . who are you?" he said in a monotone. After attending endless movie parties, I had heard this question asked, in all its blunt honesty, at least three hundred times. I was prepared to answer this oft-asked query in a way appropriate for a studio-bankrolled writer.

"A friend of Charlie's," I said, smirking.

"A friend of Charlie's," he said, relishing the phrase, turning it over in his mind as if he were looking to see if it had holes in it. To see if it was a lie.

"From the studio," I said.

"Who isn't?"

I looked around and saw he had a point. I tried to make myself more believable. I gave myself a name. I showed that I had no fear of being no one.

"David Garrison. I'm a writer at Touchstone."

"Good luck. All they produce is crap. Programmers."

I turned around, startled by this sixteen-year-old's incredibly sharp observation. Where does a teenager pick up a term like "programmers"? My God, I thought, did his parents get him a subscription to *Variety* for his birthday?

"Davey . . . you a breast or leg man?"

Without realizing it, I'd advanced to the head of the line. Charlie loomed in front of me, a large silver utensil aimed in my direction. He was wearing an apron with a picture of Uncle Sam on it, pointing his finger at me, admonishing me with the slogan "I want you . . . to eat!" I took a leg and stepped aside to let the world's youngest producer-in-training have his audience with Charlie.

"Any thighs left, Dad?"

My neck made an audible snap from the shock. This kid was Charlie's son. I couldn't believe I had missed it. He had the same facial features: large, glassy eyes, slanting Roman nose, ruddy cheeks. The thing that had thrown me off was the hair. Charlie was bald.

"Sure thing, Eric. You have a plate for your mother? Here, take her this . . . she loves thighs."

Charlie winked at me and I swallowed a laugh. Eric rolled his eyes, took the two plates, and walked over toward his mother and her full head of Norwegian blond hair.

I wandered off, somewhat stunned by the danger of my half-flirtations with Charlie's teenage son. I found a couple other writers from Touchstone and we sat together at one of about fifty wooden picnic tables (the kind you find in public parks) that had been trucked in just for the occasion. Eric sat at a table with Charlie, Michael Douglas, his mother, Michael Ovitz and his wife, Tom Cruise and Nicole Kidman. Eric sat attentively as Tom, who sat to his right, seemed to be telling an animated story about a thriller he'd just wrapped down in the Andes. Eric nodded and laughed and even interjected some apparently humorous remarks that Tom got a kick out of. Eric had probably called Tom's film a programmer.

I was fascinated by Eric. Fascinated with watching him. On looks alone, he seemed a quiet, reserved, and almost sensitive boy. Yet the minute he forced his way into the conversation his eyes grew narrow, his voice became assured, and he talked like— well, just like his father.

To say that I had developed a crush on him that afternoon

would be dangerous. In retrospect, I know that I did, but there were a couple small problems that kept me from admitting this. First, as a rule, it's generally illegal to date anyone under the age of eighteen. Second, in Hollywood, it's a greater rule that you don't date the studio boss's son.

If you're a man, that is.

To top off this extraordinary evening, Charlie provided his guests with a little after-dinner entertainment. Not much really. Just a thrown-together medley of country-western tunes. The crooning duties were shared by Dolly Parton and Garth Brooks.

As I sat in the grass under a melting red sky, Eric was leaning against one of the speakers and cruising me. Really. At least he stared for a really long time. There was a curiosity to his gaze, an interest to find out my "deal." That's what people actually say here when discussing the possibilities of one's sexuality: "What's their deal?" If you're lucky, you'll actually get an answer.

A minute or so later, Eric plopped himself down beside me and started talking a blue streak. It was that nonstop sort of chatter which sixteen-year-olds specialize in. It was as if he'd just realized he had the power of speech, and people would listen to him, and take him seriously if he spoke seriously—meaning, of course, if he spoke about the business. And he spoke of it as if he himself, and not his father, ran the studio.

"They're trying to put out ten to fifteen pictures a year at Touchstone, but they don't have the talent pool or the writers to come up with anything to sustain such a production schedule. The only way they'll be able to balance their books is by getting the former A's as talent, pay them just a little more than scale, and hope for a fucking miracle. Lightning does strike, but not ten to fifteen times a year, you know what I mean?"

I had no idea what he meant, but I was learning. I was learning almost as much from him about the motion-picture industry as I'd learned in four years at film school. But I was also learning something else: if a sixteen-year-old has a crush on you, he will do anything—talk, eat, aerobics—to keep from being still. It was quite clear, in a goofy sort of teenager way, that Eric liked me. Maybe just as a friend. It was hard to pinpoint his feelings toward me. I was sure, however, that he knew my "deal." He asked all the right questions.

"You have a girlfriend or anything?" he said, emphasis on the "anything."

"Nope. Just a development deal with your father."

"So where do you live?" he asked, moving onto the second gay qualifier in L.A.: location.

"Near West Hollywood," I said, trying not to completely give myself away. "The Fairfax district."

I knew I'd blown it when he came back with the next line.

"Nice. Getting kinda gentrified these days."

I have never heard of a neighborhood being gentrified without a fair share of homosexuals leading the fight. I doubt Eric even knew the meaning of the word itself, but he surely knew what it implied, how its use could ferret out information that in L.A. was generally unferretable in industry party conservations. He found out my "deal." In a way, he got me.

In a way, I wanted to be got.

The evening culminated with a backyard fireworks display set off by the Zambelli family. The finale was one of those huge metal-framed sparkler displays that form a picture or phrase when all lit up. In this case, we got mouse ears. Surprise, surprise.

Around ten, the party started to break up. I would have left sooner but I'd made an awful mistake: I'd gotten drunk. Not really all that awful in itself, but the problem was I'd driven to the party. After years of taking cabs and subways home from bars in New York, I was still not assimilated to the problem of driving home from Hollywood parties.

I confided my dilemma to Eric and he said he'd take care of it. He sprinted away, up the sloping backyard and into the house. Five minutes later he came out of the house and was out of breath. Underneath a ribbed cotton tank top, his chest heaved. Oh boy, did it heave.

"I called you a limo," he said, flipping his blond hair out of his eyes.

"I can't afford a limo!"

"It's the studio's limo service."

"But I don't want my name on this. . . . Your dad will think I'm a . . ."

"Lush?" he said and smiled. There was a silence. He started fidgeting with the edge of his tank top. "Don't worry. I gave them a different name."

I looked at him warily. I didn't even have to ask who. My furrowed brow did that for me.

"Tom Cruise," he said with a serious face.

I started to laugh uncontrollably, tears forming in the corners of my eyes. Eric began to laugh too. It was a guffaw. A big, brazen guffaw that leapt out of his throat.

It was the first truly teenage thing he did all night.

I awoke around nine Saturday morning. After taking three Advil, I went back to bed. I finally got up at eleven and went to the fridge to get some breakfast. Nothing. Just beer and condiments. I needed to go to the Mayfair Mart. I reached for the car keys and was running out of the house before I realized my car was still parked outside of Mr. Fleischer's house. I called a cab and, cursing on arrival after a forty-minute trip on the Ventura freeway, paid the driver thirty-four dollars plus tip.

The embarrassment I feared of being the single car left on the street turned out to be premature; there were still six or seven cars there, all in the same spots as they were in last night. I found out later that many of the car refugees would show up at the Fleischers' for brunch around one—it was something of a Fourth of July tradition for them.

My stomach shrinking with hunger, I jumped in the car and tore off. A couple of minutes after pulling onto the freeway, I noticed a piece of paper fluttering under my left windshield wiper. I thought it was a parking ticket—a leftover New York reaction—but on closer inspection, I saw it was smaller and had something handwritten on it. I thought maybe I had parked in front of someone's house and they'd been upset.

Looking ever closer through the windshield, I noticed that this note was written on Disney stationery, the silhouette of mouse ears visible as the paper flapped around dangerously in the wind. That's when I had my first heart attack of the morning. It surely must be a note from Charlie. My mind reeled with the possibilities. I could see Charlie's big loopy handwriting chastising me for my drunkenness, my indiscretion, my insane flirtations with his only son! I imagined myself being fired, blackballed, or, worst of all, being put into turnaround. I began to sweat.

Without even looking in the side mirrors, I swerved to the right and crossed three lanes of traffic. Horns honked. Drivers cursed. I skidded onto the shoulder, jumped out of the car, and yanked the note from the window.

The first thing I noticed was that it was not Charlie's handwriting. I read three short lines in blocky pencil print and had my second heart attack of the day.

"I would like to have sex with you. Would that be OK? Beep me at 555-3462. Eric."

I was in shock. The whole of the note was unbelievable, of course. But what really got me, what really made me crazy, was the middle line. "Would that be OK?" There was a wisp of innocence to it that, having spent a few hours with him, I never would have guessed at. Would that be OK? Like he was asking to borrow my notes from bio class or wear one of my shirts to a high-school dance. Would that be OK? Had he no idea of the unanimous "YES!" his request would receive from ninety percent of the gay male populace? Was he entirely unaware of his beauty? Was this some sort of prank?

I spent roughly three hours ruminating over these questions before my desire got the best of me. I beeped him. That was easy. Waiting for his return call drove me mad.

I paced around the apartment, washed dishes that were already clean, and even—gasp!—began to clean the bathroom. After twenty minutes of that, the phone rang. I ran to answer it but stopped a few feet away in the hall. I would let the machine take the call in case this was some sort of a setup. My father, who practices corporate law in Delaware, told me the day before my trip out west that I was never to trust anyone in this town. Suddenly, his warning echoed in my ears. I wondered if the category "anyone" applied to people who didn't even have a driver's license.

My deadpan outgoing-message voice clicked on.

"Hi, this is David and I'm in a meeting . . . Just kidding. Leave a message at the sound—"

The machine stopped and began rewinding. Whoever this was, prankster or teenage sex maniac, they had hung up. I kicked the phone stand out of frustration. The machine tumbled to the floor.

Then I remembered a commercial I'd seen on TV for a new phone service you could use when you missed a call. With logic and my father momentarily missing from my brain, I snatched up the receiver and punched in *69. One ring. Sweating again, now down my back. Two rings. A third and surely fatal heart attack coming on. Three rings. Pacing with uneven steps. Four—

"Hey," the voice said. "Is this David?"

"Uh . . . yeah, this is David. And yourself?"

"It's Eric. Remember?"

"Sorta . . ."

I was still skeptical, trying to remember the voice. There was silence on the line. I needed more information but didn't want to ask, didn't want to get trapped, didn't want to be a fool in sexual paradise. It was, however, too late. Technology had already served to make me the fool I really was. I'd *69'ed my way into fooldom. My L.A. cool, that attitude I had spent weeks perfecting, had simply drained away. I'd gone hot.

"You got my note?" he said.

"Yeah, on the car."

"So," he said, his voice rising in pitch, "would that be OK?"

He said it. The line. In his own little voice. Confirming that this was truly him on the line and not some ruse. What can I say? It killed me. I dropped the cordless phone and the call was unintentionally disconnected.

He called back immediately and, with hesitation only in my voice, we made a date. He would come over to my place Sunday afternoon around four I hung up, totally wrecked from a two-minute phone call, and collapsed onto my futon. It was not so much the call that brought on this collapse. It was the irretrievable fact that I'd just made a date to have sexual relations with a minor.

Nightmares. That's what filled my sleep that night. Pure, visceral, Freddie Krueger–strength nightmares. I can't even get into it, can't give it the awful justice those sorts of dreams deserve. I awoke from the worst one shortly after 5 A.M. and realized I had made a horrible mistake. I grew concerned that this . . . thing with Eric was just not proper. Socially, legally, psychologically—all the ly's I could think of.

I came up with a new and less illegal plan of action.

I thought that maybe Eric was confused about his sexuality and was having some trouble coming out. Maybe he needed someone to talk about sex with him. I certainly couldn't imagine Charlie having a heart-to-heart talk with his son about his homosexual tendencies. Charlie was the type of man who never even said the word "sex" in conversation. His phrase was "making it," such as, "I made it with that girl back in '54." He was from a lost world, somewhere in the middle of this century, where sex barely existed and homosexuals were all costume designers. That is, as far as he wanted to know.

I called Eric with the change in plans. I was a little crestfallen when he agreed so easily. So casually. As if we had decided to go to the Beverly Mall instead of Rodeo Drive. We would meet at a bookstore/coffee shop in my neighborhood, Big and Tall Men's Books on Fairfax. It was not an industry hangout because it was a bookstore, and no scripts were available for browsing. Thus, I knew I'd be safe from the rumor-mill aspect of this dangerous liaison. Also, I thought Eric and I could do some browsing in the store's nicely stocked Gay/Lesbian Studies section. There was also the consideration that we'd be drinking espresso instead of cocktails in my apartment. This way we could keep level heads. More than anything, though, I thought we would be able to talk this thing through, bookstores not being a place where making out is terribly common practice.

After a morning diddling around the *Old Yeller* ranch and running through some probable first-date dialogue in my head, I drove over the mountains to West Hollywood for our afternoon rendezvous. He was already there when I arrived, sitting at a wrought-iron table under the corrugated copper awning and sipping a double mocha cappuccino iced fizz. Really.

He looked very chic, wearing his Armani sunglasses (tinted red) and reading *Variety*. He greeted me with a smile and I began to have another heart attack. Yet I didn't let his charm divert me from my altruistic goal. I asked him if we could move inside, since it might be more conducive to conversation. He agreed with yet another smile (ouch!) and we moved to a booth near the Human Sexuality aisle.

I ordered an iced tea and we began to talk. Movies, scripts, seventh grade, sex.

"And now . . . you think you're gay?" I asked him.

"Maybe."

"You've had sex with other guys," I said, with a reluctant disappointment.

"Well, not really. I've rented a few pornos, and I thought it looked like lots of fun."

Fun? My reluctant disappointment dissipated like cappuccino fizz. Get it?

"So," I continued, "you've done what you, uh, saw in the pornos?"

"Sort of. Last year, I started to with one of my friends from school. He's Gary Dale's kid, from over at Columbia." That was rich. As if I didn't know who the hell Gary Dale was. Anyways— "We got naked and stoned and watched the tape."

"Then you . . . you fooled around with Gary Dale's son?"

"No. We got into a fight over, you know, who would be the man and who would be the girl."

"What?" I said, my mind drifting toward his heaving, T-shirt-covered chest again.

"You know—who does it to who. So, yeah, he basically wimped out, but we slept in the same bed. Does that count?"

I told him it did not and to lower his voice a bit. The waitress had started to stare.

We talked for a good hour and a half about his desires, my own coming out, and the per-screen averages of his father's summer releases. Walking back to my car, he drove the conversation back to the note he'd left me. The note which now held an esteemed place on my refrigerator, under the Barbie magnet. And, again, Eric asked that irresistible question: Would it be OK?

If, at age twenty-three, I had had the ability to faint, I would have. When I was nine years old, I used to have regular fainting spells at church—perfect, huh? I was once told that my fainting spells would make a great opening scene in a movie. Well, I agree, but I think you'd heighten the drama if the person fainting was twenty-three and he did so on the floor of Big and Tall Men's Books. It would be a Big and Tall fainting seizure. On the floor. At Eric's feet.

This, of course, did not happen. My life was not completely a movie. Not yet.

"I'm not sure if it would be OK," I answered, not looking at him.

"It's my father, right?"

"No. Yes, a little. But no. It's really that you're a little young."

"You're not so old yourself."

Well, he had a point there. Right? On the surface—that is, based on sheer mathematics—the number of years between sixteen and twenty-three is not immense. It is seven. Lucky seven. But those seven years between sixteen and twenty-three might as well be seventy. I think that adolescents live in dog years. Remember when you were fourteen, and you would not even speak to someone who was twelve—someone who wasn't a teenager? Those two years, in adolescent dog years, are essentially a decade to most average adults. So, math may have been on my side, but reality was not.

Eric asked me if we could at least have another date. He said he really liked talking to me. I said sure. He said there was one condition. He would get to pick the place. Again, I said sure, as long as it wasn't a bathhouse. I laughed at my own joke while he stood there with an awkward smile and blinking, beautiful eyes.

"What's a bathhouse?"

I could have said no to his idea for our next date. After all, I was the one driving. (Eric had told me he only had a learner's permit.) But I found the idea, his idea, incredibly charming and goofily romantic. He wanted to go to the planetarium at Griffith Observatory. *Rebel Without a Cause* was one of his favorite movies.

The observatory is placed atop the narrow ridge of a steep and dirty L.A. mountain, and to get there we had to drive up a winding two-lane road that did not have a center line. Navigating hairpin turns with asphalt shoulders that crumbled off into brown, brush-ridden slopes was tough for someone accustomed to city blocks. After a while, I grew dizzy from all the treacherous turns. I had to stop.

Eric and I got out of the car to take a scenic cigarette break. Looking out toward the L.A. basin, I finally understood the meaning of the word smog. The city was a great, gray, bleary mess. Not exactly scenic, but still somewhat breathtaking. The sprawl was incredible. Eric offered to drive the rest of the way. I doubted the legality of it—as if we weren't already daring the law—but he assured me that as long as someone in the car was over twenty-one it would be fine. He flashed me a real peer-pressure grin. I immediately felt like a teenager again. A co-conspirator. I tossed him the keys.

At the end of this bleak, twisty road, the observatory stood like an Art Deco temple—heavenly white and surrounded by an impossibly lush green lawn. Leading me around to the side of the building, Eric wanted to show me something. And there he was. Jimmy. A twelve-foot-tall bronze statue of Mr. James Dean. He faced west, staring out toward the valley below with sad, hollowed-out eyes. On the marble pedestal was a greenish plaque with an inscription that explained how Griffith Observatory had become a holy pilgrimage site for fans, how the grounds were a virtual shrine to the cult of Dean.

"That's one of my all-time favorite movies," said Eric as if he'd spent a lifetime screening films. And in adolescent dog years, he had. "Great casting."

"It's a pretty great film," I said, trying to muster a similar enthusiasm. Honestly, I liked the movie but found it slightly overwrought. Of course, this is why it was a hit with the teens of its time, living their overwrought lives in an underwrought era. And Eric was on the verge of this same era in his life.

"You know that James Dean was gay too," he said.

"Actually, he was more bisexual."

"No way, man," he said, adamantly. "A friend of my dad's was his roommate for a few months. Jerry Weinstein. He produced *T. J. Hooker.* He told me Jimmy used to bring different guys home all the time, and not once did he see a woman."

"Really," I said, wondering if Jerry had received a note on his windshield too.

Inside the planetarium, we took our seats in the familiar rotunda. I waited expectantly for a genial old man to assume the controls of the steel and glass contraption at the center of the room and beam us into the heavens. Just like in the movie. Modern times, however, had caught up with the planetarium. Our guide to the universe was a woman in her late twenties who was incredibly attractive. Probably an out-of-work actress.

For the next half hour, lasers were shot over our heads and stars dotted the ceiling as we were lectured on the existence of quasars, pulsars, and black holes. Every time a new laser lit up the "sky," Eric let out a little "whoa" or a "cool." At the same time, with a certain amount of subterfuge, Eric started to put the moves on me. As the woman described the nature of black holes—in an overly cheerful manner considering the subject— Eric's hand kept inadvertently slipping onto my thigh, and then sliding off, almost as inadvertently. It was all very fake-awkward. Finally, his hand landed there permanently. As the black hole on the ceiling began to suck in all the light in the room, Eric squeezed my thigh. I couldn't take it.

"Whoa, boy," I said, removing his hand from my leg. I have to admit that they were beautiful hands too, warm and smooth. His skin was the texture of soft wax. Despite this, they had to go. I turned to give him a scolding look. A parental look.

"Sorry," he whispered, "I got a little excited."

Then, we were staring at each other. Things were not getting better. Just worse. As the sternness in my face dissipated and his remorse faded, the black hole above us continued sucking up everything in sight. I felt lightheaded and lost. Lost in space. My face began drifting toward his. The gravity of our lust took hold.

Suddenly, the room was thrown into pitch blackness. We'd finally entered the black hole. I felt his lips land delicately on my cheek. He did not merely kiss me. He took a playful bite of my cheek. I did not pull away. Fortunately, for the two of us, he did, because, just as suddenly the house lights came on. The show was over.

We lingered in our seats for a while as families and children bustled around us, making their way to the same exit signs that led James and Natalie and Sal out into the world forty-some years ago. Finally, Eric turned to me again. This time there was not a trace of sex in his face at all. The kiss had been lost in the black hole. Now he was just a high school student wondering what might next preoccupy him.

"Now what?" he asked. "We gonna drive home?"

"Home?"

"Your home," he said.

It was not a question. He laid it out as a statement. A true one. I did not respond. I didn't know how to respond. I rose in silence from my seat and began to walk out of the theater. Eric sat there glumly, acting like a sad-faced Sal Mineo, staring at what was formerly a black hole. Now it was just a round, plaster ceiling. White.

"You coming," I called to him, "or what?"

After grabbing a quick slice of pizza at 7-Eleven, we took a long drive down Santa Monica and then up into the hills of Bel Air. I would drop him a couple blocks from his house. He would walk the rest of the way. Just to be safe.

The statement he'd made was not true. I did not take him to my home, and this was a surprise to him. Not to me. When we emerged out of the black hole and headed out of the planetarium, the afternoon sun was strong and blazingly bright, like a 10K. I saw him and saw his youth.

Though I was only seven years older than him, I felt that taking him back to my apartment, having him in this manner, would be unfair. To him, that is. Having sex with him would somehow deposit some of the age I had accumulated onto him. It would rub off, no matter what I did. He would grow old before his time. It didn't seem fair.

This whole semi-affair, my whole dilemma with it, was no longer about his being Charlie's son. I didn't want to sleep with Eric because I didn't want to be responsible for the premature aging of a sixteen-year-old. At the time, this change in thinking seemed like a good thing. However, it was a turning point I should never have made a turn at. Once he was removed from "who" he was, and the unique status he held in the business as heir to one of the decade's most successful studio executives, once all this was gone, he was no longer Eric Fleischer. Eric Fleischer in capital letters, Times Roman print, page two of *Variety*'s "Buzz" column. Now he was just another cute boy. A very young cute boy. A very young and charming cute boy who wanted to have sex with me.

As he got out of the car that white afternoon, he lingered a bit by the curb. Something was up. His face scrunched up as thoughts rolled freely across it. His face was like the news scroll that flashes across the Chemical Building in Times Square. The day's headlines were easily read: BOY IN LUST . . . WEIGHING HIS OPTIONS . . . OFFICIALS UNSURE HOW TO PROCEED . . . READ ABOUT IT IN TODAY'S *NEWSDAY!* Eric didn't know yet how to hide thinking.

"Something wrong, Eric?"

"Beep me tomorrow," he said quietly. "Promise?"

Suddenly, I wanted to cry, but he didn't give me the chance. He turned around sullenly and began to skulk down the street toward his parents' estate. He kicked at a stray pebble for effect. It worked. I got it. As people here are apt to say, the scene read.

A new problem was instantly clear. What I was doing was exponentially worse than homosexuality or pedophilia or whatever I was getting involved in.

I was breaking his heart.

The next day, I beeped him. Of course. In turn, he beeped his father's limo and came over to my apartment. Not what you're thinking. At least, at the time, it was not what I was thinking.

We had decided to see a movie, one of the cheap afternoon matinees. I had the paper at my house, so he came over to decide what to go see. It was summer, so the choices were fairly limited to the studios' big-gun releases—that year it was *T2*, *Regarding Henry*, and *The Hard Way*. I sat at the kitchen table going over the listings and times. He paced around the kitchen, opening cabinet doors and closing them just as abruptly. He was looking for food.

"God, don't you have anything to eat other than condiments?"

"I'm a writer, not a cook. OK, how about *Regarding Henry?*"

"Sucks. Harrison Ford is so tired."

"All right. Maybe a comedy. —*Soapdish?*"

"I'm boycotting Whoopi. You see what she said about dad on *ET?*"

And on and on—this sort of banter went on for a good ten minutes. He didn't want to see anything.

Finally I realized I had exhausted all the possibilities, having even read through the "art films" at the Sunset 5. I looked up from the *Times* and noticed that Eric had stopped hunting for food. He was standing right next to me, the crotch of his jeans level with my eyes. I looked up at him. He was already looking down at me. Had been for the last minute or so. Again, something was up.

"Eric?"

"Hmmmm."

"You haven't liked one of these movies yet."

"Uh-hmmmm," he said, nodding his head slightly.

"You don't really want to go to the movies, do you?"

"Uh-uhhh," he said, turning the nod horizontal.

"So, what do you wanna do?"

He didn't say a word. He didn't utter a sound. He didn't even move his head. All he did was unbutton his jeans with his waxy hands and let them fall to the floor. In a heap. Through a pair of immaculately white Calvin Kleins, I could see the outline of his desires. And then, just as quickly as his 501's fell, his desires were revealed to me in all their nakedness. I was gloriously shocked. I was beside myself. He was beside myself.

In the stunning pleasure of that moment I thought of a movie. Typical. I remembered seeing *Psycho* on TV when I was Eric's age. More than the rotting corpse of Norman's mother, more than the shower murder, more than anything in that masterful film, the one thing that always struck me as being scary and wonderful was the opening scene. Janet Leigh having sex in a hotel with her afternoon lover.

What struck me as odd was the very idea of having sex in the middle of the afternoon. How utterly bizarre! Maybe it was my Catholic upbringing, but I always believed that sex was something that only happened at night. Under the covers. Under the inky cover of night. In a black hole, even. I couldn't fathom it otherwise.

Watching *Psycho*, mouth ajar, I remember thinking to myself that I would never, ever be able to have sex in the glaring, high sun of an afternoon. My morals wouldn't allow it. My sense of decency would not stand (nor, as the case may be, lie down) for it. But with Eric standing by my side, naked from the waist down, my morals left me. They escaped. I felt the same sick thrill that Janet Leigh must have felt as she spent her lunch break in nothing more than panties. The naughtiness of it all knocked me down from my higher moral yearnings. The brazenness of this illegal act, in broad daylight nonetheless, secretly thrilled me. I began to sweat. All over.

It was all over.

My desire to help Eric was lost. Now I just wanted to help myself. Wanted to indulge in the seediness of sex in the afternoon. And with a startled expression, I threw my arms around his bare waist and pulled him toward me.

We fell to the floor, and did not rise for two and a half hours.

The concept of guilt is a largely American notion.

This idea, like many of my ideas, comes from the movies—*The Manchurian Candidate*, specifically. And, despite its origin in a movie, I believe this idea to be particularly true. One could even lay the blame for American guilt at the doorstep of Hollywood. During the thirties and forties and into the early fifties the content of motion pictures was held in check by the strictures of the Hays Code. This censorship code stipulated, on top of common concerns like bad language and racy situations, that films lay out a moral blueprint for the country. If a character was evil, he was to get his comeuppance in the end. If he did bad things, bad things had to happen to him.

Being an American and working in an industry that marketed the concept itself, I was feeling guilty after sex with Eric. But not only feeling guilty—I was feeling guilty that I wasn't feeling guilty enough. After our afternoon of linoleum lovemaking, it was frighteningly official. I was sleeping with the teenage son of probably the most powerful man in motion pictures since Louis B. Mayer. At least, that's what *Premiere* said.

A couple days after our liaison, as if I wasn't feeling guilty enough, I had a breakfast meeting with Charlie. First off, whoever came up with the idea of the breakfast meeting should feel a little guilt himself. I had to sit through seven of those "meetings" that summer and they are the worst. The concept, for me at least, is so off. At breakfast, I usually don't want to even speak, let alone strategize or, for God's sake, pitch. And, I can never get any food down with all the talking.

I was to meet Charlie in the lobby of the Beverly Hills Hotel at eight. I had slept maybe four hours of guilt-wracked sleep, if you can call it that. Charlie, as always, looked well rested and impeccably good-natured. He shook my hand—make that *crushed* my hand. We sat down in what was called the "diner"—coffee for $2.50 is no diner price, even with unlimited refills—and he ordered cheese blintzes and orange juice for us both. The diner, according to Charlie, had the best blintzes in town.

"And OJ! A boy like you needs his vitamins. That's my secret, Davey," he said, grasping my arm and shaking it. "Vitamin C. The thing's a cure-all. Never get sick if I have my vitamin C."

"Thanks," I said. "I could use something like that."

"You don't look so hot, Davey. They givin' you a hard time over at Touchstone?" he said, his voice rising. "If anyone gives you a hard time over there, you tell them where to put it, if you know what I mean. You've got more talent than the lot of them."

"Thanks, uh, Charlie." I struggled on his name. I almost called him Dad.

"Good, good. So how's Eric?"

He said it just as I placed a blintz in my mouth. Suddenly, I was nauseous. Cheese. I tried to swallow but it was too, can I say, cheesy? I chewed and chewed but it got worse, gaining a consistency like wallpaper paste. I swallowed hard and knew I would regret it for the rest of the day. I did.

"Fine," I said, "he's just fine."

"I really gotta hand it to you, Davey. You're good with him."

"Really?" I asked, relishing this line, thinking how it would play in the TV movie that would surely be made of this sexual misadventure. "Well, he's easy to be good with."

"He needs to relate to more people his age. He's a good kid, smart kid, but needs to stop hanging around me and all my cronies so much. He needs to be a kid, you know?"

Then, Charlie went on to some story about how during the war he hung around with a pack of kids who toughened him, made him less of a sissy, made him a man. I saw the analogy. He wanted me to make Eric a man. A man of his own and not a mimic of Charlie's business friends, gossiping about studio politics or Kevin Costner's latest pay-or-play deal. I almost couldn't believe I was hearing this. Charlie was essentially giving me permission to have an affair with his son. To make him a man. If he only knew what sort of man I was making.

"Eric said you saw a movie last night? That new Universal picture—what's it called?"

Sex with Teenagers, I thought. That's the title of this movie. This movie that had become my life.

"*The Hard Way*," I said, smiling for reasons he'd never guess.

"What'd ya think, Davey? Any good?"

"It's a programmer," I said.

CHRIST-LIKE

EMANUEL XAVIER

Things never quite worked out living with Juan Carlos in the South Bronx. All kinds of shit was going on up there. Every day, someone else got shot, stabbed, or killed in his neighborhood. Mikey was afraid to befriend any of the local drug dealers—here today, gone tomorrow. One female doctor, trying to stop a brother from stealing her car, got shot three times outside the crack house next to Mikey's building—once in the leg, once in the arm, once in the chest. Mikey was coming home from the bodega when he saw her getting slaughtered in front of him; he dropped his forty-ounce bottle of Crazy Horse. The piss-yellow liquid racing toward the pool of blood surrounding the young black woman sprawled on the ground as quickly as the stolen car speeding away; her dead, open mouth still screaming a silent shriek; eyes staring at Mikey's bloodstained brand-new sneakers.

The next day, in an effort to look really *really* tough, Mikey went down to Paul's Boutique to shave all his hair off, enhancing the scars on the back of his head from many childhood brawls and his mother's abusive fits of anger. With a thicker, fuller twenty-one-year-old mustache, goatee, and an already decadent glow in his eyes, Mikey blended in nicely with the rest of the neighborhood. Walking hard, spittin', crotch grabbin', with a slight limp for allure, down the overcrowded streets where the salsa boomed over rottweiler fights and gangsta bitches argued over imprisoned boyfriends.

Picking up welfare checks and cupones to do the compras,

playing the numbers every day in hopes of hitting the lottery, Mikey in order to survive had become everything he had promised himself he would never be. Fighting every day with Juan Carlos about going back to hustling at the piers and making enough money so that they wouldn't have to eat pan con welfare cheese again. Spending his days learning Santería rituals from Padrino, a wise thirtysomething gay santero who would eventually become his godfather in a religion which fascinated Mikey more than anything in the world. Dreaming of the day he could make a living by putting brujos on cheating boyfriends and estranged lovers while listening to the sounds of growing winds outside South Bronx windows.

Padrino was also *tryin'* to teach Mikey how to cook for Juan Carlos, who would leave him home every day and went off supposedly looking for a job and coming back with marks on his neck and the smell of someone else's cheap cologne. Mikey, unsuccessfully trying to impress him with half-cooked arroz con pollo and the worst pernil since Titi Yoli poisoned the entire family on Mami's birthday with her bacalaito cakes.

"Mira, nene, you gotta start learning how to take care of your husband, because he won't always be this healthy, you know," Padrino would lecture.

Frustrated with Juan Carlos's up-front attitude about his affairs, Mikey would spend his midnights getting stoned with Padrino in the park across the street from Yankee Stadium. Padrino filling his head with stories about rich old men coming up from the city to pick up poor little Latino boys for sex. The park was legendary for "street trade" and it wasn't unusual for Padrino to disappear behind the bleachers, leaving Mikey alone from time to time while getting sucked off by strangers, coming back with enough money for a six-pack and a dime bag.

Mikey, never a step behind, frequented the parks until he had enough money to buy a new pair of sneakers, sucking on his Blow Pops while waiting on the bleachers late at night for rich horny old men desperate for a taste of banjee heaven. He wanted to make enough money to leave Juan Carlos's tired ass and move to the big city where he wouldn't have to worry about whether or not he'd wake up alive the next day.

"Well, well, well! If it isn't the Grand Pier Queen of the South Bronx herself tryin' to work the park!"

Mikey, turning around from the bleachers where he sat to come face-to-face with Hector, a tacky cha-cha queen who lived on the second floor of their building.

"What's the matter, Mikey? Need more money to buy food at the cuchifrito so Juan Carlos won't find out you can't cook for yourself?"

"Yeah, well at least I don't be giving my ass away for some crack like you, you nasty ho!"

Hector walked away with his tight Daisy Duke shorts and flipflops, pretending not to hear him.

"I HATE MY LIFE!" Mikey broke down later that day when he opened the fridge and the milk carton spilled onto the floor.

"Here, I'll clean it," Juan Carlos offered.

"No, forget about it! Just go away!"

"Hey! Hey!" Juan Carlos grabbed Mikey by the hands as he tried to soak up the milk with a sponge. "Càlmate, okay! . . . I thought I was your life!"

Mikey rolled his eyes away from Juan Carlos.

"I love you, Mikey! I motherfuckin' love you, ah-ight, kid!" Juan Carlos was giving his best performance since Mikey's cousin Alberto busted him at La Escuelita one night with some queen named Pedro.

"It's all about you, Papi!"

Mikey freed himself from his grip and headed toward the door.

"Why you frontin'? STOP FUCKIN' WIT' MY HEAD, JUAN CARLOS! If you love me so much, then how come you have to fuck around wit' other guys? Huh? Tell me, Juan Carlos!"

"Look! If I fucked around wit' other guys it's because I'm sick, ah-ight! You know I'm sick, Mikey!"

"No, *you* look! Don't make me go off! YOU DON'T WANNA SEE ME GO OFF!"

"I'm dying, all right! I just wanted to have a little fun before I'm good and buried!"

"Ay! Not for nothing but just because you got AIDS don't mean I'm gonna let you fuck every José, Luis, and Victor you can get your dick into! That's shady, Juan Carlos! Too shady!"

"I'm scared ah-ight! I'm scared of getting too close to you so you can pick up and leave whenever the next fly papi cruises you in a club!"

"Oh! Just because other guys they look at me, that gives you the right to make a cábron out of me! I DON'T THINK SO!" Mikey picked up his baseball cap and unchained the door. "You know, maybe if you didn't think about yourself all the time, Juan Carlos, I wouldn't be going out to the clubs running into all those putas you be calling 'baby' thinking everyone else doesn't know your bochinche!"

Juan Carlos grabbed him before he had a chance to storm out, turning him to stare into his face. "I never meant to hurt you, Mikey! I said I was sorry, all right, but what do you want me to do? Can't you just let it go?"

Mikey forced back the tears. "Whatevah, okay! I'm tired of you playing me for a fool!" He pushed him off and stormed out of the apartment, running down the dark stairs as fast as he could, past all the bodega boys and drug dealers, heading toward the park.

That was the night Mikey was approached by the fiercest, most expensive car he had ever seen, an older man in the driver's seat, staring him down. Mikey's mind raced with a million and one reasons to steal his car. Mikey had never seen anything like it except on television and in magazines. The lamppost lights bouncing off the white shield of the car, glistening in Mikey's hungry eyes. The driver watching from beneath the shadow of his baseball cap, concealing his wrinkling forty-year-old face, wearing an expensive football jacket Mikey had seen on Fordham Road for like thirty dollars.

The sugar papi parked his car in front of the bleachers where Mikey sat and stared at him in the way every young boy wants to be looked at by a potential trick. Mikey stared back at him, feigning an innocent smile and giving him his best puppy dog eyes ever, car alarms ringing somewhere in the distance.

Juan Carlos had run out after Mikey, lurking underneath the bleachers. He watched the stranger in the car, thinking the same thoughts as Mikey: about what he could do with a car like that. He remained motionless in the shadows.

"WOULD YOU LIKE TO GET IN?" the man yelled out to Mikey, drowned out by the hip-hop record blaring from his speakers.

"NO!" he yelled back defiantly, like when he was a little boy and his mother asked him if he had smashed the aquarium while the goldfish struggled desperately for air.

The man bit his lip and pulled out a wad of money, flagging it at Mikey like he was about to land a plane.

"OH, COME ON! I WON'T HURT YOU!" he taunted him, as if Mikey really felt threatened by his corny old white ass.

Down below, Juan Carlos lit a joint, the smoke rising up to Mikey's attention, searching underneath through the holes only to find his cheating heart smiling up at him devilishly. Even through the darkness Mikey could see his eyebrow raised and a knowing smile on his face.

"I PROMISE I WON'T!" the old man begged, thinking Mikey was looking away in contemplation.

Mikey and Juan Carlos silently voiced the plan laid out before them with their eyes.

"AH-IGHT! BUT YOU HAVE TO PROMISE NOT TO HURT ME!" he yelled to the driver, glancing back down to lock eyes with Juan Carlos. Juan Carlos mouthed the words back up to him "I won't!" before he rose off the bleachers and headed toward the car, the old man's face crumbling into one big smile.

Mikey opened the passenger door, making himself comfortable inside, nervously glancing over at the man, trying to avoid eye contact, the smell of alcohol reeking from his slightly built older body.

"What's your name?" he asked.

Mikey was quiet, searching for any signs of a weapon while contemplating an answer.

"Ricky!" he said, using his ex-lover's name, a thrill on his rebellious face.

"Ricky?" the old man repeated in disbelief. "That's the perfect name for you!"

"Well . . . what's your name? John?" Mikey asked with a fuck-you-viejo-maricon! tone of voice.

The man cracked a smile which for a moment made Mikey reconsider his plot with Juan Carlos.

"How'd you ever guess?"

Sitting in silence for a moment, Mikey anxiously waited for Juan Carlos to give him a signal.

"Tell me, 'Ricky,' how much does a boy like you ask for these days?"

Mikey glared at him with attitude. "Oh! You mean besides the car!" he sneered sarcastically.

Mikey played it off by laughing along with him, before "John" reached over, crushing Mikey with unexpected strength, feeling around for Mikey's rising erection, lost somewhere in his over-sized baggy jeans.

Finding it, he pulled back and happily smiled down at Mikey's overwhelmed stare.

"You can have more than just the car if you play your cards right, pretty boy!"

With his other hand, he moved Mikey closer to him, forcing his tongue deep into Mikey's throat, almost choking him while unzippering his jeans.

"Wait a minute . . . Cógelo con—take it easy, ah-ight!" Mikey struggled to push him off, the old man chewing on his neck before being taken by surprise and pulled out of the car. There was a ferocious rustling sound and loud screaming outside the door as Mikey zipped up his jeans and raised himself enough to see Juan Carlos pounding the old man in the face, yelling like a bitch as Juan Carlos kicked him in the stomach.

"THE WALLET! THE WALLET! DON'T FORGET THE WALLET!" Mikey shouted nervously as Juan Carlos kicked the old man in the face again.

"SCREAM AGAIN AND I'LL KILL YA!" Juan Carlos reached into his back pocket to pull out the wallet, kicking him one last time before jumping into the driver's seat.

"HURRY UP! HURRY UP! LET'S GO! LET'S GO!" Mikey cried.

Juan Carlos fumbled with the car keys still in the ignition.

"AHHHHHHHHH!" the man screamed.

"COME ON, LET'S GET THE FUCK OUT OF HERE!" Mikey screeched.

Juan Carlos finally started the car, pulling away, leaving the old man behind, his baseball cap on the ground exposing his bald head, crying for help as blood poured out from his mouth.

They made enough money from that car to pay the rent, buy some phat new gear, reconnect their beepers, get Santería beads from Padrino, and pay off the hospital bills which Medicaid didn't cover for Juan Carlos.

Juan Carlos became worse and worse every day until finally he developed respiratory problems and his cell count dropped to only sixty-three.

"You know, Mikey, not for nothin', but he don't look too good! He ain't even gotta try to hide from da police 'cause they wouldn't recognize him if he was standing in their face. He may be whatever but he is still your man!" Padrino would tell Mikey.

So on his twenty-seventh birthday, Mikey gave Juan Carlos a surprise party. But after smoking plenty of pot, and a very revealing game of truth-or-dare, the only surprise was for Mikey.

"Truth or dare, Juan Carlos?" Padrino asked facetiously.

"Truth!"

Padrino contemplated whether or not to ask the question, until an evil glow in his eyes caught everyone's attention.

"Did you *ever* sleep with anyone else in this building other than Mikey?"

Juan Carlos's face flushing to a pale white and his mouth dropping in disbelief.

"Come on, Juan Carlos, you know you can't lie to los muertos!" Padrino insisted.

No matter what he said, he was cornered, so Juan Carlos looked over at Mikey, shaking his head back and forth begging for a no.

"Hector from 257!"

"HECTOR FROM 257! YOU SLEPT WITH HECTOR FROM 257! D-E-S-G-R-A-C-I-A-D-O!" was all Mikey said before lunging from his seat and landing on Juan Carlos.

Padrino raced to pull Mikey away, hands gripped tightly around Juan Carlos's neck, while the locas screamed in horror.

"GET OFF ME! . . . GET OFF ME! . . . I'MA KILL HIM! . . . I'MA KILL HIM! YOU SON OF A BITCH!"

"OLVÍDALO, PAPI . . . PLEASE! HE'S NOT WORTH IT! JUST LET HIM BE! HE'S NOT WORTH IT!" Padrino urged. Mikey fell into a fit of tears.

"I believed in you, Juan Carlos! I believed in you! How the fuck could you do this to me?" Tears streamed down his face.

The entire room fell silent. Padrino reached out to comfort him before Mikey ran into the kitchen, emerging with the birthday cake in his right hand and a crazed look on his face.

"NO! NO! . . . NO, MIKEY! . . . NOT THE VALENCIA CAKE! . . . POR FAVOR, NOT THE VALENCIA CAKE!"

Padrino begged as Mikey screamed maniacally, making a hundred-mile dash toward Juan Carlos's face.

"BITCH! YOU'RE CRAZY!" Juan Carlos yelled as the sticky gooey frosting from the cake glued to his gagging face.

"HAPPY MOTHERFUCKIN' BIRTHDAY, YOU HIJO DE LA GRAN PUTA!" Mikey ran out of the apartment.

That was the last time Mikey ever saw Juan Carlos. Returning to the piers, he hustled for a place to crash every night, until his cousin Alberto caught him out there one night.

"Miguelito, what the fuck is wrong with you? How come Padrino's the one who has to call me to tell me you are back on the streets working the piers?"

Mikey was too choked up to argue with him. That whole night, they sat at the piers, Mikey telling him all about his miserable life since they last ran into each other. Alberto insisting that Mikey move in with him and his lover up in Riverdale.

"I'm not taking no for an answer! I told you que ese hombre was no good for you from the get-go! He made a pendeja out of you! Ooh, if he was here I would cut him! Ay, dios mio, if your mother only knew, she would've never thrown you out in the first place!"

The following day, Mikey returned to the South Bronx while Juan Carlos was out and packed his bags with the help of a mortified Alberto and his lover, Johnny.

"You were living *here?*" Alberto's eyes bulged with terror.

"No, I was just vacationing!" Mikey snapped, tossing his suitcases into the trunk, breaking into a smile.

"Mikey! Mikey!" Mikey recognized Padrino's voice before turning around to stop him dead in his tracks with a wicked stare. Padrino's face was flushed to a sickly color, his urgent eyes foretelling the bad news he was about to unleash.

"It's Juan Carlos! He's in da hospital!"

Mikey played it off like he really didn't care by shrugging his shoulders and turning away to slam down the car trunk—his excessive force a dead giveaway.

"Mikey . . . he's got tuberculosis!" Padrino ranted on. "The ambulance came to pick him up this morning! He thought he was gonna die! They won't let anyone near him because they say it's cun . . . cun . . . What's the word I'm looking for?"

"Contagious!" Alberto jumped in.

"Yeah, that's it! Cunt-agious!" He acknowledged Alberto's presence by raising an eyebrow.

Mikey turned to look at Padrino, all dressed in white with his collares, dropping his stare to the ground and focussing on all the bubble-gum wrappers glistening like jewels under the sun. Padrino reaching his arms out for him like the Christ at the church, only Christ had stumps, not hands, since they always stole them. He felt bad about Juan Carlos, but at the same time he felt it was just another trap to keep him by his side. It wouldn't be the first time Juan Carlos used his illness to get what he wanted out of Mikey.

"Now, I'm not telling you this so you go running back to him like you always do! I'm telling you 'cause you would WANT to go check yourself, chulo! You're the one who was with him the most!"

Mikey looked away so that Padrino wouldn't see the tears in his eyes, only to catch Hector watching them from behind the curtains in his window.

Mikey, falling into Padrino's arms, embraced him, planting a tender kiss on his cheek in full public view before running away toward the brightly lit bodega.

"Mikey! This is no time for you to go to the park! Mira, nene . . . Where you goin'?" Padrino screamed out to him. Mikey returned with a forty-ounce bottle of Crazy Horse.

"This is not the time to be gettin' drunk!" Alberto insisted.

Mikey tapped the bottle from underneath three times, like Padrino had taught him, unbottling it, closing his eyes and whispering a Yoruba chant while spilling the piss-yellow beer onto the concrete ground below. When he opened his eyes he caught his cousin and Johnny's bewildered and Padrino's motherly smile.

"It wasn't for me! It was for the muertos! So that they could look after Juan Carlos while I'm gone!"

"Ay, Mikey! He'll be ah-ight!" Padrino cried. "Pero, you need to get your ass out of here before you get sucked into this life! Fuck Juan Carlos, he's a big girl! You need to follow your dreams, baby!"

Mikey pulled out a wad of money and handed it to a startled Padrino.

"Què'eso?"

"Some money left over from the viejo's car! Go buy yourself something pretty!" Mikey said, trying not to sound like the sentimental pier queen that he actually was.

"Mikey! I can't!"

"Loca . . . please!"

Padrino quickly put the money away before Mikey changed his mind.

"Don't be a stranger!"

"Jamàs!" Mikey smiled, fully aware that he would never return to the South Bronx and that this part of his life was, for better or for worse, behind him.

"Are you ready?" Alberto asked.

"Yes! . . . Yes, I am!"

With that, Mikey kissed Padrino one last time, giving Hector the finger before getting into the backseat of the car and being driven away, never looking back at the streets of the South Bronx.

ABOUT THE AUTHORS

Keith Banner was born in Anderson, Indiana, but most of his family comes from East Tennessee. He is a social worker for people labeled "mentally retarded" and lives in Cincinnati with his partner, Bill. Alfred A. Knopf will publish his forthcoming novel *The Life I Lead*. His stories have appeared in *Christopher Street*, *The James White Review*, and *The Minnesota Review*.

Shawn Behlen lives in San Francisco with Rick Welsch, his partner of many years. His short fiction has appeared in *Black Warrior Review*, *Other Voices*, *Puerto del Sol*, *modern words*, and *Press*. He is finishing a novel, *The Here and Now of Mitch Malone*, which features the characters from "Mullinville."

Michael Bendzela has had stories published in several North American journals and anthologies and was the recipient of a Pushcart Prize in 1993. He and his partner of thirteen years live on a farm in Maine.

David Bergman is the author or editor of over a dozen books, including the last two volumes of *Men on Men*. His latest book is a collection of his poetry, *Heroic Measures*. With Joan Larkin, he edits the book series OUT LIVES: Lesbian and Gay Autobiography. He is Professor of English at Towson University and lives in Baltimore.

Michael Carroll was born in Memphis and grew up in West Texas and Northern Florida. He is a graduate of Florida State University and received an MFA from Bowling Green University. He has been a waiter, a deliverer for a Chinese restaurant, a college English teacher, a gay-bathhouse attendant, a bookstore clerk, and a nightwatchman. A Peace Corps volunteer in the Czech Republic, he now lives in Paris. His work has appeared in the *Chattahoochee Review*, *The Harvard Gay and Lesbian Review*, and in the anthology *Boys Like Us: Gay Writers Tell Their Coming Out Stories*.

C. Bard Cole is a cartoonist and writer, co-editor of the 'zine *Riotboy* and the author of several illustrated chapbooks, including *Fag Sex in High School* and *Young Hemingways*. While a student at Sarah Lawrence College, he was adopted by the staff of *Christopher Street*, where his fiction and author interviews first appeared. Born and raised in Baltimore County, Maryland, he now lives in New York City.

Caleb Crain is completing his doctorate in American literature at Columbia University. He has written for *American Literary History*, *American Literature*, *Christopher Street*, *Early American Literature*, *Lingua Franca*, *Men's Style*, *The New Republic*, *Newsday*, *Out*, and *QW*. He has translated Eda Kriseová's authorized biography *Václav Havel* and Czech fiction that has appeared in *The Tenor Saxophonist's Story* (1997) and *Daylight in Nightclub Inferno* (1997). "Cocksucker" is an excerpt from his just-completed novel, *Jacob's Ladder*. He lives in Manhattan with his dog, Lota.

Allen Ellenzweig has published art and photography criticism as well as cultural commentary for over twenty years. His work has appeared in such periodicals as *Art in America*, *The Village Voice*, *The New York Native*, *PASSIONS: The Magazine of Paris*, and *The Harvard Gay and Lesbian Review*. His book *The Homoerotic Photograph: Male Images from Durieu/Delacroix to Mapplethorpe* was published by Columbia University Press in 1992.

Reginald Harris is Information Technology Support Specialist for the Enoch Pratt Free Library in Baltimore, Maryland. Born in Annapolis, he was a founding member of BUGLE (Blacks

United for Gay and Lesbian Equality) and on the Administrative Board of the William Wolfe Institute for Gay and Lesbian Studies at the Gay and Lesbian Community Center of Baltimore. He has also served on the Community Advisory Board of SHARE, an AIDS research study at the Johns Hopkins Hospital. Happily partnered for ten years, Reginald Harris has published works in *The Baltimore Review*, *The Harvard Gay and Lesbian Review*, *Kuumba*, and many other journals and newspapers. His work was included in the anthology *The Road Before US: 100 Black Gay Poets* (Galiens Press, 1991). "A Tour of the Collection" is his first published short story.

Andrew Holleran is the author of three novels—*Dancer from the Dance*, *Nights in Aruba*, and *The Beauty of Men*—and a book of essays, *Ground Zero*. He is working on a collection of stories to be published early next year. He currently lives in Florida.

Aaron Jason was born a Valley Girl in Los Angeles but has lived in San Francisco for the past seven years, where he studied philosophy, medieval literature, and creative writing at California State University, Hayward. He is fiction editor at Pandaemonium Press in Berkeley and has published work in *Watershed Literary Review*, *Occam's Razor*, and *Doorknobs and Bodypaint*, a magazine of flash fiction. In 1996, he received the Robert V. Williams Award for short fiction.

Alex Jeffers whiles away a great deal of his time impersonating a Turkish man ten years his junior, the narrator of *The Abode of Bliss*, one of a three-volume work-in-progress, from which "The Strait" is excerpted. When not inhabiting the virtual Istanbul, he lives in Boston. His first novel, *Safe as Houses* (1995), has recently appeared in paperback in Britain. His short fiction has appeared in *Happily Ever After*, *His²*, *modern words 4*, and *Men on Men 3*.

Greg Johnson is the author of three collections of short stories: *Distant Friends* (1990), *A Friendly Deceit* (1992), and *I Am Dangerous* (1996). He has also written a novel, *Pagan Babies* (1993), a collection of poetry, *Aid and Comfort* (1993), and a biography, *Invisible Writer: A Biography of Joyce Carol Oates* (1998). He lives in Atlanta and teaches in the graduate writing program at Kennesaw State University.

Kevin Killian is a playwright, poet, critic, and novelist. In 1997 he published the novel *Arctic Summer*, the collection of short stories *Little Men*, and a volume of poetry, *Argento Series*. This year Wesleyan University Press will publish the biography of the American poet Jack Spicer that he wrote with Lewis Ellingham. He is the author of an earlier novel, *Shy* (1989), and a memoir, *Bedrooms Have Windows* (1989), and is completing a third novel, *Spreadeagle*—from which "Biography" is excerpted—and another volume of memoirs, *Bachelors Get Lonely*. His story "September" appeared in the first volume of *Men on Men*, edited by George Stambolian, to whose memory "Biography" is dedicated.

Christopher Lord works for an insurance company as director of marketing and underwriting. He holds a B.A. in history from Willamette University. Having completed his first novel, *Beautiful Lies*, he is working on a short-story collection. He and his partner, Evan Boone, divide their time between Portland and Newport, Oregon. This is his first published story.

Keith McDermott is an actor and writer. He lives in New York City with his lover, the painter Eric Amouyal. He is currently working on a book about acting with Michael Egan and on a collection of short stories.

Ernest McLeod was born in Vermont and still spends most of his time there. He is a graduate of the Rhode Island School of Design and worked in architecture for ten years before receiving an MFA in creative writing from Warren Wilson College. His work has recently appeared in *The James White Review* and *The GSU Review*. Currently he is completing a first collection of short stories tentatively titled *Think of Escape*. He hopes to work next on a trio of travel novellas.

David A. Newman grew up in Michigan and now lives in Los Angeles. His story "Ice Cream" appeared in *His²: Brilliant New Fiction* (1997). An award winner in the 1995 Hemingway Short

Story Contest with "Lesser Known Toys," he is currently at work on a collection of stories.

Felice Picano, novelist and poet, is the author of fifteen books, including *Like People in History, The Lure, The Deformity Lover,* and *The New Joy of Gay Sex* (with Charles Silverstein). He is the founder of the Sea Horse Press and Gay Presses of New York. He lives now in Los Angeles.

Brian Sloan attended Boston College, where he almost published his first short story in the college literary magazine until the Jesuit moderator discovered what it was about. He served a short stint in Washington at the Pentagon's Public Information Office, where his skills as a fiction writer were further honed. In 1989, he moved to New York to attend NYU's graduate film school. His thesis project, *Pool Days,* was part of the original *Boys Life* anthology and played in more than fifty cities around the country in 1995. His short films have been screened at more than sixty film festivals throughout the world, including the Sundance Film Festival and New Directors/New Films at MOMA. His first feature-length film, *I Think I Do,* premiered at the 1997 San Francisco International Lesbian and Gay Film Festival and is distributed by Strand Releasing.

Emanuel Xavier is a poet and fiction writer living in New York. The winner of the Nuyorican Poets Cafe Grand Slam, he published the volume of poetry *Pier Queen.* His story "Motherfuckers" appeared in *Best Gay Erotica 1997.* His poetry has appeared in *Urban: The Latino Magazine, phati'tude Literary Magazine,* and *Ma-Ka-Diasporic Junks: Contemporary Writings by Queers of African Descent.* "Christ-like" is an excerpt from his novel of the same name.